SKIN DEEP

The dream began, as always, with Nina standing alone and terrified in the middle of a cemetery draped in a dense, chilling fog. Frozen with terror, she clutched the bars of a wrought iron fence, praying for an escape from the scene materializing before her eyes. Her powerlessness against the coming horror felt like icy fingers around her throat, and she struggled for breath against the blanket of absolute dread that had wrapped itself tightly around her, letting her take in only short, labored gasps . . .

She prayed, "Please Lord, let me wake up."

skin deep

Kathleen Cross

AVON BOOKS  NEW YORK

AVON BOOKS, INC.
1350 Avenue of the Americas
New York, New York 10019

Copyright © 1999 by Kathleen A. Cross
Inside cover author photo by Star Shots
Published by arrangement with the author
Library of Congress Catalog Card Number: 99-94795
ISBN: 0-7394-0632-9

For my mother and father
Thanks for making me me

While writing this book I received encouragement and support from far too many folks to name here—thank you all!

I'd also like to extend a special thanks to those who made an exceptional effort to "have my back" in this effort:

This book would not have been written without the constant encouragement and feedback from my best friend and first reader, Laura Coleman—Thank you for not letting me give up!

To my daughters, Khalia, Melody, and Akira—Thank you for sharing me with the computer. I owe you at least a hundred home-cooked meals!

To my sister, Candy—No one has been a louder voice of praise. Thank you for loving my book even before it was finished.

To my sister, Kerry—Thanks for threatening me with bodily harm around chapter 19. You helped me speed up my pace!

To my big brother, Eugene—IT'S FICTION, baby. FICTION!

To Shilloy, Denise, Renee, Melanie, and Leisa— Thank you for reading and critiquing. You made it a better book!

To Lizzy and Elaine—Your early encouragement kept me writing.

To Shadow and Billy Ray—Thank you for loving Ahmad and Nina, and caring how it all turned out.

To my agent, Denise Stinson, and my editor, Carrie Feron—Thanks for having faith in me. You made my goal a reality!

To the Leimert poets— You inspire me with your phenomenal creativity.

To Phyllis Hart—You know how to bring out the best in everyone around you, including me.

And last, but DEFINITELY not least, to Todd B.—I would never have started this project if you hadn't insisted I try. I love you, T. 28282828282828282828282828!

△▽ 1 ▽△

The sting of Derrick's sweat, which had rolled off his forehead and dripped into the corner of Nina's eye, jarred her out of her thoughts and back into the real world. *The real world. Humph. What an overstatement.* Nina lay motionless, pondering the sad truth; not much of what was happening in the moonlit darkness of her bedroom could be referred to as "real." The cool sheets beneath her naked back ... those were real satin. The hot, sweet scent Derrick was breathing rhythmically into her face was real cognac. And that really was Sade's voice crooning smoothly from the speakers mounted in each corner of the roomy master suite. But there was definitely nothing real about the sex ... at least for Nina. She had been pretty much faking her way through that for weeks.

"Whose ... name ... is on it ... baby? Huh?" Derrick grunted the words out with short, punctuated breaths that blew into her face in unexpected little gusts. "Tell ... Daddy ... whose it ... is."

"Whose name is on it? Pshhh. Where did Derrick pick up that pillow talk selection? She peeked through squinted eyelids to see Derrick's face, an inch from hers, glistening with beads of perspiration, and contorted into the unsightly grimace of an impending orgasm. He wasn't paying her no mind. His eyes were tightly shut, and she could tell from his shallow breathing and the way his pelvis had begun to grind methodically into hers that he wasn't waiting for a response to his question. *Good.* She couldn't tell him the answer that was ringing in

1

her head anyway. *"It" was not, and never would be, his.* Nina had known it for weeks, but just couldn't seem to find the nerve to tell Derrick. She couldn't marry him after all.

Well, she certainly wasn't going to break the news to him while he was lying on top of her sweating and moaning and thrusting away. Instead, she opted for ending the so-called lovemaking as quickly as possible by wrapping her legs around his back and kissing his ear with as much passion as she could muster. A sure way to drive Derrick wild was to mess with his ears, so Nina caressed one of them with her tongue until she could feel that familiar arch in his lower back that meant he was about to come.

Sade was moaning now, something she believed about a love that wouldn't last.

Nina locked her ankles at the small of Derrick's back, arched her pelvis rhythmically into his, and waited until his convulsing body was still. He would need about two minutes to recuperate, during which she was not supposed to move.

"Don't move, baby," he whispered into her neck. "Damn, girl," he breathed huskily, "damn, I love making love to you."

Damn I love making love to you? Humph. If he had any idea of the effect it had on her, he wouldn't say that shit. *Ugh.* Nina had grown to hate those words. Maybe that was because the only time Derrick seemed to be able to say the "L" word was during, or right after, an orgasm.

She actually thought it was kinda cute back in the day, how Derrick would find creative ways to let her know he "loved" her—without ever really saying it. But damn. But after a closet full of "I♥U" teddy bears, and out-and-out overkill on the "You Mean the World to Me" Hallmark cards, you'd think the brotha would've learned to actually verbalize the word "love" without the accompaniment of some orgasmic moans.

But then again, Nina knew she had to carry some of the blame. The truth was, she just stopped questioning Derrick's obvious distress about using the word, and began settling for the once-in-a-blue-moon when he might sing "I love you" to her from the stage, or dedicate one of his original songs to her at the club. Why should she get all hung up on some words anyway? The man had asked her to be his wife; he must love her. *Yeah, right.* That was assuming he even knew what love was. All that was suspect now. *Shit, after what he said to me tonight . . . not five minutes into the sex . . . ? Please.*

Get offa me, Derrick, she thought, but didn't say aloud. She really didn't want to start an argument tonight. He might end up getting dressed and going home, and then what? Tonya wasn't home yet, and Nina definitely wasn't trying to sleep in that big ol' apartment by herself and risk being alone when that terrifying nightmare struck again. The dream had begun tormenting her a few weeks after her twenty-ninth birthday, and each time she awakened from it she was more shaken and frightened than before. She needed Derrick to be there . . . *just in case.*

Damn, this fool is heavy. Why does he have to put all his weight on me like that? She sighed deeply to signal to him that his two minutes were up. "I can't breathe," she whispered hoarsely.

Derrick rolled off of Nina and onto his side with his back to her. She heard the snap of the condom as he pulled it off and flung it toward the wastebasket in the corner. It was the last sound she heard from him before the snoring started.

Nina listened mindlessly to the obnoxious noises coming from Derrick's open mouth, waiting for some sign that the loud snoring might be only temporary. She raised up on her elbows to peek over him at the clock on the dresser across the room. *It's after midnight.* She fell back to the mattress and covered her ears with her hands, as if that could keep the intrusion of Derrick's snores out of her head. It was almost 12:30, and she had to be up by 5:30 if she was going to make it to the campus on time. She was supposed to be meeting Sweet Nat and Tonya on the quad at 6:30. Sweet Nat would probably show up late, but Tonya was sure to be standing there, arms crossed and toe tapping, at 6:25. *I need to get some sleep.* Nina nudged Derrick's shoulder blade.

"Derrick. Derrick, baby, you're snoring."

He didn't budge.

She studied her fiancé's sleeping body. Damn, he was fine. His skin was the color of dark chocolate, and as smooth as an ocean-polished stone. His shoulders were the kind of thick and broad that could make a sista believe if she laid her head on his chest, and felt his biceps around her back, nothing in the world could ever make her feel hurt or afraid. *Humph. Talk about not judging a book by its cover.* Judging by looks, if Derrick was a book, you'd be sure the title had to be *Strong, Sexy Husband Material.* Unfortunately, he read more like a nursery rhyme. Just thinking about how disappointing the fairy tale called Derrick had turned out to be made Nina shake her head and roll over to the other side of the bed.

She lay there wondering how on earth she would ever tell him the wedding was off. Not that it mattered how she broke it to him. He would immediately assume it was another man. *Too bad it's not another man,* Nina thought. *That would make it easy.* If she were leaving him for somebody else, Derrick could justify all those times he had accused her of flirting with, talking to, sneaking around with, or fucking some figment of his imagination.

If he only knew. She had never even considered being unfaithful, and it wasn't because there weren't plenty of invitations. Rarely did a day pass without some man whistling at Nina under his breath, leaving notes in her office, or slipping a phone number or business card into her hand. She had numerous opportunities to cheat on Derrick, but like Mama always said, "Whatever's done in the dark, eventually comes to light." So-called cheating was really just putting off the inevitability of getting caught, hurting somebody you cared about and ultimately hurting your own self. So, despite the fact that she felt her love for Derrick beginning to fade, and other men had recently begun to turn her head, she remained true to her word, and to her man. Even after he disappeared for those three days around New Year's, and finally called with some story about him and his boy being in jail in Mexico. Even after Valentine's Day when she found an "I Love You" card addressed to him with a photograph of some naked White woman in it. She doubted Derrick's claim that it was a practical joke played on him by one of his band members, but his bass player Reginald *had* called to corroborate the story. Then there was that time she let Derrick use her apartment to throw a bachelor party for his cousin Jason, and Nina came home to find three used condoms in the wastebasket in her bedroom. Of course, Derrick didn't know anything about how they'd gotten there. He had actually been pretty good since that last one, or maybe he'd just gotten smarter, but nevertheless Nina knew it was over.

She knew it was time to tell Derrick how she was feeling about everything. But was she really ready for it to end? She had grown used to depending on him to keep her company on nights like this, when she just didn't want to be alone. And he was alright company. He didn't complain too much about watching the Discovery Channel with her, even though it wasn't his idea of entertainment. He put up with her reading poetry aloud to him in bed in the middle of the night, and even tried to act like he appreciated it sometimes. He did have a creative, romantic side at times, and he had a pretty good sense of humor. Wasn't that worth something in a relationship? *Maybe.* But a relationship was one thing, and marriage—as her daddy would say, "That's a whole 'nother thang."

Now, Daddy and Mama had a marriage. But really, who could ever hope to have a marriage like theirs? Sure, they had gone through some stormy times along the way, but they always came through the hard times more in love than ever. When it came down to it, Mama was just one of the wisest and most generous persons Nina knew, and pshhh, Derrick could live three lifetimes and never become man enough to compare to Daddy.

Got damn. Could Derrick's snoring actually be getting louder? Nina elbowed him again. "Derrick. Derrick, I've got to get some sleep."

Derrick rolled onto his back, his arm flopping wildly across Nina's chest, and suddenly, the snoring just stopped. Nina lifted the muscular limb, and edged out from under it before letting it fall with a thud against the mattress. Raising herself up on one elbow she studied her fiancé soberly. His face was beautiful. His broad forehead and high, wide cheekbones gave him an almost regal appearance, and his skin looked as if he had been dipped in a smooth chocolate coating. His eyelashes were long and thick and curled up like they were reaching for his eyelids, and his eyebrows and mustache were jet black and shimmered in the moonlight as if they had been oiled. He had a slight smile on his face, which for an instant made Nina soften as she remembered how charming he had been when they first met. It was that smile that got her into this in the first place, wasn't it? Nina's first prerequisite for attraction to the opposite sex was a healthy smile, and Derrick's had to be one of the most beautiful she had ever seen. His lips were full and perfectly shaped, and his teeth were straight and gleaming white.

Derrick had used that smile on Nina the day she met him. She and Tonya were playing tennis in the park and the man strolled right onto the tennis court in the middle of their game. Nina couldn't help but notice those muscular thighs bulging beneath the black biker shorts he wore, and the Arizona Suns tank that hung loosely from his broad shoulders complemented his well-sculpted chest. She didn't know who the tall stranger was, and was wondering if he might be a friend of Tonya's, until he walked right past Tonya, sauntered casually up to Nina, handed her a basketball, and with his stunning, dimpled smile said, "Before today, I thought playing ball would always be my first love; now I know better." He walked away and left Nina standing there, holding his basketball. No introduction. No conversation. She and Tonya both stood with their eyes and their mouths wide open as he walked away. Nina was so stunned, it took her at least five minutes to figure out that he had written his name and phone number on the ball with a marking pen. And of course, she called it as soon as she got home.

That was almost two years ago. *Two years.* Nina stared thoughtfully at Derrick sprawled comfortably in her bed. She had to ask herself why it had taken so long to admit that he wasn't the man she thought he'd be. Yeah, he was fine, and the physical attraction was strong, but that surely wasn't enough to have kept her there so long.

Nina just had to face the fact that despite the many mature and responsible decisions she'd made in her pursuit of education and in her career, her chosen life-mate had turned out to be more like a temporary playmate. The truth was, they weren't really even friends anymore. *Humph.* The past couple of months Derrick just seemed to act like a total jerk half of the time. But then, every once in a while, he'd show his sweet, gentle side and Nina would think maybe he's trying. *Maybe.* He was nearly thirty years old, but he still had so much little boy in him. It was hard for Nina not to feel like if she waited long enough, the part of him that was playful and precious might grow up. Maybe if she waited long enough, the boy in him would catch up with the self-centered, ego-driven man he was becoming.

Nina thought about the crazy-ass comment Derrick had made to her not twenty-five minutes before ... something about making White boys jealous. *Pshhh. Some things are just beyond immature,* Nina thought, allowing a hopeless sigh to escape her lips. *Maybe Derrick was worth waiting for once upon a time* ... She finished the thought in an audible whisper, "But there ain't enough waitin' in the world now."

Derrick suddenly awakened slightly, planted a sloppy kiss on Nina's breast, muttered " 'Night, baby," and got to snoring as loud as ever.

Nina lay there staring blankly at the ceiling fan as it circulated the air-conditioned coolness down onto the king-sized bed. This was ridiculous. She was sure she hadn't gotten more than four hours of sleep a night for the last week, and yet here she was again, staring at the ceiling, wide awake.

Sade was singing Derrick's favorite now. *Sweetest Taboo.* In the end, wasn't that all Nina had been to him? Some kind of tool for revenge on the Man. Just thinking about it made the hair on her neck stand up. Nina threw back the sheet, got up from the bed, and followed a silver track of moonlight into the living room. Stopping in front of the mirrored hearth surrounding the built-in gas fireplace, she spoke aloud to the picture of her father, which sat in a silver-toned frame on the mantel.

"Well, Daddy," she sighed, picking up the photo and wincing at herself in the mirror, "you tried to tell me he wasn't the one." She looked at the photo for a long moment. Her father was a handsome man; caramel-colored and clean-shaven, with faint freckles and stunning green eyes. Nina's best friend Tonya always said he reminded her of that fine-as-hell schoolteacher who sang "Shake You Down" back in the eighties. Gregory Albert or Abbott or something like that.

Over the years, Nina had studied that picture at least a thousand times, comparing her own image to his. Although she knew it was not unheard of for children with one Black parent to come out looking White, the fact that she had inherited almost no pigment and had arguably "European" features always left Nina feeling like she somehow didn't belong in her family. Not that any of the Moores made a big deal out of it. Although Nina was the palest in the clan, Mama made it clear that there would be "none of that color-struck bullshit" in her house. As far as Mama was concerned, Nina was a Black woman, and a Moore just like everybody else in the house, and that was that. So what if Nina's biological mother was White? And so what if the date of Nina's birth made it a hard, cold fact that Mitchell Moore had impregnated that White woman while he was just newly married to his wife? Evelyn Moore welcomed Nina into her heart like she was her own daughter—flesh and blood. But no matter how hard Nina tried to shake it, there was something deep down that felt disconnected and empty in her, and the feeling had been with her for as long as she could remember.

Once, when she was six or seven, she and her baby brother Nathan went to North Carolina to visit Mama's sister, Aunt Ruthie, for the summer. Auntie's nine-year-old son Kevin spent the entire vacation teasing Nina for being so light. The first day they arrived he cornered her alone on the back porch. "You ol' White girl," he hissed at her, holding her by one of the long braids that hung down her back. "Everybody knows Uncle Mitchell ain't no parts a yo' daddy." After Nina managed to jerk her hair loose from Kevin's grasp, she ran in the house crying so bitterly, she could hardly see through her tears to dial home. Her daddy answered the phone, and immediately thought something terrible had happened. When he finally realized the source of his daughter's anguish, he tried to comfort Nina, but she was inconsolable.

"B-but Daddy," she managed to sputter between sobs, "he s-said there's no s-such thing as a White girl with a Black daddy. He said everybody knows that. He said it's in the en-cycle-pedia."

Nina's father chuckled.

"It's not funny, Da—" She couldn't call him that anymore, could she? The awful idea that Kevin knew what he was talking about, and that she didn't have a real mother or a real father, stopped her mid-sentence and she started bawling even harder.

"Baby, stop crying now," her daddy crooned. "Kevin is just teasing you." Her father calmly instructed her to take the photo of him perched up on Aunt Ruthie's piano over to the mirror and hold it up next to her face.

"Nina Moore, don't you let that fool boy make you cry like that. I'm your daddy, and I always will be. Look at your face. You have my chin and my smile. And where do you think you got those drop-dead-gorgeous freckles?" By the time her daddy was finished talking to her, she was smiling and laughing, and walking around with her head held high. Kevin spent the rest of the summer trying, but never did figure out why he couldn't make her cry anymore.

"I need to call my daddy tomorrow," Nina said aloud, letting her childhood memory float away as she set the picture of her father back on the mantel next to her own college graduation photo. Once again she found herself comparing her image to his. She had a faint sprinkling of freckles like him, and her chin had a distinctive dimple in it just like his, but she really looked like her mother. There was no picture of her mother on the mantel, and Nina had never seen one. But she did know that her mother had dark brunette hair and deep blue eyes, and like her mother, Nina's skin was a pale shade of ivory and her eyes were a brilliant sapphire blue. People often told her that if you didn't hear her speak, or watch the way she moved, you would mistake Nina for a White woman.

True enough, she was genetically half-Caucasian, but there was little in her upbringing that could contribute to her being considered White. Nina remembered nothing of her biological mother—even though she was nearly three years old when the woman died. Actually, when anyone referred to Nina's "mother," they were usually talking about Mama, the only mother Nina had really known.

The influence of Mama and Daddy on the woman Nina had become was undeniable. Before their relocation to Glendale, Arizona, the Moores had been prominent members of the Black elite in Los Angeles. They lived in Ladera Heights, a small, mostly Black suburb just on the outskirts of the city, and due to Mitchell's rising fame as a jazz musician, their home was often graced by notables from the literary and music worlds.

Nina and Nathan had been surrounded by images of Black heroes and heroines as far back as they could remember, and they were both constantly reminded that as African-Americans they had no option but to succeed. And, of course, it was Mama's guiding influence that led to Nina's thirst for education. In addition to teaching them the basics, Mama taught Nina and Nathan to revere their heritage. It was through Mama that Nina learned to honor the legacy of the Africans who had survived slavery, and Mama made sure her children understood that the material and spiritual abundance in the Moore household was the result of the fortitude of the many Black folks before them who had suffered on their behalf.

It seemed strangely hypocritical to Nina that with all that lecturing about Black pride, Daddy had somehow managed to get close enough to a White woman to impregnate her with his child. Especially since he was married to Mama a full two years before Nina was even born. But no matter how hard Nina tried, she couldn't get either one of her parents to talk about the circumstances of her untimely conception. The only thing Nina could figure was either the Moores were separated not long after their honeymoon, or Daddy had some kind of one-night stand. Or maybe he just straight out had him a White woman on the side. *Cheat on Mama?* But that just didn't seem possible. Mama didn't seem like the kind of woman to put up with no nonsense like that. Sure, she was generous and loving and extremely patient, but she didn't take no shit off nobody . . . not even Daddy.

Whatever the circumstances were, Mama loved Nina and nurtured her with the same intensity as Nathan, and in the Moore household it just wasn't allowable to make any distinctions between the two children. Nathan was Nina's brother . . . not her "half-brother," and Mama was Mama, and as far as Nina could recall there was never any reference in the Moore home to Nina being "mixed." Until she arrived in Arizona it had never occurred to her that anyone might consider her to be anything other than a Black woman. And for some reason, everything and everyone in her new surroundings seemed to try to remind her of her whiteness.

In L.A. people didn't really make a big deal about the way Nina looked; even strangers assumed she was just an extremely pale sista. But in Glendale things were just different. White folks were constantly stumbling over their tongues in her presence, sure she was an "us" until she told them she was a "them," and Black folks who didn't know she was the daughter of Mitchell Moore assumed she was some kind of confused wannabe.

She made a taunting face at herself in the mirror before she announced dramatically to her reflection, "Nina Moore, confused wannabe . . . next on *Oprah*," then she fell over onto the overstuffed couch under the skylight.

She was really tempted to lay right where she was and fall asleep without the snoring Derrick beside her, but her tormenting fear of sleeping alone would never let her do that. The fear was so overwhelming at times, Nina had actually let the thought of moving back into her parents' house enter her mind in recent weeks. But at twenty-nine years old, that wasn't her idea of an impressive move. And besides, she just loved her town house too much to leave it.

Nina's home interior included an eclectic mix of furnishings with African and Indian fabrics in warm and vibrant shades. The lingering odor of scented candles and recently burned incense hung in the air, commingling with the aroma of fresh-cut lilacs, which Nina was known to keep in abundant supply. Along an entire wall of the vaulted room loomed an impressive, custom-built entertainment center that held a vast vinyl and CD collection which was as diverse as her home was colorful.

Nina's artsy décor complemented the pricey Arizona town house with its natural lines and clean angles. The apartment was of typical Southwestern architecture, complete with stone-encased gas fireplace and window-boxed cacti. But it was the high ceilings and huge windows that caught her eye first. She loved the place the moment she saw it, and rather than have to leave it, she and Derrick had planned to share it as soon as they were married. Since Daddy was picking up the tab for the place, he was not moving in sooner.

Though Nina's father never said so, he probably suspected what Nina herself was now coming to realize: Derrick, a college dropout and struggling musician, might have been hoping to live comfortably with Nina off of the Moore family bank accounts. Nina stood to inherit a healthy sum of money from her father someday, and Derrick would obviously benefit from that too, if he could manage to hang on to Nina long enough. Derrick even admitted to Nina that the thought of one day having access to all that money was exciting, and he liked to pull Nina into his fantasy-filled discussions of how with his singing talent, and her father's contacts in the music industry, they could someday make millions with their own record label.

Nina really wasn't as turned on by the money as Derrick obviously was. When it came to material things, she had never done without. Mama and Daddy were both down-to-earth people who made sure their kids had everything they needed and were reasonable about what they wanted. Nina and Nathan were rarely spoiled. And when they were comin' up, if Daddy even thought his kids considered themselves somehow better than somebody because they had a little more money . . . that was the one thing in the Moore house that could earn you a swift backhand.

Though Nina wasn't spoiled with extravagant things, she did have a relatively carefree life compared to many of her friends. Nina was a grown woman—teaching college history and literature, working on her doctorate—and her parents still supplemented her income. When she was an undergrad, she was one of the few Black students on campus who could afford to live in the Desert Mirage Villas. She loved her apartment because it was so close to the campus, and she loved it best when it was full of her "peeps"—her friends and fellow BSU members.

Back in the day, Tonya and Nina had initiated the first Black Student Union in the history of Founder's Heritage College, a small private college outside Glendale. Even though Tonya was now working on her master's in education she still served as the BSU's president, and since Nina was now a member of the Founder's teaching staff, she was the official faculty advisor to the group.

Of course, the conservative Founder's administration was overly concerned with their "intent" when the club was formed, but the BSU hadn't really done much that could be considered controversial. So far they had organized reading and poetry circles, arranged for nationally renowned speakers to visit campus, and encouraged the members to constantly question and discuss ever-changing political, spiritual, and social paradigms.

But their next agenda item was to begin a campaign to force the school administration to honor the King holiday. To do that the first order of business was to increase the membership of the BSU for the coming year. They planned to get a jump on it by starting the campaign on registration day. That was only a few hours away. Nathan had agreed to pick the flyers up from the printer, and Nina and Tonya were supposed to meet him at the admin quad to help pass them out.

"I gotta get some sleep," Nina muttered to herself. The clock above the fireplace read 12:54. She returned to her bedroom to climb in between the sheets and found Derrick still snoring away. "Please, Lord," she whispered aloud, "please let me not have that dream tonight." Even as she whispered it, she knew the prayer would not ensure her protection. She had whispered it every night for the past six months, and at least once a week Derrick had to shake her from her terrifying nightmare. Nina edged closer to Derrick and buried her face against his chest, hoping somehow his nearness could chase away her fears and she could get just a few hours of restful sleep.

△▽ 2 ▽△

Ahmad Jefferson's head hurt. No, he didn't have a head*ache*. That was something you could describe in neat little terms, like "dull" or "sharp," "vice-like" or "throbbing." This was none of those, and yet all of those at the very same time. Ahmad was sure there were no words in the dictionary (and that was a book he knew quite well) that could adequately describe the agony he was experiencing lying on his back on his shabby couch in a pool of his own perspiration.

At least he had a couch to lie on. And he was truly grateful to his cousin Dwight for renting the apartment for him. Dwight had even gotten the electricity and phone turned on a week prior to Ahmad's arrival, but the accommodations left something to be desired. The air conditioner in the tiny studio was constantly on the blink, and the ceiling fan overhead only managed to circulate the sweltering heat, adding to Ahmad's misery.

He had tried a couple Tylenol around 10 P.M. At midnight he took three more. And here he was wide awake at one in the morning wishing it were possible for a man to temporarily remove his head from his shoulders.

What a week. Ahmad could scarcely believe everything that had happened in the last seven days. He'd been released from prison, relocated to Nowheresville, Arizona, been informed that his ex-best friend Scotty had driven off a cliff on the Oregon coast, learned that his estranged wife could no longer be categorized as "missing," and had driven from Arizona to

14

California and back to pick up his five-year-old daughter he had seen only once since she was an infant.

At age twenty-seven, he would be registering for college classes, starting a new job, and beginning his first official week of custodial parenthood.

But none of that could cloud the light that easily outshone the shadowy doubts he had about taking on all these challenges at once. That light shone even brighter than the one the LAPD flashed in his face the night they pulled him over five years earlier. It was the light of recognition that with all the burdens he had to bear, at least he was finally free.

It had been a week ago to the day that Ahmad's plan to rehabilitate his shattered life took a turn for the worse. He had been a free man for all of four days when the call came. He had just made a twenty-four-hour visit with his little daughter at his mother-in-law's trailer in San Bernardino, rode the Greyhound to Glendale, Arizona, and had finally settled into his tiny apartment when the phone rang. "Is this Theodore Jefferson?" The woman's voice had sounded way too crisp. Like she had ironed it and starched it for just such an occasion. The skin on Ahmad's forehead deepened into pained furrows and he immediately braced himself. His stomach tensed into a hard knot, and he stiffened, readying himself for what this crisp-voiced woman had called to tell him.

"Yes, this is Mr. Jefferson," Ahmad replied cautiously. He didn't need to explain to the stranger that he had changed his first name nearly three years earlier, right after he lost the appeal.

"This is Ms. Cane from the San Bernadino County Department of Children's Services." Ahmad sat down. What had Chante done this time? Ebony had been removed from her custody at least three times over the five years he had been locked up, and when he visited his daughter on the day of his release, she was living with Chante's mother in a trailer. Ebony had not seen her mother in over three months.

The crisp voice started up again. "Mr. Jefferson, I regret to inform you that your wife Chante Jefferson is deceased, and we have your daughter Ebony here. We'd like for you to make arrangements to retrieve her as soon as possible." Ahmad didn't utter a sound. *Did the crisp voice say "deceased"?*

Surely she meant "disappeared." He'd expected to hear that Chante was in another rehab center, that she'd been hospitalized, or maybe even that she'd been arrested, since Ahmad knew she'd been "away" again for a few months.

"I'm sorry." The woman hesitated. Perhaps she'd realized the magnitude of her words only after they'd been spoken.

Ahmad was desperately trying to focus his attention on the crisp voice. He fought the image that had formed behind his closed eyes of Chante lying dead in an alley somewhere, finally succumbing to the addiction that had stolen her heart from him less than a year after his arrest. *Chante deceased?* But he had prayed so hard for her. Hadn't he asked God to forgive him for deserting his family the way he did? Didn't God hear him begging every night for a chance to make it up to his wife?

The voice spoke again. "I'm sorry, Mr. Jefferson," she said, softer this time. "Apparently your wife has been missing for several months. She was identified yesterday in a morgue in Bakersfield."

Crisp Voice was quiet for a moment. When Ahmad didn't speak she added, "Ebony's grandmother was hospitalized with a massive stroke last night. We are looking for the child's next of kin." Ahmad dropped his forehead to the kitchen tabletop in disbelief, still holding the phone receiver to his ear. The voice was still talking.

"Ebony's the one who informed us that you were living in Arizona. She said she was going to go live with her daddy as soon as he got on his feet. She gave us your phone number herself. She's quite an articulate child."

Ahmad was sure the walls of the tiny apartment had collapsed around him, and it must have been their weight that was crushing his rib cage. His heart tightened into a tiny stone, and no matter how he tried he couldn't find a place in it to tuck away the cold reality that Chante was not alive. All the praying and planning . . . all the hoping he'd done over the last five years had been snatched out from under him with one crisp-voiced phone call. What about his chance at redemption? Didn't his daughter deserve a normal life in a home with two parents who loved each other? *Chante couldn't leave now. Not now.* Didn't she know he was back to fix all the damage he'd done?

Ahmad choked in a labored breath and held it in his throat. If he tried to breathe out, he'd never be able to suppress the agony that was building in his chest. After everything he'd been through, was he expected to survive this too? He had to survive. He had to breathe. He had to be okay for his baby girl. *For Ebony.* Ahmad concentrated on the recent reunion with the bright-eyed little girl. Until a couple of days earlier, he had only known her through pictures taped to his cell wall.

The first thing Ahmad did when he was officially a free man was hop on a bus to San Bernardino to see his child. He hadn't seen her since he'd kissed her and her mother good night some five years earlier. *God.* If he'd only known things were going to turn out the way they did, he'd have never let Scotty talk him into that late-night ride to Long Beach . . . But the past could never be undone, and he had to take a bus ride from the pen to get to know his own daughter all over again. Ebony had been a little shy at first, but after a couple of hours of sharing her favorite toys and books, she had warmed up to him as if they were old pals. By dinnertime, she had to have said the word "Daddy" at least a hundred times. "Daddy, look at the doll mommy gave me for my birthday. Daddy, do you wanna hear what me and Grammy sing in church? Daddy, what's your favorite color?"

When it was time for him to get on the road, Ebony curled herself into a ball at the end of the sofa and just stared at the wall. Ahmad tried to explain to her how much he wished he could take care of her right away. How much he wanted them all to be together again. When he pulled her onto his lap and hugged her good-bye, she crumpled against him and let out a sob that tore his heart out. All he could do was watch helplessly as Chante's mother took Ebony from his lap and attempted to console her. Before he walked out of the tiny trailer, he wrote the phone number Dwight had given him on a piece of paper, pressed it into Ebony's little hand, and promised he'd come back for her as soon as he "got on his feet."

The woman on the phone interrupted his thoughts. "If no one comes to claim your child," she said, "Ebony will have to be placed in a foster home."

"I'll be there tomorrow," Ahmad had said quietly. He had to go back for his daughter. That poor baby had been through enough. She'd spent her young life with a convicted felon for a father and a crackhead for a mother. *And now her mother was* . . . There was no way in hell he was going to let his daughter go to a foster anything. "Tell her her daddy's coming for her," he had said softly before gently placing the phone in its cradle.

That was three days ago, and now here he was in a tiny hole of an apartment in ninety-degree Arizona heat, wishing his head would just fall off and let him out of his misery. He had to feel better by tomorrow. He was starting his new job at the Founder's College gymnasium; he wasn't registered for classes yet, and school would begin in three weeks. Damn, he had to get Ebony registered for school too. *Talk about having a renewed respect for single parents.* Did he get the right kind of cereal for Ebony's breakfast in the morning? Was the milk he put in that raggedy icebox before he drove to California and back still good? Would his supervisor understand why he had to bring his daughter to work with him on his first day? Ahmad's uncle had gone out on a limb to set up the job for him; he definitely didn't want to blow it. And what about child care? Dwight had told him about a campus child care center that was free to students with low income, but there was a possibility that it was already full. What would he do with Ebony while he was at work?

This was ridiculous. He wasn't going to get any sleep, was he? Ahmad pulled back the sheet that covered him, sat up, and swung his feet onto the floor. He rested his elbows on his knees and dropped his throbbing temples into his hands. How could anybody sleep in this hellish heat?

Ebony wasn't sleeping either. She was sitting up on her little cot under the window clutching her Cabbage Patch doll to her chest. "Where's my grammy?" she said in a clear, tiny voice. "I want to go see my grammy."

Ahmad rose quickly from his spot on the tattered couch and knelt on the floor at Ebony's side. "Hey, baby," he said softly, "it's your daddy. I'm right here, punkin."

"I know you're here, silly." Ebony smiled at her father. "I was just thinking about Grammy. You know what, Daddy?"

"What's that, baby?" he asked, forgetting that his head was hurting like hell just a few minutes before.

"I don't think Grammy knows where I am. I need to call her and tell her I'm with my daddy so she won't worry."

"I'm sure she's not worried," he said. "I told your grammy I was coming for you." It was almost true.

Ebony pulled the cloth braids on her doll's head into a ponytail, and spoke with a voice much too sophisticated for her years. "I was helping Grammy wash dishes and she had to answer the phone, and then she fell asleep on the kitchen floor and wouldn't wake up, and I was scared." Ebony let go of the braids and held the doll's arms out, slowly walking the stuffed baby back and forth in her lap. "I called 911, like they told us at school, and they came to get Grammy, but she still didn't wake—" Ebony stopped mid-sentence. She held the Cabbage Patch doll to her chest and hugged it tightly. She didn't make a sound, but two enormous teardrops filled her eyes and spilled over onto her cheeks. She asked in a whisper, her voice trembling, "Is my grammy dead?"

"No, baby." Ahmad sat on the cot and pulled Ebony onto his lap. He wiped the tears with his fingertips. "She's just very sick. The doctors want to make sure she's okay. That's why they kept her in the hospital. We'll go visit her as soon as she's better."

Ebony immediately stopped crying. "Daddy?"

Ahmad looked into his little girl's face. God, she looked like her mother. Back in the day, Chante had a smile that would light up an entire room, and a set of shining brown eyes to match. And little Ebony had her same smooth, Hershey-brown skin with a subtle red glow just under the surface. "Yes, baby?" he replied.

"Is my mommy dead?"

This time it was Ahmad's eyes that filled to the brim with tears, only he was determined not to let his daughter see them fall. "Why do you ask that, Ebony?" He tried to keep his quivering voice still.

"I heard Grammy say so right before she went to sleep."

Ahmad's insides were twisted in knots. How was he supposed to be strong for this baby, when all he wanted to do was lay down on the floor and bawl like a baby himself? Yes, her mommy was dead. And yes, it was all his fault. All Chante ever wanted was the fairy tale family they had created to-

gether, and who knows what might have been, if only . . . It
all seemed so wrong, and so unfair. Chante didn't deserve
what she got, and Ebony didn't deserve what she got, and he
. . . How could anyone deserve all this misery from one choice
made in a split second in the middle of the night?

"Is she, Daddy?" The hurt and concern that were so ap-
parent when she asked about her grandmother were strangely
absent now.

"Your mommy went to heaven, baby." Ahmad's voice was
trembling, but he managed to hold the tears back.

Ebony's forehead wrinkled into a scowl and she sat solemnly, quietly contemplating the words her father had spoken.
She reached up to finger Ahmad's tiny dreadlocks in one hand,
while she fingered the braids of her doll with the other. She
seemed to be making a comparison between the two, and Ahmad breathed a sigh of relief that she'd been distracted from
her heartbreaking question. She'd accepted his answer for
now, and maybe later they could discuss death and what it
really meant. Ebony broke the silence between them.

"Mommy went to heaven," she said plainly. "That's the
same thing as dead, isn't it, Daddy?" The calm matter-of-
factness in her voice sent a jagged blade deep into Ahmad's
heart, and he struggled to hold in the low, sad moan that ached
to be released. The way this five-year-old baby sat calmly
discussing the final disappearance of her on-again-off-again
mother told Ahmad just how much trauma his little girl had
already sustained.

Ebony's words had coaxed the reluctant tears out onto his
face. "Yes, baby," was all Ahmad could manage and keep
what was left of the control he had over his emotions. He
hadn't cried since that day in court when his world came
crashing down around him, and now that he was face to face
with the real victim of that fateful day, two streams of silent
tears ran down his face. Ebony reached her hands up to wipe
her daddy's tears away, soaking the edges of her nightgown
sleeves. "You got too many tears, Daddy," she said, shaking
her head sadly.

"I made enough for me and you, punkin," he said, and,
planting a kiss on her forehead, he put her down gently on the
cot and held his daughter until they both fell asleep.

△▽ 3 ▽△

Nina's dream began, as always, in the midst of a dense, chilling fog. She stood frozen with terror at the entrance to a cemetery, clutching the bars of a wrought-iron fence and praying for an escape from the scene materializing before her eyes. Her powerlessness against the coming horror clutched like icy fingers at her throat, and she struggled for breath against the blanket of absolute dread that had wrapped itself tightly around her, letting her take in only short, labored gasps.

The mere thought of being in a cemetery when Nina was awake made her sick to her stomach, so to find herself in this nightmare looking out at a scene taking place among the tombstones was nearly unbearable. What was most horrifying was that for the duration of this recurring nightmare, she would be aware it was a dream, but the events that followed would be completely outside of her control. Nina ached to be awakened. If only Derrick would roll over or shake her or . . .

It was too late for that now; it had begun. Through the bars, about twenty feet from her, she saw the same little girl that was always there. The child stood alone near a towering gray oak tree with her back to Nina. Nina couldn't tell how old the child was, but she seemed tiny compared to the huge gravestones standing nearby. The little girl's pale pink wool dress with matching bonnet, white gloves, tights, and patent leather shoes seemed to glow faintly against the muted grays and blues of the cemetery scene.

Nina tried to mentally will the little girl to just turn slightly, so she could find some sign or clue to her identity, but the child skipped ahead a few feet as she always did, and pointed toward a faraway tree, giggling to herself. "Lookit," the girl said aloud, still pointing.

She looks so sweet and innocent, all dressed in pink, Nina thought sadly. That's when the reality of the scene before her, and the events that were to come, shattered her thoughts and the awesome feeling of dread rushed over her in a wave.

Nina whimpered a low, soul-stirring cry like the howl of a she-wolf looking through a fence at her newborn pup.

"No. Oh God . . . No. Please. Little girl. Please listen. You have to run, baby." She called out to the child desperately, but the girl seemed not to hear her. "He'll be coming. Please run away. Oh God . . . Please.

Nina watched in horror as a tall black-suited man with ghost-white skin appeared slowly from behind the tree near where the child was playing. Nina studied his face, hoping to find some clue of his intent. The man's expression was blank and rather benign, yet his closely cropped beard, black hat and dark glasses gave him an ominous appearance, which made Nina shudder. From somewhere deep in her being, Nina knew he was going to hurt this little girl, and she was not going to be able to get to her in time to save her. She felt her legs weakening beneath her and, frustrated at her powerlessness, she leaned into the bars and whimpered to herself in a tiny voice wet with tears, "*Please* don't hurt her. Please."

Nina's fear suddenly gave way to anger. Somebody had to be responsible for this child. Who would leave a little girl all alone? Nina straightened and scanned the cemetery for a sign that someone might be looking for the child. Someone must be coming to save her from this terrible man. Weren't her mother and father worried sick about her?

Nina's stomach tensed into a hard angry fist that threatened to push its way up into her throat. *What kind of parents would allow a child to wander off in a cemetery? What kind of parents . . . Oh no. Oh my God.* Just as suddenly as her anger had risen, it dropped in a hard ball in the pit of her stomach, and was replaced again by a breath-stealing terror. Maybe she didn't have any parents. Maybe they were dead. Maybe he killed them first, and now he was coming to kill her too. Nina screamed at the man, "She's just a baby. Leave her alone, you bastard!" But neither the man nor the child heard a thing.

Nina focused again on the little girl. She had not yet noticed the man approaching and sat motionlessly, entranced by a squirrel scurrying along the fence. When it disappeared from sight, the girl dropped to her knees in the grass and picked one of the small yellow flowers growing there. She began singing softly to herself.

Nina prayed, *Please, Lord, wake me up. Derrick, somebody, anybody . . . please.* She tried closing her eyes, but she couldn't make the scene disappear. She was going to have to watch whatever evil thing the man was going to do to that precious baby, and there was nothing Nina could do to stop him.

The man moved closer to the child, holding his right hand behind his back, as if he had something hidden.

Nina wanted to control her terror, but it washed over her like an ocean wave, leaving her choking and gasping for air. She tried talking to herself between breaths. "It's just a dream. It's just a dream." She chanted the words over and over, hoping they could calm her fear, but instead the chant grew louder and louder until she found herself screaming in a loud, raspy voice.

When the stranger was only a few feet from the child, and the little girl still had not heard his approach, Nina began screaming uncontrollably. "Don't you hurt her! She's just a baby!" She wanted desperately for the child to hear her. "Run away, honey. He's going to hurt you. Oh God. He has something. He's hiding something. Please hear me. Why won't you run away?"

Nina's mind uncontrollably envisioned the torturous things the man surely had in store for the defenseless child. Scenarios sprang to life in her head, tormenting her with heinous possibilities she might have to witness. *What if behind his back he's holding a butcher knife?* Nina fought the image that had formed in her head of the stranger holding the blade over the little girl, stabbing it into the child's body again and again, while her little wool coat turned red with blood. Nina managed to purge that image from her mind, but an equally terrifying one quickly replaced it. A vivid picture of him sneaking up from behind with a thin, braided rope stretched taut between his fists began to materialize. Would Nina be forced to watch him wrap the rope around the child's neck, choking her with it until she hung limp and lifeless like a rag doll? And then what? Would Nina be a captive audience while this vicious creep molested the child's body? She fought desperately to shake those images from her thoughts.

Oh God, please, I can't take this, Nina prayed in anguish. The terror had built deep in her lungs. Maybe if she could build up enough pressure . . . maybe she could make a sound that would let Derrick know how much she needed him to save her from this horror. She held her breath, and with all her might attempted to push a scream from her throat, but there was no sound behind it.

The man moved again, taking slow, careful steps toward the child. *"No,"* Nina moaned. She tried frantically to break through the gate, which was held closed by a heavy chain and a huge iron padlock. She stood screaming, shaking the gate, and watching in terror as the man reached up with his left hand, removed his sunglasses, and placed them in the breast pocket of his coat. Then, as if in slow motion, his right hand began moving forward. Nina's heart was pounding so hard she could hear it echoing in her head. After weeks and weeks of having to endure this tormenting dream, she was finally going to see what the man was hiding behind his back. Nina held her breath in horror and steeled herself for the gruesome scene that was to come. And just as she caught sight of what seemed to be a glint of metal, as it had so many times before, the scene began to blur and Nina was awakened to the sounds of her own sobs, and Derrick shaking her from her tormented sleep.

"Damn, Nina," Derrick grunted sleepily. "Not again. Shit, and I was sleeping good too. Wake up, girl. Dammit, Nina, wake up."

Nina sat straight up, her chest heaving violently as she fought to control her terror. "He was going to hurt her, Derrick," she gasped for air. "He . . . It's just so real." She took a deep breath and forced her voice down to a calmer tone. "She . . . I . . . I'm standing there terrified . . . like . . . like whatever he's getting ready to do to her . . ." Nina fought the tears that gathered behind her eyes.

She knew how hard this was for Derrick. He was never very good at compassion or sympathy, and crying just frustrated him. When he sat up suddenly against the headboard, for an instant she thought maybe he was going to hold her . . . tell her everything was going to be okay . . . that together they could get through this thing. Instead he just looked at her for a long moment.

"What are you thinking?" Nina finally whispered.

"I think you need a damn doctor." There was a hint of disgust in his voice.

"You know what, Derrick . . ." She shook her head slowly. "You are absolutely right. A doctor is exactly what I must need."

Derrick realized his mistake, but it was too late. "Come here, baby. I'm sorry. It was just a dream, Nina. It was just a bad dream." He put his hand over his heart and gave her his best sincere look. "I was trying to make you feel better. Come on now, baby, the only doctor you need is me. Let Dr. Derrick make it all better."

Derrick reached for Nina, but she pulled away and rose from the bed just as the alarm clock on the dresser across the room began to sound.

Nina walked over to turn the alarm off. "You know, you really can be a jerk sometimes."

"And you know, I think you're even more beautiful when you're mad." Derrick laughed nervously. His eyes roamed the length of her, moving suggestively over Nina's curves. "And you look really good right now, so you must be real upset." Nina glared at him in disgust.

"Aw, baby. I'm just playing with you. Come on, girl." Derrick lifted the bedcovers up to his eyes like a child might, and looked playfully beneath them. He smiled slyly. "I've got something for you."

Nina watched Derrick from the bathroom doorway. His antics were making her nauseous. How many times in the past had his little boy charm worked on her? *Humph. This would not be one of them.* "Yeah, well, when I'm done with the shower, I'll leave the cold water on for that."

She ignored Derrick's pouting look. She knew it well. It was supposed to get her to play the "aw, let me make it all better now" role. She wasn't having it today. She went to the dresser and pulled out some underwear, while skillfully avoiding the intermittent reaches Derrick made in his attempt to get her back in the bed.

She sidestepped an especially energetic lunge from Derrick. "You better quit now. You know I told Sweet Nat I was down for flyer duty . . . and so did you."

"Yeah, yeah, yeah. I don't know why I let you and your crazy brother talk me into this Afrocentric bullshit in the first place. BSU ain't nothin' but a bunch of irritated Negroes irritating everybody else, and damn sure irritating the hell out of me."

"Don't go there, Derrick. First of all, you know I don't play when it comes to my baby brother. That's my heart. And second, if you really think being Afrocentric is bullshit, then some irritation is just what a brotha like you needs."

Derrick came back with a sarcastic grin. "Oh, all right then, Sista Soldier. The girl thinks because her daddy's Black she has to make up for all the wrongs done by her mama's side of the family."

Nina was getting pissed now. The aftereffects of the dream were gone, and Nina felt intensely irritated. How was this fool going to start talking about her mother and her daddy? She didn't want to let Derrick know he had struck a nerve, so when she spoke, her voice was calm and controlled. "Look, I didn't even know my mother. All I know is what you know; she was White, and she died when I was two. Why do you need to bring her in it anyway? Mama and Daddy raised me. And they raised me the same way they raised Nat . . . as a Black child."

Derrick knew he'd struck a nerve. "Aw, damn . . . here we go." They both knew it was too late to avoid the direction the conversation was headed in.

There was a little more intensity in Nina's voice when she spoke again. She knew Derrick had heard what she was telling him for the umpteenth time, but it was as if saying it to him once more might help it sink in. "I'm not trying to *make up* for anything. Being Black is what I know. And being Black and looking White is . . ." She looked him straight in the eye.

"It's not as easy a situation to be in as you might think. Believe me."

Derrick shook his head emphatically. "I don't know why you don't just count yourself lucky for missing out on the melanin. You need to quit trippin' and start trying to use your white skin to your advantage. I know I would if I was you."

Nina had moved into the bathroom, and had to shout her response over the sound of the shower. "Try to use it to my advantage? I don't even have to try. That's the point. My white skin *is* an advantage. And sometimes I don't have to do anything but show up. Did you know I got the key to this apartment the same day I turned my application in?"

Derrick followed Nina into the bathroom. He stood in front of the toilet taking a piss, barely paying attention to her.

Nina stuck her head out from behind the shower curtain. "Derrick? Are you even listening?"

"Huh? Oh yeah, baby, you got my full attention. Go ahead."

She returned to the shower spray, and continued trying to make her point. "Tonya had come in to pick up the application the day before I turned it in, and they told her they weren't even adding names to the waiting list until the following spring. When I handed in the application myself a couple of hours later, they showed me this place, took my check, and handed me a key. You should've seen their reaction when we were moving in, and they realized Tonya was my roommate. They were falling all over themselves trying to make up some story about how a new employee made a mistake. Yeah, the mistake was somebody noticed Tonya was Black. Ain't that a bitch?"

Derrick jumped on the opportunity to voice his dislike for Nina's roommate. "Mmmm hmmm . . . Tonya . . . yeah, that *is* a bitch."

Nina pushed back the shower curtain. "What did you say?"

Derrick was momentarily transfixed at the sight of Nina's wet, naked body standing in front of him. When his eyes finally made their way up to her face he mutttered, "Huh? Oh. I said, yeah, racism . . . that *is* a bitch."

Nina slid the curtain closed, still talking to Derrick as she soaped her body under the spray of warm water. "I'm a volunteer at the center, and I didn't even start working there until a year after Tonya became a supervisor. She trained me. I'm not the one with the child development degree, and word is they want to offer me the director position that's opening up. Why?'' Nina squeezed some shampoo into her hand and massaged it into her scalp. ''Because they don't see Tonya as 'director material.' My girl can organize the hell out of anything. Most of those dollars we're working with at the Black Student Union came from conservative White donors Tonya nurtured relationships with. Not director material? Whatever.''

Derrick didn't respond, so Nina began rinsing the shampoo from her hair. With her back to the shower spray, she closed her eyes tight and followed the flow of the thick suds with her hands. Why was she letting him get her all worked up over this conversation? It was lost on his ears anyway, wasn't it? Derrick wasn't trying to do anything for anybody but Derrick.

Nina switched her attention to the warmth of the water cascading down her back. Sliding both hands down the back of her head, she brought the suds forward over her collarbone, and smoothed the lather over her breasts. She became lost momentarily in the feel of the silky lather against her skin. The sensation of the warm spray of water, coupled with the silky lather, had created a pleasant tingling sensation in her now firm nipples. She suddenly felt a surge of self-consciousness. Was Derrick watching her? Or had he retreated to the bedroom to escape Nina's attempt at enlightening him?

He left. He's not trying to hear any of this. ''And . . . last term . . . you know Professor Sorenson?'' She was almost hollering.

But Derrick was right there, peering through the edge of the curtain. He had been watching Nina's hands glide over her glistening curves. When he finally spoke, the nearness of his voice startled her. ''Yeah, baby,'' he groaned, ''Sorenson. Writing 346.'' Derrick looked down at the erection in his briefs. ''He's hard as a muthafucka.''

Nina turned quickly to face the spray of water, hoping Derrick wouldn't notice her erect nipples and think she wanted him to join her in the shower. ''Yeah, he's real hard,'' she responded quickly. ''He gave me an A minus on a research paper that Tonya helped me write. And on her own paper she got a C.''

Derrick removed his briefs and stepped in the shower behind Nina. ''Yeah, well, the only reason they're mistaking you for White is 'cause they're not looking at the one thing you did get from your Black side.''

Nina wiped the water from her face with a washcloth and looked over her shoulder at Derrick. ''Oh, and what's that?''

''Your backside. Paiyyow,'' Derrick laughed, smacking Nina's behind playfully.

Nina looked at him with one eyebrow raised and that ''you ain't funny'' look on her face before she reached to turn off the hot water. She stepped quickly out onto the bathrug then, leaving Derrick and his erection alone in a cold shower.

By the time Nina had put on a pair of khaki slacks and a white blouse and returned to the bathroom to apply styling gel to her still-damp hair, Derrick had emerged from the shower and was standing draped in a towel in front of the double-sinked vanity admiring his reflection. When Nina leaned against the counter to reach for the gel in the cabinet above the sink, Derrick moved behind her, pressing himself against her body. He slid his hands underneath Nina's blouse rubbing his fingertips gently against her nipples and pressing his mouth into a soft, passionate tongue kiss against her neck. Nina closed her eyes on reflex, and felt a shudder of pleasure as Derrick's tongue traced a burning path slowly up the side of her neck until he was sucking gently on her earlobe. His left hand caressed her left breast, while his right hand ran smoothly down the front of her body until his fingertips stopped just underneath the waistband of her panties. He whispered breathlessly, ''Just ask me, baby, you know I'll do whatever.''

Damn, he was good when he wanted to be. As mad as she was, and as through as she was with him and his selfish ways, she knew exactly what he was offering to do to her. Derrick's tongue against her skin had caused an electric current that crept from her neck all the way down her spine, and it was resting uncomfortably between her legs in an aching throb. The image of his face buried between her thighs and him kissing between her legs the way he had just sucked all over her earlobe burned in her mind and for a split second she considered the offer. But she had no intention of giving in to the desire.

Nah . . . Unh-unh. Nina almost said it aloud. Given the fact that she was trying to figure out how to break their engagement, Nina was ashamed of herself for being so weak. True, Derrick was offering to make her the center of attention for a change. *Damn, that sounds good.* But no. In spite of the passionless sex they had had the night before, and the effort she had made to work him into an orgasm, without coming herself, she wasn't about to let him work her so easily. She didn't want to let Derrick know the physical effect he was having on her. Besides, she *had* to get to the quad by 6:30. "Sorry, Derrick." Nina tried to keep her voice light; he could act like a real baby when he was turned down for sex. "I have too much to do to be playing love slave with you all morning," she joked.

Derrick was not going out that easy. He flashed his dimpled smile at her in the mirror. "Oh, I see, so it's a slave thing now, huh? See how you White people are? Always trying to keep a Black man in bondage." He nuzzled his face in her neck. "Hmmm . . . speaking of bondage . . ."

"Very funny," Nina replied. She bent down quickly and snatched up the towel he'd dropped, handing it to Derrick with her best "don't even try it" face. He hesitated for a moment, then wrapped it around his waist with much attitude. Nina ignored his glare and tried to sweeten the words he wasn't going to be interested in hearing. "I'm serious, Derrick. We're trying to recruit from the registration lines. And we could use your help."

Derrick was not happy. He could pout for days over that kind of rejection. "I told you I'm not down with that Black Panther thang," he said abruptly. He pushed past Nina and walked back into the bedroom.

She ignored the hint of anger in his voice and returned to the bedroom to make her bed. "I don't understand you, Derrick. You attended Founder's once upon a time. I mean . . . you know what it's like for these students—to be one of only, what, maybe fifty or sixty Blacks on campus."

"And?"

"And the Black Student Union fought for the African-

American history class and the Black lit class.''

''And?''

''And if we didn't, as you say, 'irritate' the hell out of some folks, Dr. Griffin would not be on campus either.''

Derrick perched himself on the corner of the dresser and watched Nina busily tucking the sheets under the mattress. ''Okay . . . I have to give you all credit for that one. Dr. Griffin is the man. Even the reddest of the redneck White boys has to admit that.''

''They gave in on that, but we still have the King holiday issue. I can't believe they actually had the nerve last year to announce that the campus was staying open . . . but Black people could stay home.''

''So?''

''So . . . we're talking about a federal holiday. I mean, damn, we're entering a new millennium.''

''All right already, Angela Davis. Calm down, sista. Damn. I said I'd help with the flyers. I'm just gonna . . . uh . . . uh . . . Jason has some information on this producer I'm supposed to hook up with this afternoon. I'll catch up with you after that.''

Nina smoothed the last of the wrinkles from the ivory bedspread, and arranged the Nigerian-print throw pillows in a pattern against the headboard. She gathered her purse and her car keys from the dresser and started toward the door.

Derrick got up from where he had been perched on the corner of the dresser, and plopped, wet towel and all, onto the freshly made bed. Nina just shook her head in disgust. She would have to tell him tonight. She couldn't go on like this forever. She doubted Derrick would catch up, but she took her door key off her key ring and tossed it to him anyway. ''Here's my key. Be sure to lock the deadbolt. I'll see you at the quad.''

◺▽ 4 ▽◿

"*Wake up, Ebony.*" *Ahmad pressed the last* wrinkle from the tee shirt he planned to wear, and set the secondhand iron on its base. He picked up Ebony's little Cabbage Patch doll and planted a loud pretend kiss on her cheek with it. "Come on now, lil' bit, we have a lot to do today."

Ahmad had awakened at five minutes to six, just in time to turn the alarm off before it sounded. It was not quite as hot today as yesterday; his head didn't hurt anymore, and after getting in a light workout, taking a quick shower, and offering his morning prayers, he was actually feeling hopeful about the day.

Ebony didn't complain or even yawn at the early morning wakeup. She got up from the cot, kissed her doll, motioned for her father to bend down for his kiss, planted a ceremonious smooch on his face, said, "Good morning, Daddy," and headed for the bathroom all in one smooth motion, like it was a familiar routine.

Ahmad stared at the closed bathroom door and shook his head with an amused smile. *That's definitely my baby girl.* He laughed softly to himself, and went to the kitchen to see about breakfast. "Ebony, do you want Cheerios or cornflakes?" There was no answer. He opened the refrigerator and took the carton of milk out. It smelled funny. *Great.* "Ebony?" he said a little louder. Still no answer. He knocked twice on the bathroom door before peeking in. Ebony was in the bathtub washing up.

"Daddy," she complained, "I'm taking a bath. Boys aren't

supposed to see me naked.'' Ahmad chuckled and backed out the door. She sure was an independent little lady. God knows it would help him cope.

He sat down at the kitchen table and went over his registration paperwork. He'd be working thirty hours a week at the gym, and had planned to take a full load of classes, so he could finish his political science degree and finally be able to begin law school in a year or two, but that was before he knew he'd have Ebony. So, now he could only take three classes three days a week. Ebony would have to get in at the campus child care center—if there were any openings, that is. There was no way he could afford rent, utilities, groceries *and* child care. The job would only be paying just over minimum wage, and though he did have a little money left over from the welcome home envelope Uncle Three had given him, things were going to be tight in this new little Jefferson family for a while. And though he wished he could do better, he considered it a blessing to be driving around Glendale in a beat-up old Volvo station wagon that looked and sounded like it was on its last legs, thanks again to his generous and only speaking relatives.

Uncle Three, who Ahmad wasn't even sure was really related to him by blood, got his name from an accident he was in at the tobacco plant he'd worked at in Virginia. He'd lost the thumb and forefinger on his right hand, and though he got a nice settlement back in the day and invested it well, he wasn't in a financial position to do much more than he already had. The child care center was Ahmad's only hope. If Ebony could go there every day after school, and spend a few extra hours there three evenings a week, they'd manage.

''Ebony, what on earth is taking you so long?'' He knocked softly on the bathroom door.

''Just a minute, Daddy. I'm . . . almost . . .'' The door opened and Ebony was standing there fully dressed in a blue and white checkered sundress and white sandals. Her face, arms, and legs gleamed from the lotion she had generously applied, and except for a touch of toothpaste clinging to the corner of her mouth and an uncombed head, she was all ready to go.

''Well, I'll be.'' Ahmad thought he was going to have to struggle through a morning of face washing, teeth brushing, and generally undesirable task management. But Ebony had even folded her pajamas in a neat little pile on the toilet seat and her towel was folded and hanging on the rack.

Ahmad scooped his little girl up into his arms. "I just have to give you a big thank-you hug, Ms. Ebony."

"Thank me for what?" She grinned gleefully.

"For being such a big girl. For getting dressed all by yourself. And for picking up after yourself."

"Oh, Daddy, you are so silly. I always do that."

Ahmad whispered a prayer of thanks to Chante and Mrs. Taylor, her mother, for taking care of his daughter without him. Despite the less than desirable circumstances, his little girl had turned out to be a well-mannered and well-behaved little sweetheart.

"Daddy, did you hear me?"

"What, punkin?"

"I said I'm hungry, Daddy."

Ahmad wiped the smudge of toothpaste from the corner of his daughter's mouth. "First we're going to fix this hair of yours and then we're going to have a father-daughter breakfast at McDonald's."

Ebony did a little dance and clapped her hands. "Micky D's, Micky D's," she chanted excitedly. Ahmad chuckled at her display of glee as he sat on the couch and had Ebony sit cross-legged on the floor in front of him. He parted her hair down the middle and began gently combing through the tangles. Fortunately, he had learned how to braid from the guys on his cellblock, and compared to most of the heads in the pen, Ebony's thick, wavy tresses were a cinch.

Ebony could hardly keep still. She went on and on about the time she went to McDonald's with Grammy, and the Hamburglar gave her cookies and . . . Ahmad listened intently to the story. It filled his heart with a comforting warmth to hear that his daughter had happy memories she could share with him now, but it was an equally painful reminder that there were probably hundreds of seemingly insignificant moments in her short life that he'd never know about because he hadn't been there to help create them.

Let me just thank God I'm here now, Ahmad thought as he twisted the ends of her hair. He didn't even want to consider what might have happened to his daughter if he were still in prison. "There we go," he said, admiring the two neat corn-rows he'd braided on either side of Ebony's head. "Now, I just gotta put my shirt on, and . . ." Ahmad pulled the tee shirt over his head. "All ready to go." He tucked the shirt in his beige Dickies, and bent down in front of Ebony to tie the strings on his black leather boots.

"Before there was . . . any history . . . there was . . . Black history," Ebony said slowly.

Ahmad looked at his daughter in amazement.

"I'm reading your shirt, Daddy," she said matter-of-factly.

"I didn't know you knew how to read, Ms. Ebony." He wanted to ask her if it was her mommy or her grandmother that had taken the time to teach her, but he couldn't revisit the pain of Chante's permanent absence.

"Everybody knows how to read, Daddy," she replied se-riously.

"No, punkin." Ahmad picked her up. "Not everybody. I know some grown-ups who can't read." Ahmad thought of his cellmate, Dud. Dud was a stocky little brotha with jet black skin and hair that grew close to his head in tight little naps. The whites of his eyes were a pale yellow, which led people to assume he'd had some kind of problem with alcohol, but Dud didn't even drink beer; he'd just lived the hard life of the streets for too long and his soul's weariness showed through in his eyes. But you couldn't see that weariness anywhere else. Dud was strong and quick and smarter than anybody Ahmad had come across on the inside. Dud had that kind of intelli-gence that led to trouble without an appropriate avenue for its expression . . . plain old street smarts. He was an illiterate bro-tha with more heart than Ahmad had ever seen, but no matter how hard Ahmad had tried to convince him to learn to read, Dud stubbornly refused to try.

"Grown-ups that can't read? They're silly, Daddy," Ebony said, then added, referring to Ahmad's shirt, "What does that mean?"

"It means Black people were the first ones God made," Ahmad explained. "And we shouldn't forget how important we are."

"Oh." Ebony became strangely quiet, and stared at the tee

shirt thoughtfully. Ahmad wondered if wearing an Afrocentric tee shirt on his first day at the job was a good idea, but until he could get to a Laundromat, he really didn't have a choice. And besides, his boss was a brotha, and he'd be working in a gym. Who cared what he wore, as long as he did his job? "Let's go, Ebony," he said, still holding his daughter in his arms. He picked up his paperwork with one hand, bent down so Ebony could turn the front door knob, and carried her out to the car.

By the time they got in the car and Ebony was buckled in, and she realized in horror that she hadn't gotten everything, and they'd gone back inside to get her Cabbage Patch doll and her cherished little paper bag of Hershey's Kisses, and she was finally back in her seat belt, it was a quarter to seven. He feared the registration lines would be ridiculous if he didn't get to the campus soon. They'd have to drive through McDonald's. Ahmad pulled the car out into the mostly empty street and headed for Micky D's.

"There it is, Daddy," Ebony giggled. "There it is right there." If she didn't have a seat belt on, he was sure she'd be on the ceiling.

"Okay, lil' bit, I see it." He laughed at the youngster's obvious excitement. "Oh shit," he added under his breath. Just as he made his right turn onto the main avenue, a police car coming from the opposite direction turned left and changed lanes, pulling directly behind the Volvo. Ahmad's throat tightened and he felt a surge of blood race through his heart, causing an instant throbbing at his temples. He wasn't about to panic. That was all he needed. Make a sudden movement, or draw that cop's attention by seeming nervous or rigid. *Just be cool, man*, he thought to himself. He wasn't even sure if the cop had noticed him. All he knew was the last time he looked into a rearview mirror and saw a squad car in it he'd lost five years of his life.

Ahmad turned into the McDonald's drive-through and stopped at the speaker. He looked in his rearview again. The cop had pulled over to the side of the road with his engine running.

"May I have your order, please," the speaker voice asked politely.

"I want a Egg McMuffin, Daddy."

Ahmad had his eye on the mirror.

Ebony sounded tense and uneasy when she said, "Daddy?"

"What, baby? You say you want an Egg McMuffin?"

"Yes, please. And a orange juice."

"We'll have two Egg McMuffins and two orange juices," Ahmad said into the speaker.

"Two number ones with orange juice. That'll be four dollars and twenty-two cents at the window, please."

Ahmad pulled slowly around the building, losing sight of the police car. *Good. Maybe he'll lose interest and drive away.* Or maybe the cop was planning to park and go in the restaurant for coffee.

"That'll be four twenty-two." The teenager in the booth held out his hand.

Ahmad paid for the food, handed the bag to Ebony, and set the tray with the juices in it on the floor in front of her seat before pulling carefully past the building and back onto the street. The police car was still there, and it pulled away from the curb and followed behind him down the avenue. It didn't take long for the cop to make his decision.

"Great," Ahmad muttered. The flashing lights were on, and the police siren let out a shrill moan before Ahmad pulled slowly to the side of the road and cut the engine. He instinctively put both hands on top of the steering wheel.

Ahmad noticed that Ebony had become strangely quiet. "Here, baby," he said, taking the bag from her and handing her one of the sandwiches. "Eat your breakfast, punkin." Ebony didn't say a word. She slowly unwrapped the Egg McMuffin and lifted it to her mouth.

"Put your hands where I can see 'em," the cop barked in Ahmad's ear. Ahmad jerked his hands to the steering wheel. "This your car?"

"No, sir," Ahmad said quietly. "It belongs to my uncle."

The cop was staring down at the writing on Ahmad's tee shirt. Ahmad watched the sun-scorched White man's lips move slowly as he read. When the message finally registered, a pink-red wave flushed up his neck and across his face. He didn't even seem to hear Ahmad's response to the question. "Let me see your license and registration, boy," he barked.

As if Ahmad didn't have enough to deal with already. He rolled his eyes heavenward. *C'mon, now*, he thought. *Not a small-town, racist cop. Not today, Lord.* Ahmad stared straight ahead. *I can get through this*, he said silently. He'd had the inner strength he needed to survive the pen, to finally be free and to be seated beside his little girl, who, like him, could find so much joy in something as simple as an Egg McMuffin. He could certainly deal with this little redneck's verbal abuse.

"Excuse me, Officer," Ahmad offered in a calm voice. "I am a twenty-seven-year-old man . . ." He looked over at his daughter, who had her head down and was taking another bite of her sandwich. Then he turned toward the officer and looked him directly in the eye. ". . . not a boy."

Ahmad knew he was flirting with disaster. But as long as he didn't lose his temper, and he complied with the officer's requests, the cop wouldn't be crazy enough to do anything to him in front of his little girl, would he?

"Well, excuse me then. Let me see your license and registration . . ." The officer put his hand on his revolver. ". . . *man*." He spat the last word out distastefully.

Ahmad reached into the glove compartment and handed the registration to the cop. His old California driver's license was in the wallet in his lap. He removed it and handed it to the officer also, looking him directly in the eye when he said, "It's expired. I just moved to Arizona and I'm going to . . ."

The officer didn't let him finish. "Step out of the vehicle," he grunted.

Ahmad put his forehead down on the steering wheel. He sighed deeply before unbuckling his seat belt and pulling the door handle. He looked over at Ebony. She gazed up at him for a moment with a look of fear on her face, then she lowered her eyes to her Egg McMuffin and took another tiny bite.

Ahmad had barely gotten out of the open door when the officer slammed it shut and shoved him roughly against the front fender. "Put your hands on the hood. Spread-eagle . . . *man*," the officer barked. His face had turned a yellowish red color, and his neck muscles were so tensed Ahmad thought the man might be having a heart attack or something. He was scaring Ebony. Ahmad tried to get eye contact with his little girl, but she was staring at her hands, which were folded limply around the barely eaten breakfast sandwich in her lap.

The officer pushed Ahmad forward over the hood and kicked his left foot roughly to spread Ahmad's legs apart more than a foot.

"I said, spread 'em."

Ebony looked up and caught her daddy's pained expression. Her eyes began leaking tears. The look on his daughter's tear-streaked face was more than Ahmad could bear. He looked away.

"You're scaring my daughter," Ahmad grunted through clenched teeth. *Man, fuck this shit.* He felt the warmth of the hood against his face. It was cool compared to the angry heat that was spreading through his body. *I could break this little muthafucka's neck with my bare hands.* Ahmad ached to put his hands on him. If only they had met under different circumstances, in a bar or a dark alley. *Little redneck muthafucka wouldn't have the nerve to call a brotha "boy" then, would he?*

A minivan pulled slowly alongside, its White occupants of various ages gawking at the scene like they had bought tickets to a wild animal park. Ahmad caught the eye of the middle-aged woman behind the wheel. She read the aura of anger radiating from Ahmad, and stiffened instantly, gripping the steering wheel tighter. Her eyes seemed to both accuse Ahmad and thank the policeman in one glaring look of relief. Ahmad just stared at the woman as she drove on past.

The officer ran his nightstick along the inside of Ahmad's legs, putting an added nudge in when the stick reached his groin. Ahmad flinched, but didn't make a sound. When the cop was convinced Ahmad wasn't carrying a weapon, he stood back and said with feigned politeness, "You may return to your vehicle, *man.*" When Ahmad stood erect and turned around the cop added with a cold stare, "But you don't leave until I tell you to leave."

The officer sauntered back to his patrol car while Ahmad opened the door to the Volvo and slumped in behind the wheel. He leaned his head back on the headrest for a moment. The humiliation and anger he been forced to suppress had lodged in his gut, and the heat of it simmered into a sour taste that made him want to spit. It frightened Ahmad to realize

how close he could come to ending up back behind bars. One
wrong step. One caving in to the natural desire to defend one-
self . . . one's dignity . . . and he'd have been charged with assault on an officer. He breathed slow and deep, and
remembered to thank God soberly for giving him the patience
to endure.

He turned to Ebony, who was still looking down at her
hands. "You okay, punkin?" She shrugged without looking
up. "Ebony?"

The cop was back at the window. "I know you're new
around here. But don't you let me catch you drivin' 'round
my city with no expired license again, *boy*." He scribbled his
initials on the bottom of the citation and shoved it in at Ahmad
along with the registration and the license. "Have a nice day."

Ahmad let his head fall back against the headrest and let
out a long weary sigh. They sat in silence for a moment.

Ebony finally spoke. "Daddy?"

He looked at his baby girl, at her face streaked with tears.
"What, baby?"

"Are you a bad man?"

Her question hit him in the chest like the punch of a heavy-
weight fighter, only it hurt a hundred times more. It was an
innocent question from a little girl who didn't know her daddy,
and needed to ask it. How was he supposed to answer that?
If he wasn't a bad man, was he a good man? And if he was
a good man, why wasn't he in her life for the past five years?

"Mommy said you were a good man," she said softly.
"But I thought the police only got mad at bad men."

"Sometimes the *police* are bad men, baby." Ahmad
reached over and picked up her orange juice from the tray in
front of her, stuck a straw in the lid, and handed it to her, then
he pulled slowly into the street and headed for Founder's Heritage College where the registration lines were sure to be long.

△ 5 △

When Nina arrived at Founder's, the morning sun had illuminated the east wing of the administration building, casting a shadow across the lawn that separated it from the main hall where classes were held. The artistically contoured cement quad between the lawn and the administration building was already littered with tables and signs representing the various campus clubs.

It was going to be another 100-plus Arizona summer day, and even at this early hour, the hot, dry air had climbed into the low eighties. Nina walked across the lawn, welcoming the brief chance at the cool comfort of the shade. She spotted Sweet Nat and Tonya on the quad standing next to the BSU information table. Nina was a little surprised to see her brother there so early. She had to check her watch just to make sure she wasn't late. Six twenty-five exactly. She walked up to the two and kissed Nat on the cheek.

"Hey, Sweet Nat. What's up this morning, baybee?" Not waiting for a reply, Nina turned Tonya and shoved her playfully. "Hey, girl. Where'd you sleep last night?"

Nat jumped in before Tonya could answer. "Aah-iight, Nina, I told you don't be callin' me 'Sweet' in front of nobody."

Nina winked at her "little" brother. Nat was the color of dark brown sugar with deep brown eyes that twinkled with mischief much of the time. He was the kind of young man everybody loved because he was almost always in a good mood, and he got a kick out of trying to make the people

41

around him feel good too. Nat was six foot four, and weighed about 260 pounds. With his shaved head and tattooed biceps, he looked like he could tear anybody limb from limb. But to Nina he was just Sweet Nat. She had promised him she'd try to drop the "Sweet" part now that he was a junior in college and all. But she was having a hard time remembering.

"Look, I've been calling you Sweet Nat since that day I was s'posed to be watching you . . . and you turned that sugar bowl upside down on your head. Your little two-year-old sweet-toothed ass trying to get you some sugar down off the counter almost got *my* butt whupped. But I'll try not to embarrass you in front of anybody . . . Sweet . . . uh, I mean, Nathan."

"C'mon, Neen. You don't have to call me Nathan either. Do I need to put you in a headlock?" Nat reached for Nina, wrapping his arms around her in a bear hug. Her face was buried against his massive chest, and without the use of her arms or hands, she couldn't move a muscle.

"Okay, okay. Nat. Nat. Nat. I got it now, brotha . . . Nat," Nina sputtered through breathless laughter.

"That's better," Nat replied, planting an exaggerated smooch on his sister's forehead before releasing her.

Nina turned to Tonya. "So you were saying? You didn't come home last night because . . . ?" Tonya and Nat exchanged knowing looks. Nina caught the look immediately and turned to Nat. "What? Oh, hell, no," she said, playfully poking Nathan in his chest. "My baby brother is reachin' *way* up over his head for that sugar bowl now." Tonya was staring at her with that "girl, have you lost your mind?" look on her face. Nina nudged her. "T, you're not messin' around with Sweet Nat now? I know my baby brother is a big teddy bear, and you're my girl and all, but . . ."

Nat and Tonya looked at each other and laughed out loud. Speaking at exactly the same time they said, "Us?" Laughing at Nina's suggestion, they spoke again in sync—"Please"—and laughed some more.

Then Tonya spoke up. "Nina, no offence, girl, but you know I can't stand Derrick. I saw his car outside last night, and I decided I'd rather be somewhere else."

"Let's not talk about Derrick this morning, T." Nina wasn't

ready to tell Tonya about her decision to break off the engagement.

Tonya couldn't help herself. "I know you're planning to
marry him, and I'm going to have to figure out how to be
happy about that, but I just . . . I mean, I know he looks good,
but . . ."

Nina offered a weak defense for her soon-to-be-ex fiancé.
"I know he acts like a jerk at times, but deep down he's
really . . ."

Nat and Tonya stared at her expectantly.

"Well . . . he's . . ."

The two were waiting for Nina to finish her sentence, and
once again they spoke in unison. "Mmmm hmmm?" they
taunted with arched eyebrows. Neither of them liked Derrick,
and they both thought he didn't deserve Nina. She was going
to have a hard time coming up with something positive to say
to them about him.

"Damn . . . okay, well, he can sing real good," Nina joked.

They all chuckled before Nat piped in seriously, "You
know you're too good for that brotha, Nina. If he treats you
anything like he plays hoop, he's just a selfish nigga with no
heart."

"Hmmm, well, you might be right, little brother. I've been
thinkin' about that myself, especially after this morning. The
man was snoring in my bed all night, and had the nerve to
get mad at me because I woke him up crying in my sleep."

Tonya looked at her friend with concern. She had been the
one to wake Nina up on the few occasions when Derrick
wasn't sleeping over. She knew how terrifying the nightmare
was for her. "You had that dream again, Nina?"

"Girl, yeah. Scares me to death every time." Nina changed
the subject quickly. "Anyway, I know Derrick's not the one."

Tonya's jaw dropped. "Say what?" She twisted her mouth
into a disbelieving smirk. "Yeah, right. Girl, what are you
talking about? Y'all were picking out wedding invitations last
week."

"I know, T." Nina frowned. "The whole time I was oohin'
and aahin' over that catalog, I was trying to convince myself
I could go through with it. I know I can't marry Derrick. I've

known for a few weeks now. I just need to figure out a way
to let him down easy.''

Nat jumped in matter-of-factly. ''Bump that easy shit, Neen.
Kick that muthafucka to the curb.''

''That's the problem, girl,'' Tonya said. ''You're too soft-
hearted. I know you were planning to marry the man and all,
and you wanna break it off soft and sweet, but some folks
really do require a swift kick in the ass.''

Just as the words came out of Tonya's mouth, they all
looked up to see a tall light-skinned sista approaching. She
wore hazel-green contact lenses and a wild reddish blonde hair
weave. Tonya took one look at the sista, then continued, ''Ugh
. . . speaking of people needing a good ass kickin', here comes
Monique.''

Monique walked up to Nina, smiling broadly, handed her a
flyer, and, ignoring Nat and Tonya, she spoke in her best semi-
educated Valley Girl accent. ''Hi, Ms. Moore. I want to be
the first to invite you to the introductory meeting of the new
Multicultural Student Alliance.''

''The what?'' Monique was good for working Nina's
nerves, and Nina had to make a supreme effort to be cordial
to her.

''The MSA? Well, it's a support group for those of us who
come from more than just one cultural background.'' Monique
touched Nina's bare arm and looked knowingly at her. ''You
of all people ought to know that the BSU can't . . .'' She
looked at Tonya momentarily, quickly shifted her eyes to the
ground and then back to Nina. ''Well . . . I mean . . .'' She
inhaled as if she were about to dive into a deep pool. ''It
doesn't adequately represent the concerns of those of us who
aren't . . .'' She glanced nervously at Nat. ''. . . all the way
Black.'' She spat the word ''Black'' out like it was an empty
sunflower seed shell.

Nina saw Tonya's face twist into an irritated smirk; she was
pissed. Ironically, Tonya's father was Puerto Rican and her
mother was Black, which would have included her in Monique's little presentation, but Tonya was not the one to make
further divisions in the already mixed-up African diaspora.
Tonya was a sista who loved her Black self. She wore her
naturally wavy hair in short little twists, and often topped them

with a *kinte* wrap or *kufi*. She had that casual kind of "makeup-less" beauty that might be overlooked by an unobservant man, and for whatever reason, she chose not to accent her features with lipsticks, shadows, or polishes. Tonya's skin was a deep reddish mahogany, and her eyes were the color of polished oak. Her high cheekbones and full lips made her striking, and with her charismatic personality and wit, it was impossible not to notice her presence. Anybody who knew Tonya treated her with respect, and if you didn't . . . you'd better watch out, because her sense of justice was unsinkable.

Tonya's perception of Monique was that Monique thought being mixed with White made her better than people who were "all the way Black," and Tonya's response to Monique's little announcement summed it all up. "I do not believe this shit."

Monique pretended not to hear Tonya's comment and concentrated on Nina instead. "The only requirement for MSA membership is that your parents come from two different racial backgrounds. Sorry, Tonya, Nathan . . . that would leave you two out. But Ms. Moore, we're still looking for a faculty advisor, and we'd love to have you."

Nina forced a smile. "No, thank you, Monique." It was pretty clear to Nina that this so-called support group was more like an exclusive club for a bunch of mixed-up kids who considered themselves fortunate to be genetically less inferior than regular Black folks. *Monique ought to know better.* Nina had a good mind to go on and school the girl right there, but she really didn't have time to go into a lesson on "house slave/field slave" politics.

Monique looked puzzled and a little hurt. "Don't you even want to know what our mission is?"

"No, thank you, Monique," Nina firmly repeated.

"No, hold up, Monique," Nat said, taking the girl's flyer from Nina. "*I* want to know what your mission is."

Monique was all bubbly. Although Nat wasn't welcome to attend her meetings personally, she thought he might actually be interested. She tossed her weave, blinking her eyes a few dramatic times. "Well," she puffed, "we are just trying to help people see that we biracial students cannot be lumped in with everyone else."

Nat did his best "old Black pappy" imitation. "My, oh

my,'' he said with an exaggerated Southern drawl, "I do believe the house niggas is organizin'.''

Monique didn't get it. "I would appreciate it if you didn't use the 'N' word, Nathan. I find it very offensive. And so should you.''

Nat was having fun with her. "Offensive? Girl, you obviously don't know your history." He puffed his chest out and pounded his right fist dramatically over his heart. "I am proud to be a nigga. I come from a long line of proud niggas. I mean, just look at the niggas that paved the way for us. My man Frederick Douglass . . . he was a sho' 'nuff nigga. Afro parted on the side and shit, lookin' like Snoop Doggy Dogg. Only a true nigga set a trend like that.''

Monique was appalled. Her eyes were opened way too wide, and her mouth was even wider. She took a deep, dramatic breath and scolded Nat, "That is not funny, Nathan. Mr. Douglass would be turning over in his grave if he heard you disrespecting him that way.''

Nat was laughing. He had a loud, contagious laugh, and though they were both pretty shocked by Nat's comments, Nina and Tonya had to fight not to laugh along with him.

Nat continued. "Mr. Douglass would be laughing his ass off 'cause he knows I got much respect. It ain't about a word, Monique . . . it's about attitude. Niggas wit' attitude is why we're standing here now. You know what I'm sayin'? Niggas like Harriet Tubman.''

Monique turned ten shades of red.

"Tell me Harry-ette wasn't no nigga. OG on the underground 'n shit. Sista packin' a straight-up gat.'' Nat aimed an imaginary gun at Monique's face. " 'First one of y'all scary-asses make a sound, I'll blow your gotdamn head off.' Now, tell me my girl wasn't no nigga.''

Monique had had enough. "You are just so ignorant, Nathan.'' She snatched the flyer from Nat and turned to walk away.

"Mulatto callin' a nigga ignorant? Now, ain't that the pot callin' the kettle black?'' Nathan teased.

Monique stopped in her tracks, turned abruptly, and stepped right up to Nat. "Multiracial,'' she said, quite loudly.

"What?'' Nathan said, a little louder, and right in her face.

"The appropriate term is 'multiracial' . . . not 'mulatto.' "

Tonya couldn't stand it anymore. "He's just trying to remind you where you come from, Miss Thang. Same massa called us niggers called your ass a mulatto. Now you're trying not to be lumped in with us."

Nat put one hand on his hip and flipped his imaginary hair weave. "Call me multirathal," he said, with his best girlish lisp.

Monique was finally mad. "What *ever*," she fumed, and walked off in a huff.

Suddenly Nina frowned and spoke in a low, serious tone. "Boy . . . Nat . . . If Mama ever heard you calling Frederick Douglass and Harriet Tubman niggas . . . ."

"Aw, girl, you know I didn't mean no disrespect. I was just trippin', tryin' to get under her skin."

A smile broke across Nina's face. "Did you see all those shades Monique turned? I think you traumatized her."

"That shit was funny." Nat chuckled some more.

Tonya was shaking her head slowly. "Yeah, funny and yet kinda pitiful at the same time."

To remind everyone of why they were there in the first place, Nat handed a stack of flyers to Nina and one to Tonya. "Let's do this, y'all."

The registration windows were scheduled to open at seven, and the lines were already winding around the building. Nat winked at Nina and headed for a cute sista standing alone on the far side of the quad, while Tonya started toward the financial aid line. Nina saw a brotha, perhaps in his late twenties, standing in a registration line, holding a little girl's hand. As she approached, she noticed that he was wearing a tee shirt with an Afrocentric message: BEFORE THERE WAS ANY HISTORY THERE WAS BLACK HISTORY." *He's a sure bet,* she thought, smiling to herself. *And he's fine, too.* He had the build of a man who spent a lot of time in the gym, with medium brown skin, a closely trimmed beard, and short, tiny dreadlocks. Nina thought the man looked a little tense or maybe lost in thought, standing there with his full, heart-shaped lips drawn tight. *I wonder if he has a pretty smile,* she couldn't help thinking. His daughter sure did. She was gorgeous. The color of Hershey's chocolate with a smile that was as wide as it was bright. Nina smiled at the little girl.

"Excuse me," Nina said to the dreadlock man. His eyes were deep and glassy, like there was an intense emotion just behind them, and Nina found herself strangely drawn in, as if an old friend stood before her and was waiting to hear why she'd been away for so long.

But the man just seemed to look right through Nina. His face registered no acknowledgment that she had just spoken to him . . . not even an eyebrow raise.

"Hi, I'm Nina Moore. I'm the faculty advisor to the Black Student Union." She handed him a flyer. "We'd like to invite you to our annual barbecue and pool party this coming Saturday." The man didn't say a word. She continued. "It's our annual membership drive . . ." His silence, coupled with the intense stare, was unnerving to Nina, and she stumbled over her words. "T-to increase our membership, that is."

Dreadlock man made no indication he heard a word Nina said. He glared at Nina with something that looked like anger before he looked down at the flyer.

Nina began to wonder if maybe the man couldn't hear. Or maybe he couldn't speak. He could obviously read, so she decided to refer to the flyer again. "On the back there's more information about the Black Student Union. What we've done here on campus . . . what we're about."

Nina turned to speak to the little girl, since dreadlock man still had not uttered a word. "Hi, I'm Nina. What's your name?"

"Ebony Chante Jefferson."

"Ebony Chante. What a beautiful name. I was just thinking to myself, I bet that little girl has a beautiful name, because a beautiful little girl with a smile like that could not be named Edith, or Bertha, or Fred."

Ebony smiled even wider and giggled. "My daddy named me Ebony. My mommy named me Chante." The little girl looked up at dreadlock man. He returned the child's gaze with what felt to Nina like some kind of secret that Nina was not meant to be privy to.

"It's a beautiful name," Nina responded. *So, dreadlock man was cute, but he wasn't single.*

"Thank you," Ebony said to Nina politely. "Would you like a chocolate Kiss?" The child held out the small wrinkled brown bag of candy.

"Mmmm. I love chocolate."

"Do you want the brown kind, or the white kind?"

"Hmmm . . . I don't know. Which one do you like better?" Nina questioned. She saw that dreadlock man was pretending to read the flyer, but had been eyeing Nina for a while. He lifted his eyes from the flyer to look down at his little girl.

Ebony shrugged. "I don't know, they both taste like chocolate," she said matter-of-factly.

"Well . . . can I have one of each?" Nina asked.

"Okay." Ebony reached in her bag, pulled out one of each chocolate Kiss, and handed them to Nina.

"Thank you, Ebony Chante," Nina said, smiling.

"You're welcome, Nina."

Dreadlock man was finished with the flyer. But he wasn't finished eyeballing Nina. He seemed agitated when he finally spoke. "Don't you have some whales to save somewhere?"

"Whales?" Nina questioned.

The smooth skin across his forehead had gathered into tight furrows. "You're the advisor to the Black Student Union?"

"Yes. I know I don't look—"

He interrupted her. "Why in the hell would I want to participate in a Black organization that couldn't do any better than a White woman as its advisor?"

"Ouch. Well, at least a brotha is honest," Nina said, still smiling. "I guess if you gotta prejudge, you oughta be straight about it."

"Prejudge? Look, I may be prejudging, but I know there is no way you could be qualified to represent *me* in *any* official capacity. You don't know me. You don't have any idea what it is to be a Black student . . . a Black American . . . a Black *anything*."

Nina winced inwardly at the sting of his comment. She really wasn't stung so much by the words the brotha said, but by the bitter tone he'd used to say them with. "Didn't anybody ever tell you it's a mistake to judge a book by its cover?" she said, keeping her voice light, half-joking.

He responded coolly, "Books have a cover for a reason.

They generally tell you a lot about what's inside.''

Nina decided at that moment not to tell dreadlock man she was Black. It would make a difference. It always did. He would remember the history of Africans in America, and know that to be Black hadn't always meant to have an abundance of melanin. He would remember the "one drop rule," and once he knew she was a sista, he would say something like, "Damn, girl, you gotta get a darker tan and help a brotha out" or "My bad, I should have known by the way you walked up you were a sista." But now Nina was mad. *The idiot should have figured it out for himself anyway.* She decided to continue the conversation to see where it was going to lead.

"So, tell me. What do you see inside this cover, Mr. Jefferson?''

"Look, don't take this too personally, Ms. Moore. I'm sure you're a nice person. But if you're trying to snag a Black man, all you really have to do is go hang out at the gym during basketball practice. There should be plenty of sellouts there to go around.''

"Sellouts?'' This was getting interesting. "Mmnh, mmnh, mmnh. That's what you see here, huh? A White girl with jungle fever?''

"Well, if the shoe fits . . .''

This man was serious. Nina had still not seen him crack a smile. "Speaking of shoes,'' Nina quipped, "what size do you wear, Mr. Jefferson?'' She looked down at his black leather boots. "Hmmm . . . let's see. About a twelve . . . twelve and a half?''

"See what I'm saying?'' he shot back in a disgusted tone. "Oh-so-typical. Already trying to predict how big my . . .'' He looked down at his daughter. "Never mind that, Ms. Moore. Be advised,'' he said snidely, flipping the flyer toward her as a signal that she could have it back. He whispered sharply to her, "I don't do White women.''

Nina was mad now. True, she thought, the man looked good. He had a nice chest, and some sexy bowlegs, but he wasn't *all that.* She ignored the flyer and responded icily, "Don't flatter yourself. I was just looking at your shoes to determine if your big mouth was going to be able to accommodate the size of the foot you're putting in it.''

The line dreadlock man was in moved forward, and Nina stood still and let him pass. The foot in mouth statement left him with a curious look on his face. Nina smiled at Ebony and began walking away. "It was nice meeting you, Ebony Chante. Thank you for the Kisses."

"Bye, Nina." Ebony returned the smile and waved. Nina looked down at the two candy Kisses in her hand and shook her head. Something was choking her up, and she couldn't quite figure out what it was. An uncomfortable heaviness settled in her chest and she hesitated momentarily, turning back toward the man and his child, as if she weren't sure whether to walk away in a huff, or stay and try to convince the brotha that she wasn't what he thought she was. The moment passed as swiftly as it had come, and Nina swallowed the uncomfortable feeling and turned her back to the angry brotha. She looked down in her hand at the candy again. *They both taste like chocolate.* Nina put the Kisses in her pocket and went looking for more potential Black Student Union members.

△▽ 6 ▽△

Nina was exhausted, and relieved to finally be standing outside her apartment door. Despite the discouraging encounter with the dreadlock man, it had been a productive morning, and she'd run out of flyers much sooner than predicted. She, Nat, and Tonya were able to get thirty-some people to commit to becoming BSU members when the semester began in a couple of weeks, and another twenty-five or so who promised to come to the barbecue on Saturday.

Derrick never did show up to help pass out flyers and the idiot knew he had Nina's only door key. Luckily, Nina and Tonya left campus together, and Tonya was there to let her in.

"Thanks for letting me in, T. I knew better than to give Derrick my key. You know he lost the last two I gave him. But I was hoping he'd end up over at the information table helping out."

"That's just like you, girl," Tonya replied with a twisted grin. "Hoping for the good in a person to win out over the lazy, triflin', good for nothin', self-centered side." She sucked in a dramatic breath, exhaled with the words, "But enough about Derrick," laughed at her comment, and put her hand up in front of Nina to get "dap."

Nina slapped Tonya's upraised hand and laughed along with her as Tonya put her key in the lock and eased the door open. They heard music playing inside. "Damn," Nina moaned, "Derrick left the CD player running *again*." She was irritated. It wasn't the first time he'd done that. Knowing Derrick, his towel was probably still on the bathroom floor, the milk carton was out on the counter, and his cereal bowl was sitting in the sink full of Captain Crunch–flavored milk. *Oh well,* Nina thought, heading for her bedroom to shut off the CD player, *tonight's definitely the night to drop the bomb.*

The first thing she noticed when she pushed the bedroom door open was that Derrick's sweats were on the floor, and so were his Nikes. Not surprisingly, there was a trail of clothing that began at the door and led past the mirrored triple-closeted hallway into her room. But Nina stopped in her tracks as she realized that the floral print bra draped across the chaise longue under the window wasn't hers. That's when she heard Derrick's voice.

"That's it, girl. Unh. Oh yeah, that's it right there."

Derrick lay flat on his back in Nina's bed, his six-foot-four frame stretched full-length atop the rumpled ivory sheets, and a very blonde, very naked White woman was sliding her face up and down in his lap. The woman was on all fours, hovering awkwardly over Derrick's torso, her yellow hair hanging veil-like, and draping down onto Derrick's ebony skin. But it was the woman's knees that bothered Nina most; not that she was *on* her knees, but something about the way the woman's knees sank into the plush folds of the ivory down comforter gathered in a pile beneath her was pissing Nina off, royally.

I just made that gotdamned bed. Nina's feet glued themselves to the carpet and her mind shifted into pause. The scene seemed almost surreal, as if she had stepped into somebody's mental fantasy she wasn't supposed to have been invited to. Nina watched Derrick's face, framed in one of her ivory satin-cased pillows, contort into the same pre-orgasmic grimace she had peered at the night before. She heard herself speak, as if through a ventriloquist, who could have been pulling her strings from somewhere above and behind her head.

"What . . . What in the fuck . . . are you doing?" Nina's voice was low and controlled, but the disbelief and rage simmering in her throat combined to make the tone of it sound just a little tinged with insanity.

The kneeling woman's eyes opened in shock, and she fell off Derrick and rolled off the bed onto the floor, pulling the bedspread to cover her nakedness and cowering against the dresser looking terrified. It all seemed to happen in slow motion and Nina watched as if from outside of herself as Derrick's eyelids lifted and his dick shriveled up like a deflating pool toy.

He sat up stiffly against the headboard and stuttered at Nina. "B-baby, this isn't . . . I mean, I'm not . . . I—I was just mad about this morning, and . . . damn . . . it's not like I'm having an affair."

"Dare-*rick*, you said this was your brother's house," the woman whined.

Derrick's head turned sharply and he growled at the woman, "Shut up. You just keep your mouth shut."

Nina picked up one of the Nikes at her feet. "No, *you* shut up," she said venomously, flinging the shoe at Derrick's head. It struck the headboard behind him, and he quickly put his hands up in front of his face as Nina bent over to pick up the other shoe.

Derrick shrugged and looked over at the other woman. "C'mon, Nina, I barely even know her. I was just all worked up this morning, and you couldn't take time to . . ." He leaned toward Nina with outstretched arms. "We can work this out. I'm sorry, baby. You know I love you, Nina."

Did he just say "I love you?" Two years of waiting for that shit, and this muthafucka has to get caught gettin' done by this store-bought-blonde bitch to actually use the word "love"? She held the shoe menacingly above her head, fighting the urge to fling it at him with the force she intended. She might do some real damage to his face. Or better yet, maybe she'd aim at his dick. Nina looked down at the limp organ. *This idiot didn't even have the decency to wear a rubber.*

A burning fire rose from her chest and spread across her face. Nina clenched and unclenched her free hand, digging her nails into the skin in her palms as she fought to contain the rage ballooning like helium inside her. The anger was searching for an escape, and she struggled desperately to suppress it. She was teetering dangerously on a line somewhere between *act like a crazy woman and beat the shit out of this sorry-ass fool* and *just act like you don't give a fuck, and walk out.* She settled on something in the middle. Nina clenched her jaw tightly, and between her teeth, she managed to push out the words, "Derrick, you have two minutes to get yourself, your shit, and your bitch out of my house."

The woman looked doe-eyed in Nina's direction. She sensed Nina was on the edge, and seemed scared that she might attack her. She struggled to stand up without losing the protective covering of the bedspread. When Tonya walked in to see what the commotion was, the woman must have really thought she was about to get her ass whupped. She dropped the bedspread, hopped over Derrick, scrambled across the king-sized bed, and stumbled her way into the bathroom, locking the door behind her.

Tonya was in shock. "Oh, no, you didn't," she growled, looking at Derrick with disgust. "You are one sorry excuse for a man."

Nina jumped in before Derrick could respond. "Tonya . . . do you remember that Al Green thing?"

"The burning grits story? Mmmm, hmmm. Sistas can do some *shit* when we're mad, huh?" Tonya emphasized the word "shit," and looked straight at Derrick when she said it.

"How long does it take to boil up some grits?" Nina said, looking menacingly toward Derrick, who was glaring at Tonya in silence.

"Not too long," Tonya responded. "Why don't we serve Derrick some breakfast in bed?"

"Ooh, yeah . . . breakfast in bed . . . why don't we." Nina turned to leave the room, stopping to speak to Derrick. "Leave my key on the dresser." She kicked at his sweats that were in a pile at her feet. "And don't leave anything in my house you don't want the Salvation Army to get, 'cause you won't be coming back for it." She tossed the Nike at Derrick, and he reached up and caught it with one hand. He didn't say a word.

"You won't be singing your way out of this one," Nina added sarcasticaly, turning to head for the kitchen.

Tonya got the box of Alber's down from the cupboard and started cooking, while Nina just sat at the table with her head in her hands. She didn't really know what she was feeling. Shouldn't she be sad? She didn't feel like crying. *Pshhh. Cry over that loser?* She was still shaking with anger, upset at the sheer disrespect of having that bitch in her bed, but she couldn't really even be mad at the woman. The fool probably really did think this was Derrick's brother's house, and probably thought she had snagged herself a real prize. *Well, humph, she can have him.* Nina closed her eyes, and tried to calm her shaking nerves. She concentrated on the one positive aspect of the whole thing: Derrick had saved her the big breakup conversation.

Nina sat in silence. She listened to the muffled whispers of Derrick and his fling slinking out the front door. *Coward,* Nina thought. *He couldn't even think up some smart-ass remark for me on his way out.*

Tonya must have been thinking the same thing. Just as the door closed she muttered, "Pussy" and shook her head in disgust. She set a plate of steaming grits down in front of Nina. "You all right?"

"Yeah, I'm fine. I was just trippin'."

"What . . . Don't tell me you're trippin' off that B and B violation," Tonya said, shaking her head.

"Huh?"

"You know. The blonde and blue violation. Like the trust is somehow more deeply violated if the man cheats on you with a White woman."

"Come on, T," Nina replied halfheartedly. "How am I gonna go there? Blonde and blue ain't but some Clairol away from lookin' like my pale ass." Nina laughed at herself, finally feeling the tightness of her anger begin to ease. She rolled her eyes and grinned at Tonya. "It's his loss. And she can have the triflin' ho. Sistas deserve better than Derrick any damn way."

"Nobody deserves a dog like that," Tonya murmured. She quickly added, "What did the woman say when you walked in on them?"

Nina did her best to impersonate the woman, "Dare-*rick*, you said this was your brother's house."

Tonya rolled her eyes. "Girl, brothas like Derrick think they got the whole world in their hands when they're doin' a White woman."

Nina never wanted to believe that about Derrick, but . . . She remembered how he assumed she was White that day he first saw her on the tennis court. When she told him she was Black, it took him the whole evening to recover from the shock.

Tonya interrupted her thoughts. "You know you're my girl, Nina, but I've been trying to tell you about Derrick from jump. You know I don't have anything against people dating whomever they please. But until you, I never saw that fool with a sista. He always was chasin' after White women. He probably thought he had the best of both worlds with you."

Nina chuckled to herself. "That's funny."

"What?"

"Derrick told me that just last night. Those very words. 'The best of both worlds.' Right in the middle of having sex. He was mumbling his usual 'I love making love to you, Nina.' All that ever does is kill my mood, 'cause I know that's his alternative to really saying, 'I love you, Nina.' "

Tonya's mouth fell open. "Derrick never told you he loved you? Come on now. Girl, you never told me that."

"I could barely admit it to myself. He wrote 'I L-U-V you' once on a Hallmark card. When I asked him why he spelled it L-U-V, he got all twisted, like I was trying to start something. Any expression that would ever require him to take an emotional risk . . . Derrick either sang it or wrote it."

Tonya voiced her understanding. "Girl, from day one. That basketball he wrote his name on? It put all the risk in your court. So to speak." She smiled at her pun.

Nina was too intent on finishing her story to acknowledge Tonya's attempt at humor. "Anyway, there we were in the middle of all this so-called passion, when he said something about how turned on he was by seeing his dark skin against mine. I was laying there trying to figure out what the hell that was supposed to mean, when he added that line. 'I've got the best of both worlds.' He said the best thing about being with me is the way White men look at us when we're together. Then he said, 'I just get off on the fact that they're so pissed off at me being with a beautiful White woman.'

Tonya looked disgusted. "Jerk."

"He laughed and kissed me real hard right before he said, 'It's like I know *I* got something they *wish* they had.' Girl, needless to say, it killed the whole mood for me. I just wanted to hurry up and help him come so I could roll over and go to sleep. I should've knocked his sorry ass out the bed instead."

Tonya shook her head. "Damn, Nina."

Nina pushed the plate of grits away. "T, I had already decided to call off the wedding, but I was having a hard time getting around to telling Derrick. When I heard those words come out of his mouth last night, I just laid there trying to figure out how I was going to break up with him. I was planning to do it tonight."

"Derrick was using you to make White men jealous? Damn, that's pitiful."

"You wanna know what's really pitiful though?"

"What's that?" Tonya asked.

"It didn't take me two years to figure Derrick out. I knew the man was color-struck a long time ago, and I stayed with him anyway. Derrick's not the only sellout, T."

Tonya didn't say a word.

"I'm almost thirty years old. I don't want to be alone forever, Tonya."

"Nina, before you can *get* what you want, you have to *know* what you want. But more importantly, you have to know what you *don't* want."

"I know I want a good man; I want a man who loves himself and is into being about something positive; somebody like my father, proud of being Black, and giving back to the community and all that." Nina looked down at her lightly tanned arm. She studied the web of blue veins snaking up her wrist, and shook her head. "How am I supposed to find a man who isn't tripping over this? The kind of man I want . . . he ain't lookin' nowhere near my direction. All I seem to get are the Derricks. Brothas who are attracted to White women for all the wrong reasons are attracted to me, too. Them brothas with jungle fever are beating down my door."

"Maybe that's part of the problem. Nina, why are you waiting for a knock on the door? Get out and grab the kind of man you want; don't wait for chance to blow him your way. I know when I saw Rasheed, I didn't wait around for something magical to happen. I couldn't tell you if he was attracted to me physically or not, but I wasn't going to wait for him to decide I was worth pursuing. I let him know I was attracted to him. He had to decide whether he was missing out on something by not responding."

Nina was quiet. She thought about her run-in with the dreadlock man earlier. "Tonya, I met a brotha today who I have every right to despise. He was rude and presumptuous and downright callous toward me, but I can't stop thinking about him. I felt an instant connection with that brotha, but he seemed to have nothing but contempt for me. I don't know if it's crazy, but . . . I'm really sorry I didn't tell him I'm Black."

"He sounds like an asshole to me," Tonya muttered.

"I don't know . . . I wish I had the luxury of writing him off as an asshole. But I know better. I know my skin only reminded him of White folks he's had bad experiences with in the past. How was he supposed to know I could be trusted? White woman talkin' about some barbecue."

Nina laughed halfheartedly, but deep down, she was really hurt by how he'd reacted to her.

"Why didn't you tell him?" Tonya asked. "I've never seen you even hesitate to set a person straight—White, Black, or otherwise."

Nina shrugged. "Sometimes I just get tired of apologizing. Why do I have to apologize for not getting enough melanin?"

Tonya got up from the table and took the plates to the sink. "Apologize? What kind of madness is that?" She turned her back to Nina and scraped the uneaten grits into the garbage disposal. "Now, how would it sound if I told you I was walking around feeling like I had to apologize for being brown?"

"Apologize? Unh-unh. You never would."

"And you shouldn't either. Nina, you have to stop giving people room to act ignorant. That brotha had no right to punish you for being you. You don't owe any apology to anybody but yourself. Apologize to yourself for allowing the prejudice of others to affect you like that."

"We all have prejudices."

"True, and we all have bad experiences with idiots of other races, but we don't all use them as excuses to hurt other people. Nina, you're the first one to give a person the benefit of the doubt. You deserve the same and you need to demand the same. And as for men . . . believe it or not, there are plenty of them out there who don't give a damn how much melanin you have."

After a long silence, Nina spoke again. "You wanna know

why I stayed with Derrick for as long as I did?''

''I was wondering.''

Nina winced. ''It's pretty bizarre.''

''The sex was *that* good?'' Tonya asked.

''No. Hell, no.''

''What, then?''

''I know it sounds stupid. I'm a grown woman. But I need somebody in the bed with me . . . to wake me up before . . .'' Nina became silent.

''Before what, Nina?''

''I don't really know. Before he hurts her.''

''Don't take this the wrong way, girlfriend . . .''

''I know. You think I'm crazy.''

''I don't think you're crazy. But you should go talk to somebody. A professional. This dream is interfering with your life. It's affecting your decisions. Maybe a therapist can help you figure out why it's happening.''

''I know you're right, T. But—'' Nina crossed her arms in front of her on the table, and put her head down on them. ''I'm afraid to know.''

''You're afraid *not* knowing,'' Tonya asserted. ''And you can't be sleeping with me.''

''I could always give Derrick another chance,'' Nina joked, trying to sound serious.

Tonya did a quick imitation of Blondie. ''Derrick, you said this was your brother's house.''

''All right, damn. I'm goin' to see a shrink,'' Nina replied playfully. She looked at her watch. It was almost noon. She and Tonya were supposed to be at the center at two o'clock. Some kind of emergency board meeting. ''I'll call Mama after the meeting and see if she can suggest somebody.''

''You'll call your mother when?'' Tonya urged.

''I'm gonna go take a shower and throw on some jeans. I'll call her.''

Tonya looked at her. ''Mmm hmmm.''

''I'll call her, T. I will.''

Tonya rolled her eyes and dipped her head to the side for effect before looking straight at Nina again. ''You'll call her when?''

Nina reached for the phone on the kitchen wall. ''All right, dang.'' She grinned at T. ''You ol' nag. I'll call her right now.''

▽▷ 7 ▽△

Ahmad dropped the sponge into the bucket of warm, soapy water and peeled the yellow rubber gloves from his hands. Ebony had suddenly stopped playing with the Ping-Pong balls that were arranged in neat little rows in front of her on the locker room floor, and was looking up at her father questioningly. They both listened to the voice coming in on the loudspeaker. "Mr. Jefferson, I'd like to see you in my office for a minute." Ahmad's boss hesitated momentarily, then added firmly, "Alone."

"It's all right, Ebony," Ahmad assured his daughter. "I'll be right back, baby."

Ebony reached forward with both arms and swooped the rows of Ping-Pong balls into a pile. She picked them up one by one and began forming the neat little rows all over again. "Okay, Daddy," she said crisply. "I'll be right here." She watched her father start toward the big green door with the bumpy glass window. "I won't be no trouble, Daddy," she added, shaking her head slowly.

Ahmad smiled. His daughter was too bright for her five years. He'd heard the veiled impatience in his boss' voice, and he knew the loudspeaker summons had something to do with Ebony. She must have sensed the same thing. Ahmad had apologized profusely for bringing her with him when he checked into work at noon, and Mr. Haskins didn't seem too upset about it. He even smiled at Ebony warmly when he said, "As long as it's just temporary, we'll be okay."

"Of course you won't be any trouble," Ahmad assured her.

61

"I'll just go see what Mr. Haskins wants and I'll be right back." He opened the heavy steel door and stopped momentarily to study his child. She had obviously spent a lot of time entertaining herself, and probably spent too much time alone. The stoic look on her baby face made Ahmad feel proud and sad at the same time. Proud because she was such an independent little girl, and sad because at five years old, she shouldn't have to be.

Ahmad left the locker room, and walked down the gray-walled hallway to the gymnasium office. Mr. Haskins was standing in the open doorway waiting for him.

"Come on in, son." The short, round Black man had a full beard and mustache and thick, bushy eyebrows that framed his wide, round face. He put his fat little hand on the middle of Ahmad's back and directed him to a waiting chair directly across from his black leather desk chair, which he'd swiveled around to face Ahmad.

"I'll get right to the point," Mr. Haskins said firmly. Ahmad sat up straighter. Haskins ran his stubby hand over the back of his shiny bald head. "Your uncle told me about what you've been through, and I'm the first one to want to help a young brother out." Ahmad nodded at his boss, but didn't say a word. "But I can't let my concern for your situation jeopardize mine." He was quiet for a moment, reaching to straighten the row of carefully placed picture frames lining the edge of his desk. The frames held photos of what must have been his family. A stocky little molasses-colored wife and three young women. Ahmad wondered if they were his daughters.

Haskins suddenly looked Ahmad in the eye. "I started twelve years ago in the job you have now. You need to know this about Founder's: there are some fair-minded White folks on this campus, and there are some real assholes looking for an opportunity to justify their belief that Blacks are second-rate."

Ahmad still hadn't said a word. He nodded in recognition of what his boss was saying to him, but it certainly wasn't news. Hell, what he was saying applied to the entire United States of America, not just this little small-town college. Ahmad was waiting for him to get to the real point.

"My point is, we don't have any mess-up room, you and I. Now I know what I told you earlier . . . about your little girl being here."

Ahmad shifted to the edge of his chair. "It's only temporary, sir, I promise you." He needed the man to understand how critical the situation was. "I'm going after work today, to see about getting her into day care." He added, "I really appreciate you giving me this job, sir. I won't mess it up . . . for you or me."

Mr. Haskins sat back in his chair. "No one's noticed your daughter yet, Ahmad. But if anyone does, and it's brought to my attention, I'm going to have to say she won't be back."

"I understand, sir," Ahmad replied. "She won't be any trouble, sir. She's a very well-behaved child."

"I can see that, son." Haskins hoisted himself from his chair, signaling the end of the meeting. He led Ahmad to the open door and added, "We'll make this work until Friday. No one's really on campus until next week anyway." He patted Ahmad on the shoulder. "But she can't come to work with you on Monday, Ahmad. You understand."

Ahmad understood exactly what the brotha was saying. He was willing to try to help Ahmad out, but he wasn't trying to lose his own job in the process. Ahmad heard the message loud and clear. If he didn't have a place for Ebony to be on Monday, he wouldn't have a job. He reached out to shake his boss' hand. "I understand, sir."

Haskins shook Ahmad's hand warmly. "I suggest you head on over to the center right now. The waiting list to get in over there is usually atrocious, but they never have enough diversity, so . . ." Haskins stopped mid-sentence.

Ahmad knew why. He was alluding to affirmative action day care–style. *Great.* So now he'd have to subject his daughter to five days a week of being somebody's token. But what choice did he have? He didn't have any family to depend on, and the only way he could take care of her himself would be to collect welfare and food stamps, and he wasn't about to do that.

"You can head over there now if you want. You only have an hour left on the clock anyway. You can make that up another time."

"Thank you, sir." Ahmad knew he was fortunate to have walked into a situation like this, with a cool boss who was trying to help him out. Despite everything, God really was watching over him.

"You can cut that 'sir' shit out, now," Haskins said with a laugh. "Call me TK. Everybody around here does."

"Thanks, TK." Ahmad walked quickly down the corridor.

"Hey, son," the little round man hollered to Ahmad. "Love your shirt." He winked, and walked back into his office.

Ahmad opened the door to the locker room and looked for Ebony in the corner where he'd left her, but she was gone. The Ping-Pong balls were gathered in a neat little pile, but Ebony was nowhere in sight. Ahmad's heart sank into his boots.

"Ebony," he called out, his voice reflecting a suppressed panic beginning to build in his throat.

"I'm right here, Daddy." Her voice was coming from behind a tall row of lockers.

Ahmad walked around the locker row. "Aw, Ebony, what are you doing?" He had to sit down on the long, low wooden bench that separated the rows of lockers.

Ebony was standing in a puddle of soapy water, her tiny arms stuffed into the huge yellow gloves. The front of her dress was soaking wet, and she was smiling . . . no, beaming at her daddy proudly. "I was helping you, Daddy." She dipped the sponge into the bucket and rubbed it across the dingy locker door. Ahmad couldn't tell if she'd gotten more suds on the locker, on the front of her dress, or on the floor beneath her. "I'm helping you work."

"You know what?" Ahmad took the sponge from Ebony and dropped it into the bucket.

Ebony was a sight. She'd put the rubber gloves on the wrong hands, and she had them held out in front of her in a questioning shrug. Not quite sure if he was angry at her for the puddle she'd created, she looked at her daddy with a toothy smile. "What, Daddy?"

If Kodak had a contest, this would be the moment of all moments. Ahmad just shook his head slowly at her and tried to look firm, but on top of the sopping wet dress and the clown-sized gloves, she had suds on the tip of her nose. She was too adorable. Ahmad resisted the urge to scold her for making such a big mess, and started laughing instead. Relieved that she wasn't in trouble, Ebony giggled too. Before Ahmad knew it, he was laughing so hard his stomach hurt, and Ebony's little giggle mixed right in with his loud, boisterous laughter, bouncing off the cement walls.

Ebony repeated her question through her giggles. "What, Daddy? What?"

Ahmad wound his laughter down to a controlled chuckle as he pinched the gloves from her hands and put them on the floor next to the bucket. He held both his daughter's little hands in his. "Ebony." He was still chuckling at the sight standing in front of him. "I appreciate you trying to help Daddy." He kissed her lightly on the forehead. "But it's Daddy's job to work."

"What's my job then, Daddy?" she said curiously.

"Right now your job is to play, baby. You'll be starting school soon. When you go to school, your job is to learn as much as you can, and always do your best. Then we'll both be doing our jobs."

"Okay, Daddy."

"But in the meantime, let's pick up after ourselves, okay?"

"Okay, Daddy." Ebony walked over to the corner and began putting the Ping-Pong balls one by one into the wire-framed basket they'd come from. Ahmad put the cleaning supplies away, then began mopping up the soapy mess Ebony had made. He shook his head slowly as he squeezed the dirty mop head and watched the gray water drip into the bucket. *Ebony was "helping Daddy work." Unbelievable.* It was as if she knew that her presence was a problem, and she wanted to prove she was useful. Ahmad wondered if she'd ever felt that before. He prayed to God she never had to question if she was a burden, or wonder if she wasn't wanted.

He emptied the mop bucket, and returned the cleaning supplies to the storage closet. "Okay, lil bit," he announced to Ebony, who was sitting on the bench with her ankles crossed, patiently waiting for her dad to finish. "Let's go check out this fun place I heard about where they'll let you stay and play all day while Daddy's at work."

Ebony stood up and grasped her father's hand. She stated

matter-of-factly, "I used to go to day care when I lived with Mommy." She pulled her father toward the double exit doors at the far end of the lockers. "I didn't mind too much."

All Ahmad could do was shake his head again in disbelief. The child seemed to be a step ahead of him half the time. She was letting him know that the so-called "fun place" was really a place where she'd be out of the way for a while, but she understood it was necessary.

Ahmad stopped in front of the doors and grasped the bar that opened them. He squatted down in front of Ebony. "Punkin. I want you to listen to Daddy for a minute, okay?" Ebony looked at her father seriously without saying a word. "I want you to know that I love you, and I'm glad you're here with me. And Daddy's sorry he couldn't be with you before."

Ebony leaned forward and kissed Ahmad's cheek. "Mommy already told me that," she said with a smile. "She told me not to cry because Keisha Jenkins had a daddy that took her to the park after church and I didn't. Mommy said you were sorry. She told me to watch and see . . . that you would come back for me."

Ahmad leaned in to return Ebony's kiss. He loved the way this little girl could warm his heart with a mere sentence or a word. He finally understood what Chante's mother must have felt when Ahmad eloped with her daughter to Vegas. But standing here facing this child, there was no way he could be sorry they did. "Your mommy was smart, and so are you, Miss Ebony." He pushed the bar, opened the door wide, and stepped to one side, bowing low and gesturing for his daughter to go through the door ahead of him. "After you, little lady." Ebony bounced out the door, stopping to make prints on the hot sidewalk with her sopping wet sandals and watching the prints dry almost instantly. Ahmad hoped her dress would dry as quickly. "C'mon, let's go check out this day care situation." He took his daughter's hand in his and walked across the campus lawn toward the Founder's center.

◺▽ 8 ▽◺

Nina just stared at Tonya in amazement. What the hell was she doing? The faces of the nine White women and Randall Keats, the lone White man, were all smiling broadly at Nina from around the table, although Randall's grin looked as if it had been pasted on. And there was Tonya, grinning right along with them, like she had fallen through the looking glass and had some big secret she wasn't supposed to tell Alice.

Trisha Covington, a frail, redheaded woman in her mid-fifties, finally broke the awkward silence. She smiled with obvious sincerity. "We really hope you'll consider it, Nina."

Got damn that Tonya. She was still grinning. "Well, I . . . uh . . ." Nina had been sucker punched.

Christine Sears, the center's director, who was stepping down to run an art museum in Phoenix, spoke up. She reached up with a jeweled hand to adjust a hair that had fallen from the neatly wrapped blonde French knot she wore high on her head. "Darling, we know you're working on your dissertation," she crooned sweetly at Nina, "but as director you'll have plenty of leeway to craft your own schedule. Besides, once you have your Ph.D., the funders will be more eager to support our programs."

"Excuse me for a moment." Nina rose from her chair. "I need to use the ladies' room. I'm feeling a little . . ." She glanced at the still smiling Tonya, and gave her an abbreviated and private version of the evil eye before she emphasized the last word. " . . . *ill.*"

Tonya entered the child-sized girls' bathroom five seconds behind Nina with her forefinger pressed rigidly against her lips. "Shhh." She looked sternly at her friend.

Nina backed into the last tiny stall at the end of the narrow room. "How could you, Tonya?" she fumed in a harsh whisper. "If anybody should be considered for this position, you know it's you." She shook a pointed index finger in Tonya's face. "How could you cosign this?"

Tonya grabbed the finger firmly and pulled Nina closer. "This is the real world, Nina," she whispered. "This is *their* world. We *need* you to be director, girl. Don't start tripping, talking about demanding I be considered for the position 'cause you know Randall Keats will get it first."

The thought of Randall as director of the center silenced Nina. Randall was the Founder's Alumni Center for Child Development's financial administrator, and though he'd been with the center for less than a year, and had no experience working with children, his master's degree in business and his weekly golf games with husbands of board members made him the next in line for the position.

Tonya continued. "Once you're director you can make the necessary changes. I know you have a lot on your plate right now, and if you're afraid of the added responsibility, don't be, 'cause you know I got your back." Tonya looked at Nina soberly. "We need you to do this, Nina. The kids need you to. And I need you to."

"This is your position, T," Nina whispered, shaking her head. "You deserve this."

"I appreciate all that," Tonya returned, "but we have to pick our battles. I will not get this position . . . not yet. Together you and I can help change the board of directors. We can change the culture of the organization. But it's going to take a minute. And we need you to make it happen."

Nina studied the colorful chart hanging on the wall between the row of stalls and the row of miniature sinks. Tonya had created the chart to help the children remember to brush and floss after meals and snacks. *Amber, Ashley, Bailey, Brianna, Brittany, Chelsea* . . . The list went on and on. Children of the upper class mostly. Daughters and granddaughters of alumni with a few charity cases mixed in. Sure, it was a nonprofit day care center, but by the time the waiting-listed low-income students got in, most of the spaces had been filled by the not-so-needy. It was Tonya's mission to balance those scales, and to provide a sound educational foundation for poor children.

How was Nina supposed to be excited about taking the position, knowing the rightful director was standing right in front of her, and just happened to be her best friend?

Tonya nudged her. "Hey, don't get too comfortable, though, 'cause I'm letting you know right now that I'm coming after your job." She winked at Nina, who could do nothing but roll her eyes in defeat.

Nina responded to Randall's obviously feigned concern for her well-being as soon as she was back in her seat. "I'm feeling much better now, thank you."

"If you need some time . . . maybe a few days to think about it," he added, with a half-genuine smile.

"Thank you, Randall." Nina returned the smile with an equal amount of genuineness. "I won't be needing any time to think about it." Every eye in the room fell on Nina's face. "I'd be honored to serve as the director of the Founder's center."

Mrs. Sears immediately rose from the table. "Then it's settled," she spouted jubilantly, hurrying around the conference table to embrace Nina warmly. "Congratulations, Nina." Nina rose to return the hug, catching Tonya's eye over the woman's shoulder. "Of course your duties don't begin officially until the first of the month, but if there's anything I can do to help you make a smooth transition into this position, don't hesitate to ask."

"Thank you, Christine. I really appreciate your support." Nina walked around the table to where Tonya was now standing. "I'm just pleased to have Tonya here as our lead supervisor. Without her we'd be lost."

Randall looked like he wanted to vomit on Nina's shoes. His already tanless face had turned an even paler shade of ivory, and he clenched his narrow, clean-shaven jaw tensely. He reached out to give Nina a way too firm handshake. "Congratulations, Nina," he said through his teeth. He wasn't about to acknowledge the praise Nina had just given T, but Trisha did, nodding her red head in agreement as soon as Nina uttered

it. Trisha looked Tonya in the eye and said seriously, "We
would be lost." The rest of the women in the room nodded
politely in agreement with the compliment, but Nina realized
Trisha was trying to let them know; she knew the position was
rightfully Tonya's.

Tonya thanked Nina and Trisha in a very professional tone
and congratulated her friend with a firm handshake. Everyone
knew the two women were good friends, but no one knew
they were roommates. They didn't display the closeness of
their relationship to their coworkers, and given the events of
the day, that would definitely work in their favor in the future.

In the ensuing clamor of "wish-you-wells" and "so happy
for yous" Nina thought she heard a tapping sound. Randall
must have heard it first, because he was already at the side
door shaking his head vigorously and waving at someone
through the plate glass window. Was he waving someone
away? If he was, the person hadn't budged. And though he
had his hand firmly on the doorknob, Randall didn't seem to
be making a move to open the door either.

Nina walked over to see what was going on. Through the
glass window she could see the back of a tall, broad-
shouldered man with locks, holding the hand of a small brown
child. *It isn't. It is.* It was the brotha from the registration line.
The man that had been hovering in the back of her mind most
of the afternoon. And he was leaving.

"Open the door, Randall," Nina said quietly.

"There's a sign right there, Nina. It says, 'No More Spaces
Available.' Can't the man read?"

"Randall. Open the door." She repeated it authoritatively.

"Suit yourself," he snapped, before pulling the door open
abruptly. Dreadlock man turned around to face the opening
door. Randall looked him in the eye. His nose shriveled into
a sharp point and he peered through his wire-rimmed glasses
at the writing on the man's shirt. He finally announced rudely,
"Sorry. There are never any spaces available this late in the
summer." He tapped the glass where the sign was taped. "Everybody knows you have to get on the waiting list at least by
April."

The somber-faced man just stood there. He looked like he
wanted to say something. But he didn't utter a sound. He just

stood there for an uncomfortable moment looking at Randall with a pained expression on his face. He hadn't noticed Nina. At least, if he had he didn't acknowledge her. But Ebony did right away.

"Hi, Nina," the child exclaimed excitedly as she stepped through the open door to greet the friend she'd made earlier that day.

Nina noticed the child's wet clothes immediately. "Hi, Ebony. Honey, you're soaking wet." Nina looked up at dreadlock man without smiling. "Do you want to come in?"

Randall sighed in defeat and stepped back from the doorway before turning abruptly on the heel of his two-toned oxford and returning to the chattering group of coworkers and board members.

Dreadlock man stepped through the door, closing it gently behind him. *If expressions could be translated,* Nina thought, *"oops" would be written in capital letters all across this brotha's face.*

Nina ignored him momentarily. She knew he was suffering. It had hit him that this was the same woman he'd been so rude to a few hours before. And now that she seemed to be connected in some important way to this day care center, he was probably hoping it wouldn't negatively affect his obvious mission to get his daughter in under the wire.

She squatted down to talk to Ebony, saying nothing to the child's father. *Let him suffer a little longer,* she thought. "How on earth did you get so wet, baby?" Nina questioned.

Ebony giggled. "I was helping my daddy."

Nina glanced at dreadlock man quickly, then back at the child. Without looking at him she asked politely, "Do you mind if I put her dress in the dryer? I have a smock she can put on. It'll only take a few minutes."

Dreadlock man cleared his throat nervously. He looked at Ebony, then back at Nina. "Sure," he finally muttered. "Thanks."

Nina took Ebony's hand and led her toward the craft room where the painting smocks were kept, leaving dreadlock man to stand nervously by the door awaiting their return.

*   *   *

Ahmad watched as his daughter followed the woman off into another room. *Damn. Of all the stupid luck.* How on earth did he pick this woman to take his anger out on? He hadn't intended to be so rude to her. It was just that after the asshole policeman, and the gawking minivan driver, this blue-eyed White woman was in his face talking about a barbecue. He'd had enough of liberal White women trying to help him out.

"Excuse me." Ahmad hadn't noticed anyone approaching, but a sista was standing in front of him smiling broadly and gesturing toward two richly upholstered Victorian armchairs to the right of the entryway. "Would you like to have a seat?"

Now, that's a beautiful *sista*. She didn't have a stitch of makeup on and the tiny twists in her hair were neatly tied in a *kinte* scarf. Her smile reminded him of Chante and sent a twinge of longing through him. Ahmad smiled warmly at her. "Thank you, sista." He offered his hand. "I'm Ahmad Jefferson. And you are . . . ?"

"I'm Tonya. Tonya DeMontaña." She shook his hand, smiling with mock irritation at her obviously creative parents. "My parents thought it sounded catchy."

"It's beautiful," Ahmad assured her, "and definitely catchy." It had been so long since he'd been close to a woman like this.

He followed the sista over to the sitting area where she motioned for him to sit down. "Please, make yourself comfortable," she said curtly. "Ms. Moore wanted you to know she'd be back in just a moment."

Ahmad smiled nervously and nodded. "Thanks." The sista hurried off, leaving him alone. He seemed to have offended her. Yes, he was a little flirtatious, but he certainly hadn't said anything rude to her. Maybe she was just trying to be professional. *She probably needed to watch herself in front of all these White folks.*

He watched her return to the circle of people that were milling around a low oak table on the far side of the room. Bright sunlight streamed in through a long row of windows that lined the uppermost part of the wall where it met the ceiling, illuminating the huge room. The modern architecture, big-screen television, and well-stocked built-in shelves full of books and toys said this center was well-funded, and Ahmad wondered if the people Tonya was now chatting with were the source. They seemed to be ending a meeting, and several of them headed for the door Ahmad had come through. He observed them as they exchanged their pleasant good-byes and small-talked their way out the door. Tonya led the last of the remaining few stragglers. "Nina will make a great director," the red-haired woman commented to Tonya and the rude White man that didn't want to let Ahmad in before. The door closed behind the three of them.

Director, Ahmad thought, closing his eyes and sighing aloud. *You managed to offend the director of the only chance you have at keeping your job*. He wondered if God was trying to tell him something.

Ahmad's thoughts were interrupted. "Daddy, guess what?" Ebony had returned in her now dry sundress, and was holding Nina's hand tightly. She was obviously excited about something.

"What, lil' bit? What are you so excited about?"

Ebony grinned up at Nina. "Nina said I can come here whenever I want. I can come here when you have to go to work. And I can paint and play with the toys and read books and ride the bikes and play with the turtles and—"

"Ebony," Ahmad interrupted.

"Yes, Daddy?"

"Daddy needs to talk to Ms. Moore for a minute." He searched the room for a place where Ebony could wait while he spoke privately to the woman.

The woman pointed at a long, low bookshelf that lined an entire wall on the other side of the oak table. "Ebony, how 'bout if you go over there and pick out a book? You can take it over to the table while your daddy and I talk." Ms. Moore was paying attention. She sensed that Ahmad wanted to talk to her alone.

She sat in a chair across from Ahmad, and they watched as Ebony walked dutifully toward the bookshelf. "Let me get right to the point." Ahmad looked her directly in the eye. "Before we discuss Ebony. I owe you an apology for this morning. I won't try to offer any excuses or justify my attitude." He lowered his eyes to the carpet for a moment, thinking the woman would sense his discomfort and jump in to

rescue him like a good White liberal should. He should be
able to count on her for an "Oh, don't worry about it" or "I
understand. But she didn't say a word. Ahmad cleared his
throat. Still no word from the woman. "What I mean is . . ."
Ahmad continued. He looked back into the blue eyes staring
at him. The woman had her left eyebrow cocked, like she was
a little irritated. It kind of reminded him of the way a sista
would look at a brotha when he was trying to kick some game.
Damn, he thought, *this woman isn't trying to make this apology any easier, is she?* His temples began to throb. He closed
his eyes and sent up a silent prayer. *Lord . . .* was as far as he
got when from out of the blue it occurred to Ahmad that
maybe he just needed to tell the truth.

"Ms. Moore," he began, opening his eyes to look into hers.

"Nina," she asserted abruptly.

"Nina," he repeated. "When I ran into you this morning I
was angry at every White person on the planet. I'm a responsible, intelligent Black man with a young daughter to raise,
and it often seems like I just can't get the benefit of the doubt.
I decided in a split second to do the same to you . . . not give
you the benefit of the doubt, that is. It wasn't personal, believe
me." He added sincerely, "I apologize for the rude comments
I made." He breathed a long sigh of relief and waited for her
response.

She was laughing. Had he said something funny? He looked
at her face. He didn't find scorn or contempt there, but how
in the hell could she be laughing at him after he'd just poured
his heart out to her? Her eyes were sparkling like glass, and
the expression on her face was actually warm, and if it wasn't
for the fact that she was laughing at him, Ahmad might have
felt compelled to laugh right along with her.

"Mr. Jefferson—"

"Ahmad," he interrupted.

"Ahmad, I'm not White."

Ahmad stared at her for a moment. *Shit. What was she,
Latina? Puerto Rican maybe? She could be Creole. Nah.* He
usually picked up on that right away. *Man.* "What nationality
are you, Ms. Moore?" Ahmad spoke slowly, with his eyebrows raised curiously.

"Well, rumor has it that my mother was White." Nina batted her eyelashes a couple of times. "I suppose that's where these came from. But my daddy is a brotha . . . just like you."

"Oh." Ahmad smiled sheepishly. The way she said the word "brotha" cleared up any doubt he had. She was definitely a sista. He smiled apologetically and bit his bottom lip.

"How 'bout if we just start over?" Nina suggested. She reached her hand out to Ahmad. "Hi, I'm Nina. Nina Moore."

Ahmad grasped her hand and shook it warmly. "Ahmad Jefferson. I understand you're the new director of this establishment. I was hoping to enroll my five-year-old daughter."

Nina played along with him. "Well, actually we are full . . ."

Ahmad's face fell. "Really?"

Nina laughed. "Well, technically, yes."

"But . . ." Ahmad prodded.

"But every year, spaces are saved for Founder's staff. I didn't give mine away yet. Well, until I got charmed out of it about fifteen minutes ago by a very articulate and intelligent little girl."

"Thank you, Nina," Ahmad said soberly. "I started a new job on campus today, and if I didn't have a spot for Ebony by Monday morning, suffice to say I'd have been in serious hot water."

"This coming Monday?" Nina questioned.

"Would that be okay?" Ahmad's forehead wrinkled up. He shot a silent prayer up. *God, let her say they'd be open on Monday.* "I'm kind of in a real bind," Ahmad asserted.

"Well, we actually don't officially open until the first." Nina hesitated, then looked at the child quietly occupying herself across the room. "But I'll be here every day. I'd be glad to have her company. Monday it is, Ahmad. Let me just give you some paperwork, and you can bring it in with you when you drop Ebony off. I'll be here at six in the morning."

Ahmad rose from his seat. He looked in Nina's eyes for a long moment. The last five years of prison life, with its constant racial tension, had led him to equate blue eyes with coldness and hatred. It was obviously not the case with this woman. There was a comfortable warmth in Nina's eyes that drew him in. "I really appreciate this." He reached for her hand again. This time when he grasped it, the warmth from her eyes traveled across the softness of her palm to his, and sent a radiant sensation into his chest. He felt . . . Ahmad couldn't quite put his finger on it. It was as if she was an old friend he hadn't seen in years, and he had a strange urge to give her a friendly hug. He shook off the thought, smiling warmly and squeezing her hand gently instead.

Ebony saw her daddy get up and hurried over to him, still clutching the book she'd been reading. "Tell Ms. Moore thank you for helping you with your dress, Ebony. It's time to go."

"Thank you, Nina." She showed the book she was holding to Nina and asked, "Can I read this at home?"

"Only if you promise to bring it back on Monday and read it to me." Nina placed her hand gently on Ebony's head.

"I will. I will." Ebony could hardly stand still. Her little feet were tap-dancing excitedly. "I'm going to read it to my daddy too," she added.

"How 'bout if you start when we get in the car," he said, heading for the door. He was hoping to make it to the DMV before five. He couldn't risk driving around with that expired license. On their way out, Ahmad thanked Nina again for her help and for accepting his apology so graciously. When they were out on the landing, he pulled the door closed, and before heading for the parking lot, he bowed his head and thanked the Creator for consistently reminding him that when it came to the struggles he faced, he wasn't alone.

△▽ 9 ▽△

The flashing lights in her rearview mirror were the first indication Nina had that she was sharing the highway with a police car, and that she was going over eighty miles per hour. She had been distracted by thoughts of the day's events. Derrick, the director position, but most of all Ahmad Jefferson and his little girl. Once they were alone in the craft room together, Ebony told Nina all about her daddy's new job and how much she wished she could come to the center while her daddy was working. And she didn't stop there. The child was a veritable fount of information. Nina had learned that he was working at the Founder's gymnasium. That he'd just moved to Glendale. That Ebony only recently came to live with him because her daddy "had to go away for a long time," and that his wife, Ebony's mother, had recently passed away.

Nina thought it quite odd that the child seemed to have little emotion about the loss of her mother, but maybe the child didn't fully comprehend what death was. She'd calmly skipped from talking about her mother's death to telling Nina about how they'd gone to breakfast at McDonald's that morning, and how the bad policeman was "mean to her daddy." *Policeman. Oh shit.* Nina slowed instantly, switched on her right blinker, and pulled off onto the gravel on the side of the highway. She turned off the engine, and waited calmly for the officer to approach her window.

"Are you aware that you were traveling at eighty-two miles per hour, young lady?" The cop's face was old and sun-wrinkled, with a furry white mustache perched on his top lip.

77

Nina smiled apologetically before furrowing her brows into an exaggerated frown. "I'm so sorry, Officer." She opened her eyes wide and looked directly into his. They were the same shade of blue as hers. "I'm a little distracted, sir. I'm trying to get to this doctor's office before it closes, and I'm afraid I'm not going to make it." Nina handed him the paper she'd written the address on.

"You need to take the next exit. Make a right on Hope. This complex is on the left-hand side, right next to the new Cineplex parking structure. You can't miss it. Five-thirty appointment, huh? No need to speed, young lady, you'll be right on time."

Nina batted her eyelids a few times. "Thank you, Officer."

"I won't ticket you this time," he smiled. "But you slow down from now on, hear?"

"Yes, sir," Nina said, smiling back at the cop. He tipped his hat to her and returned to his patrol car.

Nina breathed a loud sigh of relief, started her car, and pulled smoothly back onto the highway. She'd only gotten one ticket in her entire life, and that was because she ran a red light and caused a minor traffic accident. She wondered how Mr. Jefferson's "bad policeman" experience compared to the treatment she'd just received. Maybe soon they'd become friends and she could ask him about it. *Friends. Right.* Who was she kidding? Nina was attracted to the man. Strangely and deeply attracted.

Unfortunately, he didn't seem to feel the same about her. He didn't make even a veiled attempt at flirtation. Well, maybe he was mourning his wife. Maybe it was too soon. Speaking of being too soon, hadn't Nina just found her fiancé in bed with another woman that very morning? How could she be thinking romantically about another man only a few hours later? *Humph.* Maybe she *was* losing her mind. Well, she was in the right place to find that out.

She pulled her silver Honda Accord into the parking lot of the medical complex matching the address she had been given by Dr. Webb's secretary. It couldn't have just been luck that she was able to get a same-day appointment with a psychiatrist who, according to Mama, was "the best." Nina figured Mama probably had something to do with it. Mama was the kind of woman who had friends that would do just about anything for her, because she was the first to offer and the last to ask for help. If Mama had to ask, you knew it was very important, and you were glad to do whatever you could, 'cause you could bet she'd already been there for you on more than one occasion. Nina wondered if it was Dr. Webb or his secretary who owed Mama the favor.

She drove past the row of parking spaces marked RESERVED and pulled around to the row designated for patients. She parked facing the front end of a gorgeous baby blue '64 Chevy Impala convertible with license plates that read FR AT LST. *Free at Last*, Nina quickly deciphered. *Maybe it's a good omen. Maybe I'll finally be free from this nightmare.*

She followed the hedge-lined walkway to the building entrance and rode the elevator to the fifth floor. When she arrived at the suite with the nameplate that read DR. WILLIAM R. WEBB, DOCTOR OF PSYCHIATRY, Nina stopped short. Her heart was pounding against her chest, and the hand that she had raised to grab the doorknob with was trembling.

Calm down, girl, she thought to herself. *The worst thing that can happen is that this brotha can't help you, and you have to live with that nightmare for the rest of your life.* She shuddered at the thought, grabbed the doorknob, and took a deep breath. "This has to work," she whispered as she turned the knob. "It has to."

Dr. Webb's reception area was not quite what Nina expected of a doctor's office. The walls were stark white, and the carpet was black. There were huge black and white photos of scenery she didn't recognize on the walls, and a long white leather couch stretched along the bottom sill of a huge window. The low, smoked glass coffee table in front of the couch had no magazines or any other kind of reading material on it, and except for a beautiful bouquet of red roses, which sat on what must have been the receptionist's black oak veneered desk, there was no color anywhere in the room.

The receptionist was nowhere in sight. There was a closed door just to the left of the desk, with a sign on it that read THE DOCTOR IS IN, only the word "in" was crossed out with a big black X, and in bold black letters the word "insane" was written under it. Nina smiled. *Well, at least this Dr. Webb has a sense of humor,* she thought.

Just then the door opened and a fifty-ish White man wearing an Adidas baseball cap and a matching blue and white tennis outfit emerged. Nina was still standing in front of the door this patient was heading for, so she stepped to one side and waited for him to pass. He didn't move. He just stood in the doorway looking at Nina. "You must be Nina Moore."

She was surprised and a little unnerved. This couldn't be the psychiatrist Mama had sent her to.

"Yes," Nina responded cautiously. "And you are . . . ?"

"I'm Dr. Webb. Your mother called me this afternoon."

Nina didn't speak. She just assumed Dr. Webb would be Black, and the fact that he wasn't bothered her. She was trying to figure out why, when he spoke again.

"Come on in my office and make yourself comfortable."

Nina hesitated, then followed the man into the other room. She was immediately stunned by how different it was from the one she had just left. The walls of the room were painted a light mauve, and the artwork that decorated them was bright and full of greens, blues, and purples. The carpet was a beautiful muted lavender, and the furniture was a mixture of styles and fabrics that gave the room a funky kind of coffeehouse feel. There were plants everywhere, and they were lush and green and obviously well cared for. The blinds were drawn, and the room was lighted with small randomly placed table lamps that glowed with soft pinkish white bulbs. There was a strong smell of lilac, which was instantly comforting to Nina. She looked around the room for its source, and finally spotted a large vase full of fresh-cut lilacs on the floor in one corner of the room. She smiled for the first time.

Dr. Webb motioned for Nina to have a seat. "Please pick anywhere you'd like to sit."

Nina chose a big purple and green plaid overstuffed armchair and settled into it. Dr. Webb sat near her on a purple suede love seat. He looked at her for a long moment.

Nina waited for the "doctor talk" to start. She cleared her throat nervously.

"Why are you here, Nina?" the doctor finally said in a smooth, quiet voice.

She searched Dr. Webb's face. She had never really been in a situation like this before. Whenever she had a problem in the past, she went to Mama or Daddy for help, or maybe Tonya or Nat. But here she was looking into the face of this total stranger, and a White man at that. *He looks harmless.* His dark hair spilling out from beneath his baseball cap fell just below his ears, and his warm brown eyes and rugged desert-tanned complexion reminded her of an older version of Andy Garcia in *When a Man Loves a Woman.* When his eyes connected with hers, Nina sensed a gentleness that allowed her to put down her guard a little. He seemed genuine enough.

"I've been having this dream," Nina began. She fingered the bracelet on her arm, absentmindedly sliding the silver bangle up and down her wrist, making it clink softly against her wristwatch. "It terrifies me," she added, without looking up. Nina silently cursed the tremble in her voice that belied the cool exterior she was trying to show. She saw the doctor look down at her wrist, watching her toy with the bracelet, and she immediately put her hands in her lap, embarrassed at her obvious nervousness. She began sliding her tiny silver ring on and off her pinkie finger. "I wake up crying and . . ." Nina paused. The doctor didn't prompt her to speak. He waited patiently for her to continue. She looked around the room nervously. *Why is it so hard to do this? He's a psychiatrist, he probably hears things much crazier than this.* She took a long, slow breath and looked the doctor straight in the eye. "I'm afraid to sleep alone." The admission bounced out of her like a tight rubber ball. "I was hoping you could help me," she added in a much softer tone.

"What is it that you want?" Dr. Webb responded.

"What do I want?" she said curiously. *Duh, this guy's deep.* What did he think she wanted? She wanted the damn thing to go away. She wanted to be able to sleep through the night like normal people.

"I want it to stop," Nina said abruptly.

Dr. Webb was quiet for a long moment. "Is there anything else you want?" He said it so plainly. Like she had just picked out pecan turtles at the See's counter.

"Like?" Nina blurted. A hint of irritation escaped along with the question.

He paused. "Like . . . would you like to know why you're having the dream?"

"I guess." She shrugged, trying to appear nonchalant.

"Can you tell me about it?" the doctor asked.

Nina began haltingly. She described the cemetery in detail for the doctor, then the little girl, and the feeling of sweet innocence that was shattered by the sudden appearance of the ominous White stranger. She tried to relay to the doctor the indescribable terror she experienced as she stood powerless, waiting for the inevitable.

Nina struggled to make it through the details of the dream without breaking down, though she stopped occasionally to fight the tears that welled up behind her eyes. Dr. Webb listened intently, not interrupting, and not responding in any noticeable way. When she had recited the dream completely, Nina pulled her knees up to her chest and rested her chin on them. She exhaled slowly and waited patiently for the prognosis.

Dr. Webb just sat motionless, with his eyes closed, not uttering a single sound. His silence was unsettling, and Nina was becoming agitated. *How hard could it be to help a patient through a bad dream? Why is he just sitting there? Speak, for God's sake.* She went back to playing with the bracelet.

Dr. Webb finally opened his eyes slowly, looking directly into hers as he spoke. "Nina, what do you think the man is going to do to that little girl?"

This was so unnerving. Was he going out of his way to make her uncomfortable, or was Nina just tripping? She answered the question. "I don't really know what he's going to do to her. But I just . . . I know he's going to hurt her."

"Why are you so sure he's going to hurt her?" Dr. Webb prodded.

"I don't know. Because he's a stranger. Because I feel so terrified. I don't really know why."

"What if he had a bouquet of flowers behind his back, or a toy? What if your fear is unfounded?"

The word "unfounded" irritated her even more. *How dare he,* she thought. *If only it was that simple.* How could she expect anyone to understand? How could anyone know what she experienced night after night? No one would be able to help her with this thing. Nina felt a surge of hopelessness, which she tried to hide when she finally spoke in a flat monotone.

"I think I'm having the dream because of something that has happened or is going to happen to me or to someone close to me. I can't explain why I feel that. I just do. And I know he's going to hurt her," she said, raising her voice for emphasis. "*Bad*."

"Who is she, Nina?" Dr. Webb asked.

"I don't know."

"Could she be you?"

Nina was never so uneasy. She had thought this therapy thing was a good idea when Tonya and Mama encouraged her to try it. But it was just too damned annoying. She didn't know if she was feeling mad or nervous or sad or . . . shit, she was feeling a little too much of all of that. His questions were getting on her nerves, and the urge to just say, "Thank you very much" and get up and walk out moved her to the edge of the chair cushion. But the good doctor was waiting for an answer to his question, and Nina was there at nearly six o'clock in the evening, which was surely because of a favor somebody must of owed Mama. *And what was the damned question in the first place?* Nina slid defeatedly back into the chair. She closed her eyes and let her head fall against the padded chair back.

"What was the question again?" Nina breathed.

"Could she be you?" he repeated.

She swallowed hard. Without opening her eyes, she whispered quietly, "I don't know. I can't see her face." She suddenly felt the little girl's presence. The child seemed so alone in the dream. *Abandoned.* A wave of sadness washed over her. "I don't think it's me," she finally added in a quivering voice.

"Why?"

She pulled at a loose thread at the edge of a small hole in the knee of her faded Levi's, silently cursing the tremble in her lower lip. "Because I'm there with her. I'm supposed to protect her. But I can't." Nina had never wanted to cry so badly. She wanted this overwhelming feeling of being alone to go away. She found herself wanting Mama. She just wanted to cry and cry and let Mama or Daddy hold her and tell her everything was going to be okay. She certainly wasn't going to cry like that in front of this stranger. She barely knew this man. She wasn't about to let him see her break down. *Come on*, she thought. *Pull yourself together. You're not a little girl; you're a grown woman.* She took careful, shallow breaths and blinked back the tears.

Dr. Webb closed his eyes and sat in silence for a moment. "You described the man as White," he finally said, opening his eyes to look at Nina, "but the little girl had no racial description. Why?"

Nina regained her composure. Relieved by the change in direction the doctor had taken, she cleared her throat with a tiny, dry cough. "I—I can't tell her race. She has gloves . . . a bonnet. I can't see her skin."

"Nina, are you afraid of White men?" he asked.

"No," she answered abruptly, and with a little more attitude than she had intended. Here was her opportunity to end this whole therapy thing. Maybe she could offend him with the truth, and he'd suggest she try another doctor. "I don't fear White men, I just don't trust them . . . I don't trust you."

He was unfazed. "Hmmm. I see," he returned. "Well, I am a White man. Why would you come to a therapist you cannot trust?" He looked Nina directly in the eye.

So much for offending him. Nina found herself admiring his frankness. "I had no idea you were White. I asked Mama if she knew a good therapist. She gave me your number. I trust her."

"I see. Evelyn is a very good friend of mine," Dr. Webb said, smiling to himself. "She helped me through a tough time with my own daughter. I don't know what we would've done without her." The admiration the man had for Mama was clear.

So that was the favor. It wasn't the receptionist, it was the doctor himself. Nina felt suddenly relaxed. The man's daughter must have been in one of Mama's classes at the parochial school where she taught part-time. "Well, if you're a good friend of Mama's, that's good enough for me." Nina straightened up and sat cross-legged in her chair. Mama wouldn't have sent her to a quack. She obviously thought this man could help. Nina found herself leaning slightly in the doctor's direction. Maybe she should give this man the benefit of the doubt. He was probably a very good therapist. "Mama said you're the best," she said with a soft smile.

Dr. Webb looked at her thoughtfully. After what seemed like a long silence he said, "Is it possible that you're sure the man is going to hurt the child *because* he's White?"

"I guess. I don't know. I never thought about it," Nina replied with nonchalance.

"Close your eyes, Nina," he said quietly.

Nina closed them.

"I want you to picture the beginning of the dream. The little girl is standing alone . . ."

"Yes." Though she wasn't quite sure what he was getting at, Nina decided to participate in whatever point the doctor was trying to make.

"Now, when he comes out from behind the tree, picture the stranger Black instead of White."

Nina sat quietly with her eyes closed. She imagined the scene in the cemetery. She saw the little girl playing quietly in the grass and the stranger coming out from behind the tree, and instead of the White man she was so terrified of, Nina replaced his image with that of a bearded brown-skinned man wearing the same hat and sunglasses.

"Is he as ominous to you now?" the doctor asked.

"Wow," Nina exclaimed in a whisper. "That's strange."

"What's that?" Dr. Webb asked.

"I'm not afraid of him."

"Why not?"

"I don't know. My initial thought was that he could be her father or an uncle, or someone she knows."

"And you don't see White men in those roles?"

"I guess I never thought about it before. I mean, I have friends who have White parents. But . . ."

"But Black men nurtured you as a child and White men . . . ?"

Nina just stared at Dr. Webb for a minute. Now that she thought about it, this was really the first time she ever had a deeply personal conversation with a White man that was about more than grades or sports.

"When I think about the experiences I've had with White

men, there's nothing to be terrified of. Nothing traumatic. I've never been physically threatened or intimidated by one.''

''I want you to try something, Nina,'' the doctor said quietly.

''What's that?''

''The next time you have the dream, try to sleep through to the end. I want you to see if you recognize the man in the cemetery. Find out what he's holding in his hand.''

''Yeah, right,'' Nina said with a sarcastic smile.

''Don't you want to know?'' Dr. Webb asked.

''I think so,'' Nina offered weakly. ''But you don't know how overwhelming the terror is. From the time I see that man creep out from behind that tree, all I want to do is wake up. I watch his hand to see what he's holding, but the whole time I'm trying to scream myself awake.''

''And you don't recognize him at all?''

''I can't see him really. He's wearing dark glasses.''

''Doesn't he remove them?''

Nina hadn't thought of it before. *He takes the glasses off and puts them in his pocket, but my eyes are always focused on what he's hiding.*

''I'm always concentrating on his hand—on what he's hiding. I never think to look at his face,'' Nina whispered.

''Will you try, Nina? Try to see if you know him.''

''I'll try.'' Nina meant it. She was curious now. She'd had the dream at least twenty times in the last few months, and it never occurred to her to look up at the man's face after he took the glasses off. For some reason, that little discovery made her feel hopeful. Maybe this therapy might answer some questions after all. ''Dr. Webb . . .'' Nina began questioningly.

''Yes, Nina.'' His eyes seemed to see deep into her. There was some strange kind of comfortable discomfort in the way he looked at her. It was as if he already knew what she needed to end the nightmare.

''Are you going to be able to help me figure this dream thing out?''

''I don't know, Nina. But we can keep trying.'' He looked down at his watch and rose from his seat, signaling the end of their session. ''If you want to come back, that is.''

''I don't want to come back,'' Nina said seriously. ''But I

will.'' She smiled sincerely at the doctor. She thought about the good omen in the parking lot. "I want to be free at last," she added.

"So, you saw my Chevy?" the doctor asked with a wide grin.

"It's beautiful," Nina replied. She'd just assumed the car belonged to someone Black. *Oh brother, what is this guy, some kind of bleeding-heart-hand-holding-Kumbaya-singing-do-gooder?* "What, did you march with King back in the day or something?" She tried not to sound sarcastic.

"No, I was one of the officers sicking dogs on Black people in Chicago."

"Very funny," Nina chided the doctor. Well, if she could be sarcastic, she supposed he could too.

"No, really. I was a racist devil."

Nina looked into Dr. Webb's face for some sign that he was pulling her leg. He was serious. She didn't know what to say.

"I was a policeman. Joined the force so I could 'clean up the trash.' I rode around with my father in that Chevy, with a Confederate flag flying off the antenna. We thought it was great fun to throw rocks and bottles at the demonstrators." Dr. Webb had a strange, pained expression on his face. He seemed lost in the past for a moment. "It took time, and a hell of a hard struggle, but I finally learned my way out of that blatant, hateful racism my family raised me with."

Nina had never heard any White man share anything so personal. She was immediately skeptical. She'd never been to a psychiatrist before, but she did know they weren't really supposed to share their personal lives with their patients. Maybe this was some kind of ploy to get her to trust him. Or maybe he was one of those White folks seeking to be validated by somebody Black; to get a little relief from White guilt. *Unlearned his racism? How on earth does a person unlearn that kind of racism?* "How?" she heard herself asking aloud.

"I served in Vietnam with some exceptional men . . . men of every race who taught me a kind of manhood my father couldn't. My wife's Asian, and when I married her, well, needless to say my father disowned me. He could never forgive me for 'sullying the bloodline.' Before he died, he cut me out of his will and gave everything to my brother."

"Damn," was all Nina could say.

The doctor continued. "My brother had a temporary lapse of animosity and gave the Chevy to me. I took the flag off and got the plates in memory of my father, who remained a racist till the day he died. The only thing that could free him from his prison of ignorance was death."

"Free at last," Nina muttered. "That's a shame," she added, shaking her head slowly. "He died hating the majority of the human race," she heard herself say aloud.

"He thought *he* was the majority, but that's the danger of ignorance. So I decided that every time someone asks me about the plates, I'd use my father's ignorance to make a point. And here in Glendale, that car and that license plate get a lot of attention."

Dr. Webb walked over to stand under a painting on the wall, and motioned for Nina to join him. She studied the painting in silence. On the lower left side of the canvas the artist had rendered the image of a small, emaciated figure. He was a shirtless, blond, blue-eyed man, wearing tattered overalls made from the fabric of the American flag. The man stood in a deserted field, surrounded by withered trees that protruded feebly from dried, cracked soil. The canvas was divided diagonally by a painted stone wall littered with fading images of the Confederate flag, money symbols, swastikas, and other graffiti. The wall hid from the man's view a beautiful valley filled with color and lush vegetation. Healthy, happy people of every hue were depicted tending the plants, enjoying an abundant feast, and bathing in a blue-white river. The images reminded Nina of the biblical hell and paradise. There was a small opening at the base of the wall, barely big enough to squeeze through, and painted above the opening in tiny gold letters were the words "The Needle's Eye." Nina looked questioningly at Dr. Webb.

"The man would rather suffer eternal loneliness, hunger, and thirst than consider bending his knees and humbling himself to crawl through that narrow opening into paradise," Dr. Webb said quietly.

Nina looked for the artist's signature. *W. Webb* was painted in tiny blue letters in the lower right-hand corner. Dr. Webb was the artist. "Is that your father in the painting?" Nina asked.

The doctor nodded. "My father was raised to believe he was superior to other human beings because he happened to be born with white skin. Unfortunately, the sins of the father really are visited on the children." He passed his fingertips slowly across the withered image of his father on the canvas. "And I know firsthand the devastation it leaves in the soul afflicted with it. Well," Dr. Webb said abruptly. He took Nina's hand and shook it warmly. "It was a true pleasure to meet you, Nina."

"Thank you for your help, Dr. Webb," Nina said, returning the handshake.

"Believe me, young lady, it's the least I could do for your mother."

"Mama is good people," Nina replied, then added, "You do know she's my stepmother? My biological mother died when I was very young."

"I'd like to explore that at our next session, if you're willing to come back."

"I'll be back," Nina said, walking to the door. "But I don't know if there's much to explore about my birth mother. I don't know too much about her." She stepped into the reception office. "I can't really see how that would have anything to do with the dream."

"Maybe nothing at all, Nina," Dr. Webb answered, "but your image of your mother may impact the way you interpret the dream's significance."

Nina stopped at the receptionist's desk to smell the roses. She wasn't sure she really had an image of her mother. "I'll see if I can get my father to tell me more about her then," Nina replied before inhaling the sweet scent.

"Call my service tomorrow and see about an appointment next week. And don't worry about payment, it's been taken care of." He walked Nina to the outer door. "You should try talking to your stepmother, too." The doctor winked; his grin looked almost mischievous. "She's a very wise woman."

"I'll be staying at my parents' home for the rest of the week," Nina said with a nod. She headed for the elevator. "I'll see what Mama knows."

△▽ 10 ▽△

Mama was standing at the stove when Nina opened the front door of her parents' sprawling, ranch-style home. The house was just under four thousand square feet, all on one level. Mama and Daddy had started designing it when Nina was barely in elementary school. Daddy's first album had just gone platinum, and he was being lauded by jazz critics as "a fresh new trumpeter on the scene." He always said that made him laugh, since he had been playing professionally for over twenty-five years before anyone noticed he was "fresh" and "new." The Moore family had been what one could consider "upper middle-class," but with Mitch Moore's album royalties, personal appearances, and concerts, he and his wife were finally in a position to build their dream home.

Two weeks after Nina graduated from junior high, they finally packed everything up and left Los Angeles to move into their newly built refuge from the materialism and crime of the city. Nina was not at all pleased with the event. While all her friends were talking about who would be going to which L.A. high school, Nina was expected to be excited about making the adjustment to small-town Glendale, Arizona. She clearly wasn't, and spent most of the summer sulking and pouting.

"Nina, someday you'll appreciate why your mama and I wanted to move you kids out of the city. I don't expect you to like it, and I don't expect you to understand it, but I do expect you to get over it," her father told her. She never really did. That was over ten years ago, and she still missed L.A. She'd spent her first two years of college at UCLA, and she would have stayed and graduated a Bruin if it wasn't for the fact that Daddy had developed diabetes, and Mama needed her close to home, and she'd gotten a full academic scholarship at Founder's, and she met Derrick, and she knew she'd never find a friend as true as Tonya, and what on earth would she do without Sweet Nat, and she loved being able to just come home when she needed her parents, like she needed them now. And come to think of it, *maybe Glendale had become home after all.*

Nina put her overnight bag down on the salmon-colored stone entryway and followed the pink-orange path into the huge kitchen. The living room had been designed to be used, not just decorated, and Mama loved to be in the kitchen, so she had the architect leave a long counter open to the ceiling between the two rooms. It wasn't unusual to find Mama in there canning her garden-grown tomatoes, or shelling pecans for a homemade pie. Today, Nina smelled onions and garlic sautéing in butter, and coupled with the strong odor of filé-seasoned seafood she knew before she even got close to the stove that Mama had decided to try to "heal" Nina with her favorite meal.

"Aw, Mama, you're making me jambalaya?" Nina cooed, greeting her stepmother with a smooch on the cheek before pinching a shrimp from the sauté pan.

"Mama, you're making jambalaya for me?" Mama repeated, correcting Nina's English. She put down her spatula momentarily to smack the back of the hand Nina had used to sneak the shrimp.

For a woman who cooked as much and as well as Mama, Nina could never figure out how she stayed so trim. She wasn't a tiny woman, but her 140 pounds clung to her five-foot-seven frame in all the right places. Though Daddy seemed to think so, Mama wasn't a beauty queen. Matter of fact, Mama looked like the stereotypical schoolteacher. Her wire-rimmed glasses framed dark, serious eyes, and her hair was usually drawn up, like now, in a tight bun at the nape of her neck. She actually looked like she might be a stick-in-the-mud, but she couldn't be further from that. Mama's sense of humor was her greatest gift. Nina loved teasing her, and the feeling was mutual.

"Mmmm, theeyum's some sure tasty scrimps you dun made," Nina said with an exaggerated Southern drawl as she smacked the tips of her fingers loudly.

"Child, if you don't get out of my hair while I'm cooking . . ." Mama swatted at Nina with the spatula. "Make yourself useful and peel those peaches over there in the sink."

"Jambalaya *and* peach cobbler?" Nina said playfully. "Dang, Mama, you must think the doctor diagnosed me with something horrific."

Mama's smile vanished. A look of concern swept over her thin, mahogany-toned face, and she put her cooking utensils down to concentrate on Nina. "What did Will say, baby? Can he help you with those nightmares?"

Nina picked up a peach and the peeler and began stripping the thin skin into the sink. "Dr. Webb thinks I should try to sleep through to the end. He wants me to try to figure out who the man in the dream is, and what he's holding in his hand." Nina stopped peeling peaches and looked at her stepmother questioningly. "Mama, why didn't you tell me he was White?"

Mama chuckled. "I didn't think about it. Will's not White. He's . . . well, he's Will." Mama laughed aloud, as though she were tickled by a private joke. "Besides, I didn't think it would bother you, baby."

"It didn't bother me," Nina lied. "Well, it kinda bothered me at first. But after a while it was okay. He asked some good questions, I guess."

"Are you going to go back?" Mama picked up her utensils to resume cooking. She was watching Nina the entire time out of the corner of her eye.

"I'm going back," Nina responded. "Next Monday. My homework is to talk to Daddy before then."

"Talk to your daddy about what, baby?" Mama was trying not to sound worried.

Nina cut a slice of peach and popped it in her mouth. "My biological mother. Dr. Webb thinks the dream might have something to do with her. He says I might be reacting to the dream the way I do because of my feelings about her . . . or something like that."

"Hmmm," was all Mama said for a while. Then she added

quietly, "Baby, if there was anything I could tell you about her I would."

"Why won't Daddy talk about her? If I even mention her to him, all I see in his eyes are anger and pain." Nina surprised herself with the tone of resentment in her voice. She had a great relationship with her father, and she loved him deeply, but was he so ashamed of what he had done with Nina's mother that he wanted to pretend whatever they had never happened?

"I didn't know your mother, Nina." Mama's eyes were fixed on the pan in front of her, and she didn't look up. "Neither your dad nor I knew you'd been born until after she died. But I can tell you this." She raised her head to look into Nina's eyes. "Your father didn't think twice about embracing you with open arms." Mama's face registered a faint smile and she shook her head slowly. "Your father's very strong, and I love that man, but you have to understand that the subject of your mother is just too much for him to deal with. Be patient with him, Nina. Maybe it's not that he won't talk about her. Maybe he just can't."

"And what about you, Mama?"

Mama was quiet.

"Mama?" Nina repeated.

"I wish I could, Nina. I really wish I could."

Mama's eyes were two glassy mirrors for a moment that reflected a hint of pain, or regret, or . . . something Nina couldn't quite read.

Nina was instantly sorry she'd caused Mama's uneasiness. *God, what if my mother was some groupie hanging out to "do" a musician after a concert? How could Daddy have done something like that to Mama?* Nina tried to sound nonchalant when she finally spoke. "Don't worry about it, Mama, I'm going to try to get Daddy to talk to me when he gets back. Is he still flying in from L.A. on the red-eye Friday night?"

"Are you kidding?" Mama answered almost before Nina could finish the question. "Why do you think he insisted on having the party here again? He wouldn't miss that BSU barbecue for anything in the world." She winked at Nina and smiled broadly. "I think he had more fun last year than you young people."

"Yeah. You were out there gettin' your boogie on real good too, Mama," Nina teased.

Mama laughed first, then corrected Nina. "No, I was gettin' my boogie on real well, Miss Nina." They both laughed before settling into a comfortable quiet. Sharing the kitchen felt good, reminding Nina of the way things had been back when she was still living at home.

Nina thought about what Mama said about her father. *It must have been an affair.* But damn, they were all adults. Wasn't it about time Nina got to know the truth?

Mama interrupted her thoughts. "Derrick called here for you earlier," she said a little too nonchalantly.

"Derrick who?" Nina replied, wondering if Mama caught her salty smirk.

She had. "I had a feeling you two might be on the outs again," Mama said gently.

"Yeah, Mama," Nina said, attempting to put a lilt in her voice, "we're on the outs all right." She popped another peach slice in her mouth and tried to look unaffected. "The waaaaay outs. The get-the-hell outs. The get-that-strange-White-woman-you-got-in-my-bed outs."

Mama looked at Nina in shock. "The what?" she said incredulously. "He didn't."

"We broke up this morning." Nina silently cursed her trembling voice. "Forever this time."

Mama put down her spatula, turned the stove off, and was at Nina's side in an instant. A tear filled Nina's left eye and pooled on the bottom rim, threatening to spill over. "I will not cry over that triflin' fool," Nina muttered at herself angrily. The tear spilled defiantly onto her cheek, and she swatted it away with the back of the hand that still held the paring knife.

"Here, baby." Mama took the knife from Nina and dropped it into the sink. "Do you want to talk about it?" She put her arms around Nina and hugged her close.

Nina sank into Mama's embrace and was suddenly overwhelmed by a heart-wrenching, moaning sob. It was the same sob that had been aching to get out when she was fighting tears in Dr. Webb's office a few hours before, only it had gathered momentum and was racking her body until it seemed that every ounce of energy she had would be needed just to release it all. The sound of her wailing cry echoed off the stone walls of the kitchen, sending a deep chill through Nina that made her cry even harder. Thank God for Mama's strong arms, because if they weren't there to help hold her up, Nina would have been on the floor in a heap. Her head hurt, and her eyes felt like there couldn't possibly be enough room in her skull for them to stay put, but still she was crying. Crying like she never remembered crying, ever. And when she felt as if she couldn't possibly stand another minute of the storm's intensity, the need to cry left her as suddenly as it had come.

Mama's hands were holding Nina up by the shoulders, and when the crying ceased, she took a tiny step back to look into her daughter's eyes. "Was all that for Derrick, baby?" Mama asked.

Nina shook her head slowly. "I don't know where that came from," she whispered. Mama led Nina over to a dining chair and Nina collapsed into it. "I guess it's just been building up. With the nightmares, and the lack of sleep, and stressing over how to call off the wedding . . ." Mama's eyebrows shot up. "Yes, I had already realized it was a mistake . . . You and Daddy had him figured out a long time ago." Nina managed a smile.

"It was only a matter of time, baby," Mama reassured her. "Men like Derrick can only keep up the charade for as long as a woman is willing to turn a blind eye."

"I can't really get too angry at Derrick," Nina returned, "because as much as I know he was taking advantage of me, lying to me, depending on me to help him with his career . . ." She hesitated. "And his rent . . ." Mama raised her eyebrows again, but didn't say a word. ". . . I see now that I was really using him, too."

"Using him for what, Nina?" Mama's look said she couldn't believe Nina could possibly have tried to take advantage of Derrick.

"Company."

This time Mama's neatly plucked eyebrows knitted together into a deep furrow, accompanied by a sideways frown. "Company?" she repeated in a low tone.

Nina wrinkled up her nose. "Not *that* kind of company.

Not really. I—I really am afraid to sleep by myself. That's how terrifying the nightmare is for me. I started having the dream at the end of February. By July, I had started doubting that Derrick and I were a match made in heaven. And here it is nearly September and . . .'' Nina hesitated, hardly believing herself the words she was going to say to Mama. "Even after I realized I couldn't marry Derrick, I stayed with him for weeks, so I wouldn't have to sleep alone.''

Mama reached for Nina's hand. "We're going to put a stop to that nightmare, baby. You cannot go on living like that. If Will says it's going to help, we'll just have to get your daddy to talk to you about your mother. In the meantime, you can sleep in my bed if you need to.''

"Thanks, Mama.'' Nina planted a kiss on the smooth brown hand that held hers. "I really am glad you suggested I stay here for a few days; it's just what I need. But I'm going to try to do what Dr. Webb suggested. I'm going to see if I can sleep through to the end of the dream. If no one is there to wake me, maybe I can finally see who the man is, and what he's hiding.'' Nina stood up. "And I really am exhausted. Do you think—''

Mama cut her off with a knowing smile. "Jambalaya tastes even better on the second day. You go on now.''

Nina kissed her mother on the cheek and headed off to bed.

△▽ 11 ▽△

Ahmad couldn't shake the eerie feeling that he was being watched. The moment he turned onto his block an uneasiness wrapped itself around his shoulders, and the muscles in the back of his neck tightened into a rigid bow. He edged the Volvo along the narrow lane to his apartment building and glanced again in the rearview mirror. There was no one behind him, and the road ahead of him was empty too. All Ahmad could see in either direction were waves of heat radiating up from the baking asphalt. His eyes quickly scanned the unpaved shoulder of the road, which was crowded with mostly worn-out cars and rusty garbage Dumpsters, but there wasn't a soul in sight. If someone was watching him, they'd have to be crooked or crazy to be out in this heat; it was nearly a hundred degrees. He pulled the car alongside the dirt strip that edged the sun-blistered patch of what was supposed to be the front lawn, and parked.

He was just returning from dropping Ebony off at Dwight's condo on the other side of town. Dwight's daughter Adrianne was turning seven, and her mother Saundra, Dwight's ex-wife, had planned a slumber party, which Ebony was invited to be a part of.

Before emerging from the car, Ahmad exhaled a loud sigh of relief. He had made it to Saturday, and except for the run-in with the policeman, and his thoroughly embarrassing encounter with Nina Moore, he had had a pretty good week. Just knowing that Ebony would have a place to be while he worked lifted an incredible burden from his shoulders, and everything

97

else he had to deal with seemed so much more manageable.

Ahmad looked over at the empty passenger seat and smiled. He missed her already. This fatherhood thing was all right. It was a little overwhelming and even a little scary at times, but he had to give himself credit. For a man who never had a relationship with his own parents, and who had no real experience with children, he was handling the responsibility of parenthood pretty damned well. It had certainly helped that he'd read all those child psychology books while he was locked up. But reading to prepare for parenthood, and actually being depended on every minute of every day by a child, were two totally different things. Fortunately, Ebony made it a lot easier than he'd expected. She was obedient and affectionate, and though she talked incessantly, and, of course, required twenty-four-hour supervision, he could see that her presence in his life was a blessing. Still, it was nice to have this little break. This would be Ahmad's first real time alone since he was released, and he planned to take advantage of the freedom.

He got out of the sweltering Volvo and stood by the car door, scanning the scene one more time for signs of any strangers. The feeling of being watched hadn't left him, but he shrugged it off and headed for his front door. He stopped momentarily to stomp his boot loudly on the cracked walkway leading to the front stoop of his apartment, and watched as a tiny salamander that had been basking itself on the hot pavement scurried across the parched grass and disappeared.

"Somebody live over there named Jefferson?" The scratchy voice came from across the driveway. A wrinkled old face was peering from around the corner of a half-opened screen door.

"I'm Ahmad Jefferson." Ahmad used his hand as a sun visor and took a couple of steps toward the woman.

"Somebody was here for you, son. Left this." She held up a large manila envelope.

Ahmad walked over to the woman's stoop. She was an old Indian woman, with leathery skin, deep-set eyes, and a small hooked nose. Two gray braids on either side of her head hung down past her waist. "For me?" he questioned. "Who?"

"White man. Black hat and sunglasses. Dressed nice. Come early. In a cab. Hung around so long, I asked who he was looking for.'' The woman's voice was low and gritty. So gritty, Ahmad wondered if it pained her to use her vocal cords. "I told him I didn't know your name. Said I didn't usually see you and the little girl back here till around six. When I mentioned the girl, he showed me your photo. He asked me if I'd see to it you get this.'' She opened the screen a little wider and handed Ahmad the envelope.

"Thanks,'' Ahmad muttered, somewhat dazed. He grasped the envelope with a dubious frown and backed away from the stoop, then stopped in his tracks. This woman had watched over his home. She was a good neighbor to have, and Ahmad wasn't acting very neighborly himself. He stepped up onto the tiny porch and extended his hand. Smiling at the old woman he said, "I'm Ahmad. The little girl you saw is my daughter Ebony.''

The woman put her bony hand into Ahmad's and grasped it tightly. She looked into his face with a steely-eyed stare. "Mankiller,'' she growled in her gritty voice.

Ahmad's eyes opened wide and he took a small step back. He sucked in a quick, shallow breath. *What the hell was this old lady talking about? She couldn't possibly know anything about that, could she?* He drew back his hand nervously, but she still had a tight grip on it.

"Annette Mankiller. You can call me Netty.'' She laughed as softly as her taut vocal cords would allow, and released his hand. She seemed tickled by his nervous response. Ahmad obviously wasn't the first to have such a reaction to her surname.

Mankiller was the old woman's last name. Of course. It was an Indian name. He managed a nervous smile. "Thank you, Netty,'' he said with visible relief. The woman didn't say another word, she just chuckled to herself and disappeared into her apartment.

Ahmad lay on the couch with his arms folded behind his head and his boots crossed. The still unopened envelope lay across his chest, rising and falling with his every breath, provoking him to just get it over with. But he wanted time to think; to be prepared for whatever might be coming at him now. He wasn't sure he wanted to know. *It's not like it could hold good news.* Who would send an unmarked envelope? If a White man brought it, it obviously wasn't from Dwight or Uncle Three. If it had something to do with Ebony, Chante, or Mrs. Taylor, why wouldn't it have come in the mail?

He rose from the couch and let the envelope fall to the floor. "I'm going to take a piece of my paycheck to the mall and buy myself some fly swim trunks for that barbecue," he said aloud. "I'm not trying to deal with one more crazy thing this week." He had been thinking of a way to attend that BSU party since Monday evening after he'd left the day care center. He hadn't remembered keeping Nina's flyer, but there it was among his papers when he and Ebony got back home from the DMV that evening. He didn't see then how he could possibly go. Not only did he not know a sitter, he didn't have any idea how much one might cost. Besides, he couldn't imagine leaving his daughter with any old body.

He had started to just toss the flyer in the garbage, and toss the idea of the party out with it. Then it occurred to him. Plenty of other sistas would be there; *and* they'd be in bathing suits. The only women in bathing suits he'd seen over the last five years were either in *Sports Illustrated* or on television. Come to think of it, could he handle all that flesh . . . in the flesh? Hell, could he handle being at a private party surrounded by people he didn't know? It was all a little intimidating, but it was about time he made some acquaintances in town. And from the looks of this tiny, nearly lily-white community, that party would be the best place to meet other Black folks. Ahmad had tucked the flyer in a drawer in the kitchen. Just in case. And as luck would have it, Ebony would be with Saundra and Adrianne until the following evening.

He walked into the bathroom and turned the cold water faucet. *Alone for the weekend.* He splashed the cool water on his face and looked up at his reflection in the cracked mirror above the sink. He studied his chiseled features, turning slightly to the left, then back to the right as his large deep-set eyes followed his movements. He stroked his chin thoughtfully. *Hmmm.* He looked at his neatly trimmed beard and tiny twisted locks. *I'm not a bad-looking brotha. I shouldn't have any trouble attracting the opposite sex. The opposite sex.* Maybe he could have a woman over. He looked at the reflection of the tiny apartment behind him. *And do what? Have sex on that raggedy couch? No.* But maybe they could go back to her place. *Sex.* The thought of it sent a shiver through his groin. *Damn.* It had been five long years. Was he ready to just jump on in like that? It was a little frightening. He definitely didn't want to embarrass himself by being too eager and not be able to please a woman. Maybe he should pay somebody first. *Nah. No way.* He'd never paid for sex in his life, and the idea of trying to find a hooker to help him get his sexual bearings was ridiculous. And what if he couldn't . . . ? He hadn't been with a woman since . . . Ahmad leaned on the porcelain sink with straightened arms and let his head hang down.

He didn't mean to invite it in, but the memory of that last night with his wife flooded in behind his closed eyes. They had made love that night. Twice. The recollection of Chante lying on her back beneath him, with her eyes closed and a satisfied smile on her lips, was still so vivid. Hauntingly vivid. Like it had just happened yesterday. He could almost hear her sighing breathlessly in his ear. It had been cool for a September evening, but Chante was drenched in sweat. She had just climaxed for the second time, and her moans had subsided into breathy murmurs. Ahmad had raised himself up on his elbows, and was just staring down at her, thinking how good it felt to be in love with this beautiful sista, to be the father of her child. He had placed a slow and tender kiss on her mouth when the phone rang. He had no intention of answering it either. Chante was the one that playfully nudged him off of her and told him to "get the damned phone." If only he had known. How could he have known that night would be their last?

Ahmad raised his head and looked into the mirror. Why was he torturing himself? Chante was gone. Gone. And the cold reality was that she had been gone for a long time. The drugs took her soul years before; the finality of death just made it more permanent. What hurt more than anything was that he wasn't just mourning the death of his wife, he was mourning the death of the hope he had held on to for all those years— the hope that he could fix everything—that he could be the reason she needed to stay clean. He just knew that together they could rebuild the shattered remnants of their happy life together.

"Stop this, man," he groaned into the sink. He raised his face to the mirror. Maybe if he could start a relationship with a woman—any woman—the torment and the bittersweet memories of Chante could begin to fade.

He splashed his face again from the stream of cool water flowing from the tap before turning it off and heading for the other room. He picked some jeans and a plain white tee shirt from among a small bundle of laundry. He'd go to the mall and get some inexpensive swim trunks. If he scrimped on lunch for the next week, maybe he could afford a little bottle of imposter cologne, too. Ahmad took out his rickety ironing board, plugged in the iron, and headed for the shower.

When he was clean and dry and his sculpted body gleamed from a healthy dose of cocoa butter–scented lotion, he stood with a towel wrapped around his waist and the steaming iron in his hand. It was then that he noticed the envelope again. It lay there on the floor taunting him. What if it was something he really needed to see? He ignored the urge to snatch it up, to put an end to his nagging curiosity.

Instead he dressed quickly, grabbed his wallet and car keys from the table, and headed for the door. He had his hand on the doorknob but couldn't bring himself to turn it. He turned to look at the envelope again. There was no way. There was no way he'd be able to relax with the mystery of its contents tugging at his thoughts all evening. Ahmad walked slowly over to the couch and sat down.

He turned the manila envelope over and over, searching for some mark that might identify its sender, but there was nothing. Finally, he ripped it open from one corner and let its contents tumble out on the floor between his boots. There lay three white business-sized envelopes, all without markings and all sealed. He opened the fattest one first. Inside were two airline tickets to Los Angeles. One was for Theodore Jefferson, the other for Ebony. The flight left Phoenix at 7:12 A.M. Sunday morning. A week from tomorrow. The return time had been left open. Ahmad searched the envelope for some sign of who had sent them, how they were purchased; a receipt or something. There was nothing.

Who wanted them back in L.A.? Other than Chante's mother, Ebony's only other family was an aunt, Marlene, in Compton, and she was on welfare. She didn't have the wherewithal to purchase plane tickets. Besides, he had just talked to her on the phone on Wednesday, and she didn't say anything about any trip to Los Angeles.

Ahmad tore open the second envelope. The sight of its contents hit him squarely in the chest, and he leaned back against the couch, holding the folded glossy page limply in his lap. It was a funeral program, and in the center of the folded-over page was a photograph of Chante, one Ahmad had never seen. She was sitting on a golden merry-go-round horse flashing her dazzling smile. The program read, *In loving memory*. He held the paper to his heart for a moment and closed his eyes.

After he'd whispered a prayer for her, Ahmad read on. The graveside funeral was set for Sunday at noon. Airline tickets and a funeral program for the same day. But how? Who? Who would have made funeral arrangements? It wasn't Mrs. Taylor. Ahmad had just phoned the hospital Tuesday. Chante's mother was still comatose, and when he'd called the coroner's office to inquire about his wife's remains, he was told a family member had already claimed the body. He'd assumed that was Chante's sister Marlene, but when he called her, she said she didn't know anything about it. Marlene had been told by the coroner's office a few days earlier that Chante would be cremated by the state since no one could afford to bury her. So, someone had claimed her body. But who?

Ahmad neatly folded the program and placed it back in its envelope before ripping open the third envelope. In it was a plain white piece of paper wrapped around several hundred-dollar bills. Ahmad counted. One, two . . . The bills were crisp and new, like they'd just come off the presses. Seven, eight, nine, ten. A thousand dollars. Who . . . ? Ahmad searched all three envelopes again, but there were no clues to the identity of the sender. He gathered up everything, and stuffed it all back into the manila envelope.

He should have waited. Damn. He didn't want to think about all this now. It was just too much. Later. He would pray about it when he got home tonight. If Chante really was being memorialized, he had to be there. But what if it was some kind of trap? Maybe it had something to do with Chante's murder. Maybe she owed someone money. No. That didn't make sense. Why would they have sent a thousand dollars? A thousand dollars. It was a small fortune to him in light of his current financial situation. Ahmad could certainly use the money. But what if it was dirty? What if it was some kind of drug money? There was no telling what kind of shady characters Chante had hooked up with since her fall into drug abuse. What if Ahmad spent it, and it turned out to be connected to some crime? Could he go back to jail for that? Was someone trying to set him up?

He had time to decide what to do about the plane tickets, the funeral, and the money. For now, he just needed to get out for a while. Clear his mind. Ahmad shoved the manila envelope under the couch. He promised himself he would not dwell on this new dilemma for now. What he needed more than anything was to relieve a little stress, and maybe, if he was lucky, find something to feel good about. Ahmad rose from the couch and mentally pushed the envelope a little further underneath it before heading out the front door.

△▽ 12 ▽△

*Nina had actually been looking forward to an-*alyzing the dreaded nightmare, but in the few nights she'd spent in her old bedroom, the only dream she remembered having was one in which Derrick's head was on the body of a strange-looking bug that had climbed in her window. She stood poised over the insect, ready to splatter him with a fly-swatter, when instead, she grabbed him gently by one of his eight (or was it twelve?) legs and flicked him out the window. That was Monday night, and the rest of the week she'd slept better than she had in months. Nina dared to hope that maybe the nightmare had bothered her for the last time.

For most of the week, she pretty much just lazed around by the pool, ate Mama's cooking, and didn't allow herself to stress too much about anything. Wednesday, when Tonya came over to work out an agenda for the party, they discussed the best way to present their King Day strategy to a group of young, mostly unenlightened college kids. They didn't want to do a long, drawn-out "soapbox thang," but they did need to make the point of the party clear. As faculty advisor to the BSU, Nina would speak to the guests about the goals for the coming year and announce the meeting schedule. Tonya would talk about the King Day "rebellion." They'd do it right before the DJ got started; around eight. Tonya had some secret plan for a live poetry reading. She promised it would be entertaining and nothing too preachy. After all, it was supposed to be a day of food and fun.

Nina had tried to wait up for her father to come in on the

red-eye Friday night, but after reading some Gibran, and writing a little poetry of her own, she still hadn't heard him come in. So, she wrote a list of questions to ask him about her mother and drifted off into a sound sleep.

When she awakened Saturday morning to bright sunlight and the loud whine of an electric leaf blower streaming through the window of her bedroom, she hopped out of bed and padded across the thick carpet to the sliding glass door that looked out onto the back patio. It was a perfect day for a barbecue. The air was clean and hot, and the wind had settled down so that a slight breeze was swaying the tips of the eucalyptus trees that lined the back edge of the acre and a half of Moore property.

Nina surmised there must have been a mild windstorm sometime after she fell asleep, because there were palm fronds scattered around the yard, the pool cover was in a heap against the side of the garage, and the water's surface was covered with debris. A team of gardeners and hired hands were busily cleaning the yard, skimming the pool, and setting up tables and cabana-style tents for the party. The sound guys had arrived to set up for the band, but Nina didn't go outside to greet them, since her father would be out there directing everything anyway.

On her way to the bathroom, Nina stopped in front of her mirrored closet door to check out her reflection. Her skin had a healthy tanned glow, and her eyes were sparkling and clear. The decision to spend a few days at home had turned out to be good medicine for her, and she was feeling better than she had since . . . well, since that damned nightmare started.

After showering, slathering her body with Quick Tan oil, and donning her royal blue bikini, she reached in the closet for her white gauze sundress and put it on over her bathing suit. The dress was slightly see-through, and a little on the short side, but this was a pool party, wasn't it? Bedsides, if by chance Ahmad Jefferson decided to drop in, she was hoping to finally catch his eye. She hadn't been able to get the man out of her thoughts since they'd had their unfortunate misunderstanding, and she was sure he had no idea the effect just holding her hand and squeezing it slightly had on her that day. His palm against hers sent a spark down her spine that could still make her shiver if she thought too hard about it. And that sexy smile didn't help. Not that he'd used it on her extensively. He didn't seem to have the same kind of attraction for her that she had for him, and she was hoping to do something about that little problem today.

She pulled her white leather slides with the inch and a half heel out of the closet. Adding a little height would help her calves look more defined. She ran some gel through her hair, applied some lipstick and a light coat of waterproof mascara, and headed outside to find her father.

"Youuu looooook maaahvalous," Nina's father greeted her with outstretched arms as he walked toward her wearing a white golf shirt and a pair of baggy Bermuda shorts. *Was he losing weight?* That was just like Daddy. Especially when he was recording. He'd spent a lot of time in that L.A. studio lately, and without Mama's home cooking, he was getting kind of bony. Father and daughter met halfway between the patio door and the pool house where he had been busily directing the setup of the band equipment. The year before, his band played all afternoon, and when they'd finally retired their instruments, and the DJ started spinning dance records around sunset, Mitchell Moore was still good to go. He partied past midnight out on the patio with the youngsters.

Nina was looking forward to seeing her father enjoy himself. He'd been traveling back and forth to L.A. every week for a couple of months now, and he was starting to look worse for the wear. When they embraced in a warm hug, Nina held the hug long, then stepped away from him, looking into his face. She noticed a sallowness in his complexion, and when she lifted his sunglasses up and peered beneath them, she saw that he had two greenish black circles under his eyes.

"You look like hell, Daddy," she complained. "Didn't you get any sleep in L.A.?"

He chuckled at his daughter. "It's good to see you, too, baby." He balled up both fists and set one on each of his narrow hips in mock offense. "I was very busy. I got a little nap on the flight, but I'll get some rest tonight." He winked at Nina and added, "After I get my party on, that is." He did an energetic but pitiful version of the cabbage patch for Nina that made her laugh.

When Nina said seriously, "I need to talk to you, Daddy . . . when you get a chance," her father's face turned paler.

"Your mother told me." He grunted. He put his hands in the pockets of his shorts and frowned. "Messing around with therapists and such. Never did believe in it," he muttered before kissing Nina lightly on the cheek and walking back over to fiddle with the soundboard.

"Am I s'posed to take that as a no?" Nina called after him. He didn't respond. Either he didn't hear her or he was pretending not to. Nina figured it was the latter. She wasn't about to give up though. She'd wait a while. After the guests were gone, and Daddy'd had one too many zinfandels. It wasn't going to be easy, but Nina was determined to get him to talk. The woman was her mother for God's sake. And even if Nina never had the nightmare again, she still wanted to know the truth. She had the right to know the truth.

By the time the first handful of guests arrived, the tables inside the air-conditioned cabana tents were overflowing with fresh fruit trays and platters of shelled shrimp, tiny quiches, quesadillas, and a variety of other appetizers. The real food would be coming out later, after the barbecued meats were ready. That wouldn't be for a couple more hours. Mama and Nina had cooked three huge pots of collard greens and four industrial-sized pans of macaroni and cheese, and Mama's famous potato salad was in the big fridge in the garage in six gallon-sized bowls. Mama was back in the kitchen this morning cooking yams, peeling peaches, shelling pecans, and baking her heart out.

Nina walked around the patio and welcomed the few guests that had arrived "early." It was two-thirty, and actually the flyer did say two, but everybody knew that really meant around three or three-thirty. Well, obviously not everybody. Nina politely guided a young sista she didn't know to a changing room around the back side of the pool house, and went into the house to get some more towels. *Where on earth are Tonya and Nat? They're supposed to be here to help greet the guests.*

In between welcoming those who trickled in, and encouraging guests to partake of refreshments, Nina introduced a tall, freckled young man named Eric to a roly-poly little sista named Naomi. Tonya's cousin's ex-boyfriend Dwayne seemed happy to meet a student from Nina's African-American history class named Geneva, and the way-too-skinny-for-his-height math major Albert Jackson was pleased to make the acquaintance of even-skinnier-than-Albert, braces-wearing Frieda. Frieda had a big crush on Nat, and though she tried to corner Nina to ask where her brother was, Nina managed to hook her up with Albert and get on out the way.

Truth was, Nina was trying to focus on being a good hostess, but every few minutes or so she found herself glancing toward the gate that led from the backyard to a long walkway around the side of the house and on to the driveway out front. She kept hoping she'd see Ahmad Jefferson walk through it, but so far only a dozen or so guests had trickled in. He might not be coming anyway. He did have his little girl. And Ebony said they'd recently moved here, so maybe he didn't have a baby-sitter yet.

Nina heard laughter, and looked again at the gate just in time to catch Tonya and Nat coming through it arm in arm. Nina headed over to meet them. She wanted to know where they had been, and what was so damned funny?

Nat cut his laughter short to head off Nina's impending questions. "To the airport, if you must know," he offered before she said a word. He looked at Tonya.

"Surprise visitor," they sang simultaneously.

Nina stood with her hands on her hips. Her raised eyebrows and sideways frown expression wasn't phasing either of them. "Well . . . ?" she finally said, impatiently.

Nat leaned down into Nina's face. "Does the word 'surprise' mean anything to you, young lady? Unfortunately, the special guest missed his—I mean, the guest missed the flight. There was another one coming in later, but we thought you might appreciate our company. So, we be here for you instead." He smiled, showing the large gap between his otherwise perfect teeth. "Surprise visitor will have to cab it."

Nina looked over at Tonya for help, but T just shrugged and spelled it out for her, exaggerating each letter tauntingly. "S-U-R-P-R-I-S-E."

"All right, Bert and Ernie. Be that way." Nina pretended to be hurt. "But speaking of surprises, Mr. Moore . . ." She

poked at Nat. ". . . here comes your girlfriend Frieda." Nina
turned on her heel, hooked Tonya's elbow in hers, and left
Nat to fend for himself.

Nina and Tonya lay side by side on lounge chairs, basking
in the sun's late afternoon rays. "Girl, you better put this stuff
on and stop trippin'," Tonya warned, straight-arming a bottle
of SPF 50 sunblock toward Nina.

Nina waved it away. "Why am I going to block the sun,
T? I'm out here tryin' to get brown, fool."

"You are going to end up with skin cancer, girl," Tonya
warned. "So you didn't get enough melanin. So deal with it.
But don't end up dying a painful death trying to get what you
obviously were not meant to have." Tonya waved her hand
Vanna-style down her torso to rub in the fact that she had
been blessed with plenty of pigment. Tonya was just teasing,
and Nina knew she really was trying to make a point. T didn't
go anywhere in Arizona without sunblock and she'd lecture a
stranger in a minute about the damaging effects of UV rays.
She wasn't about to be old and wrinkled before her time.

"All right, Black woman," Nina teased back. "You're not
just trying to keep your skin from getting darker with that SPF
five million you been slathering on over there, are you, girl?"
She raised up on her elbows momentarily to roll her eyes
playfully at Tonya.

Tonya didn't miss a beat. "The darker the berry, baby, the
sweeter the juice." She winked at Nina. "And you, my friend,
are just a sour grape. A sour *white* grape destined to become
a raisin."

"Ouch. Damn, girl, you got me." Nina laughed and lay
back down on the lounge chair in mock defeat, defiantly soaking up the sun's rays.

The two women listened to the mellow jazz tones of the
Mitchell Moore Quartet and watched the rapidly growing
crowd of small-talking minglers and well-oiled sunbathers.
Tonya joked aloud with a chuckle, "Girl, it must be the smell
of your mama's special sauce attracting all these Black folks."
As soon as Nat started barbecuing, it seemed like people just
poured out of the woodwork. Tonya did an informal head
count and came up with fifty-five. Fifty-five. And it was only

a little after six. By the time the DJ got to mixing records around eight o'clock, the yard would be filled to capacity. Nina figured word must have spread to the university campus in Phoenix, because there weren't this many young Black folks in the whole town of Glendale.

Obnoxious feedback noise coming from the huge speakers in front of the pool house caught everyone's attention. Daddy was announcing a "take five." The band had been playing steadily for over an hour, and he looked a little out of breath. "We will be back in a few." He waved at the guests, acknowledging their generous applause before stepping away from the mike and out of sight.

Nina closed her eyes and remembered her last encounter with Ahmad Jefferson. After she'd told him it would be no problem to have Ebony stay with her at the center—for a moment, she almost thought he was going to hug her, but he just squeezed her hand real friendly-like and went on out the door. *Quit trippin', girl*, Nina told herself. It wasn't like she needed to try to rush things. He just lost his wife, or at least that's how Ebony explained it, and Nina was engaged to be married less than a week ago. True enough, attractive Black men weren't overly plentiful in Glendale, but it wasn't like she needed to chase one down; she was used to being the one chased. But Ahmad didn't seem to be trying to beat her door down. Maybe he just wasn't attracted to her. Maybe after losing his wife he wasn't ready for a relationship. Or maybe he was gay. *Ooh, girl, this heat is really getting to you. You really do need to cool off.* She had been lying in the sun for quite a while.

Nina sat up on the lounge and scanned the crowd for the umpteenth time, but there was no sign of Ahmad. It was going on seven o'clock, but the temperature was still in the low nineties. Sweat had beaded in tiny droplets on every inch of her body. She was dying to go for a swim, but she was trying not to be all wet if or when Ahmad showed up. But hell, if he was coming, wouldn't he have been here by now? Nina swung her feet onto the pavement. She nudged Tonya's shoulder. "Watch out for that dreadlock man for me, will you?" Tonya crossed both her fingers and peeked at Nina through sleepy eyes. She grinned at her friend slyly. "You know I got your back, sista,'' she called out as Nina headed for the pool. And just as Nina dove headfirst into the water, Tonya looked toward the gate to catch a glimpse of a thick-chested, lock-wearing brotha coming through it.

Ahmad closed the gate behind him and just stood there trying to take it all in. What a spread. A valet had parked his car. A live band had just finished playing a damned good cover of what sounded like a Mitchell Moore jam. There was food and drink for days, and people everywhere. There must've been sixty or so Black folks of all shapes, sizes, and ages laughing, eating, and basking in the sun. And speaking of basking, Tonya, the very woman he was hoping to hook up with, was just getting up from her lounge chair, and seemed to be heading his way.

Ahmad concentrated a little too hard on not being distracted by the sista's near-nakedness, as he watched her walk gazelle-like across the expansive poolside patio, weaving through the guests and tables. He had already gotten quite an overdose of her bikini-clad body, and was relieved when she was close enough for him to focus his eyes on her face. She held her hand out to shake his.

''Welcome, Ahmad,'' she said with her beautiful smile. ''We're so glad you could make it.'' She looked genuinely happy to see him.

Ahmad wondered instantly if she'd thought about him at all since their meeting on Monday. He held onto her hand firmly as he spoke. ''Not as glad as I am,'' he said, speaking in a low tone to cover his nervousness. ''You look radiant, sista,'' he added sincerely, being careful not to look down at her breasts. He didn't want her to think he was some kind of hound dog. Especially after the little nervous tension she seemed to have at their first meeting. He felt her draw her hand away; he reluctantly let it go.

Except for a nervous little half-smile, she didn't respond to the compliment. ''Nina will be really glad to see you,'' she said without looking directly at him. She held one hand as a shade over her eyes and looked over toward the pool. ''She just went for a swim.''

Ahmad coughed nervously. ''I'm really glad Nina invited

me.'' He was trying to pick up on Tonya's body language. Either she was shy, or she just wasn't interested in him. How in the hell was he supposed to figure it out? It'd been way too long since he had to try to read a woman's cues. His sophomore year at USC was the last time, and Chante had made it pretty obvious for him.

''Nina told me about your little misunderstanding.'' Tonya smiled knowingly.

Ahmad shook his head slowly and shifted the gym bag he was holding from his right to his left shoulder. ''Yeah, I felt pretty stupid,'' he said quietly. ''I hope she wasn't too offended.''

''She's used to it,'' Tonya reassured him. ''Most of us know we come in every shade imaginable, but people here in Glendale aren't too used to seeing Black folks who look like Nina.'' She touched Ahmad lightly on the shoulder and flashed him a teasing smile. ''I'm pretty sure she's forgiven you.'' She added slyly, ''But maybe you ought to go over there and double-check.'' Tonya winked at Ahmad and motioned with a nod of her head toward the pool steps where Nina had just climbed out.

''Well, actually . . . uh.'' Ahmad was trying to think of a clever way to let Tonya know he wasn't interested in her friend, but just as he was about to open his mouth to tell her that she was the one he'd been thinking about all week, Tonya smiled broadly, and waved at someone behind him. He turned to see who, and had to blink his eyes a few times just to make sure he was seeing straight. *That couldn't be . . .*

''Hey, baby, over here.'' Tonya motioned to the bald-headed brotha entering the gate behind them. Ahmad watched the brotha approach, and stepped back in amazement as the realization of who the man was washed slowly over him. There was no mistaking it. That was Rasheed Steel. *The* Rasheed Steel. Almost involuntarily, Ahmad took a step toward him and was about to extend his hand for a handshake when Rasheed let the heavy pack he had slung over his shoulder fall to the ground. He gathered Tonya, oily skin and all, into what could not be mistaken for anything other than a lover's embrace.

Ahmad stood uncomfortably by as the embrace turned into

a lengthy and passionate kiss. He stuffed his hands deep into his pockets and looked down at the ground. With a little concentration he could block out the fact that Rasheed Steel had his hands all over the sista's coconut oil–smelling skin and that she had her luscious lips all over his and that . . . *Ah, damn.* This was more than Ahmad was prepared to handle. He needed to walk away. He scanned the patio nervously, finally spotting Nina across the deck standing very close to and holding hands with a brotha who looked to be at least twenty or thiry years older than her. Nina was waving at Ahmad to come over, and since the girl of his dreams was now absorbed in a feverish liplock, he gratefully returned the wave and headed to the other side of the patio.

Nina moved forward a few steps with her arms extended and grasped Ahmad's hands in hers, pulling him over to where she'd been standing with the older man. "I want you to meet my father." Her eyes sparkled at him playfully. She spoke in a tone that was strangely familiar to Ahmad, and he allowed himself to be pulled by the woman, as if they were old friends. Ahmad didn't remember her being this attractive at their first meeting. But then again, he had been a little agitated at the time. Nina beamed at her father. "Daddy, this is Ahmad Jefferson. Ahmad . . . my father, Mitchell Moore."

Ahmad grasped the man's extended hand, and shook his head slowly in disbelief. "You're Mitchell Moore."

The older man smiled. "I am," was all he said.

Ahmad dropped his gym bag to the pavement and added his left hand to the handshake, clasping the hand over Moore's for added emphasis. "No, I mean, you're Mitchell Moore. *The* Mitchell Moore. There isn't an album you've recorded that I don't love."

Moore put his free hand on Ahmad's shoulder and winked at him. "Well, there might be one, son. We just wrapped the last one yesterday." He poked Ahmad playfully in the chest. "Aren't you a little young to have heard and loved every Mitchell Moore album?"

Ahmad was still trying to recover from the sheer awe of the moment. Not only was Mitchell Moore standing in front of him, Rasheed Steel, one of the few poets Ahmad had read over the years that could truly grip him by the heart, was standing on the other side of the yard. To think, just two weeks earlier a prison guard was handing him his ''personals'' and wishing him a sarcastic good luck, and here he was fraternizing with some serious members of the *Who's Who* of admirable Black men. Only a Higher Power could have plotted something this amazing. Ahmad struggled to gather his thoughts before answering Moore's tease. ''My English professor at USC turned me on to your music. I've been a fan ever since.'' Ahmad felt like a fan, too. He was tempted to ask for an autograph or something, but he let the temptation pass.

Moore laughed aloud. ''That could be none other than Dr. Lenroe Griffin.''

''You know each other?'' Ahmad questioned. *This is crazy.*

Moore laughed again. ''Son, Lenroe Griffin and I go waaaay back. Before you and Miss Nina here were born, Lenroe and I were raising hell. But don't tell him I told you so. He's still trying to convince the ladies he's in his forties.'' Moore laughed again and motioned to the cabana tent a few feet away. ''Be sure to get yourself a plate. The food's going fast.''

Nina linked her arm into Ahmad's and led him over to an empty table in the spacious, air-conditioned tent. ''Make yourself comfortable,'' she said. ''I'll be right back.'' She called over her shoulder to him, ''Is there anything you don't eat?'' She was going to fix him a plate. Ahmad didn't say a word. He wanted to tell her she didn't have to do that, but by the time he'd fixed his mouth to protest, Nina was already at the buffet table, piling on the food.

Ahmad watched Nina move around the table. She smiled here and laughed there as she spoke to the guests who were helping themselves to the huge pans of food. Ahmad could have avoided the little mistaken-identity incident altogether if he'd seen her from behind in the first place. The royal blue bikini Nina was wearing was still wet, and though she'd covered herself with a short dress, the dress was white, and kind of thin, and her curves were all the more accentuated. *Yep,* he thought with a smile, *definitely a sista.*

He watched as Nina got in a play fight over a serving spoon with a huge brown-skinned brotha competing for access to the same dish. Ahmad thought for a moment that the young man might be Nina's boyfriend. That was until she popped him upside his head with what could only be a big-sisterish slap. Actually if you didn't focus on the skin tone, they did kind of favor each other. *Must be Nina's younger brother*, he guessed.

Nina said something to the young man, then motioned toward Ahmad with a nod. They were obviously talking about him. She approached with the young brotha in tow, and set a plate down in front of Ahmad before walking off quickly. She held up one finger as if to say she'd be back in a minute.

Ahmad looked down in awe at the array of soul food delicacies on his plate. Delicacies he had been forced to live without for so long. Chante's mama had fed him some fried chicken and cabbage the night he stayed in her trailer, but how long had it been since he'd seen collard greens and yams and potato salad and barbecued ribs and—

"Didn't I see you over at the Founder's gym yesterday?" The brotha that had walked over with Nina was standing in front of Ahmad balancing his own overflowing plate on one palm. Ahmad lifted his gaze away from his food. The brotha was grinning broadly at him. "I watched you swat a Derrick Davis jumper right out the sky." He laughed and added, "Nobody swats at Derrick's shit, man. They're all convinced he's Michael Jordan or something."

"Last time I checked . . ." Ahmad smirked playfully. ". . . Michael Jordan was living in Chicago." He laughed out loud and added, "Speaking of swatting, Nina got you pretty good over there."

The young man laughed heartily in response. He reached to shake Ahmad's hand firmly, and said, "I'm Nat, Nat Moore." He ended the handshake by sliding his palm across Ahmad's until their fingers clenched briefly at the knuckles. Ahmad found it refreshing to know that despite the seemingly bourgeois surroundings, so far the people he'd met were all the way down to earth. Since his so-called friend Scotty had crossed him, Ahmad had only one person in the past five years he'd considered a friend, and Dud wasn't getting out of prison for at least another five. Maybe, if he let his guard down just a little, he could make a few friends here in Glendale.

Nat put his plate down next to Ahmad's and pulled up a

chair. "It's amazing how some folks just get away with murder, ain't it?"

Ahmad choked on the bite of collard greens he'd just put in his mouth, and swallowed them, unchewed. *Shit. What is this kid talking about?* If he was trying to be funny by letting Ahmad know he'd somehow found out what he'd gone to prison for, the shit was far from funny. Ahmad just stared at him.

"But she *is* my sis. And she halfway raised a brotha, so I guess I can let her get away with a swat upside the head once in a while." He rubbed the side of his head where Nina had popped him. "No harm, no foul, right, brotha?"

"Huh?" Ahmad shook off the paranoia and managed a smile. "Y-yeah, it looked like a sisterly love tap." He recovered his cool. "Looked like quite a bit of love, too," he added joining Nat in a chuckle. *Damn.* That was the second time today he'd been caught off guard by his insecurity about his past. Would he ever be able to just feel comfortable around people again? Or would he constantly be trying to keep his secret? The answer to the question came immediately, as Nina approached the table with Tonya, who now wore a gold and blue East Indian–style sundress over her bikini. They were accompanied by Rasheed Steel who held an arm around the waist of each of the two women as they walked. Nina was fussing at Tonya for keeping Rasheed's visit a secret. "Tonya, how could you? You know how much I love this man." She pursed her lips into a pout. "I thought you were my girl."

"Nina Moore, you know good and well if I'd told you Rasheed was coming, everybody and their uncle would be here . . . and not to find out about the BSU either."

Nina rolled her eyes.

Tonya puckered her lips at Nina and made a loud smooching sound.

"Aw, Loo-cee," Tonya teased, "don't be mad, ho-nee." Her Cuban accent was pretty good. Nina had to laugh.

Rasheed was the first to speak to Ahmad, as Nina set a glass of fruit punch and a glass of water next to Ahmad's plate. "I've been trying my damnedest to recollect where I know a brotha from . . ." Rasheed stood with his arms crossed, staring down at Ahmad with a curious look spread across his face.

Ahmad decided at that moment to spill the beans. *What difference would it make?* It wasn't like these people were going to make or break his future. "We met at Chino. I participated in your poetry workshop there last year."

A huge grin broke Rasheed's puzzled expression, as the recognition of their prison meeting dawned on him. "You sat in the back . . . with that big brotha . . . Doug, Dud . . . something like that. Deep brotha, too. Talk about a natural poet. That brotha had insight for days. Damned if I could get him to write down any of that deep shit he had to say though."

Ahmad chuckled softly, then said seriously, "That was my boy Dudley, man. He couldn't write it down. The brotha can't read or write."

The two men realized suddenly that the others at the table had no idea what they were talking about, and an uncomfortable silence fell while Rasheed waited for Ahmad to clear up the confusion.

Ahmad looked first at Nina who was looking curiously at Tonya. Tonya was looking at Rasheed, so Ahmad directed the explanation to Nat. "I spent five years in Chino prison. Rasheed spent a week with us. If you know Rasheed, then I'm sure you know all about Steel Drum, and the work they do with incarcerated brothas."

Tonya twisted her mouth into a playful smirk and teased Rasheed, "Yeah, the only brotha in the NFL to leave the game in his prime." She elbowed him. "Talking 'bout God spoke to him and told him he had some other work to do."

"Well, I don't know about God speaking to a brotha directly," Ahmad interjected soberly. Referring to Rasheed with a nod he added, "But He definitely spoke *through* that brotha to me. I was about to give up on ever getting out when Rasheed brought his program to us in Chino. It might sound a little corny, but when I heard him talk about his run-in with the law, and how God turned his life around, the brotha made me believe it could happen for me. Anyone who doesn't think prayer works might want to think again because here I . . ." Ahmad looked around at the serious faces. "Here we are."

Nat reached his fist out in front of Ahmad to get dap, and Ahmad pounded the fist with his own, holding his out for a return pound from Nat. "Praise God the system didn't keep a brotha," Nat declared sincerely.

"Yeah, praise God," a woman's voice repeated. Ahmad turned to catch Nina's head still nodding slowly up and down to accompany the words she'd just spoken. She smiled warmly at Ahmad, and looked directly into his eyes. *There was that feeling again.* It wasn't physical. Well, at least it wasn't sexual. It was coming from somewhere behind his rib cage. It made him feel a strange kind of warmth. It made him want to reach out and give her a hug, like she was a good friend, even though they didn't really even know each other. But there was no way he was going to do that. Not after having his plate fixed by her and all. She might take it the wrong way. She'd probably think he was trying to hit on her, and she definitely wasn't his type. He just smiled back at her and didn't say a word.

Nina looked over at Tonya. "We'd better do this thing, T," she said quietly.

Tonya gave Nina a quick nod before she turned to Rasheed and said, "You ready?"

Rasheed voiced a solemn "Always," and Nina and Tonya strolled out of the cabana and walked toward the empty bandstand.

△▽ 13 ▽△

The sun had made steady progress toward the horizon, turning the sky lavender-orange and creating a beautiful backdrop behind the soundstage. Nina stepped to the microphone and thanked the guests for supporting the second annual Founder's Heritage Black Student Union membership drive, then introduced herself as the club's faculty advisor. She thanked her parents for their generous support and hospitality, which resulted in a wave of cheers and applause from the partygoers. When she thanked the members of the Mitchell Moore Quartet for donating their time and talent, another rousing ovation went up in the audience. Ahmad listened intently as Nina ran down a brief history of how and why the Founder's BSU was formed, and what some of their accomplishments had been over the years. She mentioned the addition of a couple of classes with an Afrocentric focus and a forum on the portrayal of Blacks in the media; a weekend conference on strengthening the Black family; a lecture series featuring prominent Black writers. Et cetera. Et cetera. Ahmad's first thought was that the events Nina referred to didn't seem like great accomplishments. When he'd attended USC back in the day, there was always some well-known Black activist, author, politician, or entertainer appearing on or near the campus. Hell, sitting through a class with Dr. Griffin was almost like sitting at the feet of Woodson, DuBois, Douglass, *and* Garvey.

"...and of course," Nina's voice had become especially energetic, "the addition of Dr. Lenroe Griffin to the Founder's faculty was our proudest accomplishment." Yet another ova-

120

tion from the enthusiastic audience. This time even the people who were seated stood up to clap.

Did she say Dr. Griffin is on staff at Founder's? Ahmad scanned the patio. It had been a few years, but he was sure he'd recognize the professor if he saw him again.

"As many of you know, Dr. Griffin was asked to serve on the president's panel to consider reparations for the American descendants of enslaved Africans. He'll be in Washington until next week." More applause from the crowd. Nina put both hands up to quiet the enthusiastic guests. "But," she waited for the applause to die down, like she had something extremely important to add, "he made me promise I'd express his regret for not being able to party with us this year." She laughed as she added, "And that's a direct quote, with an emphasis from the professor on the word 'par-tay.' '" The audience laughed with her. "But on a serious note," she continued, "our organization may not be knocking down any huge walls in the effort to dismantle racism, but this little town of Glendale, Arizona, wouldn't have been exposed to many of the ideas it's been forced to consider and reconsider without our help."

Ahmad contemplated that point and found himself nodding slowly in affirmation. He watched Nina work the crowd. She was a natural. He could only imagine what sitting in on one of her classes must be like. He made a mental note to do just that as Nina gave the BSU more props for their efforts. There was more enthusiastic applause, a few whistles, and some fists pumped in the air.

Nina continued, "And you all know none of that would have been possible without the tireless work of our queen . . . uh . . . I mean president . . ." She looked over at Tonya who couldn't help but laugh, even though she was trying to give Nina a "don't go there" smirk. "Ms. Tonya DeMontaña."

When Tonya got to the mike she was all business. The tone of her voice, and the way she moved swiftly from one important point to the next without pause, made Ahmad wonder if she was always so serious. She moved from talking about the significance of the King holiday to the many people— Black folks, Jews, Whites, people of every race and culture— that had given so much in the fight for civil rights. Referring to the Founder's administration's decision, she said, "That announcement—that the campus would be open on the holiday, but Blacks could stay home—is an insult to the dignity of Reverend King, and to everyone who fought, suffered, and died for those rights his holiday symbolizes.'' The crowd was quiet. She added solemnly, ''Anybody out there interested in being a part of the rebellion?''

A unified affirmative shout went up from the crowd and Ahmad found himself clapping and nodding his head along with them. He wondered what she meant by rebellion. Some kind of civil disobedience no doubt. He was clapping and nodding, but he knew he couldn't be down. Not with his record. He was still on parole . . . would be on parole for at least another four years. If he got arrested, for any reason, he could end up right back where he never again in life wanted to be . . . prison.

Tonya waved Rasheed toward the microphone as she backed away from it. Ahmad had gotten so caught up in his thoughts about ending up back behind bars, he missed the introduction. But judging from the response the crowd had to Rasheed as he stepped toward the mike, they were already well aware of who he was.

Ahmad thought Rasheed was slightly on the short side for an ex-football player, especially for a wide receiver. He couldn't have been more than six-one or six-two. And though he didn't appear to weigh more than 175 or 180, he was all muscle. Rasheed was a sepia-toned man with large eyes and a nose that appeared to have been flattened by the defense one time too many. He had a neatly trimmed, jet black mustache and one of those jaw-lining, narrow beards that looked as if it required daily upkeep. For a split second Ahmad found himself wondering how Rasheed had attracted a beautiful sista like Tonya, because he really wasn't all that handsome. But then again, he was an intelligent man and an incredible poet with extraordinary insight, and of course, with the manicured nails, and the crisp linen shirt, lightweight khakis, and leather loafers, the brotha did give off a certain kind of well-groomed air. And it probably didn't hurt that he was Rasheed Steel. His first year in the NFL he signed a contract for eleven million dollars over four years. Then, as soon as his contract was up, he quit. Right in his prime. All kinds of rumors had been circulated about him having AIDS or being on drugs, but when he held a press conference and announced that he was quitting to do "God's work," the media had a field day. Headlines referred to him as "Black Moses" and he must have been mentioned in Jay Leno's monologue every day for a week. When he finally appeared on *Oprah* to tell his side of the story—that he'd experienced incarceration, and felt a calling to do work in prison outreach—the media dropped him like a firecracker lit too long.

Rasheed stood before the mike for what seemed like a long moment of silence. Pulling a black Raiders baseball cap he'd carried to the soundstage with him onto his head, he finally spoke in his smooth, deep voice. "You know . . . you can never adequately punish a man who commits the crime of oblivion. You see, oblivion to one's greatness is its own punishment." He looked out over the faces scattered about the Moores' backyard before adding, "We sin against ourselves when we refuse to remember what we always knew." There was another long moment of silence sprinkled with a "Mmmm hmmm" here and an emphatic "Okay then" there.

Mitch Moore had quietly appeared on a stool a few feet behind and to the right of Rasheed. He kept his head down solemnly, silently fingering the trumpet he held loosely against his lips. When Moore blew a long, sad note, Rasheed looked out over the crowd.

"This piece was inspired by a conversation I had with a brotha in Chino prison." He looked over at a surprised Ahmad and smiled, then continued. "The brotha never learned to read or write, but he had a kind of knowledge not many of us will attain." Rasheed paused for a moment and straightened his stance. He seemed to take on a hard, almost gangsterish persona. The trumpet played a little more intensely as Rasheed thrust his muscular chest out. He pounded his fist two quick times over his heart and glared at the crowd momentarily before saying in a surly, almost threatening tone, "This one's for the homeys . . . who ain't free yet."

When the spattering of applause died down, he turned the bill of his Raiders cap to the back. The trumpet faded to a quiet moan as Rasheed began his performance.

"If I had my dignity,
I would not yell street obscenities
to assert my dominion in my streets
or paint my name in block letters
to remind you this is my block."

Ahmad marveled at the way Rasheed had instantaneously transformed his college-educated and obviously well-to-do demeanor to that of a streetwise, angry young gangster.

"If I had my dignity,
I would not sell anything
I could not sell without lies
or steal anything I could not buy."

Rasheed paused for a beat to study the young faces.

"If I had my dignity . . ."

He pointed his index finger at the audience and glared at them angrily.

"I would not feel the need
to threaten you physically
or challenge your right to survive."

He slid the baseball cap to the front and pulled it down, until the bill covered his eyes.

"If . . .
. . . I had my dignity."

He pointed haphazardly somewhere out over the eucalyptus trees and beyond the fenced Moore property.

"But they conspired to remove it from me . . .
. . . at three.
I knew even then
there was something . . .
. . . not . . .

... quite ...
white
about the color of my skin.''

The crowd was silent. Ahmad had never seen so many young people so quietly intent.

"And G.I. Joe and Ken?
They knew too.
And they screamed it loud and clear
so all the little brothers
in my neighborhood could hear ...''

Rasheed placed a hand to his mouth, megaphone-like.

''Hey boy!
If you try hard
you could be somebody
you could pump gas
fix cars
or bag groceries ...''

Rasheed removed the hat from his head and gripped it with both hands in front of his chest. He continued in a sarcastic, stepin-fetchit tone.

"Why, if you try real *hard,*
you could even be presi—
well, shucks, you could be some*body.''*

He threw the cap to the ground angrily and shouted with venom,

"And then you convinced me to measure my value
by my material things.''

Rasheed reached into his pockets, pulling them out to reveal the empty linings.

"And when I came up short ...''

He replaced the pocket linings, and stuffed his hands deep into them. Suddenly, he dropped the angry demeanor and leaned back dramatically. When he continued, his gangster persona took on a slick, cagey edge.

". . . sheeyit, my entrepreneurial spirit kicked in."

He grinned slyly at the audience, and was quiet for a moment. The trumpet wailed painfully; its voice rose soulfully over the crowd, then floated softly down to a mere hum. Still in character, Rasheed continued.

"My first BMW was black.
Jet.
As black as I could get.
To affirm that I had bought into
the huge, social lie
that you are
what you have."

He lifted a hand to his chin, and stroked his beard thoughtfully.

"And when I step back and ponder . . ."

He looked out at the crowd with raised eyebrows and teased,

"Yeah, I said ponder . . ."

The audience had bought into Rasheed being a thug, and as though "ponder" was a word he had no business using, they responded with laughter. He quickly scolded them with cocky sarcasm,

"It means 'think long' . . ."

Then he repeated the line with piercing seriousness,

"When I step back and ponder,
I find similarities in our occupations."

He raised an imaginary gun and straight-armed it at the audience.

"Me behind my 357 magnum . . ."

Lowering the gun he scowled in disgust.

". . . them behind they nine-to-five.
And I wonder if they yell street obscenities
to assert they dominion on Wall Street."

A voice in the crowd shouted, "Teach!"

"And I wonder if in Central America
they have sold anything
they could not sell without lies.
Or if in mother Africa
they have stolen
anything they could not buy."

The crowd was getting excited now. Somebody said, "You *know* that's right." Another voice said, "Tell it."

"And if they was to face me here
eye to eye,
I wonder if they'd feel the need
to threaten me physically
or challenge my right to survive."

Rasheed bent over to pick up the cap he had thrown to the ground.

"And now I realize . . ."

He took a dramatic pause. The crowd was silent with expectation. The trumpet echoed that expectation in a shrill climax, before Moore abruptly removed the horn from his mouth altogether, as if to emphasize Rasheed's next words.

"If they had they dignity . . ."

Rasheed put the cap back on and pulled it snugly onto his head.

". . . they would not have taken mine."

The trumpet resumed with a sad, soulful run, while Rasheed stepped away from the microphone waving a humble acceptance of the cheers and whistles from the crowd.

Nina watched Tonya step to the mike to rouse another round of applause for Rasheed from the audience. Then Tonya ordered the guests to have a good time for the rest of the evening and joined Rasheed and the others back at Ahmad's table. She and Nina both affirmed Rasheed's brilliant delivery of the poem, but it was obvious to Nina from the look on T's face, something had rubbed her the wrong way.

Rasheed noticed it immediately. "What?" he asked bluntly. He knew Tonya. She wasn't one to mince words.

"Baby, you know how I feel about all that 'the White man took my dignity' shit. Can't nobody take your dignity. That's something you give away. The brotha in that poem didn't *have* to live behind a 357 magnum . . . he *chose* to. And he's no better than those corporations who rape third world nations for their own material gain." Tonya wasn't trying to be disrespectful to her man's art, but her voice carried an undertone of disgust.

Rasheed's comeback was calm and controlled. Steel Drum had traveled to a great number of prisons, juvenile detention centers, and camps over the three years of its existence. He had plenty of practice in inciting, and discussing, the emotions poetry like his could arouse.

"Baby, the piece isn't about choices made by dignified men. It's about the choices men make when they never realized they had dignity in the first place."

Ahmad quietly added, "It's like . . . a brotha has to climb his way up from oppression and figure out how to be a man, without becoming inhuman along the way."

Rasheed held his fist out for a pound from Ahmad. "That's right, my brotha."

Nina added, "G.I. Joe and Ken represent the voices of an

exclusionary, racist society . . .'' Ahmad nodded affirmation of Nina's analysis. ''. . . and if they're not drowned out by supportive voices closer to home . . .''

Rasheed kissed Nina on the cheek. ''You feel me, Nina.''

Tonya didn't say a word. She wasn't upset, but she wasn't going to apologize for her opinion either. Tonya believed in bootstraps, plain and simple. According to T, Black folks just needed to pull themselves up and get on with it and pay as little attention to the Man and his doings as possible. Nina agreed with some of that, but she also knew that for too many young Blacks, the barriers to quality education were numerous and complex. And without education, how were you supposed to even know you have bootstraps?

Tonya remained strangely quiet, listening to Ahmad and Rasheed discussing the images in the poem. *Good*, Nina thought; she was relieved that Tonya and her man weren't going to end up in a long, heated debate. If she had her way, Nina was going to end up on the dance floor with Ahmad in a long, heated slow dance. Maybe she could request a lengthy tune, like ''Reasons'' by Earth Wind & Fire. *Hmmm. ''Always and Forever'' by Heatwave might be a good one too . . .* Nina thought, slipping momentarily into a little fantasy of being out on the floor with Ahmad. *Mmmph.* Her head resting on his chest, and his hands pressed softly against the small of her back . . . She was jarred from the little daydream when she suddenly noticed one of the caterers coming from the kitchen with a tray of sweet potato pies, and it occurred to her that she hadn't seen Mama all day.

Nina nodded at Tonya to follow her to the house. Mama had been in the kitchen since before Nina got out of bed, and though Nina really wanted to stay around to hear Rasheed and Ahmad's conversation, the DJ was just getting the turntable warmed up and Nina thought she'd better drag Mama on out for a little fun. When she and Tonya got to the kitchen they found a row of warm pecan pies lined up on the counter, but Mama was nowhere in sight.

The two women walked down the hallway past Nina's bedroom door and stopped outside the Moores' master suite. The door was open a crack, and the rise and fall of arguing voices could be heard on the other side.

Tonya started to turn and walk away, but Nina grabbed her arm and held a rigid forefinger to her own pursed lips. Her parents' heated discussion was intensifying, and Nina heard her name mentioned in the last sentence spoken.

Mama was talking now. "Mitch, you cannot keep this from Nina forever. It's not right."

Daddy was angry. "Don't you tell me about right and wrong. I did the right thing back then. And I'm doing the right thing now. I don't want that child to hurt any more than she already has."

"She is not a child anymore, Mitchell, but she is hurting. For God's sake, she's having nightmares. She's a grown woman and she's terrified to sleep alone. How could you let her go through this? You've got to tell her the truth."

"Enough." Nina heard a tone she recognized. She'd heard her father use it before. He was finished with the conversation, and it was quite obvious to anyone listening. Mama heard it, too.

"I'll never mention it again, Mitchell." There was silence in the room before Mama added, "But you can bet your daughter will."

Nina and Tonya stood staring at each other with their mouths wide open. They tiptoed back toward the kitchen and stopped at its stone entry. *There it was again,* Nina thought. She had heard that tone in her father's voice many times over the years when she tried to get him to talk about her mother. What kind of monster was the woman? *That's it.* Nina was determined now. She'd get Daddy out on the dance floor; bring him a few glasses of wine. Maybe she could even get him to drink a little rum. Then he'd talk.

"Come with me, T," Nina begged in frustration. Tonya followed Nina reluctantly, heading toward the bedroom again, only this time Nina spoke loudly to Tonya about the success of the party, hoping her parents would hear them approaching. Nina rapped loudly on the door with her knuckle before pushing it open.

"Hey, party animals." She tried to sound lighthearted. "It won't really be jumpin' out there until you two hit the dance floor."

Nina's father managed a smile. "Don't worry, Nina, your

mother and I will do you proud.'' Mama nodded in agreement with a forced smile on her face before she turned and walked into the adjoining bathroom. Daddy followed her.

''We'll be joining you outside in a minute, Nina,'' he said, with an obvious attempt to sound jovial. The two women had no choice but to retreat.

When Tonya and Nina returned to the patio, Rasheed, Nat, and Ahmad were emerging from the pool house dressed in their swimming trunks, and were headed toward the pool. Nina had to take a deep breath to keep from hyperventilating. *Ouch.* Ahmad had obviously been pumping weights in prison, because his massive chest was a mound of sculpted muscles, and his biceps at rest looked as if he were carrying a hundred pounds. His shoulders were broad and square, and *mmmph, mmmph, mmmph,* his abdominal muscles rippled into a tight six-pack above the waistband of his gray and maroon swim trunks. The trunks were kind of long, so she couldn't get a good look at his thighs, but she recognized the sexy bowleg-ged stance from that first day on the quad, only now she could see how long and muscular his legs really were. *Was he flexing for them? Or did his body look like this when he was relaxed?* Nina knew she shouldn't be staring so hard, but *damn.* Tonya nudged her a little on her way over to grab Rasheed's hand, letting Nina know that she, too, had noticed the man's wares.

Tonya pulled Rasheed toward the jacuzzi and urged Nina, Ahmad, and Nat to follow. When they neared the edge of the bubbling sauna, she lifted her sundress over her head and draped it over the back of a nearby lounge chair. She winked at Nina slyly, encouraging her without words to follow suit. Nina quickly did just that, pulling the gauze shift over her head and tossing it atop Tonya's dress.

Nina sat down gingerly in the Jacuzzi next to T, and allowed her toes to float to the water's surface. She pretended to study her French-tipped toenails so she could avoid looking too hard at Ahmad, who had to have noticed her staring. Nat sat down right next to his sister, leaving Ahmad to sit directly across from Nina. As Rasheed and Tonya made goo-goo eyes and whispered to each other, Nat, Nina, and Ahmad small-talked a bit. But the night was warm, and the water was getting too hot, so when Ahmad suggested they dip in the pool, Nina stood up immediately. Nobody else did. Ahmad hesitated for a moment, and looked around as if to say, "Is anybody else going to join us?" When no one else stood up, Ahmad stepped out of the water. Nina followed him out of the Jacuzzi, and as they walked toward the pool, she tried not to be too awestruck by the firm roundness of his butt.

They sat side by side on the second step, the cool water up to Nina's neck and only barely reaching Ahmad's nipples. Ahmad started the conversation.

"I've been wanting to thank you all evening for inviting me. This is the best experience I've had in years." He hesitated then added, "Well . . . except for the reunion with my daughter, of course."

Nina didn't want to pry, but she was curious. "How long were you away from Ebony?" That ought to be a safe question.

"I went to prison when Ebony was three months old. I've only been out for a couple of weeks. I was in for a little over five years."

They sat in silence for a while. Nina wanted to tell him it didn't matter to her that he'd been in prison. People made mistakes. He was obviously a good man, or he wouldn't be taking on the responsibility of a child. And how many men would take on that responsibility all alone? She wondered about the child's mother. Ebony had told Nina her mother was dead. *Oh my God*, Nina thought suddenly, *I hope he didn't do something to hurt the child's mama.*

Ahmad sensed her discomfort. "You can ask," he said quietly.

She looked in his eyes. She really wanted to ask. But no. It really wasn't her business, and if he wanted to share it with her . . .

"I killed a man." He said it with almost no emotion, like he was announcing there was nothing good to watch on television.

Nina tried not to react, but that was impossible. He killed a man? She stared into Ahmad's large, soulful eyes, looking for something that might explain how a seemingly nice guy,

a concerned father, and a murderer could dwell together behind them. All she saw was calm resolve.

"Maybe when I get to know you a little better," Ahmad's
heart-shaped lips parted in a soft smile, "I'll tell you the whole
story. But you can believe this: I'm not a cold-blooded killer."
He traced a tiny wave into the water with his hand and
watched it ripple out. Without looking up he whispered, "I
deprived a mother of her son, and some innocent children of
their father. But I didn't see any other option at the time. It
was a split second decision I'll live with forever."

Nina was speechless. All this time she'd been trippin' over
this man, and he was a murderer. Convicted. *Damn. Maybe
the best thing to do from here on out was to just be the man's
friend. Whoa, he might have some kind of serious anger problem.* After Derrick, she certainly didn't need any more drama.
Not that Ahmad didn't deserve an opportunity to tell his side.
To explain what happened. He had been released after only
five years. They must have decided he was no threat to society.
But still, friendship was a good place to start, now that she
really put some thought into it. She didn't have any business
trying to rush into something new anyway. She and Derrick
had only split less than a week ago. *Damn. He killed a man.*

Ahmad interrupted her thoughts. "You're awfully quiet."

"I—I've got some things on my mind." She quickly added,
"I'm dealing with some family drama." It was partly true.

"Drama? You seem to have the perfect family." Ahmad
pointed toward the patio, where a crowd had gathered to
dance. "Is that your mother dancing with your dad?"

Nina laughed softly. She couldn't help herself. Mama was
attempting a not-too-bad version of the butterfly, and Daddy
was, of course, slaughtering the cabbage patch. The two were
laughing and grinning suggestively at one another. Nina was
relieved that they'd decided to make up. "That's them. Well,
actually she's my adopted-mother. My biological mother is
dead."

"I'm sorry to hear that." Ahmad nodded his head slowly.
"Mine too. And my pops. I grew up in foster homes."

Now why'd he have to tell her that? All it made Nina want
to do was give him a big hug and take care of what had to be
a broken heart. *First he loses his parents, then his wife?* Nina

wondered how he could handle all that loss, and deal with parenthood, too. She finally asked, "What is it like to be a single dad after being away for so long?" When Ahmad spoke of his daughter, his whole demeanor changed. Nina could see that the little girl really was the center of his world now.

"I get such a kick out of her. She has so much enthusiasm over the simplest of events." Ahmad told her about the excitement Ebony had about going to "Micky D's." Suddenly a solemn look stole his smile. He told Nina about the incident with the officer that had led to his reaction to Nina at their first meeting. "All a brotha wanted to do was register for school and show up for a hard day's work, and a man in uniform whose paycheck includes my tax dollars wants to try to take my dignity." The rage simmered somewhere in the back of his throat, and it sprinkled his words with a tinge of irritation. He looked into Nina's eyes. His tone softened when he said, "I really am sorry for taking it out on you."

Nina was relieved to finally know why his rejection of her was so immediate . . . and so intense. And she was glad to finally be able to accept his apology and mean it. Sharing that story with her seemed to have a cathartic effect on their fledgling friendship, and the stiff nervousness they both had been safely hiding behind melted away. For who knows how many minutes, the guest-filled patio became nonexistent, and Nina and Ahmad focused on the space they occupied together in the cool water.

The conversation between them flowed back and forth now with ease as they switched comfortably from general commentary to personal, even private experiences. Nina told him about her recent breakup with Derrick, and he said how sorry he was that she had to deal with that. That's when he told Nina about the recent and tragic death of his wife. He even confided to Nina that Ebony had witnessed some pretty intense scenes with her mom, who fought a drug addiction for most of the child's young life.

"I worry about Ebony because she seems . . . well . . . too perfect." Nina opened her eyes wide and waited for him to explain. "She never disobeys or talks back. In two weeks, I haven't seen anything even resembling a temper tantrum. And given the events of recent weeks, something about that just doesn't seem right.''

Nina thought about what he said. God, that had to be frightening. To have no experience raising a child, and then to be the sole provider of psychological and emotional support for a child who was dealing with severe trauma. ''Do you mind if I talk to Tonya about that?''

''Tonya?''

''T's degree is in child development. She'd have some great insight into Ebony's behavior. But . . . I won't if—''

Ahmad cut her off. ''No. Please do. If it will help me help her through this. It's got to be devastating for a little girl to lose her mother. But Ebony seems so unaffected. I think she has built up some kind of defense mechanism to survive it.''

Nina became strangely silent. Ahmad could see that his comment had sent her somewhere else. Somewhere far away. ''Are you okay?''

Nina stared at the tops of the eucalyptus trees swaying against the star-studded blackness of the desert sky. ''I wonder what my mechanism was,'' she said aloud. It always bothered her. It seemed downright strange that she had absolutely no memory of her mother, and she was nearly three years old when the woman died. She had a vague memory of being in a big building with an elderly woman who gave her lollipops. But no memory of the woman who gave her life.

She confided to Ahmad the lifelong mystery she'd lived with regarding her mother. Ahmad looked confused. ''Your father won't talk to you about her?'' Nina shook her head. ''Have you considered a private investigator?''

Nina let the thought sink in for a moment. In her mind, all the information she needed was right there in her father's thick skull. She just needed a way to get him to talk about it. ''Well, my father knows the answers to the questions I have. Before I hire a private detective, I'd like to give him the chance to share them with me.''

Nina and Ahmad both looked toward the dance floor at Nina's mention of her father. Mama and Daddy had stopped dancing, and Daddy was bent over at the waist like he was looking for something on the ground. *What on earth was he doing now? Did Mama lose an earring?* In the next breath,

Nina watched in horror as her father sank to his knees and collapsed in a heap on the pavement.

Mama yelled instantly for Nathan. And before Nina could even stand up, Nat was already at Mama's side. As Nina rushed from the pool, she heard her mother telling her brother, "Nathan, call 911. Baby, *hurry.*" Mama wasn't one to panic, but she was obviously trying desperately to remain calm. As Nina ran toward them, she could see that her mother was really scared. The poor woman was standing as rigid as a statue near her fallen husband, calling instructions to Nathan across the patio.

When Nina pushed through the crowd that had gathered around, she found her father curled into a loose fetal position. She knelt, still dripping with pool water, and pressed her ear to his chest. His heart was beating and he was breathing. *Thank God.* But when Nina lifted one of his eyelids, she saw that his eyeball was fixed straight ahead. He was unconscious. Nina put her head back on his chest. *God, don't let it be a coma,* she prayed silently. He'd gone into shock once before, back when Nina was still living at the house. She thought for sure her father had died that day, and it was just more than she could handle. By the time the paramedics had arrived, Nina nearly had to be hospitalized right along with her father. This time, she was going to try to be strong for Mama. She looked up at her mother and nodded with assurance. "He's breathing steady, Mama."

Nathan emerged from the house with the cordless phone pressed to his ear. "Be sure to tell them he's a diabetic," Mama shouted to him. The panic was creeping its way into her throat. "Tell them he has only one kidney." She knelt on the pavement next to her daughter, taking her husband's hand into her own and holding it tensely against her cheek. Then quietly, as if she were saying it to herself, Mama whispered, "Tell them to hurry."

△▽ 14 ▽△

The palest of rays from the just-rising sun crept between the slats of the mini-blinds and painted faint strips of light across the walls of the ICU. Nina wasn't sure how long she'd been standing at the window, but the barely opened vinyl blinds had only pitch darkness behind them minutes earlier. That was when she'd decided she could no longer sit and watch Daddy sleep. She'd chosen instead to stand at the window with her back to the tubes and wires protruding from her still unconscious father, and to pray to God he would pull through. He had cheated death before. He wasn't supposed to have survived the kidney removal six years earlier, and the doctors had threatened removal of the second one on more than one occasion over the years. But Daddy had always managed to come back with a healthy vengeance. Mitchell Moore was a fighter, and Nina could remember nothing and no one that had ever been able to intimidate or diminish him. She stole a glance over her shoulder at her father's face, which looked haggard and worn in the dawn's soft glow.

Poor Daddy. He had spent so much time in and out of hospitals in the last few years. Up to now he'd been able to convince himself and everyone else that the diabetes would never keep him down for long. This time, Nina feared the worst.

She pulled down on one of the vinyl slats to get a better view of the morning sky. Her father's often spoken words to her rang in her ears. ''The fear of a thing is usually more powerful than the thing itself.'' She had to smile. It was

137

Daddy's mantra. He'd said those words to her at least a hundred times over the years. The first memory she had of hearing them was one foggy December morning back in L.A. when she'd asked nonchalantly for another ride to school. A school that was three and a half blocks away. He'd spoken the words calmly across his steaming coffee cup after Nina finally admitted why she didn't want to walk to school. A group of seventh grade girls had decided she "thought she was cute," and deserved to be tormented for looking too different from them. He did drive her to school that morning. But that afternoon, he spent an hour and a half teaching her how to use her fists.

"When you've tried this," he had said to a gangly, thirteen-year-old Nina, pointing his index finger at her heart, "and this," with another index-finger point, this time pressed gently into her furrowed brow, "sometimes you have no choice but to use these." He hid his face behind his balled-up fists for a moment before peering out from behind them with a mischievous smile and adding, "Just don't tell your mother I said so." Mama would've had a fit if she knew he was out there giving her child boxing lessons, but that's exactly what he did. The ironic thing was, Nina never ended up having to use them. The first time she stood her ground and challenged one of her tormenters to an after-school battle, they decided Nina was "cool," and left her alone.

A gurgling sound coming from her father's direction snapped Nina out of her thoughts, and she was at his bedside instantly.

"Evelyn. I said stay in the house." The words came out in a hoarse whisper. Daddy's eyes were tightly shut, and his head jerked roughly from side to side.

Nina grasped her father's limp hand and squeezed it gently. "Mama's resting, Daddy, it's me, Nina." Nat had escorted Mama, not without a battle, to a sofa in the visitors' lounge, where she promised she would try to sleep a little. Nina had agreed in return to keep a bedside vigil in case her father came to.

"I don't want you here. I told you don't come 'round here," he growled, and snatched his hand from hers. He still hadn't opened his eyes.

He must be hallucinating. She wasn't sure what she should do. She wanted to go get Mama and Nat, but she didn't want her father to wake up alone.

He grunted angrily. "Mickey? I don't know any Mickey. Get off my property."

"Daddy, it's me, Nina. You're in the hospital. Nathan took Mama to get some rest, but I'll go get her if you want." *Maybe if I keep talking he'll come around,* she thought. *Wasn't that how it happened in the movies? The loved one keeps a vigil at the sick one's bedside, and just keeps on talking until the sick one opens his eyes and everybody cries tears of joy and . . .*

Suddenly her father's eyelids flung open and his lightless green eyes focused unblinkingly on Nina's. "If you think you're coming in here to get my daughter, you've got another think coming. You'll have to kill me first." The cold intensity of her father's voice sent a shiver through Nina. She instinctively reached for the nurse's call button, but prior to actually pressing it, she withdrew her hand. Perhaps she should see if his ramblings were just that—ramblings—or if they might actually mean something. Could he be reliving a memory, or was it just some kind of feverish hallucination? Who was Mickey, and what did he or she want? And why was Daddy so angry?

"You love her?" A crazy gurgling laugh escaped her father's throat, and he repeated the words again, only they were nearly unintelligible when combined with the eerie laugh. Suddenly the laughter stopped; the head movements and body jerks disappeared, and he lay still and stone-faced. As Nina reached for the call button above the bed, she thought she heard her father say in the faintest of voices, "How could you leave me?"

The ride back to the house was silent. Mama just kept dabbing at the corners of her teary eyes with a twisted Kleenex, while Nina stared out the window, barely aware of the scenery that flashed by.

Nathan nervously flicked the radio on. Nina welcomed the noise. It gave her something to focus on besides the words that had been echoing noisily in her head; the ones her father had muttered softly before slipping back into unconsciousness. "How could you leave me?"

Who left who? Why would he say, "You love her?" and laugh the way he did? The questions careened around inside Nina's head until she shook them out in frustration. She focused intently on the radio announcer's voice. "It's ten-thirty A.M. on another fine Arizona Sunday. There's a traffic jam on I-30. Pepsi six-packs on sale at Circle K . . ." Blah, blah, blah.

Nina finally snapped out of her trance when Nathan pulled Daddy's car into the driveway and turned off the engine. He hurried to the other side of the car to open Mama's door, but she just sat there for a moment, looking at the house sadly.

"You two go on in. I just want to sit out here by myself for a few minutes." Mama wasn't taking the news well. Daddy was going to be okay. For now. As a matter of fact, he'd be coming home tomorrow. But according to the doctor, Daddy's remaining kidney was barely functioning, and it had atrophied badly since his last checkup. The doctors were going to start him on dialysis immediately. Nina wasn't sure what that meant, but she knew it involved being tied to a machine nearly all day a couple times a week, and for a man as active and energetic as Mitchell Moore, that would be devastating.

On her way up the front walk, Nina glanced back over her shoulder at Mama sitting in the passenger seat of the late model BMW sedan. She hesitated for a moment, thinking maybe Mama shouldn't be alone at a time like this, but Mama waved her on toward the house. "I'll be in in a minute," she assured them.

Nathan reached over to retrieve the Sunday paper that had been carelessly tossed behind one of the huge potted palms that stood like sentries on either side of the paneled double door. Nina waited for Nathan to open the door, and followed him into the house. He headed in silence down the corridor to his room, and Nina went straight to her parents' room and fell face-down across the bed.

"If you think you're coming in here to get my daughter . . ." Daddy's words again. Nina couldn't keep them out. *"I don't know any Mickey."* It sounded sarcastic when Daddy said it. It sounded like the way she might say, "Derrick *who?*" if anyone asked about her ex-fiancé.

Who was Mickey?

When Mama came in and set her purse down on the otto-man at the foot of the bed, Nina rolled onto her side to face her mother and propped herself up on one elbow.

"He's gonna be okay, Mama." Nina needed to hear herself say it.

Mama just nodded.

"Mama?"

Mama's eyebrows said "Yes?"

"When you were sleeping, Daddy was awake for a minute."

"We were all relieved to know he wasn't in a coma. I'm glad you were there."

"But I didn't tell you he was talking to you."

Mama smiled. "What'd he say?"

"He said, 'Evelyn. I told you to stay in the house.' "

Her mother chuckled softly. "Unconscious, and still trying to tell me what to do." She winked at Nina and added, "As if I might listen."

Nina smiled nervously. She was on shaky ground now. She didn't know how much Mama knew. And she didn't know how much of what Mama already knew was painful or sensitive territory. It was possible that Daddy had simply been talking gibberish. But she had to ask. "Mama?" Nina hesitated. Mama sat down on the bed and removed her shoes as she quietly waited for Nina to spit it out. "Who's Mickey?" Mama's eyes became two round saucers and she tried, unsuccessfully, to hide the absolute shock that had registered on her face.

"Mickey? I don't ... I'm not ... Hmmm ..." She stumbled over the words. She finally said, "Why are you asking me that, Nina?"

"Daddy mentioned the name this morning. His eyes were wide open and he was looking right at me, but I guess he thought I was someone else. He said, 'If you think you're coming in here to get my daughter, you'll have to kill me first.' "

Mama was speechless. She looked for a long, silent moment at her husband's framed photo on the bureau, and then back at Nina, but she said nothing. Nina waited patiently for something, anything. Mama closed her eyes. She often did that when she was about to make a decision she really wasn't sure about. She called it her "time with the ancestors." When Evelyn Moore needed to be able to trust a decision, she needed quiet, and time to listen. Nina didn't say a word. A few minutes passed, and Mama finally spoke.

"In the garage. In a box. The one with the old tax returns. There's a small yellow envelope. The words 'Interstate National Bank' are stamped on it in green ink. I can't tell you any more, Nina. I'm sorry. I shouldn't have told you that. I broke a solemn oath to tell you that. But it's right there in the garage. It's something you might come across on your own if you were snooping."

Nina sat up. "I never heard a word you said, Mama," she whispered. "But I do have some snooping to do." She rose immediately from the bed, leaned to kiss her mother's cheek, and headed for the garage. Daddy had kept this secret long enough. Nina had to know.

△▽ 15 ▽△

*Ebony seemed strangely quiet, and Ahmad a lit-*tle troubled and aloof, when he handed his daughter over to Nina at the center early Monday morning. He was genuinely interested in the condition of Nina's father, listening intently as she explained what the doctors said about his collapse, and the prognosis regarding his kidney.

"I'm really sorry to hear about the dialysis," Ahmad said solemnly. "I've heard that's pretty rough." He thanked her again for inviting him to the barbecue, and let her know, again, how much he appreciated being able to leave Ebony with her while he worked. After an awkward moment of silence, he bent to kiss his daughter on the cheek, and sighed in exasperation when the child didn't respond. He checked his watch nervously, looked like he wanted to say something, but didn't, and quickly backed out the door.

Nina wondered what could be bothering the man. Hadn't they had a cozy little conversation that night in the pool? They'd shared some pretty personal things, as if they were old friends. Now, all of a sudden he was back to acting like they were total strangers. And Ebony. *What on earth was going on with her?* The child had followed Nina around most of the morning, refusing to talk, and resisting all Nina's attempts to engage her in any meaningful activities. She'd barely touched the lunch Nina had prepared for her, and finally after watching an hour or so of cartoons, she'd fallen asleep on the sofa in Nina's soon-to-be new office. Nina had put in a call to Tonya to ask her what she should do about the child's strange

143

behavior, but Tonya hadn't yet responded to the page.

Nina sat at the outgoing director's desk, watching Ebony's peaceful slumber, and pondering the weekend's events. She picked up the tiny yellow envelope lying in front of her on the desk blotter, and shook its contents out into her palm. Fingering the key's smooth metal surface, turning it over and over in her hand, she contemplated what mysteries it might unlock. Mama's directions had led her right to it, though Nina had purposely rustled through boxes of photographs and offical-looking documents to give the impression that she had indeed been out in the garage "snooping"—just in case Daddy figured out that his fiercely guarded mystery was unraveling.

Nina picked up the tiny yellow envelope and read the faded green print again. *Interstate National Bank, Mid-Wilshire Branch.* Mid-Wilshire was located in the north-central part of Los Angeles, not too far from the UCLA campus. It had to be a key to a safe deposit box; she was sure of it. Mama must have thought something in that box would lead her to what might solve the mystery. The knowledge that the contents were just sitting there waiting for Nina was killing her, and she was already going over a plan in her head. She had to travel to Los Angeles to visit this bank, and she needed to go as soon as possible.

She wouldn't be able to leave right away. Not with Daddy just coming home. But maybe over the weekend. She could go on Saturday or Sunday, and return Monday afternoon after she'd visited the bank. It shouldn't be too hard to get out of town for a couple of days without rousing too much curiosity. Nina had already decided, first thing that morning, it would be a good idea to leave her parents' house, and go back to sleeping at her apartment. She'd canceled her appointment with Dr. Webb, so she could go later that afternoon with Mama to check Daddy out of the hospital. But Nina figured that if she spent too much time around the house this week, he'd know immediately she was preoccupied. She couldn't afford to have her father figure out the mission she was on. The stress alone might further complicate his condition, and neither Nina nor Mama could live with themselves if that happened.

According to the doctors, Nina's father had gone into insulin shock at the party, and though his collapse frightened everyone, it really wasn't lifethreatening. The shock was actually a blessing in disguise, because it brought him to the hospital in time for the doctors to discover the real threat to his life—the condition of his remaining kidney. The sallowness in his skin and the dark circles under his eyes were more than just symptoms of one too many red-eye flights from L.A. His kidney was failing, and his body was filled with toxins. Dialysis was no longer avoidable for Mitchell Moore, and soon—as soon as his body was strong enough to endure another operation—the diseased kidney would have to be removed.

The shrill ring of the telephone startled Nina, and she jumped to grab it before it could ring again. "You've reached the center," she said in a low voice, trying not to awaken Ebony. "This is Nina Moore speaking."

It was Tonya. "I got your 811 page. I know it's not an emergency, 'cause you would have 911'd me. What's up, girl? And why are you whispering?"

"I have Ahmad's daughter today." She looked over at Ebony. Her eyes were still closed. "She's sleeping now, but Tonya, something is very wrong with her, and I just can't figure it out."

"Very wrong?"

"T, she won't talk to me. When I ask her if something's wrong, she shrugs her shoulders. I've tried everything to get her to communicate, but it's like she's somewhere else. It almost seems like she's scared, or maybe angry." Nina hesitated. "But then she's been at my side every minute. If I leave the room, she follows quietly behind me. I'm really worried, T. Maybe something bad happened to her this weekend."

"Did her father mention anything?"

"That's the other strange thing. After we seemed to hit it off so well on Saturday, it was like he barely knew me today."

"Hmmm," was all Tonya said.

"Do you have any suggestions, T?"

"I don't know what to tell you about Ahmad," Tonya began, "but I have an idea about the little one." Nina waited in silence. "See if you can get her close to you, physically. If she'll sit on your lap, that would be great, if not, sit beside her on the couch, or on the floor.''

"Okay," Nina whispered, "and then what?"

"Tell her a story."

"A story?"

"Not a bedtime story. Tell her a real-life story about a time when you felt angry and afraid. Make the emotions you felt as real for her as possible. She'll empathize with you. Chances are, that will draw her out to talk about whatever it is that's bothering her."

"That's it?" Nina was surprised. It sounded too simple.

"Try it, and let me know how it went."

"Thanks, T." She put the phone gently back on its cradle. Ebony was sitting up on the couch looking right at her.

Nina checked her watch. *Three forty-five.* She still had a few minutes before Ahmad would be there to pick Ebony up. She stood up and walked around the desk. "Wanna come with me somewhere?" Ebony didn't say a word, but she stood up and let Nina grasp her by the hand. Nina knew the perfect spot. She led Ebony to a cozy little cloakroom where the walls were painted to look like a park, with trees and multicolored flowers. Up high on one wall and across the ceiling flew blue birds and a happy yellow kite. Nina walked Ebony over to a big, soft beanbag chair at the far end of the tiny room. The chair faced a low window overlooking the playground. Nina sat down on it and pulled the child gently onto her lap. Ebony didn't resist, but she sat rigidly, keeping her arms and hands in her own lap and not allowing herself to lean into Nina's embrace.

They both looked out at the lonely swings and empty slides, and just sat together in the awkward silence. Finally, Nina began talking. "One time, when I was a little girl, Mama and Daddy took me to a big carnival in the middle of a huge park." Ebony didn't move. She stared out the window, and gave no impression that she even heard Nina talking. "It was my birthday. I remember I was wearing a bright yellow sundress. Mama had brought it to my room that morning in a box wrapped with shiny pink paper. We had so much fun that day. I got on the Ferris wheel with Daddy and we all took pictures in the picture booth. Daddy got a rainbow painted on his face just for me, and that made me and Mama laugh.''

Nina's comment about the face paint made Ebony look up at her momentarily, but when she caught Nina's eye, she quickly turned away. Nina continued. ''They took me to a little yard where you could pet animals, and I petted the pony and the baby cow, and I held a baby duck in my hands.'' Ebony was getting interested now. She still wouldn't look directly at Nina, but Nina could tell by the way the child's body had begun to relax, and from the slight tilt of her head upward, that she was listening.

''My daddy sat down on a little bench next to Mama, and when I brought the baby duck over for them to see, Daddy said . . .'' Nina made her voice deep, impersonating her father for Ebony's benefit. '' 'Nina, your mother and I have a big surprise for you.' It was my birthday, so I thought they were going to give me a really special present, but just then Daddy put his hand on Mama's stomach and said, 'Your mama and I are going to have a new baby. Just like that mama duck had that little baby.' '' Nina's voice suddenly reflected a distance. ''I was so sad.''

She was quiet for a long moment, and Ebony shifted her weight so that her shoulder leaned comfortably against Nina. Nina continued. ''I was so sad, and I was so scared. I didn't know. I didn't know what they meant. I thought they were telling me it was time for me to go away. I thought they were going to send me away to live somewhere else.''

Finally, Ebony was looking directly into Nina's eyes, and she was listening.

''I thought, since my real mother went to heaven, and Mama wasn't really my mama, she could get a new baby now and forget all about me. I dropped the baby duck on the ground, and ran through the gate. I ran through the crowd of people until I was far away. Daddy tried to run after me, but I got away too fast. When I finally stopped running, I was far away from the carnival on the other side of the park.''

Ebony sat up in Nina's lap and turned her face upward. In a tiny voice she said, ''What happened then?''

''I sat in the grass crying and crying. Finally, a lady took my hand and walked me back over to the carnival. She took me to where some other lost little kids were; some of them were crying too. A policeman came, and he brought grown-ups with him, and one of the kids left with them. Every time he came back with a grown-up, one or two of the kids would leave. Finally, I was the only one. I was the only one whose mama and daddy didn't come. That's when I knew they would never come back for me.'' Nina felt her voice tremble a little as she relived the hurt she'd felt that day.

Ebony's eyes glazed over. She could barely whisper the words, ''They never came back for you?''

''It was almost dark, and Daddy finally came to the place where I was. I was so happy to see him, but I was so hurt and so mad, I wouldn't talk to him. He was really happy to see me, too. He hugged me really hard, then he carried me to the car where Mama was waiting. Her face was wet like she had been crying. I wanted to climb in her lap and hug her like always, but I just couldn't. I was too mad. I didn't want to talk to them.''

Ebony suddenly looked down at her hands. She realized where Nina was going with the story.

''Finally, Daddy told me that while I was lost, the police-man kept telling him there was no little girl in the lost and found that fit my description . . . a little girl wearing a yellow sundress.'' Nina smiled. ''Daddy forgot to tell them I wasn't brown. The policeman saw that Daddy and Mama were both brown, and they forgot to tell him that I wasn't. The policeman saw my yellow dress, but he just couldn't believe I could belong to two Black people.'' Nina kept quiet then, staring out the window with Ebony as they both visited their own painful memories. ''Daddy was so sorry. He said he was sorry I was so scared. He said he was scared too. He was afraid someone had taken me. He told me he didn't know what he would do if he lost me forever. Then he started to cry. I had never seen my daddy cry before. That's when I realized he really loved me, and he would never send me away.''

Ebony was staring at Nina. Her dark brown eyes and long, thick eyelashes were absolutely still. She stared for a long moment into Nina's eyes, then looked away, pretending to study the blue birds painted on the ceiling. Finally she said, ''I felt just like you.''

''You did?'' Nina asked.

"At Adrianne's." They were both quiet. Ebony interrupted the silence. "Adrianne has a mommy."

Nina just nodded.

"Adrianne's mommy gave her a doll for her birthday just like the one my mommy gave me."

Nina could feel the emotion building in Ebony. She didn't quite know how she was supposed to deal with whatever was about to happen, but she whispered a prayer, and braced herself. Suddenly, Ebony's little body began to shake, and tears rained from her eyes. She cried silently at first, but then her little voice broke through in heart-wrenching sobs. Nina fought back her own tears.

"I used to have a mommy, but she left me." Ebony managed to get the words out between sobs. She gulped in a deep breath of air before she groaned, "I used to have a grammy . . ." She buried her face against Nina and released a heartbroken moan. ". . . but she left me, too." Nina held Ebony close to her and wrapped her arms around the sobbing child until the convulsive crying slowed. Suddenly a shudder racked Ebony's body, and the crying finally stopped. That's when Ebony pressed her head against Nina's heart, and without looking up, she said in the tiniest voice, "I used to not have a daddy. Now I do."

Ahmad saw an open doorway at the other end of the huge room and wondered if Nina and his daughter might be in there. *I hope everything's okay with Ebony.* He wished he would have warned Nina about the strange mood Ebony had been in since he picked her up at Saundra's Sunday evening. He'd come to get her from the party a little later than he'd expected, and a strangely silent Ebony didn't hug him or even acknowledge him when he arrived. He thought maybe she was just tired, but this morning in the car she just stared out the window and didn't utter a word. Ahmad had tried everything to get through to her. He even did cartoon impersonations—but not even his Scooby-Doo could get her to laugh or smile. He'd asked her a million questions about the party; what games they'd played and what gifts Adrianne received, but Ebony only responded with nods or shrugs. So, he finally decided maybe the child just needed to be quiet for a while.

When he left her at the center that morning, he knew he should say something to Nina; let her know what she was in for. But he had been running late, and decided instead to rely on the hope that Nina might get Ebony to talk. Ebony really liked Nina. She'd taken to her that first day, and hadn't stopped talking about the woman the whole week. "When I see Nina, I'm going to read her my book . . . When I see Nina, I'm gonna ask her if I can paint a picture of you, Daddy . . . When I see Nina, I'm going to ask if the turtle can spend the night at our house."

But there was no chatter from her about the woman that morning, though Ebony did manage a slight smile at the breakfast table when he mentioned they'd soon be leaving for the day care center.

His daughter was obviously hungry for mothering, and Ahmad found himself wondering if Ebony's instant attraction to Nina was the result of that hunger. And actually, Ahmad could understand how Ebony felt. After he got to know Nina a little better, he was strangely drawn to the sista himself. Not that she could ever be his woman. That just wasn't going to happen. But he did feel really comfortable talking to her, and he knew instinctively that she was a sista he could trust. It was too bad they could never be more than friends.

When Ahmad thought about it he had to shake his own head in disbelief. He knew it was ridiculous, but the truth was, the woman's skin color was just too much for him to deal with. Ahmad knew that wasn't right. There was nothing that could help him feel good about the way that sounded in his head. But still, that didn't make it not true. It didn't even matter that he'd met her family—that they were strong, positive Black folks that anyone would be proud to associate with. *But . . .* Ahmad hated the sour feeling it gave him in his gut to admit what had etched itself in his consciousness as an ugly and unmendable character flaw . . . No matter how "Black" the sista was, the color of Nina's skin wasn't going to allow him to get too close to her, and he knew he would never allow himself to love her as anything more than a friend. Her whiteness loomed in front of him like a huge barrier. Her skin would always serve as a constant and sharply painful reminder of a past he had been fighting too hard to bury. And her eyes.

Nina's eyes were that same serene shade of blue as Beth Maxwell's, and they drew him in just as Beth's had drawn in a fourteen-year-old Theodore Jefferson. In his young innocence, he had looked into Beth's blue eyes and dared to believe that he could finally be cherished, loved, parented by someone who wouldn't throw him away when the going got tough, or the county funds ceased. He'd finally consented to let down the impenetrable wall around his heart that he'd built up over years of abuse and neglect in Seattle's foster care system. He'd allowed himself to believe that he, a homeless Black teenager from the wrong side of the tracks wasn't just a temporary houseguest, but had been genuinely accepted as a full-fledged member of the Maxwell household—one of the Northwest's oldest and wealthiest White families. He'd proudly shared his perfect report cards with them, and even mentioned them in his valedictorian speech at graduation. And when he'd been accepted at USC and earned a full academic scholarship, they all seemed so genuinely proud and happy for him.

Ahmad hated himself for being so blind. He wasn't a stupid man. So how could he have been so utterly naïve? He never even saw it coming. He'd let his guard down, and dared to believe he'd never again be thrown away like so much garbage. But that was exactly what Beth had done, wasn't it? The damage she'd done to him was unthinkable and irreversible. It was as if she'd just climbed into his heart where he'd never let any adult enter before—she was supposed to be in there helping to fix the cracks and fractures he had already sustained—when, without any warning, she suddenly took a sledgehammer to Ahmad's heart, and didn't stop pounding away at it until she was sure it was damaged beyond repair. And it was.

Ahmad would never forget. And he would never forgive Beth for what she had done to his life. Never. He wasn't sure that was right; he'd even prayed for help to remove the hatred from his heart, but it clung like rust to uncured iron. He'd never felt anything even close to hatred before Beth, and it was so powerful; it spilled over and clouded his ability to let anyone like her or her pitiful son ever get close to him again. He didn't need any more White friends. And he would definitely never date a White woman. That was just out of the question. He didn't believe he'd ever be able to trust another White person. Shit, as far as he was concerned, if he never had to deal with another one again, that would be all right with him. Matter of fact, he didn't even want to give the impression that anything they had was valuable to him, which they would surely think if Nina was his woman.

Nina's a sista, Ahmad. She's a Black woman. His inner voice was still trying to tell him he was just tripping. *Nina's not White.* But that was beside the point. She looked White. He had mistaken her for White his damnself. The fact that she had Black parents was the only real reason Ahmad could consent to letting himself get as close to her as he had. And he wasn't sorry about that. So far she seemed like a really cool person. She would make a cool friend. And it wasn't so bad to just be friends with a woman anyway. Every man needed at least one good female friend. And Ebony sure liked her. As long as Ahmad made it clear to his daughter that the woman was never going to be her mama, maybe Nina could help provide some of that female attention Ebony so badly needed.

Ahmad heard voices coming from across the center's huge main room, and he walked across it until he stood at the door of a small, colorfully painted cloakroom. He couldn't help but smile at the sight his eyes fell upon. Nina had done it. There at the far end of the tiny room, sitting on a beanbag chair, was his daughter, cradled comfortably in the sista's arms. He could hardly believe it. Not only had Nina gotten Ebony to just sit and be held, the child was finally crying—something Ahmad had been praying for her to do, something he was sure his daughter needed to do after everything she'd been through.

He watched, unnoticed by the two, as a familiar ache radiated through his heart. This was how it could have been if Chante had stayed clean; if she had lived. She should have been the one Ebony could turn to in times like these when she needed a woman's touch . . . a mother's touch. Ahmad hesitated at the doorway, straining to hear what his daughter was saying through her heart-wrenching sobs. She was crying so hard, he could barely make out the words.

"I used to have a mommy, but she left me." The words were followed by a pitiful moan that sliced into his heart like a razor knife. When she added, "I used to have a grammy, but she left me, too,'' Ahmad's shoulder fell against the door frame, and he let his chin fall to his chest in despair.

He fought the urge to rush into the room and scoop his daughter into his arms. He wanted to tell her he was sorry for everything she'd been through. He wished she could know how much he yearned to turn back the clock and make everything perfect for her. But it was too late for that. *I'm sorry, Ebony.* His heart ached to fix her hurt, but hell, he wasn't even able to get her to talk to him—something Nina seemed to have no trouble doing.

Instinctively, he stood silently in the doorway, waiting for the right moment to let the two know he was there. Then he heard something that made Ebony's strange withdrawal from him make sense.

"I used to not have a daddy. Now I do.'' She said it in the tiniest voice, but Ahmad heard her loud and clear. *Poor baby. She's afraid I'm going to leave her, too.*

He watched as Nina held Ebony away from her, raising the child's chin gently with her hand so their eyes would connect. "And you're afraid he's going to leave you, too?'' Nina's tone was both soft and candid, and the sound of the words had a magnetic quality to them, drawing the last of his child's pain out to the surface where it could first be acknowledged, then cast away. Ebony didn't answer right away. Her lower lip trembled, but she didn't cry, she just nodded her head slowly up and down.

Nina let Ebony's head fall back against her chest, and she held the child for a long moment. "Your daddy loves you more than anything. He tells everybody he meets that he's the luckiest person in the whole world to have you for a daughter.''

Ebony raised her face to Nina's again. "When he left me at Adrianne's, I thought he wasn't never coming back.''

"Honey, he thought you would have a good time at the party. He didn't mean for it to hurt you. If you tell your daddy it scared you to be away from him like that, he'll tell you how sorry he is.''

"He already did tell me he was sorry.'' Ebony smiled for the first time. "But I was too mad to talk to him.''

Ahmad finally understood that inexplicable warmth that had

overcome him those times before when he'd connected with
Nina. The same feeling overwhelmed him now. It had nothing
to do with physical attraction. That would be easy enough to
recognize. It wasn't her beauty or her body. It was her heart.
She had a sincere quality that could only come from what was
on the inside.

Ahmad moved slowly into the room, drawing Nina and Ebony's eyes immediately. No one said a word. He walked noise-
lessly over to the corner and sat on the floor beside the
beanbag. When he was settled next to his daughter, he picked
up one of her hands and brought it to his lips. Placing a kiss
in her palm, he said, "Don't ever be afraid of me leaving you,
Ebony." His eyes focused deep into hers, and when he spoke
again it sounded like a vow, as if there was a Bible under his
hand, and he was swearing to an unseen Judge. "I will always
come back for you."

Ebony scrambled into her father's lap and threw her arms
around his neck. They held each other in a long, intense embrace. When Ahmad mouthed the words "Thank you" to Nina
over Ebony's shoulder, Nina smiled softly and wiped a stray
tear from her cheek.

△▽ 16 ▽△

*Nina was half-tempted to ask the flight atten-*dant to pinch her, just to make sure she wasn't dreaming. Instead, she watched the polyester-vested woman lean across her to set an ice-filled cup of orange juice on Ahmad's tray table. The scene had the makings of a great dream, that was for sure. But, even better, Nina was wide awake in an aisle seat of a 737 on her way to spending a weekend in Los Angeles with Ahmad Jefferson.

"I want orange juice, too, please," Ebony piped up. The child turned in her seat to face Nina, her smile and eyes sparkling, but she was really speaking to her father when she said happily, "If Nina has orange juice, we'll all be just alike."

Ahmad turned his attention from the window to look seriously at his daughter. "Honey, maybe Nina doesn't want orange juice."

Nina nodded at the flight attendant. "Make it three." Ahmad's furrowed brow softened momentarily, and he sent a wink of defeat to Ebony before turning once more to look out the window.

He's worried. Nina knew he had good reason to be. The man had received an anonymous invitation to his own wife's funeral, and had no idea who'd arranged it. But he wasn't the only one that was worried about it. The thought that Ahmad might be facing some kind of danger frightened Nina too. Thank God she'd found out about his decision to take Ebony with him to the cemetery, before it was too late.

The flight attendant moved on to the next row of passengers,

155

and Ebony sat quietly sipping her juice, watching the clouds melt against the silver airplane wing. *Something about this feels right*, Nina thought.

Deciding to concentrate on being the man's friend had turned out to be a good idea, and Nina had arrived at the conclusion that whatever Ahmad had done that led to a man's death, it couldn't have been cold-blooded murder. *No way. He's just too calm and intelligent. Not to mention sensitive . . . and sexy as hell.*

Regardless, she had decided to go really slow this time. With Derrick, she'd let the sexual relationship influence her better judgment way too early, and it was a pattern that repeated itself until the end. *Not this time.* She and Ahmad were developing a comfortable friendship. They'd spent every afternoon that week talking and laughing and just getting to know one another.

It was Monday afternoon when Ahmad had found Nina and Ebony cuddled up together in the beanbag chair in the cloakroom, and since then, he had walked over from the campus gymnasium and spent every lunch hour for the entire week sitting with Nina at a picnic table inside the fenced playground at the center. They ate sandwiches and drank Pepsi, and watched Ebony prance excitedly from jungle gym to swing set to slide.

The child had even managed to get Ahmad and Nina to sit on either end of the wooden-planked teeter-totter. Ebony giggled happily as Nina and Ahmad sent one another high into the air, legs dangling and faces broken in laughter. Ahmad had finally seemed to loosen up, and had even begun sending Nina signals that felt like more than just friendship. But so often he seemed troubled and aloof. So Nina just tried to concentrate on being a good friend.

Finally, after he'd stared off into space with his brow tightly furrowed one time too many, and Nina had asked him two times too many if he wanted to talk about what was bothering him, he'd confided in her regarding the mysterious package he'd received the day of the barbecue.

"I'm just not sure what to do about . . ." He'd reached into his pack and pulled out the funeral program. ". . . this."

"She's beautiful," Nina said to him in a whisper. "I see

where Ebony's gorgeous smile came from." They both looked at the photo, and were quiet for a time. *Not sure what to do about what?* she thought, but didn't say. "So, were you able to attend the funeral?" Nina finally asked in a quiet voice.

"No, you don't understand. That's the whole point. The service is this coming Sunday, and I have no idea who is responsible for that." He told Nina about the mysterious stranger who'd left the envelope at his neighbor's apartment. He was obviously concerned, though he tried to make light of the possible danger. When he spoke his "what ifs" aloud for Nina, she could see that it took an effort for him to inject a hint of humor into his voice. "What if some shady character from my wife's past planned her funeral?" With a nervous chuckle, he added, "The police said it was an overdose, but what if someone killed Chante and isn't finished?"

Nina didn't find it funny. "Do you really believe that's a possibility?" She wanted to tell him not to go, but she knew she wasn't in a position to be giving the man advice about something so personal.

As if he'd heard her thoughts he said quietly, "I have to go. I have no choice. My wife is being laid to rest. I have to be there. I wasn't there for her when she was alive. The least I can do is be at her funeral to say good-bye." He looked over at Ebony, playing quietly in the sandbox. "I don't really think I'm in any danger, but I do wish I could leave Ebony here." Before Nina could comment he added, "But actually, even if I could . . . I wouldn't. Not now. You know how upset she was when I left her at Saundra's last weekend."

The realization that Ahmad was contemplating taking Ebony with him to Los Angeles to attend her mother's memorial—at a cemetery—dawned slowly on Nina, and she felt a tightness grip her throat. She shook her head slowly. She felt the same bone-chilling terror from her nightmare creeping into her chest through her lungs. "You can't take her, Ahmad." She almost whispered it.

"Maybe I'm worrying about nothing. I mean, I really don't see how it could be danger—"

"Ahmad, *please* don't take her." Nina's voice had become strained and insistent, but Ahmad seemed not to notice.

"My only other option would be to leave her with her Aunt

Marlene for a few hours, but Marlene's planning to attend the service too.'' He shrugged his shoulders and made an attempt to sound nonchalant. ''Well . . . I figure it'll be broad daylight . . . and it's not like I should have anything to fear. I mean, what kind of idiot would try something stupid in a cemetery full—''

''Ahmad, you cannot take her!'' Nina spoke the words louder than she'd intended and Ahmad looked at her like she'd lost her mind. He didn't say a word. Nina turned to look at Ebony, then said quietly to Ahmad, ''I'm sorry. I mean . . .'' They both waved at the child, who had stopped digging in the sandbox momentarily to see what the fuss was about. When Ebony went back to digging, Nina whispered, ''I'm sure if anyone tried to hurt you, you could handle yourself. But . . .'' She had to make him understand how real it all was to her. ''Ahmad, this is going to sound really crazy to you, but promise me you'll hear me out.''

''I'm listening.'' He stared at her curiously.

''It—it started a few months ago. A dream.''

''A dream?'' Ahmad's voice said he was already skeptical.

''I know in the depths of my soul it means something. It's a warning of some kind, but I've never been able to understand what it meant.'' Tears pooled in her eyes and she continued in a quivering voice. ''The entire dream is of a child in terrible danger.''

Ahmad looked blankly at her.

''The child is standing in a cemetery.''

''Hmmm.'' Ahmad was listening, but he wasn't showing any signs that he felt inclined to give too much credence to Nina's warning.

She described her nightmare in detail for Ahmad, trying especially hard to relay to him the danger that she knew was imminent for the innocent child. She explained how frustrated she was at failing to rescue the little girl; that she could have prevented the evil that was going to happen, but she couldn't get to her in time.

Another ''Hmmm'' from Ahmad.

When Nina described the man in the dream, and how he stood in his hat and shades with his hand hidden behind his back, Ahmad stopped her.

"Hold on a minute. A White man in a hat and sunglasses?" His expression told her he was finally taking her seriously. He was quiet.

"Ahmad? What? What is it?"

"That's how my neighbor described the man who delivered the package," he muttered solemnly.

Nina tried to make her voice light, to lift the gloom that had fallen around them. "Listen, I can go to L.A. with you. I was planning to go myself this weekend anyway." Ahmad looked at her with a doubtful frown, and shook his head silently as if to say that was out of the question. Nina stared back into his eyes seriously. "No, really, I have a mystery of my own to solve." She repeated to him the strange words her father had spoken in the hospital, and explained the discovery of her own mystery envelope. "I have to stay until Monday morning when the bank opens. Ebony can spend Sunday with me, and you can go to the cemetery without her. I'll even bring her back with me on Monday if you want, so you don't have to miss work."

Ahmad was reluctant at first, but he finally saw how much sense it made. He hadn't thought being at the cemetery was a good idea for Ebony in the first place, dream or no dream. She was finally beginning to show signs that her heart was mending. She was even starting to test her limits with her father, and once during the week he'd actually had to punish her for being disobedient.

Ahmad saw his daughter finally beginning to open her heart and trust him, and he didn't want anything to lead to a backslide. The hurt and confusion Ebony might feel attending the funeral of her drug-addicted, too-often-absent mother seemed an unnecessary risk. He finally nodded slowly at Nina, agreeing to the arrangement. Nina called her friend Jocelyn Rogers, a travel agent in Phoenix, who changed Ahmad and Ebony's tickets to Saturday, added Nina to the itinerary, and even threw in two rooms at the Marriott at half-price.

"We're now approaching Los Angeles International Airport." The captain's voice broke rudely through Nina's reflections. Nina looked over at her two traveling companions. Ebony had put her head on her father's shoulder to look out the window, and was now asleep. Ahmad smiled down at his daughter before looking up into Nina's eyes. His eyes looked full. Like he was holding in something that needed to be said, but couldn't be. The electricity in his gaze sent a wave through Nina that made her stomach flutter like she'd just flown down full-speed into a roller-coaster's dip, and was bracing herself for the coming incline. Was there any way this man could know the effect he had on her? Could he know how fast her heart was racing? She broke the gaze and glanced nervously at the blinking "fasten seat belt" sign above her head. Nina let her head fall back against the headrest and exhaled a long sigh. Somehow she knew the blinking message held more meaning for her than just federal safety regulations.

"Hi, Meanie." Ebony grinned from ear to ear as the heavy-set woman scooped the child up into her arms and planted a loud smooch on her neck. The tall, pecan-colored woman looked to be in her mid-twenties, and if she didn't have sixty or seventy excess pounds, Nina thought she could have been a fashion model. The thick, jet black hair she'd pulled into a smooth ponytail hung in a perfect braid, way past her butt, making it obvious that it was a fashion accessory the woman wasn't born with. Not-too-heavily-applied makeup accentuated large almond-shaped brown eyes and full lips, and the woman's skin was flawless.

"Who you callin' Meanie?" Another loud smooch, accompanied by a tickle.

Ebony giggled.

"That's not nice, Ebony," Ahmad scolded. "Don't call your Auntie names, young lady."

The woman laughed. "To Ebony, Meanie *is* my name." She kissed the child's face before putting her back down on the sidewalk. "She started talking when she wasn't barely one year old. And I mean talking. She'd tell you what she wanted for dinner, and what she wanted to wear to bed. By the time she was two, she could sing along with most everything on the radio. But she couldn't never say Marlene. So I got used to being Aunt Meanie. I've been stuck with it ever since."

Ahmad's smile was laced with pain or discomfort, Nina couldn't really tell which. But he was definitely unsettled by the comment. "I didn't know she started talking so early. No wonder she's so articulate," he said quietly.

God, that must hurt, Nina thought. To be gone so long and be so disconnected that you have to hear secondhand about your own child's language development.

A nervous little cough came out of Ahmad's throat before he said, "This is my friend Nina."

Nina thought his voice sounded a little shaky. The woman looked Nina up and down dubiously before extending her hand.

"I'm Marlene. Chante—Ahmad's *wife*—was my sister." She emphasized the word "wife" as if to make Nina feel like an intruder. It worked.

Nina shook the hand. "I'm really sorry about your sister." She wanted to say, "I've heard a lot about you," but that wasn't true. She wanted to say, "Ebony talks about you all the time," but that wasn't true either. She couldn't think of anything else to say to the woman that wouldn't sound phony, so she didn't say another word.

Marlene turned her back to Nina and motioned to a man in the driver's seat of an ancient Volkswagen van. There had to be at least five or six little sweaty faces pressed against the side windows. When they saw her wave her hand at the man, they all came piling out onto the sidewalk.

"Didn't nobody tell y'all to get out," Marlene barked at the kids, who weren't paying much attention to her. They were too busy greeting Ebony with hugs and hand-holds. One of the girls fingered Ebony's braids and another one bent down to tie her shoe. The oldest of the clan wasn't much older than Ebony. The youngest, a wide-eyed boy wearing a faded Bulls jersey, looked to be about two.

"These all yours?" Ahmad asked.

"All but one. The girl in the pink jumper is my neighbor's. The rest are mine. This here's my youngest, Jordan." Marlene laid her hand on top of the freshly clipped head of the two-year-old, who promptly squirmed out from under it and joined the circle around his cousin.

The man Marlene had waved to climbed down from the driver's seat and walked over.

"This is my boyfriend Anthony, but everybody calls him

Ant.'' Marlene pressed an acrylic-nailed hand to the man's shoulder and smiled at Ahmad. Nina thought the man looked like an Ant. He was all of about five-eight and couldn't have weighed more than 155 in wet winter clothes. He was coal black, and wore wire-rimmed glasses with thick lenses. His lips were larger than his narrow face called for and were tinged with pink where the top and bottom lip met. He wiped his hand on his faded Levi's before extending it first to Ahmad, then Nina.

"Welcome to L.A.," he said with genuine friendliness. "This all you brought?" He was referring to Nina's duffel bag on the sidewalk next to him. It was on his shoulder and on its way to the van before she could answer.

Ahmad stopped him. "Yo. Ant. We decided to rent a car after all." He pointed at the Budget lot across from the terminal. "Thanks, but we're going straight to the Marriott from here." The announcement sounded way too loud to Nina. Like in an E.F. Hutton commercial, the traffic seemed to have come to a halt, and conversations everywhere ceased, just so the world could hear that Ahmad and his female traveling companion were spending the weekend of his wife's funeral together at the Marriott.

Marlene looked dead at Nina. "Mmmph" was all she said. Ant brought the bag back and set it down gingerly at Nina's feet.

Ahmad smiled nervously. "Uh. Nina teaches history at the college where I work. She's here on business. She'll be looking after Ebony while we're at the cemetery." Nobody said anything, but Nina caught Marlene raising her eyebrows and sending a smirk over to Ant. He shook his head at his woman and frowned as if to tell her to behave.

Ahmad called to Ebony, "Ebony, come give Daddy a hug and kiss." Ebony broke from the crowd of cousins and gave her dad a peck and a quick hug. "You gonna be okay?" He held her chin and looked into her eyes. "Marlene's going to bring you back to the hotel for dinner, okay?"

"Okay, Daddy." She grinned. "I'm going to go to Meanie's with my cousins and see the puppies." Her eyes opened wide. "There's eight of 'em," she added, before hop-stepping back over to the circle of children.

When Marlene corralled the kids toward the van's open sliding door, Ebony suddenly broke from the group and ran to
Nina. Reaching her arms up for a hug she said, "Bye, Nina."
Nina kissed her on the cheek and squeezed her in a big bear
hug. Over the child's shoulder, she caught a glimpse of Marlene's face, raised eyebrows, scowling frown and all.

Ahmad knew just where he wanted to take Nina. He pointed
the rented Camry north, and headed for the 405 freeway.
"When's the last time you visited the city?" he asked his
silent friend. He himself hadn't been in L.A. since the trial, if
being jumpsuited and shackled on a sardine bus from Orange
County jail counted as a visit.

"T and I came in for the Frankie Beverly concert back in
April. It rained like hell the whole time we were here, though.
I'm looking forward to some sun this time."

"We are on our way to get just that," Ahmad teased. Nina
had given up pestering him to tell where they were headed.
When they'd realized check-in at the hotel didn't begin until
three, and it wasn't even eleven when they'd pulled out of the
Budget lot, Ahmad announced mysteriously that he had something "Nina needed to see."

As he drove, Nina stared out the window at the passing
scenery. She seemed lost in thought. Ahmad knew she had
grown up somewhere nearby. Ladera Heights was a mile or
so northeast of the intersection to the 90 freeway and they
were just passing the off-ramp. "Stomping grounds, huh?" he
asked. She just nodded. She seemed far away. Ahmad wanted
to ask her where, but he left her to her thoughts. When he
eased the car into the far right lane and transitioned from the
405 to the 10 West, Nina smiled.

"I bet it's beautiful there today," she said without looking
at him.

He laughed. *She figured it out.* "All right, woman. But
you're not just getting a trip to the beach. You are about to
embark on an official, uncharted, Ahmad Jefferson version of
a trip to the beach." They rode in silence, and Ahmad marveled at how comfortable he had become with Nina so soon.
All the fears he had about her skin color, about not being able
to overcome his initial reaction to it, seemed to fade and only

hovered in the back of his mind every now and then. Maybe he was wrong about not being able to handle it. Maybe he could be big enough to deal with it. He was right about one thing. He and Nina were already good friends, and they'd seemed to connect in a way that made Ahmad believe somehow their paths were meant to cross. A line from Gibran's *The Prophet* echoed in his head: *Your friend is your needs answered.* He pulled off the freeway ramp, glancing at a still quiet Nina. *Hmmm.* What needs in his life might this woman be meant to fill?

When he pulled to the curb on Ocean Avenue and cut the engine, Nina turned to him with a look of disbelief. She was almost teary-eyed, like she'd witnessed something miraculous or overwhelming. Without smiling, she said softly, "This is my favorite spot in all of Los Angeles." She pointed toward the freshly mown strip of lawn that wasn't more than thirty feet wide, but stretched for at least a half mile along the other side of the four-lane street. The lawn was edged by a waist-high wooden fence, meant to keep people from venturing too close to the steep cliff's edge. Along a narrow cement walkway closer to the street, there were trees with huge trunks that grew parallel to the ground in amazing twisting patterns, but Nina was pointing up, to a tall tree near the cliff. Its long smooth trunk sprouted into clusters of hundreds of thinner branches whose foliage reached upward to the sun. "That's my tree." She looked at Ahmad; only her eyes were smiling.

Ahmad was stunned. "What did you say?"

"I said, that's my tree."

Unbelievable, he thought. Ahmad wondered if he could count how many times he had referred to the exact same tree as his own. "Funny," he smiled, "I always thought it belonged to me."

They jaywalked across the not-yet-too-busy street, and stood at the curb taking in the majesty of the vast stretch of blue on the other side of the fence. The Pacific Ocean was beautiful to look at, but not clean enough along this stretch of the coast for any health-conscious swimmers, though some adventurous bodies were down there doing just that. Santa Monica Beach was considered by many Angelinos to be a touristy eyesore, but Ahmad had always loved this spot. He tried to get Chante to come down with him, but after she'd seen one or two sunsets, she'd seen 'em all. So, Ahmad had spent countless evenings standing at the cliff alone. He and his tree would watch the sky paint itself in cloudy strips of purple, lavender, and salmon, until the sun dissolved into the ocean, turning the blue water along the horizon into a sea of coral pink and fiery red-orange. Those sunsets reminded Ahmad of how truly generous God could be, and the way his tree strained upward, toward the sky, Ahmad thought it might feel the same. At dusk, it seemed to mourn the sun's passing, waiting for another day of worship. He called it his praying tree. And now he stood in stunned silence, staring up at the same tree this woman had called her own.

"I always thought it looked as if it were praying," Nina said solemnly. She turned to look at Ahmad. When her eyes met his, he was suddenly taken with a desire to wrap his arms around her; to feel her skin against his; to press his lips into hers. The urge was frighteningly intense, and Ahmad felt a shiver of desire travel up his spine, and into his chest where it ignited something that sent a warm glow through his rib cage. He was faced with the decision to ignore this urge to have her close to him, or reach for the woman and fulfill it. Suddenly, he held his hands out toward Nina, palms down in front of him, and said, "Don't move." Ahmad left Nina with a curious expression on her face as he turned to sprint across Ocean Avenue's nearest two lanes, which were empty of cars. He waited for the other lanes to clear before continuing across the street. When he returned, his camera was cocked and ready.

"What are you . . ." Nina frowned playfully at him.

"Move slightly to your left," he whispered. He found Nina's torso in his viewfinder, draped in a careless sand-colored linen sundress. The praying tree arched gracefully above her head and the blue sky and bluer ocean served as the perfect backdrop. "That's it, " Ahmad whispered. She cocked her left eyebrow. He clicked, then waited for her to smile and clicked again.

The registrar at the Marriott handed Ahmad a key to the room next to Nina's. Ahmad shook a silent "no, thank you" with his head toward the approaching bellman, and lifted both his and Nina's bags to his shoulder and walked with her to the elevator. She pressed the up arrow before leaning wearily against the wall with her head tilted back. She still had the pink and white Hawaiian lei around her neck, a souvenir from the Tahitian restaurant they'd lunched at. The flowers looked soft and almost edible draped around her shoulders. *She looks edible*, Ahmad thought. He'd been chasing images of being next to Nina's skin out of his head since the wave of desire first rushed over him under the praying tree. Lunch was especially torturous. Nina had ordered a spicy shrimp dish that was meant to be eaten with the fingers, which required a lot of licking of lips and fingertips, and Ahmad had teetered on a line between pain and pleasure through the entire meal. And that was just the beginning. After lunch when they'd walked the pier at Santa Monica, she'd stood in front of him, bending into the lens of a telescope, excitedly motioning to him over her shoulder to look at the dolphins skimming the water's edge a hundred or so feet from the pier.

How was he supposed to concentrate on dolphins, when the woman's behind was a sixteenth of an inch from rubbing all up against him? Of course, she had no idea how hard, *truly hard* that had been. He'd reached for her hand on the walk down the Venice Beach strand and could pretty much deal with that, once he got accustomed to the soft smoothness of her palm against his. And when they visited the boat docks at Marina del Rey, and fed scraps of bread to the pigeons and seagulls, Ahmad focused on remaining cool, despite the electricity Nina's nearness was generating throughout his body.

After the Marina, Nina suggested they drive inland a few miles to visit the row of Afrocentric art and gift shops along Degnan Street in Leimert Park, and Ahmad actually didn't think about sex while they were there, hardly. As they walked from shop to shop they talked about everything from art to history to the Black entrepreneurs that had rejuvenated Leimert, the quaint little area in the heart of Los Angeles' Crenshaw district. Ahmad was amazed at how much he had in common with Nina—their mutual love for literature and music—and he allowed himself to just relax and enjoy her company. But what amazed him most was that despite everything he'd feared before, he only vaguely considered whether or not people thought Nina was White. And every now and again he wondered if they thought he was with her because of the color of her skin. He had to admit that bothered him, but he really didn't understand why. Why should he let the perceptions of others get in the way of a good time with a good woman? He decided not to waste a whole lot of time trying to figure it out, and when the thought did come to mind, he simply pushed it as deep into his subconscious as it would go and concentrated instead on enjoying the afternoon with his friend.

Finally, they'd arrived back at the hotel just a half an hour before Ebony was due to be dropped off by Ant and Marlene. And there Nina was, leaning against the wall, looking sexy in a way only a woman not trying to look sexy can. She looked up at him and let out a tired sigh.

"Worn out?" Ahmad teased. He grabbed her wrist and pressed his thumb gently against the flesh just above the base of her palm. He looked at his watch with a playful smile, pretending to take Nina's pulse. "Your heart's not giving out on you, is it?" He wondered if she knew the little joke was only an excuse to touch her.

"Hardly," Nina teased back defiantly. "But it may be beating a little faster than usual." Was she flirting with him too? Maybe she was trying to let him know she was feeling the same sexual tension he'd been fighting all day. *There's one way to find out.* Still holding Nina's wrist, he dropped the bags from his shoulder and with his free hand gently grasped her other wrist too. Nina looked at him questioningly.

"Can I ask you something?" Ahmad whispered.

Nina whispered back. "Sure."

"Would you mind if I kissed you?"

"Would I mind?"

"Yeah. Mind. You know. Would it bother you, or would it please you?"

Just then the elevator door opened and a small crowd of Chinese tourists stepped over the bags Ahmad had dropped in front of the silver doors. He picked the bags up and held the elevator for Nina, then pushed the button for the ninth floor.

Nina broke the nervous silence around the fourth floor. "Please."

Ahmad shifted the bags. "Please what?" Now they were at the sixth floor.

"Please," she repeated with a nervous smile. She paused as the elevator doors slid open at the ninth floor. "As opposed to bother."

Ahmad ignored the open doors. His left hand quickly slid around Nina's waist and pulled her to him. He let the bags fall from his shoulder to free up his right hand, cupping it softly at the nape of her neck. He didn't want to kiss her all at once. He thought of the way she'd tortured him with the Tahitian shrimp, holding it softly to her mouth before gently devouring it, and he did the same to her bottom lip, licking it first with the tip of his tongue, then sucking gently on the soft flesh. A fog of desire settled around him, and he found himself falling into the center of a dizzying storm—and he still hadn't really kissed her. He was almost afraid to. Afraid he'd get lost in her. Afraid he'd never make his way back if he crossed the threshold of her lips. When Nina's lips parted in anticipation, Ahmad breathed in the desire that escaped her open mouth, and hesitated. The softness of her mouth against his drew him into the kiss like a magnet, and when his tongue was welcomed in by her own, he fell helplessly into the depth of her throat. "Mmnh." The silence of the floating elevator was broken by the tortured moan Ahmad hadn't meant to let escape.

"Get a room." The irritated whine in the man's voice brought Ahmad and Nina up for air when the elevator doors slid open at the sixteenth floor. A pasty, middle-aged couple wearing obnoxious swimwear and reeking of sunblock stood and watched the doors slide closed again.

Nina leaned into Ahmad and pressed her forehead against his chest. "Uh-oh," was all she said. It was all she needed to say. Ahmad knew exactly what it meant. *That was the first kiss?* He could only imagine how intense making love to her could be.

He reached, and pressed nine again, and stood in the middle of the elevator with Nina's forehead buried against his chest, and his head shaking slowly from side to side, until the doors slid open at the ninth floor.

△▽ 17 ▽△

Nina knocked softly on the door separating the two hotel rooms. A few seconds passed before she heard the tumbler in the deadbolt click, and the door inched open just enough for her to see the bluish glow of Ahmad and Ebony's television. She smiled. It was tuned to the same program she had been watching—a "shark week" special on the Discovery Channel. Through the narrow opening, Nina could see two double beds, and the same glass-topped table and chairs and overstuffed magenta sofa that decorated her own room. She spotted the jeans and tee shirt Ahmad had worn earlier, draped across the end of one of the beds. Nina's eyes quickly scanned the room. Ebony was nowhere in sight. Ahmad's face suddenly appeared above Nina in the door opening, but he stood mostly behind the door, as if to hide the rest of himself from her view. "Hey there." Ahmad grinned.

"Hey," Nina replied. "Uh, I was just going to order room service. I thought I'd see if you and Ebony might like to come over for dinner."

Ahmad looked a little nervous. "Um. I was going to call you as soon as I got out of the shower and ask you the same thing." He hesitated, then added, "Ebony is spending the night with Marlene."

"Oh," was all Nina could think to say.

"She caught puppy fever."

Nina smiled.

"Uh," Ahmad began. "I haven't eaten. I'd love to join you."

169

"Okay."

"I'll put my clothes on."

"Okay." *He's naked. The man is standing less than a foot away with not a stitch of clothes on.* Nina felt a wave of heat travel swiftly through her body and up into her face. *Say something besides "Okay,"* Nina thought, silently cursing her nervousness. "Uh, I'm having the grilled snapper and a Caesar salad," she finally said. "Have you seen the room service menu?"

"Snapper sounds good. I'll have the same."

"Okay."

"Give me ten minutes." Ahmad lifted his free hand to his damp dreadlocks. "Well, on second thought, I might need twenty."

"Okay." She pulled the door closed and leaned against it, breathing out a heavy sigh. *Oh my God. What have I done?* Hadn't she decided just last week to go slow this time? Hadn't she learned her lesson with Derrick? *Focus on the physical, and you risk getting in too deep, too soon.* The man was just coming over for dinner. No big deal. Just dinner. So they'd be in a hotel room alone together, that didn't mean they had to do anything. *Twenty minutes. Oh my God, I only have twenty minutes.*

Nina leapt into action, pouncing on the phone to quickly order dinner. She'd just taken a bath less than an hour before, but she hurried to the bathroom to apply a little more scented lotion to her arms, legs, and bare feet. She brushed her teeth and the back of her tongue, gargled with mouthwash, and spritzed a little Donna Karan perfume behind her ears. She called room service back to add a bottle of wine to the dinner order, hung up the wet towels she'd left on the floor earlier, retrieved the dress she'd worn to the beach from the hook on the back of the bathroom door, and stuffed it carelessly into a dresser drawer. Breathless, she finally stopped in front of the mirror. The denim shorts and white cotton tank top she'd put on when she thought she was having dinner with Ebony and her daddy suddenly seemed too plain. *Oh well, too late to change now.* She applied a thin layer of lip gloss and a little blush and decided she needed to try to relax, and just be herself. When she'd finally settled down on her bed to stare absently at the hammerhead mating ritual on TV, there was a soft knock on the front door.

Nina pulled the door open wide to let the server in, but was noticeably surprised to find Ahmad standing at the door instead. *Who needs room service?* Nina thought. *This man looks good enough to eat.* His crisply ironed khakis and black tee shirt were simple and oh-so-sexy, and the sight of him made Nina swallow hard and clear her throat. The man had one hand upraised and pressed against the door frame and was leaning casually against it—like he was posing for an Armani ad. The other hand was held behind his back. Nina noticed a tentative smile on his pursed lips, and wondered what it meant. Before she could spend too much time wondering, Ahmad's hidden hand moved slowly forward and held a single red rose out to her.

She smiled and reached for the flower, her eyebrows arched into a question.

He answered it instinctively, his eyes twinkling with mischief. "A meager and immensely insufficient gesture of gratitude for the luscious kiss you bestowed upon me earlier."

Nina laughed. " 'Meager,' 'immensely,' 'insufficient,' 'gesture,' and 'bestowed' all in one mouthful? Mama would love you."

"Don't forget 'gratitude.' "

She batted her eyes. "Oh, and 'luscious.' "

Ahmad puffed his chest out dramatically. Speaking in a purposely phony British accent he announced, "I majored in English at USC."

"I won't hold that against you." Nina held the flower to her nose and inhaled. "I was a Bruin," she explained, referring to her two years at UCLA.

"Well, if I were to hold something against you . . ." He grinned playfully at Nina. ". . . it certainly wouldn't be that."

Nina laughed. She'd already fallen in love with the man's sense of humor.

"On the real, USC gave me a damn good start." He winked and added, "But five years in the pen with a dictionary didn't hurt a brotha's vocabulary none either."

Nina smiled nervously and didn't say a word. His light-hearted reference to incarceration was begging for a comeback. *Say something to let him know you're not trippin' about it, Nina.* She wanted to say she wasn't holding his prison time against him, but the words wouldn't come out. She wasn't sure they were true. Not that she was passing judgment on the brotha. She just needed a little time, and she definitely needed to know what happened. What had led him to take another man's life? Whatever the circumstances were, she had already decided she was going to be the man's friend. That was certain. There was enough between them already to establish that. But the electricity that had been flowing between them all day felt less and less like friendship and more and more like a potential relationship. *And that kiss.* Day-um. Talk about wanting to just let yourself fall head over heels . . . *Head over heels? Get a hold of yourself, girl. No way.* There was no way she'd take that plunge—allow herself to even consider getting in too deep—until she knew what he was really made of; until he felt comfortable enough with her to tell her what really happened.

Nina looked at the warm, sexy smile Ahmad was beaming her way. It sent a shiver down her spine just to look at him. *Of course, there'd be no harm in flirting with the man a little, would there?* And maybe she didn't have to run too fast now that he finally decided to chase her.

She held the rose up to her lips, and brushed the petals lightly across them. Referring to his sweet-smelling gift and the reference he had made to her kiss, she repeated his words. "Immensely insufficient?"

"Mmmm, not even close." Ahmad bent down and pressed his lips to Nina's for an abbreviated version of what had occurred on the elevator a couple of hours before. Nina felt the same dizzying cloud of temptation envelop her, and the kiss left her breathless, and wondering whether to bless or curse the interruption of the red-vested man pushing the room service cart.

When Nina had finally stopped picking at her mostly uneaten fish, and Ahmad transferred the white cloth napkin from his lap to his empty plate, he continued his story.

"Chante didn't even complain when I told her I needed to take a quick drive with Scotty. I was up, and pulling my Levi's on, when she blew me a kiss. And before she tugged the covers up over her head, she smiled at me and told me to be careful. I bent over Ebony's crib, and kissed her little cheek.''

Nina watched Ahmad's eyes grow watery as he cleared his throat. ''That was the last time I saw my wife alive, and the last time I saw my daughter until a little over two weeks ago.''

Nina's eyes widened with disbelief. ''You never saw her again?''

A vacant expression settled over Ahmad's face like a misty veil. Nina saw him disappear for a moment. It was as if he'd taken a dive into the depths of those traumatic events from his past, and Nina knew she could only wait for him to resurface.

He took in a labored breath, and exhaled it slowly, lifting his eyes to look into hers. ''Chante refused to come to the trial, and she wouldn't come see me in jail. It was like—as soon as I was arrested, I didn't exist for her anymore.''

Nina shook her head slowly. She felt his pain, instantly identifying with what must have been an aching feeling of abandonment. But just as quickly, a thought invaded her head. *What did he do that would make his own wife desert him like that?*

''Not long after my sentencing, I found out she'd started leaving Ebony with neighbors and not coming back for days. She was partying and hanging out, and seemed to just lose interest in being a mother. She finally lost custody of our baby. That's when I found out she'd been smoking crack. After a year or so, she entered drug rehab to try to get Ebony back, but the state awarded custody to Chante's mother.'' Ahmad was silent for what seemed like forever. When he spoke again, his voice was edgy and tight, like he was fighting the pain that wanted to erupt from his throat, but wouldn't. ''I'll never forgive myself for what I did to her.''

The look on Ahmad's face pierced Nina to the core. He had loved his wife deeply; still loved her. And he was still mourning the loss, even after all those years.

''Chante used to say I was her knight in shining armor. I was the one who was supposed to rescue her from South Central, and carry her into what she'd always dreamed of: a loving family and a home of her own with a picket-fenced lawn. I almost did it, too. We put a bid in on a little two-bedroom house in Inglewood. Chante was so excited—already putting furniture on layaway. But I barely had enough money for the down payment. I was attending USC during the day and stocking grocery shelves at night. Then Scotty told me of a little job he'd heard about. A courier job. He said we could each make over a grand a month for just a couple of hours of work on the weekends.''

Nina's eyebrows raised suspiciously.

"Yeah. I thought the same thing. Like, what kind of criminal activity was he talking about? I knew Scotty's family had finally gotten sick of footing the bill for his lavish, unemployed life-style. They had money. Big money. And they had spoiled that boy rotten. Then they suddenly cut him off without out a dime. I knew Scotty was hard up for cash, but I never thought he'd resort to anything criminal.''

Nina interrupted. "Ahmad, who's Scotty?''

Ahmad's eyes turned glassy, and a tension in his throat made the words sound forced. "He was my best friend. From the day we met in junior high, we were like brothers. Or so I thought. His mother Beth was the closest thing I ever had to a real parent. If I had only known then . . .'' Ahmad's voice trailed off and Nina saw a look flash across his face that was almost frightening; something intense and angry. Then just as quickly it was gone.

"Scotty and Beth Maxwell were the two worst things that ever happened to me.'' He looked down in his lap, and shook his head slowly from side to side, as if he were being told something horrible about a loved one that he didn't want to believe. When he lifted his head to gaze up into Nina's face, he continued, "I asked Scotty if he was sure the job was legitimate. He said we'd be couriers for a film company. We'd be delivering something called 'dailies.' I'd never heard the word before. It had to do with film reels. The film crews would shoot all day, we'd deliver the reels to editing, and then we'd deliver edited tapes to the set before sunup for the actors to review prior to the next day's shoot. We'd have to be on call and we'd have to be willing to drive around in the early morning hours. Two hundred and fifty dollars per delivery. It sounded like the answer to my prayers.

"That night, when Scotty called, I felt a little uneasy. Something told me to stay right there in that bed with my wife, but she urged me to go on and go. Chante was counting on me to come through for her on that house. It wasn't like we could afford to turn down such easy money.

"So, I swung by Scotty's to pick him up and we drove to a seedy little area just off the docks in Long Beach. I asked Scotty if he was sure we were in the right place. Why would they edit film in that part of town? He said they were shooting on location—filming on the *Queen Mary*—and not to worry about where we were. That's when he reached into his jacket and pulled out a gun. Just in case somebody tries to 'jack' us, he said." Ahmad let go of a stifled laugh. "That skinny little sheltered White boy from Seattle, Washington, got a kick out of using the word 'jack.' I didn't see it at the time, but he was all hyped up on the element of danger. Unfortunately, I had no idea just how much danger we were really in. Scotty disappeared into the building; I waited in the car. When he came out, he wasn't alone."

Nina lifted the bottle of wine from the table and poured herself another glass. When she tipped it toward Ahmad's empty glass he nodded yes to a refill too.

"Scotty's eyes were bulging like the life had been strangled out of him. Or like it was about to be. A huge brotha in a black stadium jacket stood behind him, and he had Scotty's neck jammed tightly in the crook of his elbow. I saw a glint of metal in his other hand, and that's when I realized there was a gun being held to Scotty's head. Scotty didn't say a word, but he looked right at me, his eyes pleading for help. When that brotha pushed Scotty to the ground and aimed at him, it didn't take a thought. I reached for the gun Scotty left on the seat. Before I knew it, I'd pulled the trigger. I shot that brotha right in the chest."

They were both quiet for a long moment. Finally Nina asked, "Why did the man have a gun? What would a film editor need a gun for?"

"He was no film editor. He was a drug dealer. Scotty was delivering all right. But it wasn't film. I killed a drug dealer, who probably would have killed my buddy, and killed me too, without blinking twice. I can't tell you what it's like to live with the knowledge that I actually ended that brotha's exis-

tence. I mean, he had kids. You know? But if I had to do it
over again . . .'' Ahmad didn't finish the sentence.

Nina thought about it. She might have done the same thing.
No, she probably *would* have done the same thing. *If T was
being threatened? Or Nat?* Shit, she'd have to shoot a fool.

"Scotty panicked. I wanted to stay and call 911. You know?
Make sure the brotha wasn't dead. Wait for the police to arrive
and tell them the guy was trying to rob Scotty. That's what I
thought happened. But Scotty started crying and got all hys-
terical. That's when he told me there were drugs in the car,
and that we'd go to prison for a long time if I didn't get the
hell out of there.

"It didn't take the cops long to find us, speeding through
the streets at four in the morning. I was arrested for murder,
and Scotty for accessory to murder. We weren't allowed to
see or talk to each other, and we had separate lawyers, both
paid for by Beth. My lawyer told me to tell the truth about
everything. Everything, except the drugs. He said if I admitted
that I knew they belonged to Scotty, we'd both go to prison.
So I just told the grand jury I never saw any drugs, and that
I didn't know anything about any drugs. They charged me
with murder, possession of an illegal firearm, and possession
with the intent to sell narcotics. My lawyer said I had no
choice but to plea.

"Instead of pleading innocent and facing a jury and the
possibility of life in prison, he convinced me I had to plea-
bargain. If I copped to manslaughter, the state would save a
bunch of money on court costs, and would repay the favor by
dropping the drug charges. What I didn't know until the day
I was sentenced was that Scotty had a bargain of his own. He
and Beth handed me over on a platter like a stuck pig. Scotty
was called by the judge as a witness for the prosecution on
my case."

Ahmad's voice cracked, and Nina watched a single tear drip
as if in slow motion from the corner of his eye and down his
face. He was silent for a long moment, then, with a faraway
look in his eye, and obvious pain in his voice, he said, "My
so-called best friend stood in front of that judge and told him
lies to save his own ass. He told the judge how surprised he
was to learn that I was a drug dealer. He said he waited in the

car for me, and when I came out of the building, a man ran after me with a gun in his hand, and that's when I turned and shot him. Scotty made it look like I'd masterminded a drug deal gone bad. Nina, I just sat in that courtroom with tears streaming down my face. Beth couldn't look at me. She just stared straight ahead at the judge. To this day I cannot understand how those two devils could be so callous. They sent me down the river, and left my wife and baby with nothing.''

Nina felt hot tears in her own eyes. She had never heard anything so tragic. If Ahmad's heart would have turned to stone, who could blame him? But he'd come through all that misery, and was still climbing. Already back in school and opening his arms to care for his child. *This man has heart.*

''I guess it was pretty easy for the judge to believe a blond-headed rich White boy. And that's what he did. It didn't matter that I was a student at USC with a steady part-time job, and Scotty hadn't worked a day since we both applied at McDonald's in the ninth grade. It didn't matter that I had absolutely no criminal record, and Scotty had two juvenile counts and a misdemeanor marijuana charge. I got nine years. Scotty walked. Five years later, he drove his Camaro off a cliff on the Oregon coast, and two weeks after that, mysteriously, I was paroled. I don't know if it was a mistake or a miracle. Maybe God finally heard my prayers.'' Ahmad looked heavenward. ''At least some of them. All I know is that one day I was a prisoner, and the next . . . free at last.''

Free at last. The words startled Nina. An image of Dr. Webb's father appeared suddenly in her memory. The emaciated figure in the picture frame. Nina's heart felt like lead in her chest; the tragedy of it seemed so ironic and so absolutely pitiful. *Racism's toll.* One man's family; another man's eternal life—the prices were way too high.

''Hey,'' Ahmad said quietly, sipping the last of his wine.

''Hey.''

''Would it bother you if I said I don't want to talk about this anymore?'' Ahmad got up from the chair and walked over to the window, parting the curtain to look down at the Saturday night traffic on Century Boulevard.

Nina followed slowly behind him. She could only imagine what he had to experience to get through that story. Love, betrayal, abandonment, rage. It was a wonder he was still in the room with her. Ahmad suddenly seemed taller to her. He was a bigger man now. Not because he had shared something so personal with her, but because he had been willing to be ravaged by all those intense feelings in her presence. He didn't apologize for his tears, and he wasn't afraid to let her see his disappointment in himself. Even the love he obviously still had for his wife was an honest admission that didn't need to be kept from Nina like she was an immature schoolgirl. No. This was a man standing at her window. A damn good man. She had an overwhelming urge to stand behind him; to wrap her arms around his muscular body and plant kisses against his back. Instead, she stood at his side with one hand pressed to his shoulder blade, and stared out onto the boulevard along with him. She finally answered his question. "Of course it wouldn't bother me. You got something else on your mind you want to talk about?"

Ahmad suddenly turned and swept Nina into an intense embrace, wrapping his arms around her and covering her mouth with his, exploring it with his tongue until every nerve ending in her entire body was charged with anticipation. He pulled away suddenly and pierced her with his stare, and when he opened his mouth to speak, his words were like music to her ears. "How 'bout if we don't talk at all for a while." Nina didn't say a word. She wanted him. She wanted his body to fulfill the promise his lips had made, and she let him lead her toward the bed. He sat on its edge, and pulled her down onto his lap. His lips were on hers again, and his strong hands caressed her bare legs, sending more shivers of desire through her already burning body.

It wasn't until that moment that she realized how terrified she was of him. Terrified of the desire he awakened in her— the effect he had on her body. He had no idea how much she wanted him. How every inch of her skin was crying out for his nearness. The simple touch of his lips against hers was the most intense foreplay she'd ever known. No man had affected her body like this—making her tremble with desire with just a glance. Yes, she was afraid of him. And something told her to be careful. A tiny voice. Way in the back of her mind. *Wait.*

It whispered to her like the lyrics of an old Luther song about waiting to get the chance.

It took every ounce of Nina's inner strength to stand, grasp Ahmad by the hands, and pull him toward the door to his room. She smiled apologetically. "I think you'd better go now." Ahmad tried, but he couldn't hide the disappointment on his face. Actually, Nina thought it looked much closer to pain than disappointment. Maybe he was feeling what she was feeling after all.

"I'm sorry." Ahmad looked her directly in the eye. "I meant no disrespect. I just thought you were feeling—"

Nina interrupted him mid-sentence. "None taken. And I am—" She stopped mid-sentence too. "I'm not ready, Ahmad. I'm not sure. It's not that I don't—"

"Shhh," he whispered. He leaned down to place a soft kiss on her lips. "You don't have to explain." He opened the door between the rooms and backed his way onto its threshold. "If you need me . . ." A warm smile lit up his face. "Well, just call me, if you need me for anything." Ahmad brushed his fingers across his lips and blew the kiss softly to her, and he was gone.

△▽ 18 ▽△

At first he thought it was a cat out in the alley, or maybe the sound from a too-loud television coming from somewhere down the hallway. It took a few moments for wakefulness to assert itself over the dark unawareness of sleep before Ahmad realized it was Nina. Somebody was in her room. Somebody was trying to hurt Nina and she was screaming in a voice of terrified panic.

Ahmad leapt instantly from the bed and bolted through the door. He stood in Nina's dawn-lit room wearing only a pair of white cotton boxers, and let out an exasperated breath of relief that Nina was not in danger.

She was alone in her bed, thrashing wildly beneath her bedsheet and desperately crying out for someone to help. Ahmad sat on the edge of her bed, and shook Nina gently. Whispering to her in a soothing voice, he crooned, "Hey. Shhh. I'm right here, Nina. Nina, wake up." Nina tossed wildly, still in a deep sleep. She let out a muffled moan, her body writhing as if in pain. Ahmad shook her gently. "Nina, wake up. It's Ahmad. It's okay. Nina?"

When her eyes finally flung open, she was gasping for breath, tears streaming down her face. She sat up stiffly against the headboard, clutching the sheet around her and blinking her eyes rapidly, as if she wasn't yet sure where she was. Without hesitation, Ahmad gathered her into his arms and felt her body collapse gratefully against him. Nina sobbed quietly onto his chest, her tears wetting his bare skin.

"He was going to hurt her," she finally whispered.

180

"Who?" he said softly in her ear. He held her close to him, stroking her hair, then her cheek.

"The little girl. He was going to hurt her."

"Who was going to hurt her, Nina?" Ahmad felt Nina's body convulse into sobs, this time more intense than before. He had never seen a dream have such an effect on a person. He wasn't sure what to do for her, so he just held her and waited.

"Ahmad. All this time I've been having this nightmare, and I never thought to look at his face. So, tonight I didn't focus on what he was holding behind his back. I waited until he reached for his glasses. I watched him take them off his face and . . ." Nina collapsed against him again and just held on.

"Shhh. Hey now." Ahmad held her by both shoulders and leaned away from her for a moment to look into her eyes. "It's okay, Nina. It was just a dream. Nobody's going to hurt anybody. If the little girl was Ebony, well, she'll be with you all day, right? She won't be in any danger."

Nina's face turned to stone and she closed her eyes before she whispered, "It wasn't Ebony."

"It wasn't Ebony?" Ahmad repeated.

Nina's head shook slowly before she whispered, "It was me."

Ahmad didn't know enough about what Nina was going through to really be of any help, but he knew how he felt when he woke up in the middle of the night with the image of Ron Parsons' chest blasted open before his face. How many nights had he awakened on that narrow cot in his cell wishing Chante were there just to lay with him; to hold on to him; to whisper that everything was all right?

He lay down beside Nina on the bed and pulled her closer, held her gently to his chest. "Why do you think it was you?"

Nina held the answer for a time in her throat. She looked up at his face timidly, like she was afraid to let the words spill from her mouth. With a tremble in her lower lip she said, "Ahmad. It wasn't some strange White man at all." She choked back a sob. "It was my daddy. It was my father's face, only all his color was gone. All the pigment was gone and his skin had turned white as snow, and I was terrified of him. I was still terrified, even after I realized it was him. I saw my father's face, his eyes, and I feared him. I *knew* he was going to hurt her ... me ... Oh God. I don't know. I don't know what any of it means. I just want it to stop.''

''It's gonna be okay, Nina,'' Ahmad said, gently wiping her tears with the back of his hand. He said the words like he knew what he was talking about. Like he was telling her what time the sun was scheduled to rise that morning. Like you could set a watch by it.

''It's gonna be okay?'' She smiled softly. The look on her face said she might actually believe him. Ahmad watched her smile broaden until its light spread into her eyes. ''You say that like you know what you're talking about.''

''I do know.'' He kissed her lips gently. ''I don't know why I do, but I know it's gonna be all right.'' Ahmad suddenly realized something he hadn't noticed until that moment. He had been holding this woman for nearly ten minutes, and it didn't occur to him until that moment that beneath the thin sheet covering her she was absolutely naked.

The realization must have hit her at the same time, because she stiffened nervously for a fraction of a second. Then suddenly, Nina relaxed into him. She pressed her body close, until he could feel the soft heat of her through the sheet, warming the length of his own scantily dressed body.

He tasted the sweetness of her on his tongue before he realized that he was kissing her neck, and she arched into him, tugging the sheet away until the softness of her breasts pressed against his bare chest, tempting his mouth away from her throat. His lips and tongue traveled quickly to her waiting nipples, which were hard before he got there. When he suckkissed his way from the left to the right one, Nina let out a soft moan, and that's when the thought occurred to Ahmad. He wanted nothing more than to make love to this woman. Love. It had been too long since he'd known the ecstasy of it. He wanted to savor her. To be savored by her. He wanted to taste her everywhere—every inch of her needed to be explored with his tongue, and then he would enter her. He would make love to her until they both experienced the ecstasy he had lived without for so long ... He'd barely had the chance to wonder if Nina was thinking the same thing when her hands began tugging at the waistband of his boxers, pulling them down past his hips. He slid them off quickly and lay against her naked skin, cradling her head on the inside of his bent arm.

His free hand stroked the back of her head, roamed the length of her back, held her to him. He reveled in the feel of her smooth heat against his flesh, and his pelvis began rocking slowly against her. Without entering her, his erection found a warm refuge against the soft skin between Nina's thighs and as he kissed her, he tantalized himself with short quick strokes that in the past would have been mere foreplay. But that was five years ago, and in his rapt desire, he'd forgotten what that much time could do to a man's stamina.

Before he even felt the rush of adrenaline that used to come early, to warn him before it was too late, Ahmad's groin jerked forward in a tight cramp, and a stream of fluid escaped onto Nina's skin. *Damn.* For a split second he wondered if she would show her disappointment; if she would question his manhood. She didn't. She simply caressed his back with her smooth palm and planted a kiss against his neck. "How long ago since . . ."

"Five years, three months, four days, and six hours."

"Well, maybe we'll get an opportunity to try this again." Nina's eyes sparkled mischievously at him. "Only we won't wait that long."

Ahmad smiled back at her, but didn't say a word. Instead he got up from the bed and went into the bathroom, turning the bathwater on full blast. He twisted the crystal knob until the water was just the right temperature.

When he returned to the bedroom, Nina was lying on her back with her eyes closed. In one fluid motion Ahmad lifted her from the bed, carried her to the bathroom, and, kneeling on the plush bath rug, placed her gently into the tub. Nina had a look of absolute disbelief on her face but she didn't say a word. When he softly rubbed the waterlogged washcloth across her breasts, down the length of her legs to her feet, and back up between her thighs, Nina's head tilted back against the tub, and she let out the tiniest moan of pleasure.

Only after he'd caressed every exposed inch did Ahmad step into the tub. He stood over Nina, pausing to drink in the sight of her before reaching to pull her up by both arms. When she

was standing, he turned her gently to face the wall. He reached
again for the cloth and squeezed it softly at the nape of her
neck, releasing the warm water to run like a tiny waterfall
down the arch of her spine. Ahmad traced the trail of water
with his tongue, stopping at the crack of her behind for a split
second, only to drop to his knees right there in the tub. He
hadn't planned it that way; he was heading for something a
little more traditional. At least something on the bed. But Nina
was moaning at his every touch now, and there was no thought
in his mind that didn't have something to do with bringing her
pleasure. He whispered to her to turn around, and Nina wordlessly obeyed. When his tongue slipped into the wetness between her thighs, she moaned as if in pain, her legs trembling
against him. Ahmad finally stood and lifted her gracefully with
his strong arms until she straddled him, her legs wrapped
around him and her ankles locked at the base of his spine. He
was hard again, and he felt her hot and wet against him, and
dangerously close to drawing him inside her. But no, he wasn't
ready for that. He wasn't finished with her yet.

Wait. The voice was still there. And Nina just wanted to
tell it to shut the fuck up. Ahmad was carrying her toward the
bed, and Nina felt his rigid flesh pressed *mmnh* so close
against her. He was a fraction of an inch from entering her,
and if that happened, there would be no turning back. There
was nothing in the world she wanted more at that moment
than to have him inside her, and if he slipped in, she would
pull him in deeper and wouldn't let him go until they'd both
climaxed and . . . *Wait. Nina, you cannot let him inside you
without a condom. Shit.* She was always so careful. Even with
Derrick. *Humph. Especially with Derrick.* But she didn't want
to think about being careful now. *Not now.* Ahmad had carried
her, still dripping wet, into the bedroom, and lay Nina on the
bed on her back. He was on his knees between her legs, his
lips and tongue playing against her inner thighs, teasing her.
She was on fire now, and a battle was on with her inner voice
to let it go this time. *Just this once,* the voice was pleading
with her. *Nothing's gonna happen.* "Ahmad." Did she say
that out loud? *Damn.* "Ahmad."

Ahmad raised his eyes to hers. His eyebrows arched in

amusement, a slight smile across his moistened lips.

"I want to . . . but . . . I can't, Ahmad . . . not without protection."

Ahmad's face disappeared again. This time he didn't tease her. Just as he had kissed her mouth and sent searing waves of passion through every cell in her body, even now, with a tenderness Nina had never felt from any man, he brought her to the edge of ecstasy. And when she became the center of a powerful quake, and the last tremor shook her body, he lay behind her and held her to him, planting the softest kisses on the back of her neck.

△▽ 19 ▽△

Ahmad caught the look of disappointment that flashed across Nina's face but he could see that she was taking the news in stride. Marlene had just walked over to the car to announce harshly that Ebony would be spending the day at the beach with her cousins instead of with Nina as planned. Nina was obviously disappointed, but she smiled right past the frowning Marlene, blew a kiss to Ebony who was seated happily in the van amidst her cousins, and said quietly to Ahmad, "Ebony's with me at the center every day. She should be with her family now."

Ahmad leaned into the driver's side window and planted a bold kiss on Nina's lips. "I'll see you back at the hotel, before I head for the airport?" She nodded and smiled at him, but as Ahmad watched her pull out into the Sunday morning traffic on Florence Avenue, something tugged at his heart. Something sad, like a heavy gloom, settled around him, and if he was a superstitious man, he would've sworn it was some kind of premonition. He felt the urge to run after her, to not let her get away, but instead he raised his arm and waved a good-bye at the disappearing taillights.

Ant was also just pulling off with the van full of kids, leaving Marlene and Ahmad standing side by side in front of the red brick information building just at the entrance of the cemetery. Marlene was nearly overflowing with some intense emotion, and she stood staring at the disappearing van, shaking her head slowly from side to side. It didn't take her long to let Ahmad know the contents of her worried mind.

186

"Look, Ahmad." Her voice was filled with tension, like she'd been winding up this spring since they'd all stood on that sidewalk at LAX. "My sister's not here to take care of Ebony. I recognize that. And I know it's got to be rough on you, you just gettin' out and all. If I had any more room in my tiny house, I'd gladly fill in for Chante—"

Ahmad interrupted her. "Marlene, Ebony and I are doing just fine. You don't need to worry about us."

"Well, I *am* worried," she said abruptly. She turned to face Ahmad, putting one hand on her hip and pointing off in the direction of the disappearing van with the other. "Damn, Ahmad, hasn't that baby been through enough without you lettin' her get all attached to the first pretty face that comes along?"

"Now, hold on just a minute, Marlene . . ." Ahmad was trying to stay calm. Marlene's voice had risen just enough to let him know she was really irked about Nina coming along on this trip, but Ahmad wasn't about to get in a shouting match with the woman outside the busy cemetery office. He glanced at a few mourners who were filing slowly out of the open door and lowered his voice to a near whisper. "Nina is good with Ebony. And Ebony likes her. What's wrong with the child getting as much love and healthy attention as she can?"

Marlene lowered her voice too, only it came out harsh, like a librarian's scolding. "I'll tell you what's wrong. I walked in on your child this morning telling my Jessica how much she wished she was white and pretty like Nina."

Marlene's words pricked Ahmad's heart and it sank in his chest like a deflated balloon. He stared into Marlene's fiery brown eyes for a long, silent moment. A painful throbbing sensation set in at his temples. "She said that?" he muttered in sad disbelief.

Marlene's tone softened a little. "Yeah. Right before she said, 'I wish Nina could be my mama.' "

Ahmad let out a weary sigh. He had feared Nina's white skin for all the wrong reasons. Nina's skin. *Mmnh.* He had awakened that morning reveling in his nearness to it. The sweet smell of her next to him and the warmth and soft smoothness of her felt so much like everything he was missing. Everything he wished he could come home to after long days at work and long nights at school. He lay there in Nina's arms only a couple of hours earlier, and had seriously considered putting his guard all the way down to let the woman in. His worries about her skin tone had melted into nonexistence in the heat of that early morning tenderness they'd shared, and he knew then that he'd been tripping over absolutely nothing. He couldn't care less what anyone thought about his feelings for her. She was a sista he could be proud to be with, and he didn't give a damn what color her skin was. Until now. Until the words that had just dripped out of Marlene's mouth ran like sludge to muddy his only recently clear waters. All that time he'd been afraid for himself. It never occurred to him that he should be afraid for Ebony.

Marlene wasn't finished. "I just think the baby's been through enough. My sister was sick with that crack shit, then Mama goes to the hospital. Who knows when she'll be well enough even to recognize her grandkids again. Now you got this child all sprung dumb on a White woman who may or may not be around for a minute. And what if she is around, Ahmad? Is Ebony gonna be sixteen, tryin' to bleach her skin and get her some blue contacts?"

"Nina's not White," Ahmad muttered.

Marlene hesitated for a split second, like she was just a little punch-drunk from Ahmad's quiet words. But she recovered quickly. "I don't care if she's Puerto Rican, Jamaican, Indian, *and* Chinese. The sista look White. And Ebony's watchin' you, Ahmad. You all she got. And she seein' you sniffin' all up behind what she ain't nevva gon' be. You ever tried convincing a little brown five-year-old that they skin look just fine the way it is? Ever had to explain why it ain't nobody in the movies . . . at least nobody they wanna be like . . . ever look like them? Ever tried tellin' 'em why they hair ain't nevva gone cascade down to they butt lest they buy it that way?" Marlene poked an airbrushed acrylic nail up into the huge knot of synthetic hair on top of her head, adjusting the already perfect bun. "I love that baby girl like she was my own, Ahmad. Please don't let her grow up hatin' what she is."

Marlene waited for the comeback. It never came. She felt the weight of Ahmad's silence, and looked sorry for a split second. Sorry that she'd expected a fight from him and got only a worried silence in return. She said softly, "I—I'm not tryin' to get all in your business. I just thought you should know. I know you doin' the best you can."

Ahmad muttered a troubled "Thank you" to Marlene and started toward the office door. "I'll think about what you said." He would. He had to. But for now, it was time to do what they'd come there for. It was time to bury Chante.

"Somebody went all out," Ahmad heard Marlene whisper. He nodded in agreement, thinking to himself that someone did indeed go all out on the funeral arrangements. But whoever that person was, they were nowhere in sight. A serious-faced minister in a black suit and collar, and a portly sista standing solemnly at his side, had already made it known that they were hired by the mortuary and had no idea who was responsible for the cost. Ahmad and Marlene were the only other people standing beneath the tarpaulin covering meant to shade the funeral patrons from the blazing August sun. There were a dozen or so metal folding chairs decoratively hooded in forest green rayon, but the chairs could only have been put there for effect, seeing as how there were no people there to fill them. Two huge vases overflowed with dozens of red and white long-stemmed roses, and a huge blanket of white carnations draped the onyx coffin which had been carried to the gravesite by six broad-shouldered pallbearers Ahmad didn't recognize. Judging by the shrug he got from Marlene after the young men set the coffin down and walked away, she didn't recognize the pallbearers either. The meticulously staged scene had been arranged atop a thirty-by-thirty-foot square of forest green carpet in which a neat four-by-eight-foot rectangle had been cut to leave the unearthed grave gaping in the middle of it. On the other side of the pit, a single microphone stood in front of two speakers.

The portly sista suddenly left her position next to the reverend and waddled over to the mike. She smiled serenely from beneath a thin veil of black net that draped forward across her face from a stylish gray hat perched atop her pressed-and-curled shoulder-length hair. It wasn't until then that Ahmad and Marlene realized—now that the sista had moved—she had been blocking their view of a portrait-sized, easel-mounted photograph of Chante. It was a larger version of the same picture that was on the program. Chante on a golden merry-go-round horse. She looked genuinely happy and radiantly beautiful. The sight of Chante's beaming smile sent a twinge of pain through Ahmad's chest. The knowledge that what remained of his wife was lying in that shiny black box a few feet away seemed impossible; like a reality that was just out of his reach. He heard a sniffle from Marlene, and turned to see tears falling down her cheeks, smearing her mascara into two gray pools under her eyes.

The sista behind the microphone closed her eyes. She cleared her throat to let Ahmad and Marlene know they should be seated. They sat in adjoining chairs and watched the woman ready herself to play her part in this well-planned affair. She tilted her head back, and unaccompanied by any music, began singing an old Temprees' song in a crystal-clear voice.

Dedicated to the One I Love. Ahmad and Marlene stared at one another in disbelief. The two of them knew that was Chante's favorite song. Chante would play the damn song over and over until Ahmad thought he'd go crazy. Every time she started the record again, Ahamd would cover his ears and tease his wife about reaching way back before her time for some oldie but goodie music she was too young to know anything about. Anybody close to Chante would know that song, but that could only include himself, Marlene, Mrs. Taylor, Scotty. But who else could . . . ? Ahmad's head swung around and his eyes roamed the hilly green expanse of Inglewood cemetery. There were at least three other graveside services being performed over on the Manchester Avenue side, but there wasn't a soul out of place anywhere nearby. Ahmad heard Marlene begin to make soft sobbing sounds, and he instinctively reached his arm around her shoulder to comfort her, still scanning the area for signs of movement.

The singer was really feeling it now. Her voice rose and fell in sharp punctuating gales that sounded as if she was sending up her own heartfelt version of a prayer to heaven.

Ahmad couldn't put his finger on it, but something about all of this was really bothering him. He was suddenly sorry he'd come. He didn't need all this to say good-bye to his wife.

What he needed was to be alone with her. To come back here when all this pageantry was over with. If he hadn't been dropped off by Nina, if the rental car was parked over where that long black limo across the road was parked, he'd get in it and get out of there fast. Get out from under the suffocating cloud that had suddenly overtaken him. The cloud that was interfering with his right to mourn his wife properly. He scanned the cemetery again. Not a soul. Finally, he recognized the tension he felt. It was the same strange feeling he'd had that day outside his apartment before Netty called him over to get the package. Ahmad felt his neck muscles tighten, pulling his shoulder blades into knots. *Someone is watching this,* he thought. *Watching me.*

He looked again at the black stretch limousine parked forty feet or so from where they stood. Its motor was running, probably keeping it an air-conditioned cool for whoever would be returning to it after saying good-bye to their loved one. Or maybe someone was sitting in it. Maybe someone was watching his every move from inside that very car. *Who would be watching from a limo?* Suddenly, it all began to fall into place in his head and a boiling rage began simmering in his gut. In the calmest voice he could find he said to Marlene, ''Don't move. I have to go now. You all go on without me.'' Before he knew what he was doing, he was on his feet and running like a madman toward the idling limo. He covered the forty feet in a few seconds. Just as he neared the car, he watched as a window in the back slid slowly closed, but not before he got a glimpse of a white woman with blonde hair and tortoise-shell sunglasses. It was her.

''How could you come here?'' he screamed at the closed window, beating on it with his fists. He wanted to break it, break the neck of the devil behind it. ''You killed my wife! You killed Chante!'' The anger he had bottled up for five long years erupted into a crazed rage and Ahmad scrambled around the car, pulling at the door handles and beating on the hood, the top of the car, the trunk. ''You killed Chante!'' he repeated over and over, screaming with so much venom, his voice finally gave out. When it quieted to a raspy whisper he was still repeating the words, ''You killed her, you killed Chante.'' Ahmad finally collapsed against the limousine's hood, and buried his face in his crossed arms. When he was completely quiet and absolutely still, one of the limousine doors finally opened. A black-suited, sunglass-wearing White man emerged from it and called Ahmad to come over. Ahmad didn't raise his head.

"Theodore, please," the driver called again. "It would be so much easier on everyone if you would cooperate. Please get in the car."

Ahmad straightened. Wordlessly, he walked to the open door. He knew he had to speak to her. He had to free himself from the questions that burned in his soul. Questions that tormented him through his days and visited him in the middle of the night, nearly every night for the last five years. Questions he'd given up on finding any rational answers for. At this point, he'd take whatever answers he could get. With a tired sigh of surrender, Ahmad stepped in front of the limo driver, slid into the coolness of the air-conditioned limousine, and faced his dragon.

She looked like shit. She seemed to have aged twenty years and then some since that day in court when she couldn't look at him. And she could barely look at him now. Her blue eyes were puffy and red, and they seemed reluctant to spend too much time in one place. When they did finally settle on Ahmad's own eyes, he just glared at her. All the angry venom he'd felt just a few minutes before had mostly dissipated into numb exhaustion and left him with only a smoldering look of hatred behind his eyes.

"Theo, I know you must hate me. And I don't blame you." Her voice reflected a dull sorrow. She sounded as numb as he felt.

"Don't call me Theo," Ahmad quickly interjected. "Theodore Jefferson died in prison. My name's Ahmad. And yes, you made sure I had every reason to hate you." Ahmad didn't blink. "And if you're here to ask me to forgive you for what you did to me and my family, you're wasting your time."

She was quiet. She raised a trembling hand to smooth her gray-tinged blonde hair back behind her ear. When she turned to look out of the tinted window toward Chante's gravesite, Ahmad's eyes followed hers. They could both see Marlene, still seated, being comforted by the minister and the singer who were now seated on either side of her.

"I've caused more pain than I can ever be forgiven for," Beth began. She looked down at her hands. Every nail was bitten down to the fingertip. Finally she looked up at Ahmad. "I can't be forgiven, son," she said matter-of-factly. "That's not why I'm here."

The sound of the word "son" was like a heavy mallet landing with a distant thud somewhere in Ahmad's heart where Beth used to be. "Why *are* you here, Beth?" He growled the words at her angrily.

"When I found out about Chante ..." Her eyes glazed over, but not a drop fell from them. "Scotty didn't want a funeral, you know. Before he killed himself he called me and told me all about his plan. He said if he went off the cliff at top speed, he figured he would just sink to the bottom of the ocean and never be found. He made me promise I'd have him cremated if they discovered the car, and that I'd scatter his ashes where they could be washed away. All he wanted was to be washed away. He made me promise." Beth closed her eyes. Ahmad watched her sullen face. The skin that used to glow from weekly facials and expensive anti-wrinkle creams was now leathery and cracked. Where high, fashion-model cheekbones and a dimpled smile used to be were two sunken caves of drooping skin, and a permanent frown.

"The lawyers told me Scotty would never survive prison. He was so slight, so thin. They said he'd be raped the first night in, and he was sure to be some man's slave for years. He'd be lucky to come out alive. Scotty was the last Maxwell son, you know. Bert had all girls and Reginald's son Chris died of leukemia."

Why on earth was she telling Ahmad all this shit he already knew? Of course he knew Chris died of leukemia. Hell, he was the one who stayed up all night in the hospital with Beth while she cried onto his seventeen-year-old shoulder.

"I was against it from the start, Ahmad. You have to know that. And so was Scotty. But he was scared. He was more scared than I'd ever seen him. Grandfather Maxwell and his pit bull lawyers with their visions of rape and torture. They said no one would mess with Theo. 'He's tall and strong.'

Being Black would keep you safe if you did go to prison is what they said.''

Ahmad glared at Beth. Her eyes gazed lifelessly into his.

"They convinced Scotty that you wouldn't get more than two or three years for the involuntary manslaughter, and that with your squeaky-clean record, you'd never serve a day in prison. We believed them, Theo . . . Ahmad. God help us, we believed them, son.''

"I'm not your son. Never was.'' Ahmad wanted to hurt her. He wanted her to feel the venom he'd stored for her over five long years of sleepless prison nights.

Beth made a tiny choking sound in the back of her throat. "I kept quiet. I could have spoken up for you, I know, but I kept quiet. Even after I heard the judge say nine years. I thought somehow it could all turn out right. I—I knew Scotty was guilty. I knew you'd never have anything to do with those crimes you'd been accused of. I kept quiet. I let them send one of my sons to prison and the other one . . . I might as well have pushed the car over the cliff myself.''

Ahmad didn't say a word. He wasn't going to help this woman feel better about what she'd done to him, and he knew there was nothing he could say to make her feel any worse. So he stared at her in silence.

Beth looked back over at Chante's coffin. "I tried to help her while you were away, you know. I tried to give her money, but your mother-in-law let me know that I was only helping her buy drugs. It seemed like nothing I did turned out right. I made Scotty promise to stay away from her, though. I did that. I knew all about those two. They'd been doing that crack stuff together long before you met her, you know. I told him I'd give him whatever he wanted if he'd stay away from your family. We'd already done enough damage . . .''

Her words finally sunk in. "What do you mean they'd been doing crack before we met? What are you talking about, Beth?''

"Honey, Scotty was supplying Chante with drugs the whole time you were married, and long before that. You and Chante meeting at USC wasn't by chance, you know.''

"That's crazy. I introduced Scotty to Chante. Why are you

saying they knew each other before?'' He hated that Beth had
something he wanted. But she did.

''Scotty made plans to make a delivery to Chante that day.
He was supposed to meet her outside the entrance to the gymnasium, and meet you there an hour later, only he was late
showing up. He never planned for you to get there first, but
you did . . . and . . . well, the rest is history.''

Ahmad closed his eyes and sank into the darkness of a
memory he wished he didn't have. A memory of the day he'd
''introduced'' Scotty to the beautiful girl who'd asked him out
within the first ten minutes of their conversation. Ahmad had
instantly recognized something that looked like discomfort in
both of their expressions, but he had chalked it up to a little
healthy rivalry on Scotty's part, and maybe some kind of
White-boy phobia for Chante. The discomfort wasn't there
long. They all got along like best friends in no time.

''What else do you know?''

''Scotty told me everything. Everything.''

Ahmad was getting impatient. ''What do you mean, everything, Beth?'' His voice rose with anger, and the burly driver
seated next to Ahmad scooted forward in his seat, in case
Ahmad got any ideas of hurting the woman. But hurting her
was the furthest thing from his mind.

''Chante tried to quit, you know. While she was pregnant
with your daughter. But Scotty never did. We finally stopped
sending him money. We thought it would make him take responsibility for his future. You know? Make him step up to
the plate. But it only made him turn to crime. He started sell-
ing the drugs heavy. After your daughter was born, Chante
went back to the drugs too. While you were at school . . .
work, Scotty and Chante would be at your apartment. Scotty
told me so just before he died.''

''I don't believe you.'' Ahmad turned to look out the window. He believed her. He didn't want to. He never wanted to
believe Chante was doing anything harder than the marijuana
she said she only did ''occasionally'' but he always wondered.
Always had a nagging doubt in the back of his mind.

Beth was quiet. After a few moments she whispered, ''Your
wife never put any furniture on layaway, son.''

Ahmad leaned forward between his knees with his head in

his hands and fought the tears. He wanted nothing more than
to lapse into some kind of coma. If he'd had a million years
to prepare for it, it wouldn't have made a bit of difference.
There was no way he'd have been any more ready to hear the
words Beth Maxwell had just spoken. Chante and Scotty. How
could he have been so blind? Toward the end she was always
asking for money. A few hundred at a time. She'd say it was
for the furniture. To pay the layaway installments. *Goddammit.*
Beth was telling the truth. *What a sucker.* He couldn't choose
a trustworthy loved one if he tried, could he? First Scotty, then
Chante, and finally Beth. They'd all betrayed his trust. They'd
all taken him. His so-called marriage was a sham, just like his
so-called family before it. The only bright spot in any of it
was the daughter he and Chante had produced. Ebony was the
only sure thing he had. When Ahmad finally raised his face
from his hands, and looked up, Beth was holding a white envelope out to him.

"Please don't refuse this, Th—Ahmad. If you don't want
it, if you don't want Ebony to one day have it, then find a
charity, any charity. Just . . . please take it. Please."

Ahmad stared at the envelope for a long moment.

Beth finally began to cry. She looked as if she had been
doing nothing but crying forever. He felt a sharp twinge of
pity for her, and he heard himself offer a silent prayer: *God,
help her.* As if she'd heard it too, she stopped crying as suddenly as she'd started, cleared her throat, and spoke to Ahmad
in a trembling voice. "I know I stole your life from you. Your
education. I took your potential to provide for your daughter.
I took it. I won't say I'm sorry. Those are empty words to
you, I know. Please take this. Please. Ebony deserves it."

Ahmad finally reached for the envelope. He didn't take his
eyes off Beth as he grasped the thin piece of paper inside.
When he pulled it halfway out of the envelope, he glanced
down, peeping just enough of it to let him know it was a
check. When his eyes fell on the figure, he didn't say a word.
He turned his head to stare out the window in silence.

"Scotty's life insurance. I know it isn't enough," she said.
"It could never be enough. But I can't keep it. I'd never spend
a dime of it. I sincerely hope you will."

Ahmad fought the urge to tear Beth's offering into a thousand pieces, and folded the envelope in half instead. He stuffed it into his back pocket, and without a word to Beth, he pulled the door handle, stepped out of the limousine, and left Beth, Scotty, and, yes, even Chante, in the past.

△▽ 20 ▽△

Nina swallowed hard, choking back the urge she felt to say out loud what was in her head. *Mmmph. Why in the hell didn't I see this coming?* She didn't say a word, and instead just gazed out the passenger-side window at the thirsty browns and beiges of the Arizona scenery whizzing past.

Ahmad was staring straight ahead, gripping the wheel of Nina's car tightly as he navigated the Monday afternoon traffic back to Glendale. He had driven Nina's car home from the airport Sunday and returned to pick Nina up as planned, but their reunion wasn't quite what she'd imagined. Her lonely flight back from L.A. had seemed to last forever, and Nina spent most of it occupying herself with memories of waking to the warmth of Ahmad's embrace and thoughts of being in his arms again. But when he greeted her at baggage claim, all she got from him was a stiff hug, no kiss, and a strained look of discomfort that suggested she might want to stand back a foot or two. She wanted to ask him why he left the hotel without saying good-bye. She wondered whether he learned who had sent the envelope to him, and she wanted to know where Ebony was, but his strange attitude made her keep an awkward distance from him all the way to the car. Now here he was, driving along the stretch of I-30 that would get them to Glendale, telling her that what they'd shared in L.A. was a mistake.

"It's not you, Nina." He maneuvered around a slow-moving station wagon that was moseying along in the fast lane, and glanced over his shoulder to ease the car back over to the left. He still hadn't looked at her.

Nina kept her eyes glued to the road ahead. She wasn't about to look at him either. She didn't want to see those dark eyes that had sent shivers through her with just a glance, or the lips that had melted her with so many tender kisses. The man who only a day ago had bathed every inch of her body had just informed her that he needed to not "see" her anymore. He wasn't ready for a relationship, and he hoped she wouldn't be too angry with him if she didn't see him at all for a few weeks. Well, he'd have better luck hoping for world peace, 'cause she was beyond angry. She was through. *Damn, Nina, you sure know how to pick 'em. First Derrick, now this? Well, shit, I just kicked a fiancé to the curb. This ought to be a hell of a lot easier than that. I'm just glad I didn't let the man all up inside my body. What kind of fool would I be feeling like right now?*

"I just realized it." His voice was calm and quiet, which was actually pissing her off more. The least he could do was sound a little nervous or unsure. "It's not that I don't really like you . . ." He finally snuck a quick look in Nina's direction before returning to the straight-ahead stare. ". . . because I do. Really. It's just that I . . ."

"Look, Ahmad." Nina turned to look straight at him. "You don't owe me anything. We let things get a little out of hand. It's no biggie. If you want to forget about it . . . let's forget about it." She tried to sound convincing.

Ahmad finally made eye contact. "I don't regret what happened between us, Nina. It's not that." The look in his eyes said he might be telling the truth. "I'm not trying to forget about it, either. I'm just not ready for anything like this. I can't do a relationship, and I can already see that you and I . . . Well, I just need to concentrate on Ebony. My daughter really needs me right now."

Nina had nothing to say. What *could* she say? They never talked about "doing a relationship" anyway. True, she had assumed that that's exactly what they were headed for—after the intimacy they'd shared—but it wasn't like she was trying to tie the man down or anything. He was the one that had awakened Sunday morning talking about how glad he was that

Nina had come to L.A. with him. He was the one that ran his hands along her naked skin, humming soft "Mmmms" in her ear. If they hadn't slept so late, and if he didn't have to hurry to get to the cemetery, his ass would've been at 7-Eleven picking up some condoms, and there would have been some serious lovemaking going on in that hotel room. It was a major accomplishment just to get Ahmad to go to his room to shower and dress, and to get him to the cemetery gate in time for the service. The cemetery. *Something happened at that funeral.* That was the only explanation Nina could find for this sudden change in Ahmad. *This has something to do with his wife.*

They rode in silence for a long while until Ahmad finally spoke again. "I'm sorry about checking out of the hotel without saying good-bye. And I hope you don't mind that I paid your hotel bill. It was the least I could do."

The least he could do? What the hell was that supposed to mean? She fought the urge to tell him to go straight to hell, and take his apologies with him; she didn't want to give him the satisfaction of knowing how deeply affected she was by his rejection. If he could sit there all calm, cool, and collected, she'd have to try her damnedest to do the same. She managed a weak "Don't sweat it," before the silence enveloped them again.

When they finally arrived at Ahmad's apartment, he pulled into the crumbling cement driveway behind the Volvo and cut the engine. Turning to face Nina he said, "I'm not sure how to say this . . ."

Nina held her breath. Shit, he didn't seem to have too much trouble spitting out any of the last few sentences. What on earth did he want to say that could be more difficult than what had already been said?

"I left Ebony at Saundra's today. She'll be there tomorrow too."

"What?" Nina looked at him like he was crazy. After all that "I can't do a relationship" shit, this fool wasn't trying to get her to come in his apartment, was he? *Ugh.*

"I left her at Saundra's because I'm worried about Ebony spending so much time with you, Nina."

Nina just looked at him. The raw pain of his words burned her eyes like freshly sprayed Mace, and she fought to hold back the tears that were welling up behind them. *He's worried about Ebony? What the hell would I do to Ebony?*

"I mean . . . I can't afford to do anything that might hurt my daughter."

The reality of what Ahmad was trying to say to her finally sunk in. *He's protecting her from me.* The baby had just lost her mama and her grandmother. He didn't want his child to get attached to Nina. The concern he had for Ebony, and the look of pain on Ahmad's face, only made him more attractive. Nina could hardly bear to look at him.

"I understand." She cleared her throat and did her best to sound businesslike. "With classes starting I will actually be spending less time at the center from now on. Tonya will be the lead staff person, and there are four other employees who provide the direct care for the children. I might see Ebony once in a while, but it won't be anything like it was last week."

"I appreciate you being so understanding." Ahmad's voice wavered slightly, like maybe this wasn't as easy for him as he was trying to make it seem. "I hope we can still be friends."

They both sat in silence. Finally, Nina pulled the door handle and walked around to the driver's side of the Honda. Ahmad got out too, and stood with his hand held out to Nina. "Friends?"

She put her hand limply in his, and he squeezed it gently, his smooth palm only serving as a painful reminder of the way his hands had felt against her skin the day before.

"Friends," was all Nina could say. She didn't look at him. Managing a half-smile, she released his hand and slid behind the wheel of her car. As she turned the ignition, she hurriedly wiped a stray tear from her cheek that had somehow escaped her eye. When she'd eased the car into reverse, and backed out of the driveway and into the street, she hesitated for a moment to watch as Ahmad walked slowly toward his front door. An overwhelming feeling of dread washed over her— something sad, like a heavy gloom, sat on her chest—and Nina felt a strange urge to stop him—to not let him walk away from her. Instead, she slid the gearshift to drive, headed toward home, and didn't look back.

*   *   *

Nina took another sip of coffee and winced at Tonya. "Girl, all I know is I'm glad I didn't let that man all up inside my body."

Tonya nodded in agreement. "You know that's right."

Nina raised the cup to her lips again. *What difference does that make now? He's all up inside my head . . . and my heart.* She put the mug down a little harder than she'd intended, and barely noticed as coffee sloshed out on to the table. "Ugh. I could just kick myself, T, for being so gotdamned stupid. I know better. You know I know better."

Tonya got up and walked into the kitchen, yanked a paper towel from the roll on the counter, and walked back over to Nina to hand it to her. When Nina grasped it, Tonya held on to her end of it as she raised one eyebrow at her friend. "Sometimes the recipe for knowin' better turns out more like a dinner of doin' it any damn way."

Nina yanked the towel from her. If this was T's attempt at being supportive, she was going to have to work a little bit harder at it. "Thanks, T, that really makes me feel better," Nina responded sarcastically.

"Aw, girl, you know I'm just messin' witcha." Tonya chuckled, then looked at her seriously. "I do want to know one thing, though."

"What's that?"

"Was the dinner delicious?" She laughed.

Nina was trying not to laugh, but she had to join in. "Hmmm, the way it went down," she quipped, "you should be asking Ahmad that question."

"The way it went down, huh?" Tonya's laughter was ringing now. "You mean the way *he* went down, don't you?"

Nina laughed a little harder too. When silence settled down around them, Tonya asked, "Girl, did the man really bathe you?" She shook her head in disbelief.

"Yep."

"And he let you see him cry?"

"Yep."

"It ain't over." Tonya raised a knowing brow.

Nina wanted to cross both her fingers, blow out some candles, toss a coin in a fountain, wish on a twinkling little star, and pray to God that Tonya had some kind of psychic soul connection. "What makes you say that?" She managed to sound nonchalant.

"Please," Tonya moaned. "The man is sprung. He just ain't admitting it to himself yet. He probably really is worried about Ebony, but I think he's just using his daughter as an excuse to protect his own damn self."

"If that's the case then it *is* over." It needed to be. The man was trouble. Damaged goods. Shit, he just got out of prison for killing a man, and he was still in love with a dead woman. He was dealing with too much loss to be emotionally reliable. She needed to just move on to the next one and learn her lesson from this one. "I learned my lesson, T. First Derrick with his lying ass. Now this little one-night stand with a smooth operator? I'm just going to be celibate from now on. No sex for nobody. I gave up too much too soon. I swear, T, the minute you get intimate with a brotha they wanna start trippin'."

"Girl, that's why I made Rasheed wait so long." She shook her head at Nina. "But I don't think that's it, Nina. Not this time."

Tonya's confident tone was intriguing. "Why do you say that?"

"Ahmad wasn't just trying to get some."

"Okay, Dr. DeMontaña, how do you know that?"

"He told Rasheed he would never consider dating you."

Nina's face fell. "What? When did he say that?"

"At the party. He told Rasheed he could never date you. He said he thought you were attractive, and intelligent and a nice person and all, but that it was really unfortunate that your skin had no trace of melanin in it. He said you weren't and never would be his type."

Tonya's comment stung. If Nina would never be his type, then why did the man fall asleep in her bed with his arms all wrapped around her? He must have just been taking advantage of a convenient opportunity to get him a little piece of ass, seeing as how he'd gone without it for so long. How could she have been so wrong about the man's intentions, when he seemed so sincere? Nina could feel the heat rising in her face. "T, you are really not making any sense. So, how do you come to the conclusion that it ain't over? Shit, if he really did say all that, that's a good reason why it really *is* over. Or that it needs to be."

"Nina. The man wasn't attracted to you initially, right?"

"Definitely. I practically had to hit him over the head with an 'I want you stick' to get him to notice me."

"And when did he finally begin to show signs that he was feeling something?"

Nina thought about it. "I think it sort of began when we were together in the cloakroom that day. When he found me mothering his child. But come to think of it . . . it was really the day we spent out at Santa Monica when something clicked. I could feel him change. The way he looked at me. The electricity between us. It started there, and just kept getting deeper."

"I'll bet my next paycheck that's because it finally hit him that you got it goin' on on the inside. He fell in love with the inside of you, girl, and he's scared of you. He let that melanin thing go with a quickness. But he's scared of something."

"Like?"

"Hell if I know. But that's not for you to worry about. There's nothing you can do but leave him alone and hope he deals with it before you finally move on to someone else."

"Hope he deals with it before I finally move on? It sounds like you think I should wait." Nina heard the Luther lyrics in her head again.

"I'm saying it ain't over." Tonya was as serious as Nina had ever seen her. "It ain't over, Nina. But you need to be careful. He needs to be the one to come back for you. He broke it. Now, let him think it's beyond repair. When he realizes how valuable it is to him, he'll try to figure out a way to fix it."

"Please. I'm not about to hold my breath for that day." Nina rolled her eyes.

Tonya winked at her and grinned. "That's the spirit, girl-friend. Now you got the right attitude. Make the brotha believe he doesn't have a chance in hell."

Nina remembered the anticipation she felt when she walked up the airplane ramp expecting to be in Ahmad's arms again, and the way her heart dropped when he wasn't there at the gate waiting for her. And at baggage claim, when he barely even hugged her? And then he let her sit in silence in the car for at least fifteen minutes trying to figure out what she could have done to make him act so distant . . . The way she'd been treated was just plain cruel. After all that passion and ecstasy from the morning before, Ahmad acted like it wasn't going to phase him a bit to not see Nina anymore. *What kind of heartless shit is that?* She wouldn't have to work too hard to make the brotha believe he didn't have a chance in hell. The reality was, the way she was feeling about what he'd done, she wasn't sure he did have a chance. As a matter of fact, the more she thought about the roller-coaster ride Ahmad had taken her on over the last couple of days, the angrier she felt. ''Make him feel like he doesn't have a chance in hell, huh?'' Nina smirked at Tonya. ''Humph. Well, girlfriend, that really shouldn't be too hard.''

△▽ 21 ▽△

Dr. Webb reached forward to hand Nina the box of Kleenex. She pulled a few sheets from the box and dabbed at the drops that had leaked from her eyes.

"I did what you suggested, Dr. Webb. I focused on his face and . . ." Nina closed her eyes and sat in silence, recalling that awful moment in the nightmare just before Ahmad had shaken her awake. The white-faced man she had been so terrified of was not a faceless stranger at all, but her own father. *What possible meaning could there be in that?* If the dream did carry some message that she was supposed to be able to decipher, she just wasn't getting it. Nina opened her eyes suddenly and found Dr. Webb's warm brown eyes staring directly into hers.

"You focused on the man's face, and . . . ?" Dr. Webb prodded.

"The man I've been so terrified of all this time . . ." She took in a labored breath and pushed the reluctant words off her tongue. ". . . was my father." More tears dropped from her eyes, and she wiped them away quickly. "His face was as white as . . . as white as mine. But . . . those were Daddy's eyes. And his . . ." Nina lifted a hand to her chin and pressed her palm softly against it. ". . . our chin." She shot a nervous smile at the doctor before continuing. "But he looked strange. Not strange really. Different, you know? But it was my father. I knew, and . . ." Nina didn't want to let the words she was thinking come out of her mouth. She held them until the silence was unbearable. Finally, she finished the sentence. "I knew it was my father and I was still terrified of him, Dr.

206

Webb. I was so terrified of what he was going to do to me."

Dr. Webb raised his eyebrows into two questioning arches. Nina answered his question before he could ask it. "I know. I said me. I know. I think the little girl . . ." She looked into Dr. Webb's eyes and held his concerned stare. "No, I *know* the little girl in the dream is me."

The doctor didn't say a word.

"I guess I knew before, but . . . I—I didn't want to admit it to myself."

Dr. Webb nodded at Nina, as if he were praising her for finally admitting something he'd already thought was true.

"A part of me wanted to believe she was someone else." Nina thought of Ahmad, and that moment of freedom she'd felt when he mentioned taking Ebony along to her mother's funeral. How relieved she had been to think the dream could have an explanation. That the whole tormenting ordeal might end with Nina protecting Ebony was something Nina needed to believe.

"As crazy as it sounds, I wanted to believe I'd somehow been 'chosen' to protect someone else's child from some avoidable doom. But deep down . . ." Nina stopped talking. Two tiny streams made their way from the corners of her eyes and she didn't even attempt to dry them. "I knew who that little girl was. Standing all alone. So naïve, so unaware. She never even knew she had something to fear. I felt her, you know?" Dr. Webb nodded and sent Nina a comforting smile. Nina twisted her wet Kleenex into a tight string. "I just hate that I'm so afraid of this thing. I want to understand. If the stranger isn't a stranger at all . . . why am I still so afraid of him?"

Dr. Webb rose from the suede love seat and walked over to the window. He removed his "Just Do It" cap from his head and ran his hand through his wavy brown hair. He was quiet for what seemed like too long. Finally, looking directly into Nina's eyes, he said, "Did your father ever do anything to hurt you when you were a little girl?" His words were coated with smooth nonchalance, but to Nina they sounded harsh and accusatory.

Maybe he didn't mean for that question to sound so loaded. He wasn't accusing Daddy of anything. He just had to explore

that possibility, didn't he? To venture down all the avenues a
therapist was trained to explore. But to Nina the question was
just plain unnecessary. Of course her father had never done
anything to hurt her. He'd saved her, hadn't he? He'd come
to her rescue when the woman who'd given birth to her left
her alone.

"Daddy? No. Never." Nina knew she'd said it with a little
too much passion. She closed her eyes and let out a tired little
breath that said she was hoping the doctor wouldn't spend too
much time fishing there. She wanted Dr. Webb to move on to
another subject now. Her daddy was the best. He was her
protector and her model of a good man. He loved her, and
that was that. *He's hurting me now*. The thought entered her
mind in a near shout, but she didn't dare say it aloud. She
shifted uncomfortably in her seat, twisting away at the shred-
ded Kleenex. The reality was, her father was hurting her in a
way no one else could. The pain she was in—not knowing
where she'd come from, *who* she'd come from, was gnawing
away at her more each day.

"He's hurting you now, though, isn't he, Nina?" Dr. Webb
shot a look of compassion at Nina that softened his words just
enough for her to be willing to acknowledge them.

Nina nodded her head slowly, as more tears spilled out onto
her cheeks. "It's just like in the dream. He's holding something behind his back. He *is* hiding something from me, Dr.
Webb. He's hiding the truth. And I'm so afraid of what that
might turn out to be."

"But you do want to know, don't you?"

Nina nodded. "I went to L.A. this weekend hoping to find
out. But . . ." She sighed a long, loud sigh of disappointment.

Dr. Webb waited.

Nina told him about the key Mama had led her to. She
explained her reason for the weekend trip to L.A., leaving out
the romantic interlude she and Ahmad had shared. She wasn't
ready to talk about that.

"So, what did you find in the safe deposit box?" Dr. Webb
asked.

Nina answered him in nearly the same bland tone the bank
manager had used to explain to her why she couldn't retrieve

the contents of the box when she'd gone to the bank early that morning.

"Since there was no activity with the box in over twenty-five years, the contents were sent to a clearinghouse in Omaha, Nebraska, to be inventoried for auction."

"Auction?" Dr. Webb sounded almost as hurt by the explanation as Nina had been. "I'm so sorry, Nina. You must be so disappointed."

"Yes. I was so sure I'd come back home with at least a clue to my mother's identity. I *am* disappointed, but he said it's not too late. They hadn't publicly announced the sale yet, and legally they have to, before they can proceed. The man made a copy of my key, and took my signature and my request for the contents. He assured me he would locate them and have them shipped to me as soon as possible. But it could take anywhere from three weeks to three months."

Dr. Webb asked a question then that made Nina's heart skip a beat. "Nina, deep down you have a feeling about the contents of that box, don't you?"

She couldn't speak for a moment, and managed only to nod an affirmative response.

"What do you believe you'll find?"

"It's going to sound crazy, Dr. Webb."

He smiled. "You're in the right company to share crazy thoughts."

"I'll just have to answer your question with a question, if that's okay."

Dr. Webb motioned "of course" with a single nod of his head.

"Have you ever felt like you had unfinished business with someone you don't even know? Like some kind of reunion or something with a stranger who's really not a stranger at all?"

A slight smile appeared on Dr. Webb's face, and his head nodded slowly up and down. He looked up at the painting of his father on the wall above Nina. Motioning toward it with a nod of his head, he said in the softest of voices, "Yes, Nina, I believe I have."

Nat pressed the tiny buttons wildly, sending Nina's ninja fighter to the ground in a puddle of blood. "Gotcha, Neen.

That's twenty-three to twenty. You're slippin', big sis.''

Nina was having a hard time concentrating on the game or she would have put a little more effort into whupping Nat's ass. When Nat first bought the PlayStation, Nina told him he needed to grow up and put away the childish games. That was before she sat down and played with him. Nina liked to pretend her interest was mainly in the logic and trivia games like Tetris and Jeopardy, and she'd spent hours playing them. But over the few months since Nat had hooked the contraption up on the big-screen TV in Mama and Daddy's den, she had become quite an expert at the shooting, slicing, stabbing, punching, and kicking of what she had once sarcastically referred to as the ''kill 'em up games.'' Now, Nina and Nat were in the midst of an ongoing competition, and up until Nina's most recent bloody fatalities, they had been tied twenty games apiece.

''You just caught me on an off day, Sweet Nat. Don't get cocky now.'' Nina tried to sound playful.

Nat put the play pad down on the carpet and looked at Nina with concern. ''You all right, Nina? You seem like you got a load a shit on your mind.''

''A load of shit?'' Nina laughed.

''Yeah. Mental constipation.'' Nathan's gapped smile flashed at his sister. ''You get it from holding on to your thoughts for too long. As long as it don't stink, you can let some of it out now if you want.''

Nina reached her bare foot across the space between them to kick Nat playfully. ''My shit don't stink, baby brother, you know that.''

He grabbed the foot and wouldn't let go. ''Spit it out, Nina. What's bothering you?''

''Can I ask you a question?''

He was still holding the foot. ''Shoot.''

''Would you date a White girl?'' The question came out urgent and irritated, not calm and nonchalant like she'd intended.

Nat let go of her foot. He didn't answer for a few seconds. Then: ''Why are you asking me that?'' He sounded just a little bit defensive.

She wanted to hear him say something harsh. Something

like what Ahmad had said to Rasheed about her. If Nat said "Hell, naw. Not enough melanin. Definitely not my type," then she could ask Nat the next question: What about if she only looked White? If she was pale like Nina, but was a bona fide sista, could Nat get over the physical appearance and deal with the person inside?

"You said you wanted to help. So help. Answer the question. Would you date a White girl?"

"I have."

Not the answer she was looking for. "No you haven't. I've seen you date sistas, and that one Mexican girl. I've never seen you bring any White girls around."

"I don't bring 'em around."

Nina kicked him again. "Quit playin', Nat."

"Nina, I live in Glendale, Arizona, and the pickins are slim when it comes to sistas. I *have* dated White girls."

"So, you've never been serious about any of them?"

Nat picked up the play pad and started a one-player game. "Nat."

He halfheartedly punched and kicked at the sword-carrying samurai that was trying to behead him.

"Once," he muttered without looking up. The computer avenger let out a shrill cry and swung at Nathan's character's head. The head rolled off the character's shoulders, blood spurting out of it, as Nat's fighter expired.

"And . . ." Nina prompted. She couldn't remember any White girl Nat had dated, and she had no idea who he could be talking about being serious about. This must have happened after Nina moved out, while Nat was still in high school.

"Her name was Amanda Winston." Nathan dropped the game pad and began picking at the fibers of the plush ivory carpet like he was looking for something he'd lost. "Daddy found out I took her to her junior prom and almost had a heart attack."

"Daddy was mad?"

Nathan let out a stifled laugh. "Yeah. You could say that."

"Why?"

"He made it clear to me that White girls were off limits back when I was in the seventh grade."

Daddy wouldn't do that. Nina could remember no such con-

versation being had with her about choosing a boyfriend.
While she was in high school she had dated Blacks, Latinos,
and a Filipino . . . They were equally scrutinized, but their eth-
nicity was never mentioned. She'd never dated a White boy
though. Maybe if she had, Daddy would have had the same
talk ready for her too. But that just didn't sound like something
Daddy would do. Sure, he was proud to be Black, but Nina
couldn't remember him ever sounding like that kind of bigot.
"What did he say, Nat? I mean, I just can't picture Daddy
telling you something like that." Nina used her best menacing
vampire voice when she added, " 'Nathan, I vawnt you to stay
avay from thoze *eeevil* Vite vimmen.' "

Nat smiled at Nina, then shook his head and said seriously,
"He didn't say it like that. But he made it obvious in his own
way. He called me into this very room and closed the door
behind us." Nat managed a slight chuckle. "When I was
twelve or thirteen Lindsey Fortson's father had called him,
furious as hell, to tell him I was caught kissing his daughter
on the lips."

"That little country-club hot mama?" Nina remembered
Lindsey Fortson from Nat's high school football games. The
sun-kissed, rumored-to-be-scandalous cheerleader was on the
arm of a different jock at the end of just about every game.
She was known to have a thing for Chicano boys, but Nina
had seen her with a brotha or two across the seasons.

"Daddy said I could save myself a whole lot of pain in the
future if I left White women alone. You know how Daddy has
that way of making a mandate sound like a suggestion?"

Nina nodded. Their father didn't really interfere in their
lives much. But when he did, his so-called advice always rang
with an overtone of ultimatum. It was as if going against
Daddy's will might lead to some dire unforeseen consequence.
Like when he "suggested" Nina not let Derrick move into
her apartment. She had no idea what the repercussions would
have been, but she wasn't about to try to find out either.

"He didn't say anything to me about taking Amanda to the
prom, but he was obviously very upset about it. He didn't
speak to me for a week."

Nina was quiet. She studied her pale toes and shook her
head slowly. How on earth was Daddy going to prohibit Nat

from doing something he obviously had done himself? "What did Mama say?" she asked.

Nat looked Nina in the eye. "Please. You know Mama would have a fit if she knew Daddy told me to leave White women alone. Mama wants me to date whomever I please. As long as the girl's respectable, Mama doesn't care. She just wants her baby boy to be happy."

"Did you love her?"

"Mandy?" Nina watched a dark cloud settle on Nat's face when he mentioned the girl's name. The experience had obviously been painful. "I don't know." Nat shrugged. "I liked her a lot."

They were both quiet for a while.

Nina shook her head slowly. Nat had been warned. Whatever dabbling Mitchell Moore had done over on the "other side" hadn't turned out in his favor, so he was going to "save" his son from making the same mistake. *So what . . . ? Did Daddy think he could just dip a toe or two into the "whites only" pool before settling down for the long haul with Mama? If so, he musta got pulled in over his head. Nah. Not Daddy. Not Mitchell Moore. Maybe some other triflin'-ass Black man, but not Daddy. Not over some strange White woman's snatch. Then again, maybe the woman set him up. Maybe she got him drunk or something. But for what possible reason? Daddy wasn't famous back then, and he sure didn't have any money.* The questions were beginning to burn in Nina's veins, and the longer they went unanswered the more impossible it was becoming to ignore them. Why should she have to suffer because of some terrible shame her father was walking around with? It wasn't fair. So what if he followed his dick somewhere it wasn't supposed to go? If he was so ashamed of what he had done, then he shouldn't have claimed Nina at all.

"Daddy's sorry he made me." Nina muttered the thought aloud. It came out sounding very matter-of-fact.

"What?" Nat's surprise sounded almost angry. "That's ridiculous. You're Daddy's pride and joy."

"I may be his joy," Nina turned her arms over in front of Nat so the lightest shade of pale beige on the inside of her forearms made her next point, "but I'm definitely not his pride."

"Come on, Nina. You know that's not true. He's not sorry he made you, and he's not ashamed of you. He just gets a lot of flack about it."

"Flack?"

"You know. People talking behind his back. They see you and they question his integrity, his pride in being Black."

"He told you that?"

Nathan nodded. "People call him a sellout. Sometimes to his face."

Nina shook her head. "There isn't a man on the planet prouder of his Blackness than our father."

"True that."

Nina hated it. She hated the way it made her feel to know her existence was some kind of awful payback for somebody's sin. *No wonder he doesn't want to talk about my mother; she was obviously a mistake he wished he could forget.*

"But you know what, Neen?"

"What?"

"I'm glad he made you."

Nina puckered her lips and smacked a kiss at Nat. "Ju so sweeeeeet." She grinned.

"Know what else?"

"What?"

"Everybody gets dealt a hand in life. You gotta play with the cards you got. Even if they seem like shitty cards."

"Oh, so you're majoring in philosophy now, huh?" Nina teased.

Nat puffed his chest out and tried to sound erudite. "Yes. As a matter of fact I am. And that little tidbit of shitty card wisdom is from a new school of thought."

"What school is that?"

"The School of Shit Happens."

"Shit happens, Nat?" She shot him a twisted grin.

"Yeah, Neen." he nodded matter-of-factly at his big sister. "Yeshshitduzz."

△▽ 22 ▽△

Ahmad fell hard to the gym floor and skidded, his elbows and hands hitting about the same time his butt came down. He lay flat on his back for a minute, trying to let the pain of losing the top layer of skin on his elbows dissipate. *This asshole really thinks he's gonna intimidate me.* Derrick had fouled him for the fifth time. Ahmad sat up.

"That's another two points." Derrick was grinning stupidly at him. "That's twelve up, man."

Ahmad shook his head. "Naw. Hell, naw. You know it's my ball."

"You weren't set, man." Derrick knew he was lying. He had way too much momentum coming in for that layup. He knew he fouled Ahmad again. He just didn't want to give up the basket.

"So, what's up? I have to bring my own ref to get you to play square?" Ahmad was getting pissed. The first few fouls were irritating. But five in a row? It would be different if the brotha was trying to admit to at least one or two of them.

Derrick threw a smirk Ahmad's way. "Nigga, you should quit trippin'."

Ahmad was on his feet in a split second. He got up in Derrick's face and growled at him. "I got yo', nigga." He was half-hoping Derrick would put his hands on him. Push him back, or shove him with a shoulder. That way, when he knocked Derrick's ass out, it wouldn't be considered a sucker punch.

But Derrick just shrugged at Ahmad. "I quit anyway." He

215

walked over to the bleachers and grabbed his jersey from the bench. "I hate a cheater."

"Yeah, I bet you do," Ahmad sneered sarcastically. "There's a psychosociological term for that syndrome."

Ahmad's words might as well have been said in a foreign language. Derrick stared blankly at him.

"It's called *self*-hatred."

Derrick waved a hand at Ahmad in frustration and stomped off toward the locker room.

Just then, one of the double doors that led to the parking lot opened wide. The sun glaring brightly behind the open door made it difficult to make out the shadowy figure, but when his eyes finally made the adjustment, Ahmad's heart jumped up into his throat. He hadn't seen her in weeks.

Nina didn't come in. She motioned for Ahmad to come over to the door. "Ahmad." She shouted over the noise of a volleyball class being held on the other side of the gymnasium. "Can I talk to you for a minute?"

Ahmad had managed to avoid Nina for over two months. The memories he had of her were torturous enough. The smell of her. The taste. The feel of her soft skin pressed up against him. Thinking about Nina for even a minute created a dull ache in his chest that haunted him for hours, and it hadn't gotten any easier to stay away. If anything it was getting more difficult by the day. Every time Ebony mentioned Nina, which was still at least once a day, Ahmad fought the urge to pick up the phone and call just to hear her voice. But the fear of being with her was far greater than the pain of being without her, so he'd managed to stay away. Everyday, after picking his daughter up from morning kindergarten a few blocks from the campus, he'd been dropping her off at the side door of the center, knowing Nina's office was on the opposite side of the building. And in the afternoon, when he came back to get Ebony, Nina was already on campus teaching her classes. The plan to avoid seeing her for a while had gone pretty smoothly. Now, here she was standing in front of him. She'd sought him out. But for what?

When Ahmad reached the doorway, he felt a strong urge to get a "long-time-no-see" hug, but the beige double-breasted suit Nina wore made that a bad idea, since his Kmart shorts

and tee shirt were still sweat-drenched. He held his hand out
to her instead. She reached for it, simultaneously sliding her
tortoiseshell DKNY sunglasses up on to the top of her head
with the other hand. Ahmad knew he shouldn't, but couldn't
resist looking directly into Nina's eyes. He'd forgotten that
they were the same shade as an evening sky, and the moment
they met his, they pierced him with an intense look which he
tried, but couldn't read. An electric current raced through his
body when she grasped his outstretched hand. He cleared his
throat nervously. "Hey, Nina. How have you been?"

She shook his hand briskly, then pulled hers back quickly.
When she spoke, her tone said she had come on business.
"I'm fine, thanks. Listen, we've got a slight problem."

Ahmad's pulse quickened. "Is Ebony all right?" The
thought that something bad happened to his daughter made the
words come out urgent and tense.

"Tonya is taking the kids on a field trip today, and Ebony
doesn't want to go. They'll be leaving in about an hour, but
she said she wants to stay here and take a nap. T said Ebony
seemed to be okay this morning, but now she's saying she
doesn't feel well."

Ahmad's eyebrows shot up, and his brow wrinkled in concern.

"She doesn't have a fever; I checked. But she's saying
she'd rather stay and lie down for a while." Nina's voice lost
its businesslike tone for a split second. "She could stay in my
office for the afternoon, but . . . I know how you feel about
her spending time with me, so—"

Ahmad cut her off. "Ebony was feeling fine this morning,
Nina. She's not sick. She just misses you." *I miss you too*, he
thought. He wanted to say it out loud. He wanted to reach
across the huge divide he'd created between them and take
her in his arms; taste her kiss again. Instead he said quietly,
"I didn't mean I don't want you around her at all, Nina."

They were both quiet.

Finally Ahmad said, "I don't think it could hurt for her to
stay with you for an afternoon."

Nina smiled softly. "I was hoping you'd say that. I've already arranged for one of my students to take over my
classes."

An uncomfortable silence engulfed them and they both looked as if they were searching for something meaningful to say, when suddenly, from behind Ahmad, Derrick shoved his way rudely through the doorway, knocking Ahmad brusquely into Nina. Ahmad had to put his arms around her to keep her from falling backward, though he might have put a little more enthusiasm into the embrace than was necessary, because he could smell her perfume wafting up from behind her ear which was pressed tightly against his chest. It was the same scent she'd worn the last time he held her in his arms in the hotel room, and when Ahmad breathed it in, a warm glow spread through his body. When he realized Derrick was standing there looking stupid, Ahmad, still holding Nina tightly, growled at him, "You could at least say, 'Excuse me.' " The anger between the two men from their earlier disagreement hadn't dissipated.

Nina had recovered her balance, and didn't seem as comfortable with the embrace as Ahmad so obviously was. She immediately peeled Ahmad's arms from around her waist and took a step backward, the whole time watching Derrick. She too was waiting for some kind of an apology.

"Excuse me." Derrick said it to Ahmad sarcastically. Then he looked at Nina. "I need to talk to you."

"I don't have anything to say to you, Derrick." She looked up at Ahmad, then back at Derrick. "Can't you see I'm in the middle of a conversation?"

Derrick grabbed Nina's arm. "You can't take five minutes out of your . . ." He shot an angry glance toward Ahmad. ". . . busy schedule to talk to me?"

"Let go of me, Derrick." Nina tried to pull her arm back, but Derrick had a tight grip on it.

"Man, what's wrong with you?" Ahmad was in Derrick's face now. "Didn't you hear the sista ask you to let her go?"

"You need to mind your own business, Rasta man." Derrick puffed his chest out, like he was really going to do something.

"Well, maybe I'm making it my business." Ahmad stepped into Derrick, puffing his chest out too.

"Ahmad." Nina said his name softly. She was trying to keep things from escalating, but the tension between the two men made them both momentarily deaf. "Ahmad," she repeated a little louder.

Derrick shot Nina an angry look. "Ahmad," he mocked her in a syrupy, girlish tone. Then, pointing a stiff finger in her face, he growled, "Damn, the body ain't even cold on our dead relationship. You doin' this brotha already?"

Ahmad heard the sickening thud of knuckle against flesh before he realized he had already made the decision to knock the shit out of Derrick. The blow spun Derrick around and he lurched sideways at the impact, nearly falling to the ground, but he caught himself on one outstretched hand first. When he stumbled back into a standing position Ahmad was in his face. "Don't even think about hitting me back, fool. The hospital is not a great place to spend the night."

Derrick didn't want none. He knew he didn't have a chance in hell against Ahmad. He held one hand to his jaw, not realizing there was blood dripping from his busted lip. When a stream of it ran down onto his hand and it finally occurred to him that he was bleeding, Derrick backed his way into the gymnasium, hollering at Ahmad as he retreated.

"Oh shit. You busted my fuckin' mouth. You're gonna hear from my lawyer. That's assault, nigga. You're gonna pay for that shit."

When Ahmad turned his attention to Nina, he was sure the look of disgust and contempt on her face was directed at Derrick, until she opened her mouth. "You didn't have to hit him." She shoved past Ahmad and hurried into the gym to catch up with Derrick.

Nina's heart was in a panic. The talk of Derrick getting a lawyer, of pressing charges against Ahmad . . . What in the hell was Ahmad thinking? He was out on parole. He couldn't get an assault charge. He'd go back to prison. And what would happen to Ebony? A foster home no doubt. Ebony would lose her daddy after losing every damn-body-else she ever loved, and it would be all Nina's fault. Nina had to do something.

"Derrick. Derrick, wait up." The click of Nina's heels against the gym floor slowed as she caught up with him outside the locker room door. She pushed the door open and walked in ahead of him, grabbing him by the hand that wasn't holding his bloody jaw. Ignoring the fact that she was in a men's locker room, she pulled Derrick toward a bench, and left him momentarily to grab a handful of paper towels from the dispenser above the sink on a nearby wall. She wet the towels and was back at Derrick's side, dabbing one of them at the blood that was beginning to coagulate on his lower lip.

"You know you had that coming."

Derrick grabbed the hand that Nina was using to swab his face and held on to it. "Are you?" He looked her in her eyes. She could see the pain behind his, and it wasn't the pain of getting hit in the mouth.

"Am I what?"

"Doing him?"

Nina yanked her hand from Derrick's grasp and went back to dabbing the wet paper towel on his swelling jaw.

"You've got a lot of nerve asking me that. I'm your ex, Derrick. If I was doing him, that wouldn't be any of your business."

Derrick looked like he wanted to cry. "I miss you, Nina."

"We really should get something cold on this." She acted like she didn't hear him. "Before it swells up."

"No, I want it to swell up nice and fat." He was nodding his head emphatically with every word. "I'm going to take a nice picture of it for my lawyer."

"You can't press charges against Ahmad, Derrick."

"The hell I can't. You saw him hit me first. That's assault."

"Okay, but you did kind of ask for it. You disrespected me. Ahmad was just making a point."

"Well, the nigga shouldn't of put his hands on me. Now I got a point of my own to make."

Nina knew she had to be careful about how she worded it. But no matter how it came out, Derrick was going to think Ahmad was her man. But what difference did that make now? She couldn't let Derrick walk out of that locker room until she'd at least tried to change his mind. There was a possibility he was just bluffing, but what if he wasn't? What if he went straight to the police station and Ahmad ended up in jail?

"Derrick, please don't press charges against that man."

"Why are you so worried about it, Nina? Is he *your* man?" Derrick looked in her face, waiting to see her reaction.

"He has a five-year-old daughter. He's a single parent."
Derrick just looked at Nina with a "so the fuck what" expression plastered across his face. "He's on parole, Derrick.
He'll go to jail, and then he'll go straight back to prison. Ebony will go to a foster home."

Nina's eyes searched Derrick's for some sign that his ego
might retreat momentarily and allow his heart to function. But
his face was stone. Nina's voice quivered slightly. "The
child's mother is dead, Derrick. Her grandmother's in a
coma . . ."

Derrick's expression had softened just a little. Nina knew
she was getting through to him.

". . . and . . . he's not my man."

A gleaming smile dawned slowly across Derrick's face.
"So, what do I get out of dropping it?"

Nina didn't like the tone in his voice. "What do you want?"
she asked suspiciously.

"Dinner."

"Dinner?" She thought he was headed somewhere much
cruder than that. "Derrick, please . . ."

"Damn, girl. I'm not trying to stalk you. I just want you to
have dinner with me."

"Is dinner all you want?"

"Saturday night. Eight o'clock. I'll pick you up."

Nina nodded hesitantly. "Dinner, Derrick. Just dinner."

△▽ 23 ▽△

"My daddy has a picture of you." *Ebony*
stopped coloring the tree on her side of the coloring book to
make that announcement. Lying next to Nina on the soft reading rug, Ebony crossed her little stretched-out legs at the ankle
and reached into the crayon box for the brown crayon.

Nina stifled the smile she felt, and continued drawing a careful yellow line around the sunflower on her own side of the
book. "He does?" She didn't look up from her work. Instead
she filled in the center of the flower, applying a light pressure
against the crayon, moving it back and forth inside the yellow
outline in broad quick strokes.

"Yep." Ebony nodded her head emphatically. "He looks
at it a lot."

"He does?" Nina glanced nonchalantly at Ebony, and
reached for the green crayon. She had just begun outlining the
flower's leaves with it when out of the corner of her eye she
caught a glimpse of Ahmad tiptoeing quietly into the tiny
cloakroom. Ahmad held a finger mischievously to his lips as
he moved slowly toward them. His gesture asked Nina to keep
his presence a secret, so Nina quickly turned her attention back
to the coloring book.

"Yep. My daddy thinks you're pretty," Ebony exclaimed.

"He thinks I'm pretty? Did your daddy tell you that?" Nina
glanced over Ebony's shoulder to find a surprised look on
Ahmad's face. He shrugged as if to say he had no clue where
Ebony got that idea, but his guilty smile said his daughter's
comment was correct.

"Nope." Ebony rested her chin on her hands and stared thoughtfully into Nina's face. "He didn't tell me. I can just tell he does." She was still staring into Nina's eyes when she added, "You *are* pretty."

"Thank you, baby." Nina stared back into Ebony's sparkling eyes. "And you are pretty, too."

"But I'm not *your* kinda pretty." Ebony shook her head and said it with such matter-of-factness it hurt Nina, and she winced up at Ahmad who now stood directly over his daughter with a pained expression on his face.

"You are the prettiest girl I know," Ahmad said quickly to his daughter.

Ebony looked up in surprise. "Hi, Daddy."

Ahmad forced a smile for Ebony's benefit, but his voice and his stiff demeanor said his child's words more than bothered him. "It's time to go now, Ebony."

Ebony didn't get up. Instead, she looked at Nina and asked, "Daddy, how come God didn't make me white like Nina?" The question came out tinged with a wistful sadness, as if she had already come to the conclusion at age five that her brown skin was some kind of deserved punishment.

The look of pain on Ahmad's face turned into something closer to anger, and he repeated himself in a low, tense voice. "I said, it's time to go, Ebony." He forced a smile at Nina. When he said, "Thank you for giving up your afternoon," Nina heard the angry regret in Ahmad's voice. He was obviously sorry he had agreed to Ebony spending this time alone with Nina.

Nina sat up quickly. Ahmad's agitation was filling the room like smoke and Nina breathed it in, nearly choking on its thickness. She was surprised by his willingness to let something so obviously important go unchecked. Didn't he understand what Ebony was asking for? Nina had asked Mama a similar question around the same age when she and Nat returned from their summer visit with Mama's sister Ruthie. Nina knew it was her white skin and the way people pointed out her so-called "good" hair that led other kids to taunt her. She didn't know why blue eyes were considered "pretty" and she didn't understand why grown-ups made such a big deal about it. Nina just wanted to have brown skin and brown eyes like the other kids. She didn't like being different, and she didn't like having her feelings hurt. And when she asked tearfully why she was different from all her friends, Mama didn't hesitate to do her best to help Nina feel better about it. In a split second, Mama explained to her that sweet things come in all different flavors and colors, but some people get stuck on one flavor and think it's better than the rest. She took Nina into the kitchen and together they searched the cupboards for every delicious thing they could find that came in shades from black to brown to tan to white. By the time they were finished, Nina was munching on marshmallows and chocolate chips, caramels and licorice, and dipping her little fingertips into every shade of sugar from white to dark brown. That's when Mama explained to Nina about recipes. "Baby, everything in a recipe is different, and everything is important. When God made this family, it was like he was making a recipe for something delicious. All of us are different in our own way. You're different too. You're not more important than anyone else in the family, but you were certainly too important to be left out of the recipe."

Nina looked into Ahmad's scowling face, then she looked at Ebony. The child was waiting wide-eyed and expectant for a response to her question. Nina wished she had a well-stocked kitchen to take Ebony into, but she didn't. She had to come up with something Ebony could understand. She looked around the tiny cloakroom before settling her eyes again on Ahmad's angry expression. "Don't leave, Ahmad." Her voice was calm but insistent. She nodded toward Ebony. "Ebony asked a good question. Do you think it's wise to leave it unanswered?"

Ahmad's face registered an emotion that Nina could only interpret as fear. Either he was afraid of what he might say to his daughter, given his agitation at her question, or he was afraid that there was no answer to give her. It was quite obvious from Ahmad's scowl that if Ebony's question was going to be answered, Nina would have to be the one to do it.

She turned her back to the child and spoke softly to Ahmad. "Ahmad?" He hadn't said a word, and he hadn't made a move. "Can I speak to you outside for a minute?" Nina motioned for him to join her outside the door, then she turned to Ebony. "Honey, why don't you put all the crayons back in the box for me, okay? Your daddy and I need to talk.''

Ebony nodded obediently and sat cross-legged in front of the pile of crayons. She was obviously upset by her father's reaction to her question. She looked as if she had been scolded and was fighting the urge to cry. One by one she picked up the crayons and slowly placed them in the yellow-orange box.

Nina walked quickly out of the room, and stopped far enough from the open door so Ebony would not hear her. Then she turned to Ahmad. Her voice was tight and controlled, and the impatience and anger she felt was brimming in her throat. "What are you doing, Ahmad? How can you punish her for not being sure? She's just a baby, for God's sake. She doesn't know. Haven't you ever asked a question like that?''

Ahmad didn't look directly at Nina; instead his eyes roamed the huge main room of the day care facility. When he spoke, his whisper was cool and emotionless. "I was afraid this would happen. I knew better than to do this to her.''

Nina stared at him blankly, waiting for him to explain.

"I can't let my baby grow up hating what she is, Nina. I have to do something. I have to get her out of here. I need to get Ebony away from all these white faces before the damage is irreversible.''

"Get her away from these . . .'' A knife of realization plunged itself into Nina's chest, and the pain of it spread across her face. "You mean this white face, don't you?''

Ahmad didn't say a word.

"You mean me, don't you, Ahmad?''

He didn't answer her question, and he didn't look at her face.

"Well, I'll do what I can to prevent you and Ebony from having to see this face too often.'' The hurt and anger Nina felt made the statement come out with more of a sting than she'd intended.

Ahmad turned to face her and whispered harshly, "Look, Nina. You don't know what she's going through. You can't know what this is about. Just being around you makes her want to be like you . . . look like you . . . It's not fair to her. She loves you already, and that's only going to hurt her in the end.''

Nina instantly thought of Mama. How many times had she

dressed herself in Mama's clothes and painted Mama's brown pancake makeup on her own ivory face? Sure, she wanted to be like Mama. She wanted to look like the woman who taught her to read, who comforted her when she was hurt, and put a note in her lunch pail every day before school. And yes, she still found herself wondering what it might be like to not be so different. To not stand out like a sore thumb in family pictures, or not be so readily rejected by her own people—like Ahmad had done at their first meeting. The bottom line was that Nina could not imagine a life without Mama. What if she had been raised by a mother with a skin tone more like her own? Who would she have become? What view might she have of the world? Of her own racially mixed self? Mama and Daddy were both brown, and yes, that did make Nina value brown skin, but it didn't mean she didn't love her pale self. It didn't make her ashamed of the color that had been chosen for her by God.

Chosen for me by God. That's it. In a flash of inspiration, Nina knew what she was supposed to do. "Ebony needs us to be real about this, Ahmad. She needs us to deal with it. I'm asking you to trust me to do the right thing." She hurried back to the cloakroom, not looking back to see if Ahmad was following.

Nina sat next to Ebony on the floor and motioned for Ahmad to do the same. She turned her attention to the child as Ahmad just stood there looking down at her. The anger in his face was gone, but it had been replaced by a look of doubt. Finally, he seated himself on the rug and pulled his daughter onto his lap.

Nina questioned Ebony matter-of-factly, "Ebony, tell me some of the things God makes."

Ebony looked first at her father, then at Nina. In a tiny voice she began rattling off a list to answer the question Nina had posed. "God makes butterflies and kittens and goldfish and clouds and . . ." She pointed an index finger at Nina's page in the coloring book. "And sunflowers."

"And you and me?" Nina added for effect.

"Yep." Ebony smiled. "And Daddy too."

"And do you think God is pretty good at making things?"

"Yep. God is *very* good at making things." Ebony said it like there could be no doubt.

Nina picked up the brown crayon Ebony had used to color her tree's trunk and held it next to the child's skin. "Hmmm. So, why do you suppose God chose to make Ebony brown?"

Ebony frowned. Her large, deep brown eyes turned glassy before she finally said, "I don't know" in the tiniest of voices. "He didn't make you brown, or Kristin or Heather." Ebony was referring to the two little girls who were her daily playmates at the center. Nina had watched the three of them playing house that very morning. Ebony had draped a length of yellow cloth over her head and gathered it into a "ponytail" before announcing to Nina that she now had "hair like my friends." Though Nina responded by kissing the child's forehead and telling her she liked the hairstyle her daddy had given her much better, it was now clear that Ebony was asking for more than that. The child was asking that potentially soul-shattering question too many children of color eventually come to ask—especially ones that are surrounded by people they looked nothing like—that questioning of worth. Was there something inherently more valuable in having pale skin, light eyes, or long flowing hair like White folks? Ebony was plainly asking it.

The child didn't know anything about Europe or Africa or slavery or affirmative action. But she already knew to ask why God didn't make her white, and she was searching Nina and Ahmad's faces for an answer. A look of quiet anticipation held Ebony still, and her eyes begged the two adults to know. Why did God see fit to make her brown?

"Well, let's see." Nina's face wrinkled into a thoughtful scowl. She raised her eyebrows dramatically at Ebony. "We can't ask God face to face, can we?"

Ebony shook her head sadly.

"Hmmm. Well, we can see that some of the most important things in the whole world are brown. Maybe that's why God chose brown for you."

"What things?" Ebony asked curiously. "What important things?"

Nina pointed the brown crayon at the tree in Ebony's coloring book. "Ebony, what do you know about trees?"

Ebony thought a moment, then exclaimed, "Trees are tall!"

"Trees are tall," Nina confirmed, "but there's something more important about them that you should know."

Ebony shrugged.

"Take a deep breath like this." Nina breathed in and held it in puffed-out cheeks. Ebony followed her lead and puffed her cheeks out too. When they couldn't hold it any longer they both exhaled with a loud gush of air. Ebony giggled.

"What if we couldn't breathe in again?" Nina asked seriously.

Ebony looked first at Nina, then at Ahmad, with round eyes. "What? What would happen, Daddy?"

Ahmad had a curious look on his face. He didn't seem sure where Nina was going, but he answered the question. "If we couldn't breathe in, punkin, we would die."

"Trees make the air we breathe in their leaves. It's called photosynthesis." Nina stated the fact like she was talking to a class of college students, not a five-year-old child.

Ebony attempted the word but it came out sounding more like "phodo-sis-tha-niss."

Nina smiled. "Without photosynthesis nothing could breathe. If there were no trees everything would die, Ebony." She looked at Ahmad, who seemed to have lost some of the tension that had gripped him just minutes before. But the look on his face said he still had no idea what any of this had to do with his child's fear that God had somehow cursed her by coloring her brown.

Nina whispered dramatically to Ebony, "If there were no trees, everything would die. So, how important are trees?"

Ebony whispered her answer dramatically too. "Trees are really, really important."

"That's right. And what color did God choose to wrap a tree in?"

Ebony looked at the tree painted on the wall of the tiny cloakroom, then down at the one in the coloring book under Nina's index finger. "God chose brown." Ebony's expression said she was paying attention and that she made the connection, even if she wasn't totally following where Nina was trying to get her to go.

"And what about dirt?" Nina looked at Ebony's scrunched-up nose and had to laugh. "Oh, you don't think too highly of dirt, huh?"

The child's head shook slowly from side to side and the scrunched-up nose stayed scrunched.

"Well, dirt is also called soil, and soil is what helps everything grow. If there was no soil, there'd be no trees. Matter of fact, if there was no soil, there'd be no fruit or vegetables or anything to eat. And what would happen if we couldn't eat?"

Ebony looked at her daddy again. He was smiling now. He knew where Nina was headed, and his eyes shone with admiration that she'd had the presence of mind to help Ebony deal with her question in a way she'd be able to understand. "What, Daddy? What would happen if we couldn't eat?"

"If we couldn't eat, we'd die," he said matter-of-factly.

Nina whispered the dramatic whisper again. "If there was no soil, Ebony, everything would die. How important do you think soil might be?"

This time Ebony spoke her answer loudly and with feeling. "Soil is very, very, very, very important."

"And what color did God choose to make soil, Miss Ebony?"

Ebony's eyes lit up with the recognition of what Nina was trying to get her to see. With awe in her voice she exclaimed, "Brown! God chose brown."

"And of course, there's another very important thing."

Ebony looked questioningly at Nina.

"What do you think is the tastiest flavor of candy or ice cream or any sweet delicious thing?"

Nina knew Ebony's love for chocolate would lead her to answer in just the way she needed to close out her dramatic explanation. And sure enough, Ebony exclaimed, "Chocolate! Chocolate is my most delicious flavor!"

Nina grinned. "And what color did God choose to make chocolate?"

By now Ebony was up on her feet and dancing her tap dance of excitement. "Brown. Brown. Brown. God made chocolate brown. God made chocolate brown, like me." When she said "me," she pointed at herself and turned to her daddy with a huge grin. "God made chocolate brown, like me."

Ahmad swept Ebony into a hug and planted a smooch on her cheek. "God knew how important and pretty and sweet you'd be, Ebony. So brown was the best color in the universe to make you." He kissed her cheek again and smacked his lips playfully. "Mmmm. You are my sweet brown-sugar baby."

Ebony giggled, then kissed her father's cheek, mimicking the smacking noise he'd made. "Mmmm. You are my sweet brown-sugar daddy." She giggled again then pointed at her daddy's cheek where she'd kissed it and said to Nina, "Daddy tastes sweet too, just like me." She pressed her fingertip into Ahmad's dimple, just above the line of his beard. "Kiss Daddy's cheek right here, Nina. Daddy's chocolate. He's sweet like me."

Nina's reaction was a stiff, awkward silence. Her uneasiness surged around her like an aura, electrifying the air and sucking the happy laughter from the tiny room. She suddenly felt exposed, as if Ebony's innocent little matchmaking attempt had peeled back the layer of nonchalance Nina had been trying all these weeks to maintain. In a split second, all that was left of her cool façade was the naked rawness of the hurt and anger Ahmad had left Nina with when he banished her from his and Ebony's lives. Nina wished she could plant a careless kiss on Ahmad's cheek, but she wouldn't dare. She wanted to look boldly in Ahmad's eyes, but she couldn't let him see the raw emotion she was hiding behind her own. She wanted desperately to be able to just laugh the whole thing off and say, "Oh, Ebony, you are so silly," but she was sure the words would never make it out of her mouth. So, instead, Nina kept her eyes from Ahmad's face and silently gathered up the box of crayons and coloring books from the floor.

Ahmad grasped his daughter's hand. "C'mon, lil' bit," he said sadly. He knew instantly that he was the source of Nina's discomfort, and he couldn't handle the weight of it. "Let's go get your things." Without another word, Ebony quietly followed her father out of the room.

Ebony clearly realized that her request for Nina to kiss her daddy's face had left the two grown-ups wrapped in a strange blanket of sadness, because as soon as she got in the car, she just lifted up a corner of that blanket and burrowed right in under it too, staring quietly out the window at the passing cars. Ahmad too sat in silence, trying to deal with the thoughts that were competing for attention inside his head.

He glanced over at Ebony quietly watching the passing scenery. *My brown-sugar baby.* The thought of how naturally Nina had dealt with Ebony's question sent a warm wave of calm through his heart. How ironic that with Nina's creativity and a few sincere words, she wiped out every trace of the fear Marlene had filled his heart with so many weeks before. *I was confused then. And afraid.*

He'd really thought he was ready to deal with whatever fears he had about Nina's skin, but . . . then . . . Marlene was so convincing. It didn't take much for her to persuade Ahmad that Ebony was vulnerable and needed to be protected—that Nina was a threat to Ebony's self-esteem. The argument that his child would never be able to grow up feeling good about herself if he kept Nina around frightened him. It sounded so rational and reasonable to him then. But the truth was, the entire time he spent trying to stay away from Nina, a quiet inner voice continued to tug at him . . . making him constantly question if he was doing the right thing. The voice stayed in his head, and refused to go away. It whispered to him on late evenings when he pretended to be browsing through pictures of Ebony and the cousins in L.A.—knowing every time he opened the envelope of photographs he was merely trying to relive for a brief moment the wind of longing that Nina had swept over him when he snapped her picture under the praying tree.

That same voice had continued to nudge him over the weeks. It tried to convince him of what had just been made so perfectly clear. Nina wasn't any threat to his daughter's self-esteem. The scene he'd just witnessed told him everything he needed to know about what kind of an influence in their lives Nina could be. But hadn't he really known that all along? From the moment Nina claimed his tree? Didn't he decide then that it no longer mattered that she was wrapped in pale skin? It was just that . . . skin. Beneath its surface was a real sista. A real woman.

What an asshole Nina must think I am. One night I'm bath-

ing her and telling her how glad I am to have her in my arms, and the next day . . . Ahmad wanted desperately to turn the car around and go tell Nina he was back. He wanted her to realize he had finally returned from the place of fear he'd retreated to. He wanted to take Nina in his arms and tell her how much he wished they could start over . . . how much he missed her friendship . . . how much he missed *her*. But Nina didn't seem to be feeling the same way. The look on her face—that look of hurt and anger Ahmad had seen—made him wonder if it was too late to fix the damage he'd done.

Damage. He remembered the incident with Derrick outside the gym. *She wasn't too happy about the damage I did to her ex-boyfriend's face, either.* As if on cue, the knuckles on Ahmad's right hand began to throb painfully, causing him to remove the hand from the steering wheel momentarily to flex and shake it as if he might actually be able to shake the swelling and discomfort out. But that only made the throbbing worse.

Ahmad knew he should have iced the hand right after he hit Derrick with it, but he didn't want to have to explain to Mr. Haskins why he'd need to walk around with an ice pack on his fist. If his boss ever found out that he'd been involved in a fight while he was on the clock, he'd probably lose his job. So Ahmad had just decided to endure the painful swelling around his knuckles, and even though it had been at least six hours since he'd smashed Derrick's face with them, they were still sore as hell.

Nina was pretty disgusted with me. Ahmad wanted to apologize to Nina for punching Derrick in front of her like that, but he never got the chance. She took off running after her ex like she was scared Ahmad had done some real damage to him or something.

I barely even tagged that sorry fool, Ahmad thought. *And he had the nerve to threaten to go to the police.* Ahmad figured that's all it was—an empty threat. Derrick had his hands on Nina, and Ahmad would just have to say he believed Derrick meant to do her harm. All he was doing was defending the woman. From everything Nina had told Ahmad about the way Derrick treated her, the punk deserved that shot in the mouth, and Nina ought to be thanking Ahmad for serving it up.

So why did she run off after Derrick like that? And what was the look of disgust she shot at Ahmad before she did? *Maybe she still has some kind of feelings for Derrick.* Ahmad hoped that wasn't the case. Not now. He was ready now. All his heart really needed was that reassurance he'd just gotten back there in that cloakroom. He was scared of only one thing now, and that was not being able to convince Nina how sorry he was for pushing her away. All he needed her to do was give him a chance to show her how wrong he had been about everything.

As if Ebony somehow heard his thoughts, she turned to face her father as he pulled the Volvo into the driveway of their apartment building. "We made Nina sad, Daddy."

Ahmad parked the car and turned off the ignition. "What makes you think so, Ebony?"

"Nina misses us. And that makes her sad."

"Nina misses you, punkin." Ahmad leaned toward Ebony to plant a kiss on her forehead. Before he could straighten again, Ebony reached her arms around his neck and held on. With her face two inches away from his, she said seriously, "Nina misses you, Daddy. Why didn't you tell her you miss her too?"

Ahmad could only smile at Ebony's naïve meddling. He nodded silently at his daughter's question, then he pressed his forehead against hers. Finally he whispered, "Well, lil' bit, that's something I might just have to do."

◸ 24 ◿

Nina slammed the receiver down so hard, the steel insides of the old-fashioned phone made a ringing sound that echoed off the stone walls of Mama's kitchen. Daddy was just coming through the doorway, and the noise startled him enough to make him jump.

"Hmmm. Somebody gon' get it," he whispered playfully at Nina as soon as he recovered from the shock.

"Sorry, Daddy." Nina patted the phone like it was a puppy whose tail had been accidentally stepped on. "Those ass—I mean, those idiots are really going to be sorry."

"Hmmm. Somebody *really* gon' get it." He pulled out a chair, seated himself at the table, and waited for Nina to explain what had made her so angry at whoever was on the other end of the phone line.

"Founder's idiots." Nina poured two cups of decaf, and brought them over to the table. She set one down in front of her father, and seated herself in the chair across from him. "Tonya and I have been trying to arrange a meeting with admin since September, but they keep putting us off. That was Dean Pritchard. He said he wanted to give me a little advice."

Mr. Moore tightened the belt on his terry cloth robe, leaned his elbows on the table, and, holding the cup with both hands, took a sip of coffee before he finally asked, "What kind of advice?"

"He said we should just give up on the meeting. He spoke with Rudyard. He said there was no way the president was

234

going to back down. They know we want to meet about King Day, and they don't want to waste our time."

"Well." Mr. Moore cleared his throat. "It sounds to me like he might be doing you a favor."

The weakness in her father's voice frightened Nina. He sounded almost fragile. It must have been the dialysis appointment he'd had the day before. The treatments seemed to be increasingly draining his energy.

Nina raised herself from her chair and headed for the refrigerator. She had come to the house to make sure Daddy ate something nutritious. Mama had gone to some kind of meeting in Los Angeles, and she'd asked Nina to come to the house on her lunch hour. Nina opened the refrigerator door and searched the shelves for something appetizing before she finally commented on what her father had said. "Dean Pritchard? Doing us a favor? How is that, Daddy?"

"The decision to keep the campus open has been made. If you meet with them, they'll ask what you plan to do when they refuse to give in to your demands."

She stopped her search to look at her father with a thoughtful expression. "Good point. And we will be 'asked' to cease and desist."

"Exactly. This way no one officially knows your plan ahead of time, so you can plead ignorance when they try to come down on you later."

Nina nodded at her father's words. "How 'bout a tuna sandwich and some fruit salad for lunch, Daddy?"

"I'm not hungry."

"Daddy, I'm going to fix you some lunch. I promised Mama. You don't want her mad at me, do you?"

Mr. Moore picked up the TV remote and pointed it at the television mounted in the corner of the breakfast nook.

"Daddy."

He turned to a Raid roach spray commercial and stared at it. Without looking at his daughter he said, "Sounds delicious, baby."

When the commercial ended and the faces of soap opera actors appeared, Mr. Moore quickly turned the television off and slammed the remote down on the table.

"Daddy, are you all right?"

"You know how I feel about that trash, Nina."

Nina didn't want to get him started on that subject. She didn't want to see her father get upset, and a conversation about the entertainment value of soap operas was sure to raise his blood pressure. Nina loved them, and in the past she might have tried to debate with Daddy about it. He'd argue that they were overly dramatic, valueless, and materialistic . . . But what on television wasn't? Nina found them to be a great escape from reality, and she was known to tape her favorite ones on her VCR while she was at work. Daddy's emotional reaction to them seemed pretty irrational to her. He could watch all the evening television in the world, but don't let Daddy walk in on you watching a soap opera. It was like waving a red flag in front of a bull. Nina didn't want to do anything to upset her father, especially now that his health seemed to be deteriorating more and more each day, so she changed the subject.

"Would you like sweet or dill relish in your tuna, Daddy?"

"Hmmm. Dill sounds good and a little tomato." He was eager to change the subject too. "So tell me about your King Day plan."

"Well, we're having a little dissension in the ranks at the moment." Nina put the sandwich on a plate, spooned some fruit salad next to it, and brought it over to the table. She put the plate down in front of her father before answering his questioning eyebrow raise. "There are some new members of the BSU that only want people of color involved in the plan."

"Only people of color?"

"Mmmm hmmm. Black folks. Native Americans. Latinos. But no White folks."

"That's not too smart. And I don't think that's how King would have wanted it. What are you going to do?"

"Well, it's only coming from a couple of the members. A freshman from one of my classes is the main ringleader. He says, and I quote, 'White folks don't count as humans because they don't have no hue, man.' "

Her father chuckled, but Nina didn't join in. "He's serious?" he asked in disbelief.

"Yes. He believes being melanin-deprived is equal to being depraved. You know. White man is the devil and all that. He makes allowances for me, though—blue eyes and all."

Mr. Moore picked up an apple slice and popped it in his mouth, while gesturing with his raised eyebrows for Nina to explain.

"I get to be an exception to the rule . . . but only because of my inheritance of freckles from you." Nina laughed at the absurdity of the statement. "What's ironic about it is the brotha ain't but a shade away from my skin tone."

Nina's father nodded his head knowingly.

Nina sucked her teeth. "He doesn't see that in excluding White folks he's pretty much suggesting we do the same thing admin is doing in singling Black folks out. Tonya and I tried to reason with him, but he's threatening to stage his own protest. He promised it will be something 'far more revolutionary' than what we have planned."

"What *do* you have planned?"

"We're calling it 'Hands Around the Campus.' Our goal is to have enough people joining hands to form a barrier. Anyone who attempts to attend classes on King Day will have to pass through our barrier. We won't hurt anybody, or prevent anyone from breaking through it, we just want folks to realize what they're choosing to do when they come to attend classes on King's holiday. We want to remind them that they are actively participating in disrespecting his legacy. They'll be forced to make a statement most of them won't want to make."

"I like it." Nina's father nodded. "But that campus is at least two square miles. That's a whole lotta hand-holdin'."

"Actually, it's three and a half miles if you include the athletic fields. But we're just trying to block access to the classrooms and admin buildings. We figure we'll need at least twenty-five hundred people."

"So you'll have to actually stand on the campus grounds then?"

"Yep."

"That means they can accuse you of trespassing on private property, Nina. Somebody'll get arrested."

"We thought about that, Daddy. But those of us who work or are students at Founder's have every right to be on that campus. They're choosing to keep the campus open that day— so they can't call us trespassers."

"Well, trespassing or not, you know can count me in. Your mama and I had our share of close encounters with the cops at demonstrations back in our day."

Nina winked at her father. "I'll count you in, Daddy. But only if you eat that tasty gourmet lunch I prepared for you."

He took a bite of the sandwich and grinned at her. Without chewing, he mumbled, "Okay. I'm in."

Nina laughed. "Thanks. Only twenty-four hundred ninety-nine more hand-holders to go."

"And I'll even hold hands with a White person," he joked.

"Very funny, Daddy." *I guess so*, she thought sarcastically. *You've certainly done a lot more than hold hands with one.* Nina instantly felt guilty for thinking it, but she couldn't help herself. The thought just popped in her head out of nowhere. It only proved that her resentment hadn't gone away. As a matter of fact, it just seemed to be building day by day, and if her father's health wasn't so fragile, she'd just go on and have it out with him. *I deserve to know. I've been patient long enough.*

Nina stared into her coffee cup and considered whether or not to just go right on ahead and try it. Why should she have to wait for some clearinghouse in Omaha to give her the information she needed, when all the answers to her questions were sitting right across the table from her? She looked at her father, and felt the questions rising to the back of her throat. *How'd you meet my mother? What kind of person was she? Why didn't you know I existed until she died?* Nina tried to picture herself asking him, "Daddy, who's Mickey?" But no matter how she tried, she couldn't find a voice for the questions. *I can't. I can't risk upsetting him. Maybe when he's stronger. After he's adjusted to the dialysis. Maybe then.* She took a sip of coffee and the two of them sat in silence for a moment before her father finally spoke.

"I know you're upset with me, Nina. And I'm not saying you don't have good reason to be." His green eyes were faraway and glassy, and for a split second Nina thought he wanted to cry. "I can't explain anything to you, Nina. I can't. If I could I would. But I can't, and I won't." He had obviously picked up on her vibe. He was feeling everything she was trying so hard to keep to herself on the other side of the table.

"Daddy . . . I . . ." Nina started to respond, but her father put a finger up to his lips and shook his head slowly. She wanted to tell him that however disappointing or embarrassing the truth about her mother might be, she didn't care. She wanted to know it. She needed to know it. But the look on his face told her it would never happen. Behind her father's eyes was an immovable resolve. She'd never get the information from him. Never.

"No matter what happens, you believe this, Nina. You are my daughter and I love you more than you'll ever know. And when the day comes when I'm not here anymore . . ."

"Daddy, stop . . ." Nina put her hand up. She didn't want to hear anything about him not being around.

"Listen to me, Nina. When that day comes, I want you to know . . . I love you, baby girl, and I'd never do anything to intentionally hurt you." Nina watched a tear pool and then drop from her father's eye. He quickly wiped it on the sleeve of his robe and barked at her. "Now, I know you left work to play nursemaid to me. I promise I'll finish my lunch. You get on back to your students, and leave your old daddy be. Do we have a deal?"

Nina smiled stiffly at her father and watched him take another bite of tuna sandwich. She knew he was asking her to leave it alone. To let the secret die. To never ask him about it again. She heard him saying he wasn't young and healthy anymore. He wasn't sure how much longer he had to live, and however long it was, their time together needed to be savored and appreciated and not filled with resentment. Nina heard her father's request loud and clear and she wanted her answer to him to be the same. She rose from her chair, moved to her father's side, and, wrapping her arms around him, she planted a kiss against his stubbly cheek. She knew that what she was about to say would seal it forever—like a heavy stone sealing the tomb where the secret of her mother lay. So at the same time she whispered the words "You've got a deal, Daddy," Nina prayed that whatever was in that clearinghouse in Omaha could somehow roll that heavy stone aside.

△▽ 25 ▽△

Ahmad lay quietly in the darkness, counting his heartbeats and trying unsuccessfully to talk his pulse into slowing down a little. *Calm down, man. You can do this.* It wasn't that he was afraid . . . He really had nothing to be afraid of. He couldn't do much more damage to his friendship with her than he'd already managed to do. Actually, the more he thought about it, the more it seemed he really had nothing to lose by calling Nina out of the blue. *Yeah, right. Nothing to lose.* If that was the case, why had he been trying for the last fifteen minutes to pick up the telephone and dial her number? And why, every time he managed to press the seventh digit, did he slam the phone to the cradle before the call could go through?

Ahmad rolled suddenly onto his side and propped himself up on one elbow on the couch. He reached again for the phone, picking the receiver up with his free hand. Cradling the receiver to his ear with his shoulder, he reached to press the lighted digits again. *This time,* he thought, as he began dialing for what must have been the fourth or fifth time, *I'm not hanging up. What's the worst the woman could do?* He didn't really want to think about the answer to that question, because under the circumstances, he wouldn't be surprised if she hung up in his face . . . and if she did, he couldn't really blame her, could he?

When Ahmad slowly pressed the last digit, he took a deep breath and waited for the call to connect. There was no answer on the first ring. *Hmmm. Maybe she's not home. It is almost eight o'clock on a Saturday night.* On the second ring there was still no answer. *Maybe she has that I.D. thing—she knows it's me calling and she doesn't want to talk to me.* Ring number three. *Okay, she's not home. So, when the answering machine comes on, do I leave a message or should I call back?* Ring number four . . . *And if I leave a message what the hell am I going to—*

"Hello?"

Nina's actual voice wasn't what Ahmad expected to hear after all those rings, and he waited a long time to say hello back. Too long.

"Hello?" she said again. This time there was a hint of impatience in her voice.

Ahmad's abrupt transition to a sitting position made his voice sound shakier than it already was. "Uh . . . hello, Nina. It's Ahmad."

There was an uncomfortable silence. Finally, Nina said blandly, "Oh. Hello, Ahmad."

"Uh . . . Listen, Nina. I was wondering if I could talk to you." He knew he sounded nervous. But there was nothing he could do about that.

"Oh-kaay." The stiff, professional tone said Nina was questioning whether she really wanted to hear what Ahmad had to say. The last couple of "we need to talk" conversations they'd had hadn't ended too well.

"Uh." Now that Nina was actually on the phone, he suddenly needed to see her face. He needed to be able to communicate with her in person. This wasn't the kind of conversation you had on the phone—this required eye contact. Finally Ahmad said softly, "Nina . . . I . . . I don't think I can really communicate what I need to say to you over the phone. Is it possible for me to see you? Are you busy?" He listened to the silence on the other end, and when Nina didn't respond, he added, "I mean, it doesn't have to be tonight, but as soon as you have some time . . ."

"I have plans tonight, Ahmad."

"Oh . . . okay. Well, how 'bout tomorrow? Maybe we could have lunch or . . . ?"

"I'm sorry, but I'm going out to my parents' house tomorrow."

Ahmad was beginning to wonder if she was trying to tell him she really didn't want to be bothered. Maybe he'd waited too long to come to his senses. Maybe she was seeing someone else. But wasn't all of that beside the point? He needed to see her. And he was willing to wait until she was ready. "Maybe sometime during the week then?"

"Next week is finals. I—I'm pretty busy with my students during finals week."

"Oh. I see." He cleared his throat nervously. If the woman was trying to discourage him, it was working. But he'd gone this far; he wasn't about to give up now. "Well, maybe during the holiday break?"

"Ahmad, is this about Ebony?" There was that businesslike tone again.

"No, Nina. It's not about Ebony." Ahmad hoped she'd hear it in his voice. Hear how ready he was to make things right. "It's about me, Nina. It's about what happened in L.A. It's about everything."

Another long silence. Ahmad wished he could see her face ... read her expression. Finally Nina said softly, "Um ... Well ... Actually, I have a meeting this evening that shouldn't take long. I should be back home pretty early. If you don't mind waiting for me to—" Nina stopped talking suddenly, and Ahmad heard what sounded like a doorbell ringing in the background. "I guess if it's not too late, you could come by for a cup of—" The doorbell rang again, and Nina said quickly, "I'm sorry, but I have to go, Ahmad."

"Okay, Nina. Listen, Ebony's at Adrianne's tonight and I'll be right here at home." Ahmad thought to tell her he'd wait up all night if he needed to, but he didn't.

When Nina said, "Why don't you call back ... around ... say ... nine-thirty or ten?" something in her voice made Ahmad feel hopeful. Something said maybe she was missing him as much as he was missing her.

"That's cool, Nina. I'll talk to you then."

When Nina's good-bye came through the receiver, Ahmad could have sworn he heard a smile come through with it.

Nina had spent the whole day hoping Derrick would forget about their dinner arrangement, and when the phone rang, she thought it might be him calling to cancel at the last minute. But no, Derrick showed up at her door right on time, interrupting her short phone conversation with Ahmad and looking drop-dead gorgeous. She stood in the doorway for a moment and looked Derrick up and down with her eyebrows raised in surprise. Derrick's usual outfit of sweatshirt, jeans, and tennis shoes had been replaced, and Nina was standing there staring at the most luscious ivory cable-knit sweater she had ever seen. The thick pullover hung from Derrick's broad shoulders like silk to just below the pockets of his black corduroy slacks which sat handsomely atop new leather boots. He'd topped the whole outfit off with a quilted butter-soft black leather jacket, and with his recently grown beard and wire-rimmed glasses, Derrick actually looked like a man. But Nina knew better.

She stepped stiffly out into the porch light wearing a conservative black wool pantsuit, and as Derrick moved his eyes over Nina's body approvingly, she quickly pulled the front door closed behind her . . . just in case he had some idea that he was going to be invited in. When he leaned in close to her, she turned her head at just the right moment so the kiss Derrick had planned for her lips fell on her cheek instead. Unruffled, Derrick stepped back and smiled.

"You look beautiful, Nina."

"Thank you," she responded curtly and started down the walkway toward the curb. The coolness of the desert night air felt refreshing on her face, and Nina stood under the blinking lights of the Christmas-decorated maple trees in front of her building exhaling a long, slow sigh. *What a beautiful December night*, she thought. *I should be curled up in front of the fireplace in someone's arms on a night like this* . . . She thought of Ahmad instantly. He wanted to see her tonight. *He wants to talk. Finally. Tonya predicted it, and sure enough . . . the man was finally coming around. Damn. If I didn't have this so-called date with Derrick* . . . She stopped in front of a gleaming black Mustang convertible and looked around for Derrick's beat-up Tercel, but it was nowhere in sight. To her surprise, Derrick approached the Mustang and opened the passenger door, flashing his sexy grin at Nina.

"Nice car," Nina said dryly. *Probably belongs to some hoochie he picked up last weekend.*

"I got it last weekend," he replied, waiting until Nina was buckled in before he closed the door. He stopped at the trunk to open and close it, then walked around to his side of the car. When he got in behind the wheel, he handed Nina a delicately wrapped bouquet of white long-stem roses and shot her his dimpled smile as he pulled away from the curb. "A peace offering."

Nina didn't say anything at first. She just looked at Derrick sitting there grinning at her like it was their first date. Was she supposed to act like she didn't already know his tactics? Who knew better than Nina that Derrick's romantic charm was just another familiar weapon in his war to get what he wanted? *If this fool whips out a Hallmark card and starts singing, I'm gonna throw up.* Nina cleared her throat and finally muttered unemotionally, "The roses are beautiful."

After riding in silence for a few minutes, Derrick reached forward and pushed a cassette into the tape deck. Minnie Riperton—cued to the song Derrick knew was one of Nina's favorites. Nina wondered if he caught her rolling her eyes in disgust. *Come on. He really doesn't get it, does he?* Derrick turned the volume up. "Loving You." She listened for as long as she could stand it before she reached for the eject button and popped the tape out.

"What'd you do that for?" Derrick looked genuinely baffled.

"Derrick. Let's not beat around the bush, okay?" Nina reached behind him to deposit the bouquet on the backseat. "I only agreed to this so-called date to influence you to do the right thing. I don't know what it is you're after, but I don't want to play games with you."

"Why does it have to be about games, Nina?" Derrick turned the car into the driveway of the Red Lobster, pulled into a parking space, and turned the motor off. Reaching up suddenly with his right hand, he positioned the rearview mirror so that his face was reflected in it. With his left, he rubbed the freshly-healed bump on his lip where Ahmad had slugged him, and smiled at her. "I'm glad that happened, Nina. And I'd take another punch if I knew it would give me a chance to . . ." Derrick grasped one of Nina's hands in his. "I'm trying to show you . . . to tell you I realize now how stupid I was.

I miss you, Nina, and I just want you to let me make it up to you. I want things back the way they were before.''

Nina stared hard at Derrick in disbelief. *After all the lies and manipulation . . . Shit, after being caught with another woman in my bed . . . This fool actually thinks he can buy a few flowers and pop in a Minnie Riperton cassette?*

Derrick finally responded to Nina's stare with a nervous ''What?''

''Pshhh.'' She pulled her hand free from his grasp. ''I don't believe you. You want things back the way they were before?''

''Yeah. What's so unbelievable about that?''

She laughed softly and shook her head. ''Before what, Derrick? You want things back the way they were before *what*? Before you got caught with that woman going down on you in *my* bed?'' Derrick didn't say a word. Nina waited for his excuse. She expected some sorry story. She knew there was no way Derrick would take responsibility for what he had done to help destroy their relationship, so while Nina waited for him to come up with what was sure to be a fantastic lie, she amused herself by imagining her own sarcastic version of how Derrick might apologize. *No, Nina . . . you've got it all wrong . . . See . . . the woman you saw me with was actually a backup singer who was only there to rehearse . . . I don't know how it happened . . . But when I asked her to perform—orally—she must have misunderstood . . .* Nina smiled sarcastically at the scenario going on in her head before she said coolly, ''I can't hear you, Derrick. The way things were before *what?*''

Derrick looked deep into Nina's eyes. Without breaking his stare, he said quietly, ''Before I messed everything up. Before I disrespected you and your home. Before I was stupid enough to put some weak-ass sexual satisfaction before my commitment to you.'' Derrick's voice wavered slightly when he added, ''Before I realized how much I really do love you . . . how much I need you in my life, Nina.''

Nina was stunned. Derrick had never given such a humble and remorseful version of an apology. Never. Usually, when he'd done something that required one, he was trying to make up a zillion reasons why his mistake was somebody else's fault. He had never been able to admit to being wrong about anything, and of course he had a creative excuse for doing whatever stupid thing he was apologizing for. But here he was now, laying it all out there on the line. And to top it all off, he was actually saying the "L" word . . . with all his clothes on. Nina couldn't help but feel a twinge of pain for what she was about to say.

"I don't love you, Derrick."

"Nina, please. I know it's crazy . . . what I did. I don't deserve another chance but . . ."

"Derrick. This isn't about what you deserve. And it's not even about what you did. I'm not in love with you, and I'm sure I never will be. And there's nothing either of us can do about that."

Derrick sat quietly, trying to take in what Nina had so calmly announced. She knew he had never seen her so detached, so self-assured. He clutched the steering wheel tightly with both hands and tried to sound calm when he asked, "Is it that dreadlock dude? Is that it?"

Nina shook her head. "No, Derrick, it's not about anybody else. It's us. You and I . . . We're just not . . ." Nina studied Derrick's handsome face. He was as fine as ever, and the sight of his dark, mysterious eyes and his luscious lips could still make her heart skip a beat. But that was all his gorgeous looks would ever do for her heart. It had taken a while for her to figure that out, but she knew it now. "This relationship was based on physical attraction, Derrick. And we both know it."

"And what's wrong with that?"

"I'm not saying physical attraction's not important, but I want more than that. Don't you?"

Derrick didn't answer. He leaned his head back on the headrest in defeat and exhaled loudly, but he didn't say a word.

"Derrick, I'm going to ask you a question, and I really, *really* would like it if you would just answer it honestly . . . for old times' sake if nothing else."

He raised his eyebrows and smiled nervously.

"Have you ever dated a Black woman before me?"

Derrick turned his head away from Nina and looked out the window. "No," he muttered quietly.

"Why not?"

"I never met one I wanted to date."

"You met me."

He looked at her and cocked an eyebrow. "But you're fine as hell and I thought . . ."

"You thought I was White."

"Yeah. So? Now I know you're not and it doesn't make a difference to me. So . . . what's your point?"

Nina was almost sorry she'd asked. Derrick really had no idea what the point was. *What's my point? Isn't it obvious? My point is there's something wrong with you.* "Derrick, don't you think there's something strange about a Black man who isn't attracted to Black women?"

"People have preferences, Nina. What's wrong with people dating whoever they please?"

"It's not about you being attracted to White women, Derrick. And I'm not saying you shouldn't date them. There are plenty of attractive White women in the world, and if you . . . if you find them beautiful . . . I can't say that's wrong. But something *is* wrong with not being able to recognize beauty in women who God didn't create to be pale-skinned, light-eyed, and silky-haired."

Derrick reached for his door handle. "There ain't nothing wrong with me," he said, jerking the handle. "Can we finish this conversation over dinner?"

"Why don't you just save your money, Derrick."

"Nina . . . come on."

"I really do just want to go home. Really." Nina wasn't even mad at him anymore—just disgusted. She had actually been engaged to this man—a man who never would have looked twice at her if she had just inherited a little more melanin from her father . . . *Ugh.* All Nina could do was cringe and shake her head at herself in disgust.

"Fine." Derrick sighed in defeat, closed his door, and turned the ignition. He gunned the engine and drove the car out of the parking lot and back toward Nina's apartment. They drove in an uncomfortable silence, making Nina wonder if Derrick might actually be thinking about what she'd said to him, or if he was just too upset to talk. When he finally pulled up to the curb at her place, she turned to him and stared, as if she was waiting for him to say something. When he finally looked in her eyes, she asked calmly, "Do you think you're a racist, Derrick?"

"Do I think I'm a racist? What kind of question is that?"

"Well, you exclude Black women from your list of prospective partners, and . . ."

"Look. Who are you to scrutinize my dating practices? How many White men have you gone out with, Nina? *None* . . . *so?* Does that make *you* a racist?"

"That's different. I'm not saying I won't date one. I'm just—"

Derrick jumped on the comment. "You're just not *attracted* to them. So, why is that different? Maybe I'm just not attracted to Black women."

"But you *are* black . . . There's something wrong with that, Derrick. I'm attracted to men who resemble the people who raised me . . . who loved me . . . My father is Black . . . It makes sense that I—"

"The man who raised you is no different than me, Nina. Don't forget what kind of woman your daddy had to be attracted to to create you. Maybe he and I are more alike than you want to believe."

Derrick's comment stung worse than a slap, and Nina pulled her door handle to get out of the car and the situation before she did something crazy. The anger rose like a hot flash from her gut, and she wanted to slap Derrick's face for daring to compare his trifling self to her daddy. She jiggled the handle angrily and pushed her shoulder against the door to escape.

When it didn't unlock or open right away, Derrick reached calmly for the door's autolock button. Before pressing it he said, "You want to leave me with your words of wisdom about my racial preferences, but you don't want to hear any words of wisdom about your own."

Nina turned toward him abruptly. "You've got some wisdom for me, Derrick? Please, I'd love to hear this."

"The reality is, Nina Moore, you are not just a Black woman. You are *half*-Black. Half of you is White, and whether you like it or not, that's something you need to deal with."

"*Need* to deal with?" Nina smirked at Derrick. "Okay, while I'm dealing with that, why don't you deal with the fact that you're a Black man who's so busy running after every

White woman who comes along, he'll never figure out what he's running *away* from.''

"Okay."

Derrick's cool comeback knocked most of the venom out of Nina's voice. "Okay, what?"

"Okay, I'll deal with it," he countered matter-of-factly. "Why do you think I'm so busy running after White women, Nina? What do you think I'm running away from?"

Nina didn't hear any sarcasm in his voice, but she figured the sincere tone was only another ploy to get his way—to manipulate her. "That's not for me to say. You need to deal with it yourself."

"But I'm sure you have an opinion about it."

Nina did have an opinion. But she didn't think Derrick really wanted to hear it. "Derrick, why don't we just leave well enough alone? Why don't we try to end this as friends and just leave this whole conversation alone?"

"No. I want to know what you think."

"Okay. Fine. I think you don't want to be what you are. I think deep down, you think there's something better about . . . I think you wish you were anything but Black." Nina paused, and Derrick was strangely silent before she added, "And I think you hate Black women for reminding you that no matter how hard you try, you cannot run from yourself."

Derrick was quiet for a few moments. He stared straight ahead and sat motionless, momentarily lost in the glare of Christmas lights twinkling above the windshield. When he finally spoke, it was as if he wasn't even talking to Nina. His deep, gritty voice sounded like he was on the verge of tears, though there wasn't a drop of wetness in his eyes.

"Did I ever tell you the earliest memory I have of my mother?" He stopped then, like he wasn't sure he wanted to venture any further into the dark cave he was about to enter. When Nina responded by shaking her head slowly in answer to his question, he continued. "I was three and a half. We were standing in line at the grocery store and this White woman behind us tapped my mother on the shoulder. The woman had this long, golden hair, and she . . . she was standing there staring at me with these shining blue eyes. I remember thinking she looked like the angel my mother put on top of our Christmas tree every year. The lady smiled down at me. Then . . . I remember . . . like it was yesterday. The way my mother's hand felt.''

Derrick finally looked at Nina. It was the first time Nina could remember Derrick sharing anything about his mother, and it reminded her of that little boy in him that was so precious to her once upon a time.

"She called me beautiful." Derrick looked into Nina's eyes for a long moment before he continued. "My mother was holding my hand in hers, and when the woman called me beautiful, Mama squeezed my knuckles together so hard it was a wonder she didn't break my fingers. I don't know if she knew she was really hurting me. I wanted to cry, but I didn't. I looked up at my mother then, but she didn't look at me. Instead, she just looked at that White woman like she was crazy . . . She didn't crack a smile. In the hardest, coldest voice my mother had, she barked at the woman, 'Derrick? Beautiful? Shit. That boy's black as the devil and twice as bad.' ''

Derrick disappeared somewhere for a long moment. He held his left hand in his right, gently massaging the knuckles as if they still stung with pain after all those years. He stared straight ahead for a time before he turned to Nina and added, "My mother made it her life's work to remind me . . . to punish me for coming out so dark.''

The two sat in silence. Nina watched the reflection of Christmas lights twinkling across Derrick's face, competing with the shining glow of his deep brown skin. He really had no idea. *How sad to be so beautiful and have no idea.* Derrick was still looking for that woman who could convince him that what that White woman saw was true. It was a shame that his mother, the woman who should have said those words to him herself, never saw her son's beauty in the first place, so now Derrick was looking past her for a woman who could. Nina leaned over suddenly and planted a kiss on Derrick's cheek.

"Memories are supposed to remind us, Derrick. But they don't define us. Mama heard the same messages when she was a child, but she was determined not to pass them on to me and Nat. Your mother probably heard them, too. She just didn't know how to be better.''

"Well, I'm going to be better then, Nina. I'm going to do

something she didn't do. I'm going to make sure my kids don't have to deal with this.'' Derrick held his ebony-toned hand out in front of Nina.

"Derrick. Marrying a White woman . . .'' Nina placed her ivory-beige hand on top of his. ''. . . or even a white-skinned Black woman . . . that's not going to undo what your mother did to you. That's not going to fix anything. I know you're thinking I don't have any idea—me with my white skin—I don't have any idea what it's like to get the hand you were dealt . . . and that's true. I don't. But I do know you have to be better. Before you marry anybody. You have to be better or your own kids will be telling a story like this one day.''

When silence settled down around them once more, Nina pulled the handle and opened the car door. Derrick got out quickly and walked around to her side of the car. She said softly, "Let's just say our good-byes right here, okay Derrick?''

Derrick wrapped his arms around Nina and hugged her tight. He held on for a long time, but he never said a word. Nina knew why he wasn't talking. There was really nothing left to say. She was glad she'd agreed to go out with him. She was glad to finally feel like Derrick didn't have to be a disgusting memory swept under the rug. Nina hugged Derrick a little tighter. She had to feel compassion for him. She could understand what had happened that might make him the way he was, but she was also glad it was over. It *was* over. And she wasn't sure if he really understood that yet. Finally, she whispered, "Good-bye, Derrick. I hope you . . . I hope we both find what we're looking for.'' She turned and walked away, leaving Derrick watching sadly until the front door closed behind her.

Ahmad had decided he couldn't sit still long enough to wait to call Nina. Instead he had showered quickly, put on a pair of clean, but threadbare Levi's and two of his warmest sweatshirts, and headed out his front door. After stopping at the grocery store for some breath mints and an inexpensive bouquet of plastic-wrapped roses, he drove over to Nina's house, and sat in the car watching the Christmas lights along the street flash and sparkle against the dark sky.

Ahmad waited anxiously, and a little uncomfortably, in his chilly car, anticipating Nina's return. He was glad she suggested they meet right away, because there was no way he could hold on to all the thoughts and feelings dancing around inside of him for much longer. *Finally.* He was finally going to be able to tell Nina what had happened at Chante's funeral and to apologize for the pain he'd caused her. He knew she'd understand. At least he hoped she would. She'd realize that it was the stress of everything he was dealing with that had driven him to run from her, and he'd admit to her that it was his own insecurity that kept him away for so long. He needed to explain his fears about Nina's skin . . . about the foster homes . . . then Beth and Scotty. He wanted to make sure Nina knew that his issues had nothing to do with her. He wanted her to know how he really felt about her, how often she was in his thoughts—how much he ached to begin again where they left off.

Ahmad had driven across town with a grin on his face and hope in his heart that finally, he could tell the woman how much he had been missing her. Finally, he could do what his heart always knew was the right thing . . .

But now that the moment had finally arrived—now that the opportunity to clear everything up was actually before him, he didn't know what he was going to do. Everything that was so clear only minutes before blurred before his eyes as he sat in his car halfway down the block across from Nina's apartment and watched her emerge from a brand-new black Mustang.

He couldn't make out the identity of the driver until the man got out of the car and walked over to wrap his arms around Nina in a tight hug. There was no mistaking it—it was Derrick. Ahmad had watched her lean across her seat to kiss him, and now that they were out of the car, she was wrapped, willingly, in his embrace.

Damn. Maybe I'm too late. Ahmad blew a warm breath into his hands and held his eyes closed for a moment, as if maybe, when he opened them again, the scene before him might miraculously disappear. But when he looked again they were hugging even tighter, and . . . *Humph.* Nina seemed to be whispering something in Derrick's ear. *She can't still have feelings for that fool? Not after . . .* Ahmad began to wonder

if maybe all Nina's talk about Derrick being shallow and immature was just that—talk. Maybe she was just using him,
Ahmad, to get over Derrick—or worse, to make Derrick jealous. Maybe the night Ahmad and Nina had spent together in
Los Angeles meant a whole lot more to him than it ever did
to her. Maybe he was kidding himself thinking Nina would
consider the little apology he had prepared for her. Even
worse, maybe there was nothing to apologize for.

Meeting, huh? This looked suspiciously like a date. What
if these two were planning to reconcile all along? If that was
the case . . .

The threat Derrick had made to press assault charges against
him echoed in Ahmad's head. ''You're gonna hear from my
lawyer. You're gonna pay for that shit.'' What did he really
mean? Pay how . . . with money, or with freedom? Either way,
Ahmad couldn't pay the price. If Derrick and Nina were back
together, would that mean that Nina might have to defend her
man? Could Nina cosign something so ridiculous? *No way.
Nina would never do that . . . She loves Ebony too much. But
then again, what if she's sprung on this dude?* Ahmad hated
the thoughts that were running through his mind. He hated
how easily the feeling of vulnerability swept over him—how
quickly the fear flooded in and how willing he was to allow
it to. He believed he did the right thing when he pulled that
trigger to protect Scotty, and it was the same instinct to protect
a loved one that had made him punch Derrick in the face. The
bottom line was, if he had it to do over—he'd hit him again.
He'd just have to trust that Nina believed he did the right
thing, too.

Ahmad watched as Nina walked slowly toward her front
door. Derrick looked after her, like he wanted to follow, but
he didn't. He just stood there watching her walk away. Ahmad
let out a long sigh. *So maybe she really did break up with
him.* Maybe it wasn't a date after all. She said she had a meeting and it would be short. *If this was a date, wouldn't Derrick
be following her into the house, not hugging her good-bye on
the sidewalk?* Maybe they had some loose ends left over from
the engagement that needed to be tied up. *I'm just going to
wait until Derrick drives off and just go on and ring her . . .*
Ahmad's thoughts were interrupted by the realization that Der-

rick wasn't leaving after all. He watched as Derrick pulled a bouquet of what looked like incredibly expensive roses out of the back of his car and headed with them in hand toward Nina's front door. Ahmad looked down at the pitiful bunch of roses wrapped in plastic on his front seat. He looked at his shabby sweatshirt and faded Levi's and glanced back up at Derrick's obviously expensive outfit and beautiful leather jacket. Ahmad had never felt inadequate before now, and it never occurred to him that Nina might think he was, but suddenly the Volvo seemed too old, too raggedy, and too dirty, and the clothes Ahmad wore seemed like rags. And come to think of it, what did he have to offer the woman, really? Nothing that she didn't already have. What reason could a woman like Nina have to be attracted to a poor ex-convict? A woman with as much going for her as Nina obviously had . . .

When Ahmad raised his head and looked toward Nina's door, Derrick was standing on her front step ringing the bell. Ahmad watched as Nina opened the door, smiled at Derrick, and took the bouquet from his hand. But when she leaned forward to plant a kiss on Derrick's face, Ahmad had seen enough. The warm anticipation he'd felt on the drive over to her house had suddenly cooled. The decision he'd made—that he was ready to finally let Nina all the way in his heart—had evaporated into the cold night air, and the belief he'd held that Nina might actually want to hear what he'd come to say evaporated along with it. He wasn't ready. And the sight of Nina in Derrick's arms was enough to prove it. *I've got some work to do*, Ahmad thought as he turned the ignition. *Sorry, Ms. Nina Moore, but I'm not quite ready for this.* Ahmad was glad he decided to show up early, and the last thing he wanted to do was to wait around to see how the scene in Nina's doorway would end. He wasn't about to throw in the towel, but he knew what he had to do to. Ahmad Jefferson pulled the Volvo out into the street and took a very long way home.

△▽ 26 ▽△

Ahmad watched the face of the Interstate Na-
tional Bank's manager turn an unusually deep shade of pink.
The round-faced man cleared his throat, then blinked several
times at Ahmad before he tried to speak. After a dramatic
swallow, he half-whispered, "Did you say you want cash?"

Ahmad gave each end of the check he held tightly in both
hands a sharp yank, making a loud snapping noise with it. "I
said I want to deposit this, please, but I'd also like a cashier's
check for forty-three thousand, five hundred and seventeen
dollars." That was the exact amount he had been quoted for
the fully loaded Lincoln Navigator he'd test-driven on Sunday
afternoon.

As he handed the check over and watched the bespectacled
man examine it carefully, Ahmad tried to come to grips with
what was about to happen to his life. With the simple scribble
of a signature on the back of a three-by-seven-inch piece of
paper, at age twenty-seven Ahmad would be forever leaving
poverty to join the ranks of the financially well-off. Now that
he was actually in the bank and the reality of what was happening was becoming more tangible with each passing minute,
he silently cursed himself for taking so long to come to his
senses in the first place.

He tried not to think too hard about what had prevented him
from making the decision earlier. The resentment toward
Scotty and Beth and what they'd done to his life was surely
a factor, but more than anything, it had just been too painful
for him to accept the reality that he would be benefiting from

255

Scotty's suicide. And rather than force himself back into the painful past, for over two months he'd kept the check stuffed in a shoe box on the top shelf in his closet.

It took that long for the reality of the situation to sink in, and it did, all at once, like a thunderous announcement from the heavens. It came to him in a very loud and clear voice as he sat outside Nina's apartment and watched her emerge from Derrick's car. *The Maxwells owe me.* They had taken his life, or at least what felt like a huge chunk of it. The fact that Scotty's death was the source of Ahmad's newfound financial security should actually have felt like some kind of ironic justice to him . . . but it didn't. He just decided it was time to embrace the reality that if it wasn't for Scotty and his courtroom lies, he, Ahmad, would have graduated from USC years ago, and surely would have had his law degree by now. If his life hadn't been swept out from under him like it was, he would have been in a position to take care of his daughter in a manner that she deserved.

"Enough already." He had whispered those words aloud to himself in the cold interior of the Volvo as he sat outside Nina's apartment. Hadn't he driven Ebony around Glendale with no air-conditioning and no heat for long enough? It was time.

The manager led Ahmad to an office along the back wall of the bank and motioned for him to seat himself in a plush leather chair. "It's not every day we get a customer asking to deposit such a large amount of money." The round-faced man was absolutely jovial. But Ahmad didn't say a word. It wasn't that he was trying to be rude. Actually, the polyester-suited, paunchy little man exuded that nervous kind of friendliness that was almost likeable. Like maybe if their lives weren't so radically different from one another's, there might be enough shared humanity between them to find some kind of common ground. Maybe a ball game to talk about, or the latest swimsuit issue of *Sports Illustrated*.

The man finally interrupted Ahmad's thoughts with a nervous attempt at small talk. "So, are you an athlete or . . ." He dipped his head from side to side and grinned expectantly, waiting for Ahmad to fill in the blank.

So much for the wasted romantic notion of shared humanity.

Black man with a lot of money ... can't be anything but an athlete? Why didn't he ask me if I just won a Pulitzer ... or a Nobel prize? Or, gotdammit, maybe I just sold my excess Microsoft stock. Ahmad felt his anger rise with a painful throbbing at his temples, and for a split second he fantasized about knocking the idiot out. But when he remembered why he was standing there, he grinned like a jester instead and said with obviously too much enthusiasm, "Why, yes, as a matter of fact I *am* an athlete. Olympic swimmer," Ahmad gibed. "Synchronized swimming to be exact. That check is the payment for my Wheaties shoot."

The bank manager's silence let Ahmad know the dart hit its mark. There was no more small talk. When the man was finished typing Ahmad's information into the computer, he said quietly, "Fortunately, this check is drawn from one of our banks, Mr. Jefferson. I see you have Arizona identification and legal proof of your name change. There should be no problem. I just need to call the branch manager in Seattle for clearance, and your seven hundred thousand will be deposited here immediately. Do you want that in checking, savings, money market account ... ?"

"Just put the bulk of it in savings for now. And I'd like twenty thousand in checking."

"Yes, sir, Mr. Jefferson, sir. No problem." The man left him alone then, and Ahmad watched through the windowed wall as the manager scurried from the new accounts desk to a teller window and back to the new accounts desk. Then, waving Ahmad's check in the air like it was on fire, he disappeared into an office along the same row as the one Ahmad was in and closed the door.

The check had been like fire to Ahmad too. It had burned a hole in his thoughts since the day Beth handed it to him, but he hadn't been close to cashing it until now. He hated to admit it, but seeing Nina with Derrick was what finally did it. It brought everything into perspective for him. He had felt so naked sitting there in the dark watching Nina. And it wasn't just about the material things—the car and the clothes. No, it was everything. It was seeing Nina locked in Derrick's embrace. It was the memory of Derrick's threat ringing harshly in his ears. It all blended in together to finally jolt Ahmad out of his stubborn unwillingness to spend Beth's money. And what he finally had to see—the greatest jolt of all—was that if something tragic did happen, he had no way of protecting his daughter's future.

Though he believed Derrick was really just blowing smoke, that threat to press charges did make Ahmad think. What if he lost his job? Or what if, God forbid, he did go back to prison? What would happen to his child? From the moment Ahmad had pulled away from the curb outside Nina's apartment, he'd begun planning. Not only did he want a better standard of living for himself and Ebony, he needed to work quickly to try to clear his name for his daughter's sake.

Ahmad had already put a deposit down on a roomy two-bedroom rental near the campus with an option to buy. Even if he bought the car and the house with cash, he'd still have over five hundred thousand dollars left. With that he'd be able to hire a real lawyer, and if he had to subpoena Beth and all her Maxwell cronies, he'd finally be able to clear his name. It might take a year or two or maybe even more, but any judge hearing Beth's testimony would be sure to have all charges dropped against him, and Ahmad could be free to raise his daughter in peace.

Then, of course, there was the matter of Nina. He certainly wasn't trying to run from her anymore. The truth was, someday Nina would be his woman. And if Ahmad had his way, that someday would be very soon.

The bank manager returned to the office where he'd left Ahmad and handed over the cashier's check, two credit cards, and a checkbook. "Here's your Visa debit card. If you'd like to apply for our platinum card, you would most certainly qualify for our optimum line of credit."

"That won't be necessary." Ahmad pocketed the items, and stood up.

"Here's my business card if you need anything else. My direct line is right there at the bottom. If you have any questions or problems please don't hesitate to call."

"Thank you very much," Ahmad said politely. He shook the man's outstretched hand, took the business card, and headed for the door. As he stepped out into the crisp, sun-drenched December air, Ahmad made a mental list of the things he still needed to do. He had to pick up the new car, and take a check to the furniture store before noon. The real estate agent was scheduled to meet him at his new place to hand over the key at three o'clock, and the furniture he'd already shopped for was scheduled to be delivered at four. Now that he knew exactly where he was headed—what direction he wanted his life to take—Ahmad was on a mission. And when everything was finally taken care of, and he was sure beyond a shadow of a doubt that everything was in place, he had a very important message to deliver.

Looking up into the cloudless December sky, Ahmad suddenly remembered an even more important message he'd neglected to send. Without hesitation he whispered a prayer of thanks for the steady stream of blessings that continued to be sent his way, then he let the bank's heavy glass door close slowly behind him and he started on his way.

◬ 27 ◭

The first bouquet of flowers arrived at Nina's door at nine in the morning, and by noon her living room looked like a florist's shop. The white carnations had come first, tied with a lavender satin bow and accompanied by a note card with only one word on it: *Please.*

With the arrival of a gorgeous daffodil arrangement came a second note, again with one word, only this time the word "have" was written in bold letters on the card. By the time she'd received the box of purple irises, the giant basket of daisies, a crystal vase filled with multicolored tulips, and a beautiful lush hanging fern, the message *Please have dinner with me tonight* was spelled out with the notes she'd arranged on the kitchen table.

Around one-thirty a colorful arrangement of exotic passion-flowers arrived. This time the card featured a typewritten address: 31424 Palm Canyon Drive. Shortly after that, Nina's living room resonated with the thick, sweet scent of lilacs. Those came with a note that read, 8 p.m.

When Tonya walked in the door at two o'clock, Nina was sitting on the couch, still in her pajamas, waiting for the final card that would tell her who was asking her to dinner.

Tonya took a long, slow look around the room, her face contorting into an almost painful look of bewilderment before she finally said, "Day-um. Who's sorry?"

"That's a good question." Nina fanned the cards up to Tonya like she was revealing a winning poker hand as she explained how they'd arrived.

260

"So . . . is this ol' Diehard Derrick trying again?" Tonya dropped her purse on the floor by the couch and stopped in front of the vase of lilacs on the coffee table. She bent over to inhale their sweet aroma.

"If it *is* Derrick, he's reached a whole new level of creativity." Nina shook her head knowingly at Tonya. "But I don't think so, T."

"Ahmad?" The look on Tonya's face said she didn't see how it could be him.

Nina shook her head again. "Ahmad doesn't have this kind of money." They both looked around at the obviously expensive collection of flowers filling up every empty space in the room.

Tonya pointed at the passionflowers on the floor near the bookshelf. "This time of year . . . Sheeyit, that arrangement alone is over a hundred dollars."

"We're looking at a good six or seven hundred dollars worth' of flowers, T."

"Somebody really wants to have you for dinner, girl. *Bad.*" Tonya chuckled. "Maybe it's that old coot in the English department. What's his name? Professor Pinkney?"

"Very funny." Nina rolled her eyes in disgust. "I had to threaten to tell his wife. He hasn't bothered me since."

They were both quiet, each trying to be the one to guess who the mystery date might be. When the doorbell rang, they jumped nervously, but neither of them made an attempt to get the door.

"T, you get it—just in case it's him."

"Who's saying it's a *him*. It could be a *her*."

"Shut up, T."

"You know that Cassandra woman from your literature class last year . . . She was way sprung on you." Tonya cracked up at the peculiar expression on Nina's face, and she was still laughing when she walked over to see who was out there ringing the doorbell for the second time.

Nina followed behind Tonya, and was peering over her friend's shoulder when she pulled the door open. When they saw who was standing there, and what he was holding, they both made the exact same sound at the exact same time. It was just a quick rush of air—the sound of an inhale that didn't quite make it all the way to the lungs.

"Damn, Nina." Tonya didn't move.

"Damn." Nina crept out from behind Tonya.

"Another delivery for you, Ms. Moore. And again, the tip has already been taken care of." He reached out to hand Nina the flowers—a silver foil box holding one dozen of the most beautiful red long-stem roses Nina had ever seen. Each of the rose stems had been individually wrapped in florist's silk, and each of the buds glistened with tiny beads of dew. Nina backed into the house and sat on the couch with the box of roses across her lap.

"Well?" Tonya urged.

Nina found the tiny envelope among the bed of baby's breath and pulled the card out. She read it silently and looked up at Tonya in amazement.

"Well?" The eagerness in Tonya's voice said if Nina didn't hurry up and tell her whose name was on the card, she might just come over and snatch the card out of Nina's hand.

"It says, 'Please come. I need to talk to you.' " Nina grinned and waved the card in front of her face like a church fan.

"I'm gonna hurt you, Nina. *Who* needs to talk to you?"

"Ahmad."

"I knew it. I told you he was sprung." Tonya's face lit up with a smile that said she couldn't be happier for her friend. Suddenly Tonya's smile was replaced by a look of suspicious concern. She nodded in a quick, curious gesture at the roses on Nina's lap. "How'd Ahmad manage all this?"

"Hmmm." Nina's voice held the same concern. "Wouldn't we both like to know?"

"Didn't you tell me he was a starving student?"

Nina glanced around the room at all the flowers, then studied the roses in her lap. "His application for the center says so. He barely makes enough to live on. I mean . . . I always assumed he filled that app out honestly."

"What are you saying, Neen?"

"Nothing." Nina pulled one of the roses from the box and held it to her nose. When she breathed in its scent, she inhaled with it the memory of the single rose Ahmad had brought to her door that night at the Marriott. A shiver ran down her spine at the thought of Ahmad's soft lips against hers. *Everything that night had been so perfect. Maybe too perfect.* She went over Ahmad's story in her head. *He wasn't doing anything wrong. He had been set up. Yes, there were drugs in the car, but Ahmad didn't know anything about them. He wasn't a criminal. He had to plead guilty. He had no choice.* She believed him then—she believed every word he said beyond a shadow of a doubt. But now . . .

"What is it, Nina?"

"Tonya, how on earth are you supposed to know when you're being deceived by a man? Why is it always so hard to figure out what's really going on with them?"

"I'm telling you—that man is sprung, Nina."

"Maybe. Maybe he's just trying to play me."

"You don't believe that."

"How am I supposed to know what to believe? What the hell is wrong with expecting men to just be . . . just be human for God's sake."

"Girl, you know men are from Mars."

"Yeah, and I must be from Pluto." Nina tossed the box of flowers to the carpet and tossed the rose she was holding into it. "South Pluto."

"What are you talking about?"

"What am I supposed to think, Tonya? First the man virtually ignores me. Then he nearly inhales me. Then he disappears for weeks at a time. When he finally resurfaces, I wait up all night for a phone call that never comes. And now, nearly two weeks later, he's showering me with flowers he supposedly can't afford, and is asking me to come to dinner at an address I've never heard of, and all in less than . . ." Nina glanced dramatically at her watchless wrist. ". . . in just a few hours? So what? Am I supposed to ask the man how high he wants me to jump?"

Tonya stared at Nina thoughtfully. Finally, she cocked one eyebrow, and with the slightest of sarcastic grins she asked, "What are you going to wear?"

"I was thinking maybe my black knit dress." They both burst out laughing.

"Ya gotta do what ya gotta do." Tonya waved dramatically

at the roomful of flowers like she was a TV spokesmodel. "At
least give the brotha a chance to explain."

"What if that man is the opposite of everything I wanted
him to be? What if he really is some kind of criminal?"

"Or . . . what if there's a reasonable explanation for everything?"

"Yeah, right," Nina chirped sarcastically. She got up from
the couch and scowled at Tonya as she headed for her bedroom. "And what if I could beat Michael Jackson in a moon-
walking contest?"

"So, you're not going to go?" Tonya hollered down the
hallway at Nina.

"Nope," Nina hollered back. "I can't go." She tiptoed
back down the hallway and peeked around the corner. "I
mean . . ." She grinned at Tonya. ". . . I can't go like this.
Ain't you gon' help me pick something out?" Before the
words were out of Nina's mouth, Tonya was already on her
feet and headed in her friend's direction.

Ahmad basted the broiled salmon steaks with melted garlic butter then covered them lightly with a foil strip before
sliding them back into the warm oven. *I hope she likes
salmon.* He had considered preparing the smothered chicken
and buttered potatoes he'd become so famous for when he
worked chow duty in the pen, but he remembered Nina or-
dering snapper at the Marriott and thought fish might be a
better choice.

He gathered up a folded stack of table linens and walked
around the tiled counter that separated his new gourmet
kitchen from the adjacent dining room. Ahmad had chosen
to decorate the dining room sparsely, selecting a glass table
atop a granite rectangle base. The table complemented the
room's floor-to-ceiling slate fireplace which separated the
dining room from the living room, leaving an entryway on
either side. The armless chairs were upholstered in a pale
gray fabric—an excellent contrast to the black and amethyst
stoneware the Pottery Barn salesgirl had helped him pick out
a few days before.

Ahmad checked his watch. *Seven forty-nine.* Ten minutes
to spare, and except for the linens in his hand, everything was

in place. He carefully arranged the placemats and napkins at either end of the table, took one last look at his handiwork, and seated himself in one of the chairs. Ahmad imagined Nina at the other end of the table, gazing at him the way she had in L.A.—looking into his soul with that naked innocence that said she could be the one to actually stay. *The one to stay.* How ironic that it was that same look that made him have to get away from her. *Hindsight. Humph. If I knew then . . .* He missed everything about her. Her smile. Those eyes.

A flash of headlights shone in the dimly lit living room and Ahmad rose immediately just to see if it might be Nina, but the headlights moved on past the house and down the street. He stepped around the fireplace into the living room and stopped in front of the undecorated Christmas tree that filled most of the huge picture window that faced the street. He and Ebony had made plans to decorate the tree together as soon as she returned from her visit with her family in L.A. *We're going to decorate the Christmas tree together.* Ahmad smiled to himself. *Ebony's first Christmas with her daddy.* He loved the way the words sounded in his head. *Together. With.* Ebony would spend Christmas *with* Daddy, not with a handmade card full of phrases like "I'm sorry" and "I wish." This year, he and his daughter were going to celebrate Christmas the way he prayed they one day could, and though the sad memory of Chante might linger in each of their hearts, they would be happy to have one another and to have so many things to be thankful for. *So many things.*

As difficult as it was to do, Ahmad had been trying to reel himself in almost daily to keep from overdoing it on the present buying. He was so excited about the prospect of seeing Ebony's happy little face on Christmas morning, he had already packed the hall closet with gifts for her.

Ahmad walked around the tree to stand at the window, trying hard not to allow himself to feel discouraged that Nina had not yet arrived. He looked out at the empty curb, then down at his watch. It was eight o'clock exactly. *Maybe she's not . . .* He stopped himself. He knew better than to doubt. He knew she'd come. Just like he knew she'd forgive him for pushing her away, and he knew someday she'd be his woman.

The truth was, Ahmad had already pictured a day when Nina would be his wife. He'd terrified himself half to death with that thought the day they stood together under the praying tree in Santa Monica. The moment Nina called the tree hers, he realized there was something magical happening. He'd forced himself to banish all those crazy thoughts from his head as quickly as they had entered then; after all, he hadn't even buried his first wife—how could he already have been thinking of a new one?

Ahmad couldn't find any rational explanation for the strong feelings he had developed for Nina so soon. In the one day they'd spent together she had become totally irresistible to him, and the night they spent he could not get out of his head. Since that weekend, thoughts of Nina could only be banished with concerted effort, and they never stayed away for long. Each time he looked at that photo he'd taken of her, he had to admit to himself that there was something more than special about this woman who had happened into his life.

Ahmad never thought he'd allow himself to believe in anything like love at first sight—or even two people being destined to meet each other, especially after what had happened with Chante. But he was young back then, and inexperienced. This was different. These emotions that washed over him every time he'd been in Nina's presence were undeniable. Despite all the energy he had expended trying to avoid the inevitable, the realization of who Nina was had taken hold of him with a fury. It was as if somehow he had known her all his life. And looking back on it all now, he realized why he was so willing to push her away so quickly. It had all come too fast. First Scotty's death, then Chante's. He'd barely had a chance to adjust to being a free man, to being a father and a widow.

Marlene's warning to save Ebony from Nina was like the lifeline Ahmad was reaching desperately for—the first excuse he could find to back away from Nina—and he had clutched at it hastily. In a strange way it had been a lifesaver; it had given him the time he needed to step back and see the truth. It took him a little time to figure it all out, but he finally did, and in his heart he knew—there was no way on earth Nina wasn't going to show up tonight. *She'll come.*

As if on cue, a glow of headlights shone from behind the barren Christmas tree and illuminated the entire room as Nina's silver Honda pulled slowly up the block and finally hugged the curb in front of Ahmad's house.

Nina sat stiffly on the edge of Ahmad's calfskin sofa, inhaling the delicious smells wafting in from his kitchen, and marveling at his home's décor. *How has he managed to do all this in what must have been very little time? And with what money?* As her eyes moved slowly around the softly lit living room, she found herself trying hard to chase the images from her head of Ahmad masterminding some clandestine drug deals or some other illegal activities that could have led him to reap such rich rewards in such a short time. She had promised herself she would reserve judgment and just let Ahmad explain everything to her without jumping to her own conclusions. And the mere fact that she'd decided to come at all was because she'd decided to just go on and give the man the benefit of the doubt. But *damn*, she wasn't expecting all this. She did come to one very firm conclusion right away— *if the man is some kind of smooth-talking criminal, he's a criminal with some excellent interior decorating skills.*

Ahmad's living room featured a gleaming wood floor, bleached to a pale ash blond and lightly varnished. The stark white walls held framed prints of some of Nina's favorite contemporary black artists, and a bookshelf on the wall behind her was already half-filled with a variety of books. The baby-soft, plum-colored leather sofa Nina was seated on faced two light gray linen-upholstered accent chairs, and in the middle of the seating configuration was a glass-on-slate coffee table holding a small crystal-framed photo of Ebony hugging one of Marlene's puppies.

In front of the living room's huge picture window was a naked Christmas tree, whose branches, despite their lack of ornaments, gave life to the room and emitted an aura that looked unconcernedly hopeful, as if it knew it wouldn't be left undecorated for long.

On either side of the tree, across a high platinum-colored steel rod, hung generous, tied-linen window coverings. Their washed-ivory hue, coupled with the smooth lines of the pale wood floor and the abundant use of gray and white, gave the entire room a kind of "minimalist chic" feel, which made Nina want to take her knee-high leather boots off and stay a while.

Nina especially liked the offbeat splashes of color Ahmad had placed in various spots in the room—a large burnt orange candle on a tall, wrought iron stand near the door, and a funky purple and platinum wall sculpture hanging across the hearth of the beautiful floor-to-ceiling slate fireplace. The fireplace, which glowed with cool blue-green gas flames, separated the living room from whatever room was on the other side of it— Nina guessed it was the kitchen.

Whatever the room was, Ahmad had disappeared into it right after he welcomed Nina in with an enthusiastic hug, muttered something about the oven, and asked her to have a seat. She was waiting now, nervously, for his return.

"Your home is very beautiful . . ." Nina's voice echoed loudly, bouncing up at her from the smooth wood floor, but she wasn't sure if Ahmad was in range to hear since he didn't respond. A few seconds passed before he finally reappeared from behind the slate wall holding one hand behind his back.

"This is for you." He held a not-too-neatly-wrapped Christmas gift out to Nina and waited for her to reach for it.

She didn't. "Look, Ahmad." She could barely stand to look at him. The vanilla rayon shirt he wore, untucked, draped his muscular chest, then fell loosely over caramel-colored slacks. The dimmed track lighting coming from the cathedral ceiling above made Ahmad's chocolate skin shine with a delicious glow, and Nina struggled just to get the next sentence out.

"I appreciate the flowers, and . . ." She still didn't reach for the gift he held toward her. She had more pressing business on her mind. "I mean, they were really beautiful and I know you must have spent a fortune—"

Ahmad interrupted her. "If the flowers have anything to do with why you're sitting here in front of me . . ." He sat down a few inches from her on the couch. ". . . they were well worth it. It's just money, Nina. I wasn't trying to show off; I really just wanted to get your attention."

Nina hoped her face might reveal the battle that was going on in her head. She begged Ahmad silently to guess her burning questions and answer them one by one until she knew with a certainty exactly who he really was. But then what? What if there were reasonable explanations for everything? How would she ever be able to get past the hurt, and the doubt? She wanted to feel the way she did those months ago that now seemed like years—when Ahmad was an exciting mystery waiting to be revealed. Now, there was only one mystery she seemed to be able to focus on—*How on earth did this man afford all of this?*

Ahmad placed the gift he was still holding in his hand onto Nina's lap. "Please accept this. I know it looks a little . . ." He apologized for the disheveled wrapping job with a sheepish grin, then added, "Ebony helped me wrap it."

Nina's smile was wide and genuine at the mention of Ebony. "How is she?" She picked up the gift and examined the awkwardly taped ribbon and off-center bow.

"She's fine. She's staying with Marlene for a few days. Her grandmother asked for her."

"Her grandmother? But I thought . . ."

"She was in a coma? Yes, but only temporarily. Marlene said the stroke hit her pretty hard, and she didn't want any of her grandkids to see her in that condition. She couldn't move a muscle and she couldn't talk. She didn't want that to frighten the little ones. Now that she's recovered movement on her right side, and can speak . . . well, according to Marlene, the first person she asked for was Ebony." Ahmad's dimples deepened as his smile spread quickly across his face. "I talked to my baby this morning." He was obviously tickled at the thought of whatever conversation he had had with his daughter. "She said to tell you hi and she misses you."

The light that shone from behind Ahmad's eyes as he

looked deeply into Nina's was nearly blinding her. She blinked a few times and had to turn away, hoping he didn't notice how glassy her own eyes had become. She didn't say a word, and she didn't look back up at Ahmad. She couldn't. Instead she studied the happy little elves that smiled up at her from the gift-wrapped package on her lap.

"And," he added, "she made me promise to let her know if you like the present."

Nina tugged nervously at the hem of her mid-thigh-length cashmere dress. She had argued with Tonya about whether to wear it or something a little more conservative, but Tonya convinced her that it brought out the blue in her eyes. *Yeah, right.* Nina wore the dress because she knew it was feminine without being too sexy. It accentuated her hourglass shape without making her look sleazy, and even though Ahmad hadn't mentioned her physical appearance when he greeted her at the door, his eyes said he approved of her choice.

The nervous silence between them bordered on painful, and Nina found herself pretending to pick lint off her hemline to relieve some of her tense energy. But all that did was instantly draw Ahmad's attention to her bare thighs which were only partially covered by the gift balanced on top of them.

When Ahmad nervously lifted his eyes to hers, and stared at her in silence, Nina wondered what he could be waiting for. He wasn't waiting for her to speak, was he? Maybe he was waiting for her to open the gift. But Nina wasn't ready to do that either. She wanted some answers. She had come for answers and she wasn't ready to do anything with, for, or to this man until she got them all.

Ahmad smiled softly at her and reached for her hand. He squeezed it gently in his, but Nina didn't squeeze back. She scooted a tiny bit toward the center of the couch, trying desperately to put a little space between her and this man whose gaze was still enough to make her melt.

She had barely survived the enthusiastic hug Ahmad greeted her with, and the intense surge of longing it sent through her had made her take a few defensive steps backward just to get her bearings. She wasn't trying to go there with him. At least not yet. Tonya's words were as true now as they were when she'd said them nearly four months before: "He broke it . . .

let him think it's beyond repair.'' So when the man greeted
her at the door, she put on her best nonchalant face and managed to swallow all the angry questions she'd been holding
on to. She'd also avoided asking any questions about the
brand-new Navigator parked in the driveway of his gorgeous
new home, and she made no mention of her suspicions about
Ahmad's new designer clothing and his obviously deep pockets. She'd managed to get through the nervous small talk, had
been asked to accept a gift, for which she had not brought
anything to give in return, and after what felt like a very long,
uncomfortable time, she still had no idea why she was there.
And she had no intention of asking. It was Ahmad's turn to
talk.

Finally, he broke the silence with a simple sentence.
"Would you like for me to start at the beginning?"

Nina didn't smile and she didn't make a sound. She looked
seriously into Ahmad's eyes, which had become two deep
pools of mystery. *Start at the beginning?* she thought. She
wasn't sure if she was ready for whatever that meant. *Start at
the beginning.* Finally she slowly nodded, and waited for him
to do just that.

Nina didn't know if it was the part about being left by his
mother in a grocery cart on a busy Seattle street and never
seeing her alive again, or the awful abuse he'd suffered in
each of the five foster homes he'd been placed in before the
fifth grade. It could have been the terrible stories he told her
of hoping each time to be loved, and ultimately being disappointed again and again by a series of foster parents who were
more devoted to the cashing of the check they received each
month than to the little boy who depended on them for care.

She didn't know if it was the dreadful scene Ahmad re-
created for her of his encounter with Beth Maxwell in a limousine in the Inglewood cemetery, or the truth he was forced
to face about the disloyalty and the tragic deaths of his best
friend Scotty, and of his wife Chante.

Nina wasn't sure what part of his account had caused the
one lonely tear to slide slowly down her face, but whatever it
was, when Ahmad finally took the story back to their day
together in L.A. and admitted to her the thought that occurred

to him as he stood facing Nina under that tree in Santa Monica, he too had tears on his face.

Did this man just say the word 'wife'? She stared speechlessly into Ahmad's face.

"I know. I thought it was crazy, too. Which is why I tried so desperately to convince myself that I needed to stay away." Ahmad took a deep breath, and finally, stopped talking for a long moment. He looked down at the wrapped present Nina still held gingerly in her lap. "Before I go any further..." He nodded at the gift and pleaded with his eyes. "Please open it. It will tell you everything I'm trying to say."

Nina carefully lifted the taped edges of the elf wrap and unfolded each crumpled end. When she gently tore the paper away, a soft smile turned the edges of her mouth up ever-so-slightly at each corner. Finally, she lifted the silver frame from the paper and stared at her own image staring back at her from under the glass.

"What do you see?" Ahmad whispered.

Nina studied the photograph soberly. It was the one Ahmad had snapped of her at Santa Monica, under the praying tree. She saw it. Anyone with eyes could. The reality of how vulnerable she had been then was undeniably clear, and suddenly Nina felt bare again, overexposed. She looked across the room, fixing her eyes on the undressed Christmas tree.

"What do you see, Nina?"

Nina looked deep into the photograph again. She remembered that moment as clearly as if it had just happened. "I see a woman who was full of hope."

"Is that what that is?" Ahmad shook his head slowly and gently took the frame from Nina's hand, placing it on the coffee table next to his child's framed photo.

He stared at the picture for a few moments longer before he finally turned to look in her eyes. "That's not hope..." He reached for her hands and held them in his. Bowing his head to first place a soft kiss in each palm, Ahmad then held Nina's fingers to his lips, and when she didn't resist, he left them there, against his mouth, for a time. Finally he whispered, "That's certainty."

He leaned into Nina then, the space between his chest and hers suddenly shrinking to a mere few inches, but just as suddenly, she leaned away. Placing her extended hand, still held firmly in his own, against his chest, she said plainly, "Then why, Ahmad? If you saw how vulnerable I was, how could you . . . How could you be so intimate with me and then just push me away?"

"I . . ." His head shook slowly from side to side. Nina wondered if that "I" was the beginning of "I'm sorry" or maybe an even weaker "I don't know."

Nina held her breath and waited for him to finish.

"I was certain I would love you, and I was afraid." He squeezed her hand gently when he said "afraid," as if to emphasize the word.

Nina avoided Ahmad's eyes then, and allowed her gaze to travel across his muscular chest, down the massive biceps bulging powerfully against the ivory-colored fabric of his shirt and to his strong hand surrounding hers. *This is a man.* He was a man in every physical way a man could be described. But even better, he was man enough to let the words "I was afraid" spill from his lips.

She was suddenly overwhelmed with the urge to taste his lips, to explore his body the way he had explored hers what seemed like so long ago. She forced the thought from her mind, and instead, looked boldly into Ahmad's shining eyes and asked, "And . . . are you afraid now?"

In the split second it took Ahmad's mouth to find hers, Nina knew the question never again needed to be asked. He had heard and answered every question her heart had been whispering for agonizing weeks on end, and as Nina sank deep into the familiar sweetness of Ahmad's kiss, she finally remembered why her face had held an undeniable look of certainty under the praying tree that day. And now that she was back in Ahmad's embrace, she remembered what certainty felt like, and realized at last that Ahmad had never really gone away.

There could be nothing on earth closer to heaven—nothing. With his eyes still closed, Ahmad emerged from his sound sleep and inhaled deeply, breathing in the sweet scent of Nina. The aroma of her cologne, blended with the sweat, tears, and passionate lovemaking from the night before, created an en-

velope of satisfaction around them, and Ahmad sank deeper
into it, exhaling a contented sigh.

When he finally opened his eyes to the first rays of morning
light spilling into the room, he raised himself up on one elbow
to gaze down at Nina, sleeping so peacefully in his bed. He
leaned down slowly and placed a tender kiss on her lips, half-
expecting her eyes to be open when he straightened again. But
she just moaned slightly and nodded her head. She was still
sound asleep.

Ahmad smiled. Nina had good reason to be tired. They had
been up most of the night. Making love then talking. Talking
then bathing. Bathing then making love and starting the cycle
all over again. It had to have been after three in the morning
when the last moans of pleasure escaped from their mouths,
and sleep was finally allowed to cement them into one another's arms.

Ahmad looked over at Nina's dress and the rest of her things
in a pile on the armchair near his bed. The sight of them filled
him with an uncomfortable distress. They were a reminder that
this new feeling of completeness he'd found would be dis-
turbed soon, and Ahmad gazed down again at Nina, dreading
the thought of watching her rise from his bed.

A shrill ringing noise came suddenly from the pile on the
chair, causing Nina to stir, her eyes slowly opening to the gaze
of his.

"Good morning," she whispered, a shy smile on her face.

"Good morning." Ahmad bent to place a kiss on her forehead. "I think someone's trying to get ahold of you."

Nina's eyes flung wide open and she sat up suddenly in the
bed. "Did my cell phone ring?" She seemed close to panic.

"Yes, it rang once just now."

Nina yanked the comforter back and was already standing
at the chair, digging in her purse for the phone, when its shrill
ring sounded again.

"Hello?"

Ahmad watched Nina's look of dread slowly turn to calm.
When she spoke, her voice was cool and serene, as if she were
trying to calm the person who was on the line at the other
end. "Is he going to be okay? Of course I will. Of course
not."

Nina looked up at Ahmad and smiled softly at him, sending him a look that said "sorry if I scared you, and everything's okay." "Yes, Mama. I know I don't, Mama. I want to do this. Don't worry. I'll be there at eight."

She returned the phone to her purse and stood near the armchair for a moment. She closed her eyes, and Ahmad was sure she was whispering a prayer. He loved the way she looked just then, with her hair curled in tight little ringlets around her face, her makeup-less face turned heavenward, and the way her body held the drape of his XXL Hanes tee shirt.

When she opened her eyes again Ahmad asked with concern, "Is everything okay?"

"Yes. And no. It's Daddy's remaining kidney. It's scheduled to be removed in a couple of days."

"I'm sorry." Ahmad motioned for Nina to join him, patting the bed next to him and lifting the comforter to make room for her to climb back in.

She came to him, but sat on the edge of the bed near Ahmad instead of climbing back in with him. "I've got half an hour to get to the hospital. I'm being tested at eight o'clock to see if I'm a tissue match."

"A tissue match?" Ahmad echoed.

"They don't want to have to open him up again for the transplant; it's best if they can do it right away. Nat's being tested too. The doctors want the best possible odds for compatibility."

"Are you talking about donating?" Ahmad couldn't hide the look of concern on his face.

"It's perfectly safe."

Ahmad sat up suddenly against the headboard. He looked at her a long time, his eyes roaming the length of her slowly, as if he was examining her body from head to toe. "I hope this doesn't come out wrong . . . but . . ." He grasped her hand and held it in his. "If . . . well . . . would you still be able to make some babies with me one day?"

Nina smiled. "Don't you worry about that. You know a kidney is just like a woman."

Ahmad's sidewise smile and arched eyebrows said he didn't get the comparison.

"You only need one good one," she said seriously. Nina leaned over and planted a kiss on Ahmad's lips before she rose from the bed and headed for the shower.

△▽ 29 ▽△

Nina dropped the UPS package on Tonya's bed, hoping the soft thud it made would wake her friend. Tonya stirred, but didn't open her eyes so Nina whispered, "T. I need you. *Bad.* You gotta get up, girl." Nina sat on the edge of the bed and shook Tonya's shoulder gently. "Wake up, T."

Tonya finally pried her eyes open. She squinted at the clock on the bedside table and saw that it wasn't quite 10 A.M. "Go away," she growled, "I'm on vacation." She yanked the covers up to her neck and started to roll over and go right back to sleep, but when she saw that Nina was still wearing the dress she'd worn to Ahmad's the night before, and when she caught the dazed and nervous look on Nina's face, Tonya sat up quickly and attempted to shake off her groggy sleep. She said with husky-voiced concern, "What happened? Nina, are you okay? Did something happen at Ahmad's?"

Nina didn't say anything at first. She just picked the box up and held it in her lap. "It's not Ahmad." She smiled slightly and added, "He was perfect. And you were right about everything." Tonya glanced down at the package, and back into Nina's face, realizing Nina's skin had paled to the color of the eggshell white walls, and her eyes were glazed and opened wide. The only words Nina could manage were, "It's from Omaha, T."

"Omaha? It's from the bank?" When Nina nodded weakly at her, Tonya climbed out from beneath the covers and sat next to Nina on the edge of the bed. They both sat there, Tonya in her gray flannel pajamas and Nina still wearing the

278

dress and boots she'd just tiptoed into the house in. They stared at the box on Nina's lap, as if it were going to reveal its contents to them without any action on their part. Finally, Tonya reached into her bedside drawer and pulled out a pair of scissors. She held them out to Nina, but Nina didn't move.

"How old am I, T?" Nina finally said softly.

"You're almost thirty, Nina."

"How long have I been waiting for this day?"

"As long as I've known you. At least fifteen years."

Nina sucked in a short, determined breath and grabbed the scissors from Tonya's hand. "The wait is over. I know it's in here. The truth about my mother is in this box."

Tonya stood up suddenly. "Wait, girl." She ran from the room and into the adjoining bathroom. When she returned, she was holding a box of tissues. She sat back down on the bed and held the tissue box in her lap as Nina began sliding a scissor edge under the packaging tape.

"To be holding so much," Nina commented quietly, "it isn't very big." The box was ten inches by twelve inches and about an inch and a half high. When the last of the brown tape had been cut away, Nina opened the box flaps wide and reached for the manila envelope inside. She looked at Tonya soberly, but neither of them said a word. Nina tossed the empty box to the floor, opened the envelope flap, and, holding her breath, she let the envelope's contents tumble out onto the bed.

There were a couple of official-looking documents and some sentimental knickknacks: a playbill from a 1958 San Francisco performance of *West Side Story*, a stack of photographs held together with a large paper clip, and a necklace with a tiny, diamond-encrusted "M" hanging from it. *Hmmm. M for Moore? Mickey?* Nina picked up the necklace first, slowly fingering it in her palm, but it was the eight-by-ten page with the word "Kodak" printed across it that held her attention. She hesitated only a moment before she dropped the necklace into her lap and reached for the stack of face-down photos.

When she turned the stack over, she realized instantly that she wasn't prepared. There was no way she could have braced herself for the impact made by what she was holding in her hand. Nina sat as still as stone, looking at the color photo of the woman smiling up at her—the ivory-toned face, smooth skin, and high cheekbones, the thick black hair swept back in a headband, and those blue eyes. The likeness was almost exact. Except for Nina's dimpled Moore chin, this woman's face was as close as one could come to being a carbon copy of Nina's own. *My mother. This is my mother's face.*

Nina could only tremble in silence as emotions she didn't recognize staked their claim on her. She'd suddenly become like a cartoon character whose chest was split wide open, separating at the edges like torn cloth, and as she clutched involuntarily to somehow hold the edges together, she inhaled a sharp, deep breath.

Tonya pulled several sheets of tissue from the box and waited. She knew her friend would fight the tears first, but when they eventually came, they would surely come in a flood. They both stared at the picture in silence before Tonya finally whispered, "She's beautiful, Nina. You look just like her."

Nina's few tears fell quickly, and Tonya reached with the handful of tissues to wipe them before they could spill down onto the picture in Nina's lap. Nina herself expected to cry bitterly, to sob in mourning for the mother she had waited so long to meet, but these five or six quiet tears were all that came. And instead, Nina just disappeared somewhere. She was caught in a place she didn't recognize. It was as if she was struggling to grasp hold of memories that were just out of reach. For a moment she thought she remembered her mother's voice . . . a soft voice long forgotten. Then in an instant the memory was gone and Nina didn't struggle to bring it back. She sat in silence, staring down at the photo, not sure if she should be angry or relieved.

In the sudden wave of emotion, two strong urges filled Nina's mind, each equally confusing. One was telling her to shred the photo of this White woman into a thousand tiny pieces and forget it ever existed, and the other, much stronger urge said to clutch it to her chest and rejoice at finally laying eyes again on the face of the woman who had given her life.

She didn't respond to either. Instead she sat there statue-

like, staring at the striking photograph and trying to remember
what she had so completely forgotten. *Who was my mother?
Who was she? Did she love me?* A wave of emptiness swept
through Nina, and all she could manage to do was look up at
Tonya with an expression of absolute helplessness.

Tonya quietly reached for the stack of pictures in Nina's
lap. She placed the photo of Nina's mother gingerly on the
bed and stared long and hard at the one beneath it before
handing it to Nina. It was a promotional photo. The kind a
star would give a fan. And in the shot was the same woman—
Nina's mother—standing next to a handsome White man with
his arm wrapped tightly around her shoulder. The type at the
bottom of the picture said *Victor and Vanessa Gains*—The
Young and the Beautiful—*1964*. In bold cursive writing were
the words, *To many more happy years together—love forever,
Morris.*

Tonya and Nina looked at each other in wide-eyed disbelief.
"Do you know who that is?" Tonya whispered. Of course
Nina knew. It was Morris Michaels. It was a much younger
version, but it was definitely Morris Michaels, the actor and
star of Nina's favorite soap opera, *The Young and the Beautiful.* Morris Michaels played the character Victor Gains, the
handsome and debonair patriarch of the richest and most
scandal-infested family on daytime television. Nina and Tonya
had watched the show since high school.

Nina looked carefully at the photo. "Vanessa Gains?" she
said aloud. Nina didn't remember any such character. "Victor" was currently married to that witch Corrine who everyone
knew was only trying to get pregnant by him before divorcing
him and getting what she really wanted—a piece of his riches.
Victor had been married a few times over the years, but Nina
didn't remember a Vanessa. But in the world of daytime television many actors and actresses came and went.

"Victor Gains? Tonya, do you believe this? My mother
worked with Victor . . ." Nina's head shook slowly from side
to side. "I mean," she corrected herself, using the actor's real
name, "she worked with Morris Michaels."

Tonya grinned at her friend. "Damn. What a trip, girl. Your

mother was an actress. A soap opera actress. No wonder your father . . ." Tonya's smile disappeared and she left the sentence unfinished.

"You mean, no wonder my father hates soap operas so much? Humph. Apparently they remind him of her. And she's obviously not someone he wants to be reminded of." Nina heard her father's delirious, anger-filled voice in her head. "Mickey? I don't know any Mickey." *Is that her name? Is my mother's name Mickey?* Nina looked again at the photograph, but only the soap characters' names were printed there. "What was her name, T? Do any of those have her name on them?"

Tonya handed Nina the photos. There were three more in the stack, but they were pictures of some elderly White people that were probably long dead. Nina shuffled slowly through the photographs until her mother's face was back on top. The two women looked at the image for a long moment, neither speaking. Then, simultaneously, their eyes fell on the documents that had fallen out of the envelope with everything else. Nina didn't move, so Tonya reached forward and picked one of them up.

"What does it say?"

"Michelle Rene Bouvier," she began. "Born February third, 1937 . . ." Suddenly Tonya was silent.

Michelle Bouvier. Mickey? "Her name was Michelle? Tonya. She's Mickey. She's got to be." Nina's voice rose with enthusiasm. "She's the person Daddy was screaming at that day. I had a feeling about this, Tonya. Like there was some kind of reunion involved. What if that day in the hospital Daddy was actually reliving something that happened between my mother and him? Maybe it was her he was yelling at not to come on his property. What if my mother was trying to come for me?"

"I don't think so, Nina. I don't think he could have been talking to her." Tonya shook her head, raising her eyes from the document to look compassionately at Nina.

"What is it? What does it say?"

"Your mother was born in Providence, Rhode Island."

"And?"

"It says she died in San Francisco, California, on September sixteenth, 1971 . . .'' Tonya handed the death certificate to Nina. ''. . . of asphyxiation.''

Nina was quiet. ''Asphyxiation?'' she finally whispered, staring wide-eyed at Tonya. ''Isn't that like being strangled or drowning or something?''

''It could be. But I think asphyxiation also could be suffocating or choking. It looks like your mother might have died in some kind of accident.''

''My mother died in some kind of an accident . . .'' Nina began, ''. . . or . . .'' She stopped mid-sentence and let silence fill in the rest of the words. *Could that be why Daddy's been so tight-lipped about everything? ''I can't talk about it, Nina, and I won't.''* Suddenly other words rang clearly in Nina's ears. ''If you think you're coming in here to get my daughter . . . you'll have to kill me first.''

A look of absolute horror spread slowly across Nina's face, and Tonya responded to it in a near whisper. ''Nina, what is it? Girl, are you okay?''

''Tonya, maybe my mother's death was no accident at all.''

''What are you saying?''

''I'm saying what if someone killed my mother, and what if my daddy had something to do with it?''

''Nina. You can't be serious.'' Tonya's expression said she was having no part of it. ''Your father is no killer, and you know it.''

Nina closed her eyes then and relived the moment of terror she had faced over and over again over the last few months in that awful nightmare. The paralyzing fear she felt waiting to see what the man held behind his back, and the final horror of realizing that the man she feared so deeply was Mitchell Moore.

Nina exhaled a long slow sigh and turned to her friend. ''What do I really know, T? I'm not sure I know anything anymore.''

''Are you saying you don't know your father? You don't know the man who loves you more than anything in this world? Your father would never hurt a soul. I'm not even his daughter and I know better than that.''

''I'll tell you what I know, T. I know my daddy, whom I loved and idolized my whole life, spent nearly thirty years hiding all of this from me. I know that. And I know one other thing.''

Tonya didn't ask, but her eyes did.

"I'm going down to that hospital, and I'm not leaving until one of my parents gives me the answers I need.''

△▽ 30 ▽△

Nina stepped boldly through the door of the private hospital room and stopped in her tracks at the sight of the freshly made, empty bed in front of her. "Where's my father?" She spoke the words aloud, though there was no one else in the room to hear them.

She made her way in a hurry to the nurses' station and tried to attract the attention of the woman behind the counter. When Nina's presence was not immediately noticed, she cleared her throat and sent a stiff "Excuse me" in the woman's direction.

"Yes?" The young nurse turned to Nina. "Can I help you?"

"Can you tell me where the man in 202 was moved?"

A nervous expression draped the woman's face, and she stood up immediately. "Are you with the press?"

"No, I—"

"I'm sorry but unless you are related to Mr. Moore I cannot give you any information."

Nina glared at the woman. *The press? Why would she ask* ... Suddenly she remembered. Of course the woman thought she was a stranger. The woman would have to be awfully observant to see Nina's family resemblance. "No, you don't understand. Mitchell Moore is my father."

The tiny woman stood as tall as her five-foot frame would allow. She looked sternly at Nina and breathed an exasperated "You people" before she firmly repeated herself. "I'm sorry. I cannot give you any information."

Nina reached to her hip for her purse. She would have to

get her identification out and prove to the woman . . . *Shit.
Where's my purse?* It wasn't hanging from her shoulder where
it should have been. She had been so upset, and so intent on
getting the answers to her questions, she remembered to grab
the envelope containing her mother's photo, but had mistak-
enly left her purse in the car.

"Mitchell Moore *is* my father," she announced firmly to
the unbending woman, trying her damnedest to rein in her
irritation. "My name is Nina. Nina Moore. Pull his chart if
you have to. I can tell you anything personal about him that's
on it. Home address. Home phone. Just please tell me. I have
to know what's happened."

"Humph, you have to know, huh? So, you *are* with the
press." The nurse slammed the chart she held onto a low desk
on her side of the counter and growled at Nina, "Then you
know the hospital's position on releasing information to you
people. And you also know you can be escorted out of the
building." She picked up a telephone and began dialing.

Nina didn't wait around for security to arrive; instead she
hurried away from the counter and ran toward the lab where
she and Nat had undergone testing for the tissue match earlier
that morning. The technicians there could surely vouch for her,
and maybe someone could explain to her why the information
about her father was so top-secret. The press? *Why on earth
would the press be interested in an aging trumpet player's
kidney operation?*

Nina's breakneck pace slowed suddenly, and just as she
stopped outside the double-doored entrance to the laboratory,
she leaned back against the wall to steady herself, and let the
reality of the question that had just occurred to her linger in
her brain. *They wouldn't be interested in an aging trumpet
player's kidney operation. The press would only want the story
if* . . . Nina felt the blood drain instantly from her face. She'd
suddenly forgotten the fiery mission she'd been on to confront
her father and cried out in her heart for him instead. *Oh God,
please don't let Daddy be dead.* She struggled to stay on her
feet, as she fought against the dizziness that threatened to steal
her consciousness away.

Suddenly the lab doors swung open, and two technicians
stood, one on either side, holding the steel doors apart to clear

the way for an orderly struggling with a heavy supply cart. Through the emotional fog that had enshrouded her, Nina clearly heard one of them speak her name. It was the curly brown-haired man holding one side of the open door. "Better than Jerry Springer," he said with a tsk, tsk, tsk of tongue against teeth.

"I wonder if anyone's going to tell her. Mmmph. That poor thing." Nina recognized the woman's voice. It was the nurse who had drawn her blood earlier that morning.

Nina was nearly struck by the opening door, and she pressed her back closer to the wall, still unnoticed by the two technicians facing each other in the doorway. *Tell me? Tell me what?* Nina had meant to say it aloud, but no voice came out with the words that rang in her head.

"Well, I did the test myself, *twice.*" The curly-haired man was talking again. "And there is no way. And I do mean no way. Blood tests don't lie. Those two might have the same last name, but that woman is not Mitchell Moore's daughter."

Nina gave up the struggle for consciousness then, and as her palms slid down the cool smoothness of the corridor's wall, she let go of her hold on everything that had ever held her upright.

She awakened in a darkened room, with a throbbing headache and a desperate, sunken feeling, an aching need to emerge from the depths of a groggy haze. She recognized nothing in her surroundings, and though she knew she was in a strange bed, still she tried to focus, to find something in the room to connect herself to, but she just couldn't get her bearings. The struggle to come fully awake was too much like fighting to cast off a heavy blanket, a blanket she just couldn't seem to get all the way out from under.

She'd felt this feeling before. Sedated. Drugged. Like when she had her appendix removed. Pills to calm her down before surgery. *Surgery. hospital.* The words floated around in her head and she grasped at them for support, leverage to help her climb out of her drugged confusion.

I went to the hospital. Daddy's having surgery. She remembered her father's empty room. Searching the corridors for someone to tell her why he had been moved. *Blood tests don't lie. Same last name. Better than Jerry Springer. Tsk, tsk, tsk. Not Mitchell Moore's daughter.* The words she had overheard flooded into the place of darkness behind Nina's closed eyes and she fought them—demanded them—begged them to please get out of her head. "No. No. Please, God. No."

Nina's lifelong premonition that she somehow didn't belong in her family had finally come to pass. It had been hanging somewhere high over her head for all those years and had just plummeted down onto her with a force far too great for her to bear. Nina's moan of agony filled the room, turning into sobs that ripped their way up from deep in her chest, spilling out into the pillow where she had buried her face.

Not Mitchell Moore's daughter. The man said it like there could be no mistake. *Blood tests don't lie. No way.* She'd give anything not to have heard any of it. She ached to send those careless words back into the mouth from which they'd come.

Not Mitchell Moore's daughter. Same last name. Over and over the words battered her mind. Demanding to be heard. Demanding to be understood. But Nina just refused. She wasn't ready to consider any of it. She wasn't ready to make sense of anything so absurd. Instead, she sank under the weight of her anguish and buried her face in the sterile whiteness of the pillow beneath her, until her weary sobs turned to silence and Nina fell again into a fitful sleep.

What a crazy dream this is. When Nina opened her eyes to the soft reflection of morning light against the pale yellow walls of her hospital room, she knew the scene before her heavy-lidded eyes could only be the makings of some kind of drug-induced dream.

Not four or five feet in front of her, near the room's open door, Mama stood wrapped in a tearful embrace—in the arms of a strange White man. Nina struggled to open her eyes wider, to make out the man's identity. When she realized it was *The Young and The Beautiful*'s Victor Gains, a crazy laugh burst from her mouth. *Talk about an outrageous dream. Mama and Victor? Daddy would have a cow.*

"Nina, honey. I'm so sorry, baby." Mama ran to Nina's side. Stroking her face gently with a soft palm she said, "We never meant for you to find out this way.'' Mama looked expectantly at Victor, so Nina looked at him too, waiting for him to say his lines. He looked nervously toward Nina, then at Mama, and without saying a word he just looked down at a piece of paper he held tightly in his hands.

What kind of dream is this anyway? Nina thought. *Victor Gains has never once blown his lines on television. How's he gonna come in here and mess up my scene?* Nina frowned then. She looked again at a still silent Victor, then back at Mama. Deciding to contribute her own dialogue to what was turning out to be a pretty weak script, she whispered to her mother, her voice heavy with drama-filled accusation, ''Mama, what are you doing with Victor Gains in my dream?''

Mama sat on the edge of Nina's bed. Taking her daughter's hand in hers she said firmly, ''Nina, this man's name is not Victor, and you are not dreaming.''

Nina smiled knowingly. ''Mama,'' she scolded, ''I recognize Victor Gains when I see him.'' Just as the words were out of her mouth, from the corner of her eye Nina caught sight of the manila envelope lying on the table beside her bed. The one that held the photograph of her biological mother—standing on the arm of Victor Gains. *To many more happy years together—love forever, Morris.*

Morris Michaels? Is this for real? Morris Michaels in the flesh? What is he doing in my room? The events of the last two days flooded suddenly into Nina's head. The UPS package. Arriving to an empty hospital room and searching for her missing father. She remembered the awful moment when she wondered if her father might be dead, and then . . . the last horrifying memory . . . someone saying the words, ''Not Mitchell Moore's daughter.''

''Where's Daddy?'' Nina pushed the scratchy-toned words from her throat. Her eyes begged Mama to tell her that it would all be okay.

''Your father . . .'' Mama glanced at Morris Michaels, still standing awkwardly across the room. ''He's going to be just fine. The transplant is scheduled for tomorrow.''

Why was Morris Michaels in Nina's hospital room? And why was he comforting a tearful Mama?

''You're here to tell me about my mother, aren't you?''

Nina studied the man's aging face. She had seen him on television countless times over the years, and always thought of him as quite attractive for an older White man, somehow ageless and eternally self-possessed. But close up and in the flesh, he looked disappointingly regular. Except for the youthful light shining from behind familiar green eyes, this Morris Michaels looked like a nervous old man.

"Can I . . . be alone with her for a few moments?" Michaels asked Mama in a low, quiet tone. When she didn't respond right away, he added, "I've kept my side of the bargain. Evelyn, please?"

Before Nina could protest, Mama turned to leave the room. She whispered, "I'll be just outside if you need anything, okay?"

Michaels stepped slowly toward the bed. He stopped first to pick the envelope up from the bedside table, then came to stand near Nina, smiling nervously at her.

When he pulled out the photo of Nina's mother and held it in one trembling hand, Nina watched his eyes glaze over suddenly, and a wince of pain registered across his face. He finally spoke in a voice Nina knew so very well.

"I met your mother at a *West Side Story* audition in 1957. She played Maria and I was Tony." He smiled then, staring into Nina's face with a strange look of longing. "She was so beautiful. Radiant ivory skin and blue eyes . . . She was beautiful, just like you. I loved her instantly."

Nina was beginning to feel uncomfortable and a little afraid. She sank deeper into the pillow behind her head and was silent, wanting desperately for Mama to come in the room again.

It was then that Nina noticed the small white square of what looked like paper held tightly in one of Michaels' hands. She focused on it curiously, and when she raised her eyes to his again, his pale bearded face with its piercing green eyes was staring directly into hers, with that desperate look of painful longing.

Something about this man's face tugged at a memory Nina had buried somewhere very deep, and in a split second she was drenched in a terror that swept over her in a wave. She'd suddenly become a woman standing in a nightmare at a wrought-iron gate, waiting and watching for something awful to begin, and knowing there was nothing she could do to prevent it.

He held the paper out to her. Just held it out in midair. The sad, painful look on his weary face didn't look so threatening then; Nina managed to push her fear aside, and sat up straight in the bed. When she reached for the paper and grasped it between her thumb and the index finger of her right hand, she realized instantly from its smooth, padded feel that it wasn't a piece of paper at all but a Polaroid photograph. She turned it over slowly, and when she saw the tiny face looking up at her, she could do nothing to stem the flow of tears.

Nina recognized the child instantly. The pale pink wool dress and matching bonnet. The patent leather shoes. And the sapphire blue eyes. The child's face beamed with a look of absolute delight, and the sight of it made Nina's heart balloon with a furious pain. *I remember this. I remember this day. He pulled a camera out from behind his back. My father took my picture and left me in the grass to play.*

The sudden rush of memories threatened to shatter what was left of Nina's composure—her soul filled to overflowing with the aching feeling she'd experienced at the end of that awful, traumatic day. *Surrounded by strangers.* An old woman bribing her to be quiet with lollipops and promises of ice cream. *Daddy. I want my Daddy.* She fought the sob building in her chest—building and building and searching for an escape.

"Where did you get this?" Nina demanded suddenly. She made no attempt to conceal her rage. "Who gave you this photograph?"

Michaels didn't move. He spoke in a low whisper, as if the words coming out of his mouth could be taken in better if they were softly spoken. "I took that picture at your mother's funeral. And all these years . . . it's been the only thing I had to remember my daughter by." He reached his trembling ivory hand out for hers. "I—I'm your father, Nina."

"No, you are *not!*" The picture flew at his face and Nina shouted at him to get out of her room. "You are not my father!" She reached behind her to grab her pillow and flung it at him too. "I said get out! Get out of here." She screamed then. A loud wail, like that of an animal wounded and trapped.

The shrieking cry was loud enough for anyone out in the corridor to hear.

"Get out," she screamed again and again. "Get out of here." Nina cried hysterically then, filling her room, and the hallway beyond it, with her tortured sobs. Mama rushed in just in time to catch Nina's arm rearing back to heave a vase filled with flowers in his direction.

"Nina. Nina, stop it now." Mama wrestled the vase from her daughter's hand, and set it safely down on the table beside the bed. When Nina suddenly fell back against the bed in silence and stared unblinkingly at the ceiling above her, Mama began to cry. She kept repeating the same words over and over in Nina's ear. "I am so sorry, baby. I never wanted you to hurt like this. I am so sorry." She tried to get closer, tried reaching to comfort her daughter, but Nina just jerked the covers up around her ears, rolled over to face the wall, and refused to hear or utter another sound.

△▽ 31 ▽△

Nina acknowledged no voices and refused the visits of everyone she knew. Each time a delivery of flowers arrived, she found a spot on the ceiling to study until the deliverer realized she wouldn't join in any polite conversation, and couldn't care less about looking to see "how beautifully they were arranged." She lay for hours in the same prone state, and when the sedatives began wearing off she simply sobbed uncontrollably until a nurse appeared to re-sedate her.

She knew she could not go on like this for much longer, pretending not to have a grip on sanity. Despite the effect of the drugs, she was all too rationally aware of her condition. But she needed to stall—needed time to decide what the hell a sista was supposed to do now.

You're not a sista, Nina. The mere thought was like a knife blade twisting deep into her shattered heart, which, combined with the trauma of knowing she no longer had a family to call her own, brought a fresh wave of tears to her eyes. *Yesterday you were a Black woman; today . . . today you're the "them" in "them White folks, Nina Moore."* No, not Moore. *What was she supposed to call herself? Nina X? Then again, maybe Malcolm wouldn't much appreciate that. White woman can't have the last name X. Malcolm don't belong to you no more either. He belongs to that "us" you used to be a part of.*

The door to Nina's room opened a crack just then, but she refused to turn her head, and had to catch Tonya's approaching figure out of the corner of her eye. She continued staring up

293

at the ceiling, closing her eyes when Tonya pulled a chair close and sat down rigidly at its edge.

"I got you, no matter what, Nina," was all she said. When the minute or two of silence turned into ten, and that ten turned into twenty, an hour, and finally they had been sitting together in silence for an hour and a half, Nina glanced briefly over at Tonya, then back at the ceiling again.

"Are you just going to sit there?" Nina finally said.

"I said I got you, and yes, until you talk to me, I'm not going anywhere."

"And what exactly are you waiting for me to say?"

"Whatever a sista feels like saying."

The tears rolled down then. Streams on either side of her face. Still staring at the tiled ceiling above her, Nina didn't bother to wipe the tears away, but let them soak into the pillow beneath her head. "You can't call me sista anymore, T."

"Bullshit."

"Sistas are . . ." Nina stopped, her throat choking at the words. *Sistas are women of color—and that no longer refers to me.*

"Sistas are sistas," Tonya announced matter-of-factly. "How could you have been my sista yesterday afternoon, and something comes up that makes you not my sista today?

"I guess Mama didn't tell you . . ."

"Your mother didn't have to tell me. It's all over the papers. Famous Black trumpeter raises White child of Morris Michaels and the late Michelle Bouvier."

Nina finally turned her head, looked into the warm compassion of Tonya's eyes. "What am I supposed to do now, T? Who am I supposed to be?"

"Who were you yesterday?"

"Yesterday I was Nina Moore, daughter of Mi—" She stopped mid-sentence, unable to speak his name."

"Are you different now? What has changed about you beside a name?

"*Everything* has changed. Everything I've ever held dear; everything I was ever proud to be does not belong to me anymore."

"Says who?"

Nina folded her arms across her face and moaned painfully, "Emmett Till."

"Emmett Till? What are you talking about, Nina?"

"The first time I heard the story of Emmett Till I was just a little girl. I thought of him as my brother. I pictured him in that casket, and I saw me and Daddy and Mama trying to figure out how we were gonna live without him. It was just as if he was my brother, T. And all I could do was cry and ask Mama why *they* killed him." Nina's stream of tears began again. "Only, they're not 'they' anymore, Tonya . . . they're me."

"Nina . . ."

"Malcolm, Martin, Medgar, Harriet, Sojourner, Ida B." Nina's voice was shaking with anger, with too many painful emotions building in her chest. ". . . Woodson, DuBois, Douglass, Toussaint . . . Shit, Tonya, even Rodney King. All of them. I lost them all in one day. And I hate my fath—I hate Mitchell Moore for taking them all away."

"Bullshit. Black history is everyone's history. Isn't that what you tell your students, that all human beings are descended from Africa's womb? Don't we tell White folks the King holiday belongs to them too? Nobody can take those people you love away from you, Nina. Besides, Mitchell Moore is the reason you even know those names. That man raised you as his own. He withstood all those rumors, that vicious ridicule. He lived with the knowledge that even his own daughter had convicted him of cheating on his wife. He sacrificed everything for you, Nina. Maybe before you pass judgment on him, you should find out why."

Before Nina could respond, the door swung open, and a nurse entered carrying another beautiful bouquet. "Ms. Moore, there's a Mr. Jefferson . . . I know you said you don't want to see him, but he said he'll just wait."

"Tell Mr. Jefferson I said to do himself a favor and go away."

"Nina, don't. He's been here all night; hasn't slept a wink. He said to tell you—he wants you to know that no matter what, he really loves you. Nina, you can't send that brotha away."

Nina waved the nurse out of the room and Tonya just shook her head at her friend.

"You don't understand, Tonya."

"Bullshit."

"I should just do him a fav—"

"Listen to me, Ms. Nina Moore." The tone in Tonya's voice made Nina stop mid-sentence. "For as long as I've known you, you've wanted nothing more than to be accepted for what's on the inside, not what happens to be on the surface. Now I'm telling you as someone who knows you better than most. I understand you're hurt. But in time you will get over this pain. And when you do, you'll remember that what's most valuable about you has nothing to do with your last name, or the tone of your skin. It's not something you inherited from anyone, and it's not going to disappear because you have genetic material that's a little different than you originally thought.

"I could care less who your biological daddy and mama happen to be as long as you continue to be Nina. As your best friend who you *know* loves you, I'm asking you to get up out of that bed, and be you. That's all you can do . . . That's all any of us are asked to do."

Tonya reached to the floor for a duffel bag she'd brought in with her and dropped it with a thud on Nina's bed. "I brought you a change of clothes. Now, come on, girl. Your daddy is asking to see you."

△▽ 32 ▽△

Nina sat patiently in a chair in her father's room, watching him sleep. The words he'd uttered to Nina across his kitchen table only a few weeks before echoed softly in her head. "You are my daughter, and I love you more than you'll ever know." Mitchell and Evelyn Moore had raised her as their own, and in all her anger, it hadn't occurred to Nina—until the words came out of Tonya's mouth—that her father had endured so much for her. If he wasn't her real father, why would he and Mama have welcomed her in? Especially given what Nat had said about people questioning Daddy's integrity. And what secrets about her mother's death still remained?

Too many secrets, Daddy. Kept too long. She thought of the words little Kevin had taunted her with so many years before—"Uncle Mitchell ain't no parts a yo' daddy." Even way back then, something about his cruel words rang true. But today in the face of that awful truth, none of it made sense to Nina.

As if he had overheard her thoughts, Mitchell Moore's eyes opened suddenly, a soft smile lifting the corners of his mouth, accentuating the dimple at the end of his chin. "My baby girl." He whispered it, barely loud enough for her to hear.

"Daddy." She was relieved to be able to say that word again.

"I'm going in for surgery soon. And in case I don't come back . . ."

"Daddy, please don't . . ."

"Let your daddy talk, now." Her father's voice rose to an

intense height, and Nina nodded silently, acquiescing to his demand.

"If it was up to me, I would have died with all of this. It just don't make no sense to put you through all this hurt. Some things you just leave in the past, because they fit better there. But your mama tried to tell me it would all come undone. I guess I should've told you when you first started asking about it." Mitchell Moore was quiet for a moment. "You know . . . Mickey and I used to be inseparable. We were all each other had back in the day."

Nina watched her father's eyes glaze over as he disappeared into the past.

"Mickey . . . Daddy, who's Mickey?" Nina had been waiting too long to speak those words. This time they slipped easily out of her mouth.

"Mickey . . . my brother; he was my fraternal twin. My mama's only sons—Michael Anthony and Mitchell Isaac—the only children she ever bore."

Daddy always said he was an only child. *A fraternal twin brother?* Nina slid her chair closer.

"Your grandmother, Virginia, was what they called a 'domestic' back then. She worked for a man who owned nearly half of the little town of Fernwood, Texas. A White man named Isaac Moore. To hear my mama tell it the man loved her like a wife, he just couldn't make her one officially—not if he wanted to hold on to his fortune . . . and his life."

Mitchell Moore made an effort to raise himself into a sitting position, and with a little help from Nina, managed to prop himself comfortably against the pillows she'd adjusted against the headboard behind him.

"When we twins were born, the whole town was buzzing. Word was, one of the babies came out caramel-apple brown, and the other—white as snow. Pretty soon folks had to come out to old Isaac's house just to see if the rumor was true. Well, even if he would've tried, Isaac Moore certainly couldn't deny us, 'cause there was no doubt whose babies we were. Despite the difference in our skin color, we both had our daddy's green eyes, and this here Moore dimple in our chin."

Green eyes; Moore chin. Of course, Nina whispered to herself. *It's finally beginning to make sense.*

"Well, when they saw how he had my mama living up in the house like she was his wife . . . they got it in their heads that Isaac Moore needed to get run out of town on a rail. My mama said they lynched him to get at his property and his money. Some say he just run off and left us. Either way he was never seen again, and Mama ended up raising the two of us alone."

Nina watched her father's eyes shine and then grow dim. He was quiet for a time before he began again.

"In some ways Michael just had it worse off. Folks always assuming he's White till they saw Mama and me. Being invited in in the beginning, then having to endure that rejection time and time again. My poor brother didn't know whether to hate us for the suffering he got, or hate himself for wanting to be accepted by them White folks so bad.

"When our mama passed away, Michael and I moved together to California, and for a while everything was going just fine. I started college, and he got a few odd acting jobs, and we had great laughs about how those Hollywood types thought he was a White man.

"My brother and I were best friends then—all each other had in the world. Till he met this actress woman, and everything between us changed. I knew he had it bad for her, 'cause he just flat-out refused to bring her around. All the time he's telling me how sweet and good she is to him, but the whole time he was afraid to let her know his brother, afraid she'd realize her beau wasn't White.

"Around that time, Mickey landed a big part on one of those soap opera things. He was playing the part of a rich White man. And it was a role that suited him just fine. When he called me a few weeks later to tell me he was getting married, he said he was sorry, but he didn't want me at the wedding. He asked me to forgive him and then he just went away. I never even had an address to send a congratulations card."

Nina watched as tears welled up in her father's eyes.

"You can't even imagine my pain, baby girl. I had nobody else in the world. I never even knew your mother, but a part of me hated her for taking my brother away. He had become a White man who didn't want to be a part of me anymore. I had to let him go. I finally just had to convince myself Mickey didn't exist anymore. I married your mama, and I never told her I had a brother; for the longest she thought I was an only child.

"A couple of years later a man shows up at my door with this pretty little blue-eyed White child talking about how she belonged to me. Said she was my brother Michael's daughter and since her mama had just died, and her daddy had disappeared, they asked should they take her back over to the orphanage, or did I intend to take the child in."

Nina watched an expression of pure delight spread across her father's face then. "You called me Daddy the moment you looked in my eyes and you just wouldn't leave my side. There wasn't even a question in my mind about whether to take you in; and your mama and I didn't once regret the decision to make you our own child. Our only fear was that someone could come to take you away again, so we told people you were mine, and we made a sworn oath to each other that you would never know any different.

"I don't know if it was right to keep it from you all these years, but God help me, Nina, I just never wanted you to feel my pain. I never wanted you to know your real father had abandoned you the same way he abandoned me."

"Daddy . . ." Nina moved to her father's side and sat softly on the edge of his bed. "My real father is the one who raised me. My real father never went away."

"There's more, baby." Nina's father picked up one of her hands and held it firmly in his own. "The part I didn't ever want you to know. I didn't know if you'd be able to understand. I hope you can forgive me for this, Nina. Your father . . . Mickey . . . he tried to come back for you. Showed up at my house talking about how much he loved you and had come to take you away, and that's when I chased him off my property. I told him I'd kill him if he ever came back."

"I hope you don't still mean that, Mitch." A startlingly loud voice sounded from the bed Nina had assumed was empty on the other side of the room. Morris Michaels pulled the curtain divider back.

"Everything my brother said is true. Except the part about me not wanting him at my wedding. I wanted him there desperately, but I couldn't face what that might mean. I wanted to have the courage to tell your mother the truth, but I was terrified she'd be like the others; I was terrified she'd reject me too.

"Your mother was everything to me. I never knew I could love anyone so much. It was all I could do to get up and leave her to go to work. And when I got the part on *The Young and the Beautiful*, I eventually got her a job with me on the set, playing Victor's wife."

Morris Michaels is Michael Moore. "You're Mickey?" It came out sounding like a question, but Nina didn't really mean for it to be one. She knew exactly who he was. The familiar green eyes should have told her right away. And if he wasn't wearing a full beard, Nina guessed there'd be a Moore cleft right in the middle of his chin.

"Mickey." Michaels smiled softly. "Only your father ever called me that. And Nina, he *is* your father. I might have been the one to bring you into this world, but he was willing to do the job I didn't have the courage to."

"What happened to my mother?" Nina asked bluntly, watching his face carefully, looking in it to find the truth.

"I finally did it," Michaels said, shaking his head slowly. His face clouded over with pain and in a quivering voice he added, "I finally found the nerve to tell her the truth. I told her my mother was a Black woman, that I was half Black. I don't know what devastated her more, that I had lived the lie for so long, or that I wasn't the white man she thought she'd married."

Nina didn't say a word, but questioned Michaels with raised eyebrows. "She said she needed time. She needed to go away, to sort everything out. She took a trip to San Francisco to visit her father. Two days later I got a call that she'd been hospitalized, but by the time I arrived there, she was dead." Michaels' ivory face clouded over in pain. "They had found my Michelle in the garage with the car running. I was devastated. Barely able to function. I had to take a hiatus from the show, and then I just disappeared."

"And you took a hiatus from your daughter, too?" Nina blurted the words out with more venom than she'd intended.

"I'm sorry, Nina, I couldn't—I—It took years before I recovered any semblance of sanity. I married a neurotic little movie starlet. She played the role of a mother in a film and got it in her head that she wanted a little girl, but she didn't want to experience childbirth. We talked about adopting, but my selfish idea was to just show up out of the blue to reclaim you.''

Michaels gazed sadly at Mitchell Moore, who was listening quietly behind glazed eyes. ''Fortunately my brother knew I was still self-centered and immature. He knew I didn't have what it would take to raise a child. He said if I was there to get his daughter, I'd have to kill him first. I left that day, and I never came back. Later, when age and regret began sinking in, I sent Evelyn a bank deposit box key in the mail. In case you ever asked about your mother, I thought you should have a few of her things.''

''And now? Why are you here now?''

''Evelyn came to see me on the set a few days ago. Said my brother was in need of something I had. Something that could keep him alive. Thank God I am a compatible donor. The truth is I'd give my brother both of my kidneys if there was some way it could let him know how much I regret his absence from my life. But . . . I—I told Evelyn I had only one request.''

Nina aimed a questioning look at him.

''I just wanted to look at you was all. I just wanted to see my daughter again. All I have left of your mother are memories, you know. And here you are, the one beautiful, tangible proof I had left of my Michelle, and I was so focused on my own pain, the best I could do for you was to leave you behind.''

Nina's head swam with the details she'd been asking for that had now suddenly all been laid bare. She looked back and forth between these two men who in their own ways had so impacted the woman she'd become.

She was still reeling from the trauma of the day spent believing she was not a Black woman, and how it threatened to disconnect her from everything that made her who she was. From this day forward the lines for Nina between ''them'' and ''us'' would forever be blurred by the irony that if she had lived her life with Michael Moore, she would have been raised

White, with no tie to anything or anyone Black. And in the midst of all her reflecting, her brother Nat's words occurred to her—about getting dealt what might seem like shitty cards and playing the best you can with the ones you get.

Nina looked first at the Moore who raised her, and thought of all the sacrifices he endured to welcome her into his life. She gazed then, sadly, at the Moore who would have been her father and felt a strange wave of pity for him—for the sacrifices he felt he had to make in his own life.

And finally, Nina closed her eyes and whispered a silent prayer of thanks that Michael Moore took only a photograph, and left his child in the cemetery that day.

△▽ 33 ▽△

Nina held her breath as the officer ran the metal detection wand across her chest and down the front of her body then up the back of her legs to the top of her spine. "Clean," he muttered to himself, right before he grumbled, "Stand right over there, in that line." She had never been a visitor in a prison before, and Ahmad felt horrible for asking her to go through it.

"I'm sorry you had to experience that, baby." Ahmad was on one knee, talking to Nina's belly. Actually, he wasn't talking to Nina, he was aiming the words at their baby growing inside. "You too," he said, smiling up at his wife. He rose from his knee to plant a tender kiss on Nina's lips.

"Don't worry about us, we're okay," Nina said quietly, grabbing her husband by the hand.

He grabbed her other hand too, then standing eye-to-eye with her he said solemnly, "I love you, Nina. And I want you to know I appreciate you for understanding how much this means to me."

Ahmad had barely spoken the words when the officer finally muttered, "Come this way."

Ahmad led his wife then through the heavy steel door to a place he swore he'd never see again. Chino prison. The inside.

They entered the windowless, white-walled visiting room and scanned the cafeteria-style tables that were arranged in long, obedient rows. Ahmad spotted a stocky bald-headed brotha seated at one of the tables toward the back, and led Nina over to meet his friend.

304

Nina stood back while the two men exchanged energetic hugs. Ahmad put his arm around his wife. Placing one hand on Dud's shoulder he said, "Cellmate . . ." then, beaming with obvious pride, he added, ". . . meet soul mate." Ahmad winked at Nina, who first gave her man and then his friend a kiss on the cheek.

Dudley embraced Nina warmly and sent a nod of approval Ahmad's way, a man-to-man "you dun good" which made Nina laugh.

"Congratulations on the new baby, Dr. Jefferson," Dud said to Nina with a grin, then to Ahmad, "It's good to see a brotha doin' so well.

"You know I would've come sooner, but I had to wait until that felony was cleared before they'd let me visit. Beth's lawyers took care of everything."

Dud held one hand over his heart and looked Ahmad in the eye. "Good to know you worked through all that old stuff. And even though you couldn't come in person thanks, man, for all the letters and cards you sent. And the pictures of Ebony and little Theodore."

Ahmad felt a little twinge of pain in his heart then. Dud's words reminded him of a time when Ahmad was the only one Dud trusted to read his mail to him, and he was a little envious, but relieved, to see that he had obviously been replaced.

Dud turned again to Nina. "Saw your picture in the paper, too." He was referring to the press photo taken of Nina standing arm in arm between a fully recovered Mitchell Moore and a proudly beaming Morris Michaels on the steps of Founder's Heritage College at the fourth annual "Hands Around the Campus" Martin Luther King Day celebration.

Ahmad began explaining to Dud how the event had started out as a protest the first year, and that when Morris Michaels announced it during an interview on *Good Morning L.A.* and the press got ahold of the story, it attracted busloads of people from all over the country, and the school was forced to close its doors. "The funny thing is, even though it's no longer a protest, every year people still come, so now Founder's closes its campus and officially hosts one of the country's largest annual celebrations of the Martin Luther King holiday—"

"Ahmad . . ." Dud finally interrupted him. "I know the

story. It was in this morning's paper.'' Ahmad heard a hint of
indignation in his voice.

Ahmad was quiet then. It hurt him to the core that Dud still
had to have the paper read aloud to him, and he certainly
didn't mean to remind the brotha of his humiliating handicap.
A nervous silence engulfed the table until suddenly Dud's face
broke out in a huge grin and he spouted excitedly, "So, did I
tell you they're granting my parole?"

"No, man. When?"

"March. Two months from now."

Ahmad was on his feet instantly, welcoming his buddy up
into a congratulatory hug. "We want you to know, bruh."
Ahmad sat down next to Nina and grabbed his wife's hand.
"We have a spot for you. I mean, we want you to come to
Arizona with us."

Ahmad wasn't sure if Dud had ever even been on a job
interview, but he did an awfully good impression of a serious
interview voice when he replied, "Well, Mr. Jefferson, sir,
why don't you let me know what you've got in mind." His
face broke into a wide smile when he added, "You know.
Determine the most advantageous options available to a brotha." He grinned at Ahmad playfully.

Nina explained what Ahmad meant by the offer. "Ahmad
and I have just opened a center for troubled youths in Phoenix.
We desperately need someone to coordinate our poetry work-
shops. We were hoping you . . ."

"Hmmm. And what exactly are the qualifications?" There
was that interview voice again.

Ahmad looked at Nina first, then deep into his buddy's eyes.
"We're in desperate need of an intelligent brotha with a whole
lot of heart. Somebody good with words who understands
what's going on with folks . . ." Ahmad tapped his index finger against his heart. ". . . on the inside, where it counts."

"That's it?"

Nina and Ahmad looked at each other uncomfortably.

"A brotha don't have to know how to read and write?"

"Well . . ." Ahmad didn't know how to say it. Dud would
have to at least promise to try.

Before Ahmad could finish his sentence, Dud got up
abruptly from the table and walked toward the small desk

where the guards were waiting to escort prisoners out of the room. He said something to one of the guards who reached into the desk and handed something to him.

When he came back over to the table he was smiling from ear to ear. He put the pad of paper down on the table, and Ahmad and Nina watched what a man's reclaimed dignity looked like—materializing right before their eyes. With a look of what couldn't be mistaken for anything but intense pride, Dud put the pen to paper and wrote these words: *In regards to the position being offered—you can count a brotha in.*